FLICKER

a post-apocalyptic novel

cameron
TROST

BLACK
BEACON
B O O K S

Flicker
Published by Black Beacon Books
Cover design by Cameron Trost
Copyright © Cameron Trost, 2023

Black Beacon Books
blackbeaconbooks.com

ISBN: 978-0645247145

Flicker is dedicated to Emilie Brossais, a friend endowed with vision, creativity, and a solid work ethic. When she told me to write a post-apocalyptic novel, I knew it was advice not to be ignored, but neither of us had any idea the seeds she had sown would grow into this fiery tale of survival and rebellion.

Cameron Trost is an author of mystery, suspense, horror, and post-apocalyptic fiction. *Flicker* is his third novel, and his first set in a post-apocalyptic world. His previous novels are *Letterbox* and *The Tunnel Runner*. He has also written three collections, *Oscar Tremont, Investigator of the Strange and Inexplicable*—four puzzles featuring his intrepid private detective, *Hoffman's Creeper and Other Disturbing Tales*, and *The Animal Inside*. He runs the independent press, Black Beacon Books, and is a lifetime member of the Australian Crime Writers Association. Originally from Brisbane, Australia, he lives with his wife and two sons near Guérande in Brittany, between the rugged coast and treacherous marshlands.

camerontrost.com

PART ONE

1. The Burning Car

On a cold night, between the bleak shell of a forgotten warehouse and the slick scar of an empty street, no sight is more bewitching than a burning car. There's something in the way the flames lick at the paintwork and crack the windscreen. The tyres, steering wheel, and dashboard relax, before completely melting like ice cream dropped on hot asphalt. I stand well back, but close enough for the smell of plastic and petrol to fill my nostrils, and for the heat of the blaze to warm my skin.

This is my story, and it's not one I'm willing to share with the world, for reasons that shall become all too apparent. My friends called me Flicker. That's right, *called* me. I haven't seen them around in quite a while. We used to go raiding and burning together. We'd get drunk and nostalgic—you know how it is. They've dwindled of late; either been taken away or wiped out. The latter being more likely. I'll tell you more about them some other time. I probably won't tell you much about my parents, which I know is a shame, but I don't really remember them. I don't know if I have brothers or sisters out there. I grew up with other children but I can't recall their names, or even their faces. I think they were just neighbours from the same floor in our building. I don't know my date of birth, or how old I am now, but judging by vague memories of good times before The Breakdown, I must be in my early forties. According to old books I've managed to find stowed away in ruined mansions and derelict distribution platforms, it's an age at which a man usually had a home and family in the old days, sometimes even a swimming pool and pet dogs or cats. I wonder if you know what a swimming pool is, or can imagine keeping a dog or cat for company. Drinking water must have been in abundance in those days, and meat not a luxury for the elite. I guess my parents could have told me about life back then, about their childhood. Even if they never had the chance to live like that themselves, they must have seen such things. I guess I'll never know, because all that remains of them is the empty concrete shell of the building I grew up in and this unforgettable sense of hidden fear and open rebellion, both for my sake, I'm sure. I can't picture them, and don't know if I take after my mother or father, or am a mix of both. I'm probably a tad taller than average, and slimmer than I'd like to be, as is just about everyone I've ever known. I have brown hair which I keep clipped short—again, like pretty much everyone else these days—and brown eyes. I so wish I'd been able to find just one photograph of my parents. I don't even know what they called me. John or Liam, perhaps? Ben or Steve? I don't remember that little boy. The only story I can tell you is Flicker's.

This has to stay between us, even though by the time you read this, I'll most likely be well and truly beyond recrimination. All the same, I'm ashamed of much that I've been and done. I'm sharing it with you for one reason and one reason alone—because you are the only person who needs to know. That's understood, isn't it? Right then. Where was I? I was on the topic of fire. Of course I was.

Most people aren't willing to admit it, but deep down inside, we all get a kick out of watching flames consume a luxury automobile. For me, however, it was much more than just a cheap thrill. I was enthralled. I was obsessed. Fire has always held me spellbound. There are many names for us. Arsonist. Firebug. Pyromaniac. But I've never felt that any of them really fit. When you think about it, and if you're honest with yourself, you have to acknowledge the truth in what I'm saying. Whenever there's a riot, that's how it starts. It grips us to see the foremost god of the modern world crushed by prehistoric might. The burning car is the single most poignant representation of the post-industrial psyche.

No matter how poor you are, and how disenfranchised, all it takes is a match, a little stolen fuel, and a hood to cover your face from all those CCTV cameras perched on poles like Odin's ravens. Funny, isn't it? Facial recognition technology. I guess somebody—or some automated system—knows who I am. My real name might even be on record somewhere. Almost makes you laugh. Just a little. Technology was in everyone's hands when I was boy. That I remember. Everybody was connected.

That's the beauty of fire. It can't be shut down or requisitioned. It truly belongs to the people, and setting it free is an amazing release from the dullness of life on the city outskirts. From the moment you strike the match, releasing that potential force from its little pinhead prison, all your pent-up frustration bursts into flames. For a few minutes before you hear the sirens or the low whirring of drones, you are almighty, and you *matter*, and after that, you're *wanted*. Preferably dead.

It's only worth setting fire to luxury cars. That's obvious enough, isn't it? You want to piss off the rich bastards for a change, so they know what it's like to be left out. They need to know how it is for the rest of us. The more expensive the ride, the more spectacular it looks as it goes up in flames.

The one that really stands out was an Audi. It was the one that changed my life. I can say that without any fear of exaggeration. It makes me smile just to think about it. It also makes me cry. I can't help it. You can't possibly understand how bittersweet a memory it is.

The Audi was white at first, gleaming and spotless under the soft light of those streetlamps they leave on all night for no good reason in supposedly secure private estates. I caught a glimpse of it through the wire perimeter fence. There were other expensive cars parked nearby but this one caught my eye. That often happened. There was no rhyme or reason most of the time. Choosing a car to burn is like falling in love. You just feel it, pulling you in. This private estate was one of the most exclusive in the city, with two eighty-floor towers and a third with eighty-five floors surrounded by kept gardens and sports facilities. I'd targeted it numerous times before, always leaving several weeks —but never exactly the same number—between strikes. There was a flaw in their security system, and the body corporate never cottoned on to it. There were motion-activated surveillance cameras placed at intervals along the fence, but the line of sight of the one nearest an ancient oak tree was blocked by the long leafy limb stretching over the razor wire.

I climbed the tree, crawled along the limb as far as I could be sure it would carry my weight without moving too much, and dropped to the impeccably maintained lawn below; soft grass that was guaranteed frequent watering thanks to an automated sprinkler set-up. Is it sad to be envious of grass? That's what's so disgusting about the world we live in. That lawn, in a way, was as much a symbol of inequality as the luxury automobile, and a much older one at that, harking back to the days of kings and barons. Days I thought only to be found in the history books I kept stashed away in an old dishwasher in the back shop of a disused white goods dealer. Days that sounded eerily familiar. Would this period in time be looked back on and labelled *post-apocalyptic neo-feudalism*? Would anybody be left to look back at all? These things intrigued me more and more. Books fascinated me almost as much as fire; perhaps because they were the only objects I'd never dream of burning. If that lawn hadn't been damp, I'd have considered trying to set fire to it instead of the Audi, but I suspect the symbolism would have been lost and my hunger for destruction left unsatisfied.

There were cameras on the nearest tower aimed at the car park, and although I was safe from facial recognition with a hood covering my head, my presence would quickly be detected. The key was to move quickly and purposefully. Get the fire started and enjoy it for as long as possible before fleeing the scene. There are dozens of ways to set fire to a car, but the most effective is to smash a side window, liberally douse the interior with accelerant, and ignite it. More artistic elaborations are best kept for low-risk situations.

That's what I did. I took my hammer, jerry can, wick, and matches from my backpack, screwed the spout onto the jerry can, and ran to the Audi. One swing of the hammer and the driver's side window shattered. The alarm was set off but I revelled in it as I jigged the jerry can up and down, spraying petrol across the dashboard, steering wheel, and seats. Can you imagine how fucking good that feels? I threw the can and hammer back behind me, to where I would stand and watch, wiped my hands, and took the matches and wick from my pocket.

This is the best part—what it's all about. This is what sends that shiver of sheer pleasure through every inch of your body and makes the fine hairs on the nape of your hooded neck prick up. The redhead flared up on the first strike and I grinned as I touched it delicately to the wick. Once the flame had been transferred, I dropped the wick inside and dashed back a few paces.

The flare of the match. The flickering flames. The beauty of the blaze. I felt so alive. So strong. While I watched the Audi being ravaged, I wasn't a nobody sleeping rough, struggling to make ends meet, but a fierce warlord claiming one small victory in a conflict he knew could never be won.

I slipped my hand into my black camouflage trousers while I watched. I can't explain it, but I was lonely and frustrated and the rush of excitement was all encompassing.

The moment was short-lived. Within three minutes, the Audi had been reduced to a blackened body, and it wasn't usually for a couple of minutes longer that a siren could be heard drawing near. But it was different this time and I knew immediately that this car had belonged to someone in a position of power. A high-ranking member of the bureaucracy. The Audi must have been connected to a control centre. A wave of whirrs reached my ears over the cracking and popping of the fire, and the sky was riddled with tiny red lights. Five. Ten. Maybe more. But by that time, I'd snatched up my gear and run back to the perimeter fence.

I shoved the hammer and jerry can into my backpack, slipped the straps over my shoulders, and jumped. It took all the strength I had to pull myself up onto that branch, but I managed to do it and crawled back beyond the fence, closer to the thick trunk and the familiar footholds that would bring me back to the verge.

The drones hovered around the oak tree, looking for a breach in the canopy. Their integrated spotlights had been switched on.

The techies guiding them weren't the usual mob. I was sure of that. Surveillance drones would hang higher up, waiting for visual confirmation—which generally meant a hooded figure running— then follow from a distance before swooping down when there was a reasonable chance of getting ahead and obtaining clear images of the suspect's face. But these drones were buzzing around the tree, just beyond the canopy, and they were evenly spread out. They were hunters, not observers. Flashes of bright light blinded me now and then as they moved around behind clumps of leaves, and I knew it was only a matter of seconds before one found a way under the canopy. There wouldn't be much I could do if that happened. There would be no chance of losing them before a mobile unit came to pick me up and get rid of me. Pest control. Waste management. That's all it was to them. One more rebellious dreg flushed away for daring not to quietly accept a life of invisible poverty. The last resort idea of grabbing the drone and smashing it against the tree trunk occurred to me, of course. But I'd heard rumours they were fitted with defence mechanisms; lethal electric discharges or miniature circle saws, depending on the version you listened to. I didn't plan on learning which was right.

A change in breeze brought the last breaths of black smoke from the Audi carcass floating in the direction of the oak tree, providing a thin screen, and at the same time, the sound of sirens reached my ears. It was now or never.

There was no need to decide where to go. I always kept an escape route in mind. The key with drones is to take cover in a building with several exits, that way it has to go up higher to see where you go. That's the idea, at least, when you have one surveillance drone on your arse. This pack of wolves was a different story altogether. Still, I didn't have much choice.

I dropped to the ground, bending my knees to soften the landing, and used the momentum to propel me forward onto the street. And I ran, straight along the street, staying out in the open. Zigzagging or sticking to walls would only have slowed me down and given the drones time to catch up. I had to get as far as possible before they spotted me.

I had a vague notion of onlookers on the balconies of their

high-class flats, but nobody interfered or even yelled at me. They never did, knowing the drones would catch me. I couldn't help but wonder whether they knew whose Audi I'd made the mistake of targetting.

The spotlights angled in and out, some crossing the surface of the street in front of me and others shining over my shoulders, letting me know just where the drones were. My feet hammered against the asphalt, unable to outrun the mechanical birds of prey —nobody's feet could. When it came to making a hasty departure, the natural advantage of the few remaining wealthy districts this side of the city was the condition of the streets. There were few potholes, cracks, or bumps. It was smooth running. The disadvantage, and it was a crucial one, was the lack of abandoned buildings. The streets were lined with high walls and locked gates. The key to getting away was finding the shortest safe route back to the outskirts.

I had an idea I'd never needed to put to the test until that night, so I ran as fast as I could towards the nearest public facility —a vast sports ground. The sirens were growing louder and I knew it was only a minute or so before the patrol caught up with me.

One of the drones overtook me just before I reached the gate to the tennis courts. I kept my head angled down, but the instant I heard the impact and the violent rattle of the fence, I knew my idea was right. The drone crashed down just inches away from me. I pulled the gate open and ran across the tennis courts, passing through each dividing gate on the way. The drones were forced to gain altitude to avoid the high wire fences.

The response unit arrived outside the sports ground just as I passed through the fifth and final tennis court. They would be expecting me to keep running across the football pitch and join the street on the other side, but I turned right and headed into a strip of woodland. It was as dark as a toad's gullet inside, but the thick foliage prevented the drones from following me.

The sirens faded as the patrol sped away to loop around the block and try to catch me on the far side. But I stuck to the cover of the woods, knowing there was a gap in the wire fence that gave access to a manmade environment that had long since been abandoned to nature.

I couldn't hear the drones now. My breathing was loud and my heart thumping. But I knew they were directly above me, waiting to pounce the moment I came into the open. I pushed the prickly branches of pine trees aside as I ran and ducked under the larger ones. When the ground started to slope downwards and a rocky bank upon which only brambles and thistles grew appeared on my right, I changed direction. The drones didn't spot me as I ran, zigzagging or hurdling to avoid the thorny brambles.

I almost crashed into the fence but managed to negotiate the slash in the chain and slip through it. A few feet further and I was inside one of the dozens of disused greenhouses; row after row of once almost transparent semi-cylinders, now dirty and torn and overgrown with vines, creepers, shrubs, and weeds of every description.

If it wasn't possible to lose the drones in here, it wasn't possible anywhere. I'd be done for. The patrol would quickly catch up and I'd be whisked away. Presumably, my pitiful existence would be put to a swift end and my disappearance would go completely unnoticed by anyone other than those burdened with the task. My legacy? My fires. The blackened shells of luxury automobiles, many irreplaceable because they were no longer in production or imported. Drone production, on the other hand, was going strong. Private enterprise was making a killing on that line, furnishing a desperate and crumbling administration with the means of observing the ruins of a society it was incapable of controlling.

I stopped and scanned the sky as best I could through the grime-covered plastic of the half-tube greenhouse. Only the faintest residual light from the private estates and soft LED streetlamps reached this forgotten place. And to think one of the old books I'd found discussed the problem of light pollution and talked about solar energy as a means of enabling habits of waste to continue. It was really quite bizarre.

I took a deep breath, released it, and listened before drawing another. Not a sound. Had they failed to spot me leave the strip of woods?

It was almost as dark in the greenhouse as in the woods. The soft glow outside couldn't penetrate the filthy plastic. Years of dust blown in from the ruined outskirts and bird excrement had accumulated and hardened. There was a torch in my backpack, but I couldn't use it, of course. All I could do was listen, between breaths, for that ominous droning sound I knew so well, hoping that when I heard it, it would be coming from outside the greenhouse and would quickly move on, having failed to make visual contact.

I waited for I don't know how long, standing there among the shadowy tendrils of vines and creepers, and the outstretched feathery leaves of bracken. I must have looked like the statue of some classical deity, but as a man of flesh and blood, I was tired and hungry, and only the souvenir of the blazing Audi reminded me that it had all been worthwhile.

The sound of at least three drones reached my ears and I caught a glimpse of their unclear silhouettes as they passed overhead. They didn't stop, but seconds later, the whirring grew again and one came back and hovered over the greenhouse, slightly to my right, just above a hole in the plastic—not big enough for the drone to pass through, I told myself. I remained frozen, staring at the dark patch hovering outside, waiting for it to move along to search elsewhere. I started counting silently, and at seventeen, the drone drifted back towards where the other two had gone.

How long would I have to wait before daring to leave the greenhouse and wend my way back home? Was it safer to keep moving or stay put? Would a ground patrol come after me? When we'd first started raiding for food and razing the icons of the wealthy, the patrols had used dogs to track us down. They were more effective than any drone, strange though it may seem. But there were no dogs now. They'd all be killed and eaten, and I often wondered if not by their own masters. Without them, ground patrols were considerably less successful at tracking than drones.

The whirring of a single drone grew again and made me once more question the likelihood of leaving the greenhouse any time soon. That's when a voice answered me.

'Hey, you! Are you trying to get us both killed?'

I spun around and tried to make out who it was, but I could see only a metal ranging table covered with what looked like empty pots, tins, and crates held together by a mesh of brambles. A rusted wheelbarrow was leaning against the table and the voice had come from within that makeshift cave.

'You realise those are tracker drones, don't you?' she asked. 'I don't know what you did to deserve the considerable honour of putting them on your trail, but they're equipped with infrared cameras, so would you kindly join me under this table and stop standing there like an idiot.'

The drone was almost directly overhead.

'Now!'

I dropped to my knees and crawled under, joining her in the dark.

2. Fugitives

'Who are you?' I couldn't help but ask, whispering it as though it were an act of rebellion in itself, and fully aware that it was also an odd question to ask under the circumstances. But as pointless as it was, it seemed only natural, and it came out as an apology rather than a greeting.

'You can call me Flame.'

If not for the impenetrable darkness, she'd have been able to see my face and the surprised expression it bore.

'Flame? My friends called me Flicker.'

In answer, there was the flare of a match, almost blinding against the pitch black, and she touched it against the wick of a small lamp, which she held between our faces.

'You're Flicker?'

I nodded, frowning. 'You've heard of me?'

Her green eyes were catlike and peered at me suspiciously from under her hood, the flame giving them a fiery edge. But she relaxed and a smile touched her lips. With her free hand, she wiped her dirty cheeks, almost as though wishing to look more presentable, and I wanted to tell her not to bother, that it wasn't necessary, but I couldn't think of what to say, and I think see saw that.

She drew a breath and informed me quietly and seriously that if I was the Flicker obsessed with burning every icon of greed and wealth to the ground, then she had indeed heard of me.

'Judging by your name, we share this obsession.'

She nodded. 'I guess the flames are spreading.'

'Do you know your real name?'

'Cara. That's all I know. I've never had a family.'

'We have a lot in common then.'

She raised her gaze to the filthy underside of the metal table above us. 'Except that I know how to keep away from tracker drones.'

'Thank you, Flame. I owe you my life.'

She laughed. 'Cut the dramatics. We don't know that for certain.'

'It sounds like they've given up the chase.'

'Perhaps. All the same, best we stay put,' she said, glancing around the makeshift shelter. There was probably just enough room for us to lie down, side by side. 'Do you have any food or water?'

'Sorry.'

'Never mind. So, what did you burn to put them on your arse? You were at Paradise Towers, I take it.'

'That's what they call them, is it? I never paid attention to the name of the place.'

Flame rolled her eyes.

'There was a white Audi I just had to burn.'

She smiled. 'Do you know who it belonged to?'

'No idea.'

'It must have been someone important.'

'I've never had such a fast and forceful reaction before,' I admitted. 'The Audi must have been connected to the command centre.'

'That's pretty cool. I'd never have dared an attack like that. I stick to street strikes.'

'So do I usually, but that place has a hold on me. It's hard to resist.'

'I'd suggest you're going to have to forget about it from now on.'

Just then, a drone passed overhead.

We looked at each other—both thinking the same thing. *They're not giving up.*

'I've definitely pissed off the wrong person.'

She extinguished the lamp.

'We'd better get some rest.'

I lay down, sat back up to brush away some gravel, then lay down again. When I closed my eyes, it was no darker than when they were open. 'Sweet dreams, Flame.'

'Same to you. Oh, and don't go getting any funny ideas, Flickerboy.'

I wasn't sure how seriously to take that. Was I supposed to reply with a solemn reassurance or a light-hearted quip?

'Don't worry. I've had enough excitement for one night.'

We both lay there awake in the darkness. I was waiting for her to reply, but she didn't.

'Anyway, what makes you think I'm interested?'

'It's not about being *interested*. Men are men.'

'Fire is my mistress.'

'Right. Well, that might just be the saddest fucking thing I've ever heard.'

'No, it's just that I have this rule about only doing one stupid thing each day.'

She giggled, and I couldn't remember the last time I'd heard such a lovely sound. 'Good rule.'

'I didn't get around to asking what you were doing here. There's no food or supplies. What were you looking for?'

'That's a conversation we'll have another day,' she said firmly. There was no longer a hint of amusement in her voice.

'As you will.'

'Let's get some rest.'

A conversation we'll have another day. That made me smile.

We both lay awake. I could tell by her breathing. It was so strange to be there in an unfamiliar place with another human being beside me. I'd grown so used to my loneliness and to the safety it afforded me. Until that night, I'd always felt certain you're harder to catch when you're alone. There was comfort to be found in the knowledge that you can't lose someone when you have no one at all. And yet, hidden away under that table with a woman who shared the same troubles as me, and who shared my passion for fire, I came to fully appreciate that the flames would never replace companionship. Their heat would never be as consuming as the warmth of a fellow human, nor their roar as reassuring as a whispered word.

No more drones passed overhead, and slumber eventually began to pull at me, but I spent the night drifting in and out of a light sleep, thinking about how stiff I'd feel in the morning.

We were both awake long before dawn, if we'd ever really slept at all. Judging the lengths of the countless dips in and out of slumber was impossible. Birdsong was all around us; a reassuring and poetic contrast to the tracker drones. Less optimistically, one could say it was fate's way of lulling us into a false sense of security. Flame spoke once there was enough daylight seeping into the greenhouse for us to see each other. Golden light played along the metallic edges of the wheelbarrow and table.

'Good morning, Flicker. It seems we survived the night.'

'Where to now?' I asked, rolling onto my side to face her.

She sat up and shrugged, then slipped her hood back and ran her hands across her head. Her hair was brown and almost as short as mine.

'I live in an old house near the ring road, down by the river. It's just me now. I've barricaded it off and keep a supply of food in the cellar. We'd be safe there.'

She thought about it for a while.

'You live alone?'

She looked away, and I could tell why. She didn't want me to see it, but I understood.

'Last night, you were avoiding the open street and trying to take a shortcut through the greenhouses and down to the old timber docks?'

'That's right.'

She seemed impressed.

'The idea was to follow a covered route for as long as possible. There's an old walking track that leads through thick woods from the docks to the ring road.'

'Not a bad idea,' she admitted. 'It's worth a try.'

We crawled out from under the table and stretched. The greenhouse was attractive in the soft morning light and the birds flitting about within and without were unruffled. We both peered up through the grimy plastic covering and—satisfied there were no drones—stepped away from each other to relieve our bladders in relative privacy. It didn't take long since neither of us had drunk any water. I heard her pee spatter against the beaten

22

earth. A simple, mundane sound that was somehow as pleasing as it was prosaic. It was one of those little details of human companionship that had become so alien to me.

'You have water at your place?' she asked as she came back, tying the knot on her tracksuit bottoms. She looked back to make sure the pee wasn't flowing into view.

I placed a hand over my mouth to hide my smile, amused at her coquettishness in spite of the situation.

'There's plenty. I collect rainwater from the roof. It passes through a filter and I boil it. It was a system we set up to provide enough drinking water for six or seven people.'

She looked at the ground and frowned. I knew what she was thinking, of course.

'We have some stories to share.'

'I guess we do,' she agreed, looking up. 'In our own good time.'

'Ready to go?' I asked, grabbing my gear.

She nodded, took her backpack, and walked slowly to a slit in the plastic. She parted the flaps and peered outside. It was much the same in the alleys between the greenhouses as inside them; broken and discarded tools from those days when the greenhouses had still been in use entangled in vines, weeds, and brambles. The birds remained oblivious to our presence, chirping merrily as we dashed diagonally across the alley and through a wide tear in the plastic into the next greenhouse.

'Clear,' we whispered to each other as she looked right and I looked left along the length of each greenhouse.

Thus we continued, hopping quickly and quietly from one greenhouse to the next, jumping over the occasional upturned trolley or stretch of thorny undergrowth as we advanced, and ducking under or dodging strips of torn plastic that hung here and there like a motionless waterfall.

I kept an eye out for any items that might prove of use on our short but potentially perilous journey home, reminding myself not to let Flame down, not to let any harm come to this woman who had quite possibly saved my hide. But there wasn't much left. We weren't the first to pass through these greenhouses since they'd been abandoned.

'I think the next one is the last,' Flame said as we were about to go through another gap in the covering. 'It looks like open ground on the other side.'

'I'd say you're right. Just hold on a second, will you?' I looked back around the greenhouse we were about to leave.

'What do you want?'

'It's open sky from the last greenhouse down to the docks, and even though the woods along the riverbank are thick, it won't be enough to keep the drones off our trail if they detect us. Last night, after burning the Audi—it makes me feel better every time I say that—I climbed into an oak tree to get back across the perimeter fence and out of the estate. The drones almost trapped me in there, in one tree. If it happens again, and they get close, we should be prepared to fight back. Are you armed, Flame?'

'I always carry a knife on me.'

'That won't help much against drones.'

She raised her eyebrows. 'Obviously not. I carry it for protection against humans, not drones.'

I looked her up and down, wondering where she hid it.

'I forgot—*men are men.*'

She grinned. 'I'm a pretty good judge of character, and I don't think I'll have to use it on you.'

'Well, that's a relief!'

'Don't go proving me wrong, will you?'

'I'll try not to.'

'What have you got?'

'A hammer.'

Her eyes widened. 'Not planning on pounding me with it, I hope?' She winked.

'They should have called you *Fruitcake* instead of *Flame?*'

She laughed. 'I haven't heard that word in a long time.'

'I read it in a book.'

'Is that right? You have books at your place?'

'A lot.'

'What about cake, since you're not scared of bandying the word around in front of a famished female?'

'A little. It's probably getting stale though.'

She licked her lips and a bead of saliva stuck in the corner of her mouth.

'Let's have a quick look,' I said.

She started searching through the piles of rubbish and knots of brambles. I did likewise, foraging in the opposite direction.

'I've found a gardening fork,' she called out a moment later.

I rushed over and she passed it to me.

'Seems sturdy.'

I hefted it from hand to hand and inspected it.

'The prongs are in good nick, and the shaft. Is there anything else?'

She shrugged.

'What about this?' I pulled a weighted net from the pile.

'A fishing net? That could come in handy if a drone gets too close. I'll take that and leave you the fork.'

'Fine by me. Let's keep moving.'

We continued across to the next greenhouse, glanced up and down in case there was anything of obvious interest, but with hands already full and stomachs growing ever hungrier, we didn't stop. Beyond the last greenhouse was an open stretch of land leading downhill to where broken and jagged wooden decking lined the river. There were a few chunks of rock or concrete along the way but they weren't big enough to provide cover, only to make progress slower. All the same, the sky was clear and it was a short run down to the dilapidated port office, and from there to the old walking path.

'It almost feels too easy.'

The hairs on my arms pricked up a little at what she said. That very same thought had been nagging at us since the moment we crawled out of our hiding place that morning—the soft dawn light, the gentle birdsong. It was in such stark contrast.

'Do you think it's a trap?'

She scanned the sky in silence.

'If they'd known we were in the greenhouses, they would have sent a patrol. We would have heard voices; footsteps at the very least. They don't know we're here.'

'Let's make a dash for the dock building and catch our breath on the other side, facing the river. We go at a fast-paced run but not a sprint.'

'Agreed. There's no point going too fast with no drones in

sight. We need to negotiate obstacles on the way.'

'Now!' Flame hissed, and we ran, staying side by side most of the way despite the scattered rocks and holes we had to negotiate. I must have been quite a sight, running with the fork gripped in my right hand, and it wasn't until we reached the cover of the port building that I remembered reading about gladiators in Ancient Rome with their strange weapons like forks and nets. It was almost as though we were part of that tradition, except in a world of outright chaos, not absolute control.

We took deep breaths, leaning against the wall and staring at the river, both looking up every few seconds to check the sky.

'So far, so good,' I said, watching an automated barge that had come into view.

'Is that a risk?' Flame asked.

I shook my head. 'On the contrary, that's a supply barge. It's probably loaded with fresh produce. I sometimes swim over to them, climb aboard, and grab as much food as I can swim back with. They're unmanned but have motion detectors, so you need to grab what's easily accessible and make a getaway before the drones arrive.'

'Nothing like last night?'

'Not at all. A walk in the park compared to that. Perhaps I'll show you some day.'

She closed her eyes and smiled. 'I'd like to see that.'

The barge moved past us, heading towards the city. Its electric motor was noiseless, and only the soft lapping of water against the wooden pylons of the dock reached my ears.

I scanned the sky. The morning shadows were shorter now as the sun climbed higher, but along the wooded path, we would be hidden.

'I think we can walk now,' Flame said.

'Definitely. We'd do well to take it slow and steady along the riverbank.'

I led the way, using the fork to push back branches that had grown across the path. Every few hundred yards, there was an even less distinct track running up through the woods, presumably to a house on higher ground. These properties had been expensive in bygone days, when living by the river was a symbol of wealth and privilege. They were now considered too far on foot from the centre and hideously unfashionable. The infrastructure had fallen into a state of disrepair, and as a result, they were either unoccupied or squatted.

'This is more familiar,' I told Flame as the path swept to the left and dipped into lower, damper ground. 'Watch your step.'

A stone retaining wall that had crumbled in the middle, spilling forth a ridge of rubble, dirt, and brambles, rose beside us. But the path curved back to the right and straightened out onto flatter, more solid ground. The trees grew sparser here and a street descended through the woods and joined the river just ahead, where the houses stood closer to the bank.

'We're almost there,' I told her.

The path ended where the street touched the riverbank, bending to follow it under the bridge of the ring road a little further along. There were seven houses on that street, whose name we'd never known, but that everyone I'd ever spoken to in the area referred to as River Street. There was a kind of metal hanger with four eyelets welded to the underside—one of which had a short length of chain attached—sticking out of the water. The general consensus among the former members of my household—my missing friends—was that it was a swing, and therefore that there had been a children's playground between the street and the river's edge once upon a time. The level of the river must have been much lower in the past. Now, only the narrow street separated the water from the houses.

'Which one is it?'

'Third from the end, with the concrete wall and arched gateway.'

'You really are close to the ring road.'

I nodded. 'But I almost never go to the other side. There's just more of what's on this side, but no luxury cars to burn. Have you?'

'This is the closest I've ever been to the ring road as far as I can recall.'

My eyebrows must have raised themselves. She laughed.

'I've only heard tales about the outskirts and what lies beyond.'

'Likewise.'

But she was no longer looking up at the ring road, or at me. Her eyes were glued to the house—to the roof.

'Flicker,' she whispered, and even before I'd followed her gaze, the palpable dread in her voice told me what I was going to see.

'Shit!' I groaned. 'I've been identified.'

It wasn't hovering overhead. It was perched—a single drone perched atop the highest chimney stack.

'You mustn't have covered your face as well as you thought.'

'But that means I was already in the system. They knew where I lived.'

'Most of us are probably in the system, but it wasn't until last night that they linked you to the fire bombings. That's my guess.'

The drone lifted off the chimney and swooped down.

'It's spotted us!' Flame yelled.

But it was too late. It was already hovering right in front of me.

'Flicker,' a man's voice said. 'You have been identified as the perpetrator of an act of arson committed last night at Paradise Towers. You are suspected of having committed seventy-three previous acts of vandalism.'

I stared at the camera. No point hiding now. 'How many?'

'Seventy-three acts of wanton destruction.'

I laughed, but my anger soon mounted. 'Are you fucking serious? I've set fire to hundreds of the city's most expensive luxury vehicles—fucking *hundreds*!' I roared. 'I'm waging a war here, not playing with matches like a naughty little boy!'

'That is considered a confession. Automatic punishment will be dispensed at the discretion of the leading patrol officer. Please remain where you are.'

I didn't think twice. I thrust my fork upwards into the underbelly of the drone, making sure to hold it by the wooden shaft in case the drone could discharge an electrical impulse. I then slammed it down onto the street.

An ear-splitting alarm rang out as I brought my fork crashing down on the drone. Its four propellers were spinning at full power and I had to keep hitting it to keep it down.

Flame stepped closer and between strikes cast her net over the drone. Together, we dragged it to the river and threw it in. The alarm ceased immediately.

'It's sinking,' I said, relieved.

Out of instinct, our gaze returned to the sky, but the siren that had replaced the drone's alarm belonged to a ground patrol.

'Which way?' Flame asked.

It was coming from back the way we'd come, but higher up.

'They're already coming down River Street. They'll be here any second now. Follow me!'

And so, for the very first time, Flame ventured beyond the ring road.

3. Beyond the Ring Road

I'd watched the wastelands spread over the years. Around the ring road—which cuts deep into the earth like a garrotte—nature mounts a pathetic counter-attack on the embankments. Shrubs and brambles catch plastic bags and ensnare stolen shopping trolleys. High-tension wires stretch along the top of the embankment, suspended between towering metal pedestals. I loathed this concrete wasteland, this constructed wilderness, but it's where I belonged. It's all I'd ever known.

I'd sometimes toyed with the idea of heading out into the country. Some had told me life was better there, and fresh food easier to come by. That you could even find work. Then again, others had told me there was nothing at all, just marshes and mosquitoes, and isolated communities suspicious of and hostile to outsiders. It was hard to know who knew the truth, or whether it was an amalgam of several realities. How many of those friends of mine who had disappeared had left the city outskirts for the countryside? And why hadn't they come back; because they hadn't survived, or because they'd found a home?

At any rate, it seemed the only reasonable course to take now. We were no longer safe anywhere near the city.

The street ended soon after the ring road, where an industrial disposal plant met the river. A narrow path—really no more than a steep gap of long grass wide enough for a person to pass along—led between a chain fence and the water's edge. I headed for this path, knowing it would be difficult for the patrol to chase us along it. They would be forced out of their vehicles and would have to give pursuit in single file.

'I can hear drones on our tail,' Flame yelled from behind me.

I sped up to increase the distance between us, thus allowing me time to pause for an instant without forcing her to change her pace. I grabbed the chain fence to prevent myself from losing balance and toppling into the water as I spun around. The fence rattled and seemed to move a little under my weight, but it held fast.

I scanned the sky and then looked down. Flame had almost reached me, panting and panicked. I turned around, letting go of the fence, and started running again.

'Two drones coming from over the ring road!' I shouted loudly over my right shoulder. 'Three patrolmen on foot just leaving vehicle!'

If she answered, I didn't hear her. I think she was saving her breath.

Another barge was coming along the river, slow-moving and almost silent. I realised that if a patrol boat arrived at that moment, we'd be history. Unlikely though, as they took time to be put into action, and I didn't plan on sticking to the riverbank longer than necessary. In any case, we were heading upstream, so assuming there were no river patrols posted further inland, where I knew the river grew shallower and silted, they could only arrive from behind.

I reminded myself to be logical. Only three on foot behind us and a little way back. If we kept our pace, we'd shake them off. One or more patrol vehicles would be taking parallel streets with the aim of cutting us off. If we stayed on the riverbank, they could do this easily. The greatest threat remained the drones. If they latched onto us, the patrols would be directed to our location in a minute or two, at most. Again, the river worked in their favour, enabling them a clear passage to track us.

The fence turned inwards to the left, leaving us in an open square that looked like the remnants of one of the car parks that had been used in the past for workers who drove in from the suburbs and countryside and used public transport to take them from the ring road to the city centre. It was now empty except for one shipping container in front of which was a ring of stones with a patch of ash and blackened logs inside.

We had to find cover. Fast.

On the far side of the car park was a low rock face, as though there had once been a quarry there. It stretched up to a warehouse on the left and almost reached the river on the right. Several yards in from the river, a narrow track with rough-hewn steps scarred the face and ended at about four-times my height. There was a row of trees growing either side of a low stone wall with taller trees and stone ruins beyond.

'Yes! Up there!' Flame yelled, following my gaze.

I sprinted across the car park, pumping my legs as hard as I could. There was no need to look for the drones. I could hear them to my right, coming up from the river as expected. I used the fork to help me clamber up the high stone steps, moving quickly but carefully. A twisted ankle now and it would all be over. I would finally know the unknown fate reserved for dissidents or—as we were more likely considered—street vermin.

One drone caught up with me as I reached the top. The other was hovering next to Flame, who was struggling, I could tell. We were thirsty; hungry as well, but more urgently thirsty. The patrolmen were just entering the car park and looking up towards us but without actually seeing us. I lay flat on my stomach in what was probably a vain attempt to delay being noticed by the patrolmen, who would be relying on the drones to keep track. The drone next to me dropped lower, its controller perhaps taking my posture as a sign of surrender. It was hovering just overhead.

Big mistake.

I sprang up, thrust my fork into one of the propeller rings and brought it crashing down. The other three propellers also stopped and I quickly stamped on them, snapping the rings.

'Destruction of surveillance equipment is an executable offence,' a voice told me.

A shot rang out and I heard part of the stone wall behind me shatter. Acting purely on instinct now, I grabbed Flame's hands as she reached the top of the steps and dragged her up over the edge. She cried out in pain, but getting a few bruises was better than taking a bullet. I hoped she'd see it that way later.

Once her knees were on flat ground, she pushed herself closer to me and we ran, heads down, to the stone wall. The second drone was at a safe distance behind us, blurting out warnings about our status as fugitives and the *carte blanche* now available to the patrol if we didn't surrender immediately. There were no more shots as we climbed over the crumbling wall and I assumed that was because we were no longer in their line of sight, that the men were now climbing the rock face.

As we dropped onto the far side of the wall, I wanted to tell Flame our only chance was destroying the drone, but it was hovering above the wall, well within listening range.

That gave me an idea. Did its controller know that we knew it could hear us? It was worth a try.

'Listen, Flame. We need to lose this drone and get back down to the river.'

She stared at me like I was mad, so I placed a hand over my brow as though I had a headache—which wasn't entirely false—and, knowing the drone couldn't see my face from that angle, winked at her.

'Good idea!'

I lunged at it with the fork, but missed. It hovered up higher and I jumped onto the trunk of a fallen tree and lunged again. It moved back further but hit the underside of an ash bough and bounced downwards a little. I swung again, hitting it with the tip of a prong this time. It jerked back and then retreated to just above the stone wall. Chasing it would have been futile. The first of the patrolmen would almost be at the top now.

'Let's go!' I said.

We dashed further into the grove and I soon came to understand the nature of the site we'd happened upon; a matter of a few minutes' walk from where I'd lived—and would probably never set foot again. Of course, we'd covered that distance in a fraction of the time it would take to walk. This strange place had all the outward appearances of a natural patch of woodlands, but in an area that had once been entirely occupied by industrial, commercial, or private property, it had undoubtedly performed a function at some time in the past, prior to The Breakdown. The way the land rose and fell quite suddenly, with soft mounds and winding gullies, the ruins of small buildings, and the rows of tall trees with overgrown shrubs huddled around them all hinted at its story. As I ran, following the paths that led through the lowest passages, with the tallest trees and thickest shrubbery pushing in one either side, I grew ever more certain that we were in what had been a vast and intricately planned garden.

I slowed my pace and stopped at the lowest dip in the passage. Five gigantic pines with far-stretching branches grew atop the mound to our left and a cascade of rose bushes smothered by bracken and brambles covered the slope and loomed above us like the crest of an unmoving wave. Thorns swiped at our faces. An unkempt and menacing tangle, but it was sweet protection for us. The land that rose to our right was covered in a similar, if somewhat less vigorous, mass. At the top of that mound stood a ring of junipers reaching skyward, and in the middle there was a statue broken at the waist so that only the legs and groin of that muscular man remained, now merely a monument to a ruined age.

Flame came to a stop close to me, and together we caught our breath. I tried to breathe deeply without making too much noise, scared that loud gasping would be picked up by the drone.

She looked up. 'You think the river ruse worked?'

I shrugged. One could only hope. Either way, it would keep looking, and backup would soon arrive. More patrols would also be on the way, ready and willing to shoot to kill, we had to assume.

'We have to keep running. It isn't like the greenhouses. They know we're here and they'll throw everything at us,' Flame said, sucking a breath between each sentence.

'You can do it? Can you keep going until nightfall if need be?'

She closed her eyes and frowned. It was still only early morning.

'We have no choice!' she answered, opening her eyes and boring holes in me. *If only you'd never stumbled into my life*; that's what that look said. No doubt about it. But then she smiled. 'Get moving, boy!'

I raised my fork in salute, then turned and ran along the passage, following it uphill. As I ran, ignoring the growing pain in my legs, I swore with every step that I would make her change her mind. We'd make it through this nightmare. We'd find a way out, and I'd make it up to her one day. She'd look back fondly on the day we'd crossed paths.

The passage curved up to the right and there it branched off in two directions. To the right, it led downhill and inevitably joined the river. To the left, it stayed level and followed a straight line through dozens of iron arches over which wisteria twisted.

I took the wisteria tunnel and ran like mad.

Outside the tunnel, on either side, the gardens opened out into what had been lawns but were now fields of wildflowers and weeds. Ahead of us, the tunnel joined an arcade, attached to an expansive two-storey stone building. It became clear, as we drew nearer, that the arcade wrapped around the building, and that it was clean. There was no dirt on the concrete floor, nor were there leaves or any other detritus, and stacked up against the walls of the building, between barred windows, were crates and boxes of various sizes.

I stopped, looked out at the sky and along the arcade. No drones. Nobody. I stood with my back straight against the nearest wall, between two stacks of boxes. Flame joined me.

'This building is occupied,' Flame whispered.

'Definitely,' I said. 'I wonder if there's any food or water here.'

'It's too risky. This is the first place they'll look. We can't stop.'

'She's right, you know.'

I stepped forward, fork raised. 'Who are you?'

'What does that matter? Step inside.'

It was a man's voice—calm but rough.

'Hurry up about it! Are you thirsty or not?'

I walked over to the door, which was red and spotless. I'd never seen a door like it in my life. It was ancient and new at the same time. And I'm sure it had been closed an instant earlier. We entered and found ourselves in a dim corridor, clean as far as I could tell and smelling of flowers and oils.

'Welcome to the asylum,' the shadowy form in front of us said. I couldn't see his face, and I didn't think he could see ours, but he chuckled as though able to read our expressions. 'This used to be an asylum for the mentally disturbed,' he explained. 'Funny that, isn't it? It's now where you'll find some of the sanest people left.'

He took a step closer, into the reach of the daylight. He was a tall man with broad shoulders and deep furrows in his face; a face that had known years of hardship and worries. He had long hair, all the way down to his shoulders—possibly the longest hair I'd ever seen on anybody—but he didn't smell unpleasant. The whole place was filled with spellbinding aromas.

'Who is it?' a girl's voice came from behind. It was followed by whispers, like a cool breeze, and peering past our host, we could make out a small gathering of silhouettes; a whole community.

'No time for that. Give them a flask of water each and some rations. Is someone doing that? Jump to it!'

There was a sound of shuffling feet inside.

'Thank you so much. We're forever grateful,' Flame said.

'There's no need to thank us. We know what happens to those who get on the wrong side of the powers that be. That said, we can't have them accusing us of harbouring fugitives. I heard that gunshot. You'll need to stick the provisions in your backpacks and keep moving.'

A young man hurried along the hallway and handed us the provisions without saying a word.

We thanked him and I drank some water.

'Quickly!' the man hissed. 'Go on, young woman. One sip.'

Flame did as he said.

'Put it all away now. Go on. Good. Listen carefully—you need to follow the verandah along the right-hand side. Take the path into the rock grove and follow it down, all the way down. There's plenty of cover from oak trees. After a while, the path will wind through thick shrubs, almost so thick you'll have a hard time following it, but keep going. It will lead you to a footbridge across the river. This is the only open section on your route. Look very carefully all around and directly overhead before crossing. On the other side, follow the track through the woods, and keep walking. There's no need to run from there unless you're given reason to do so. Keep on the track for about an hour until you see an old watermill. The door is left open. Inside the mill, you'll find a ladder to the attic. There's a false wall splitting it in half. You'll work it out. Did you get that?'

'Yes,' I assured him. 'We can never thank you enough!'

'Don't mention it—just go! Good luck to you.'

We took to our heels.

The way down through the rock grove was difficult. It had obviously been designed as a maze, and I wondered whether all these deep passages and winding paths were part of the therapy required by the patients who had wandered these gardens in bygone days or merely a means of making it difficult for them to escape. Why had they been put away here in the first place? I imagined mumbling old men and ageing ladies off with the fairies, young violent men and hysterical adolescent girls. Is that what they had been like? Had they been disturbed by visions of the future—images of a world gone wrong, with collapsed governments using violence and technology in a desperate attempt to retain a semblance of control, pandering to the whims of the global corporations that owned them? Had they guessed the economic machine would crumble under the weight of its own inefficiency and that the insatiable few would have to go into hiding in luxury estates to escape the world they had pushed and pushed all the way over the brink? Had they blabbered incomprehensibly about the coming of a new feudal age, where every rich fucker and his dog would scramble to become the king in a realm of ruins and disarray?

Maybe they had.

It was the difficulty of the path that reassured me. No patrol would catch as here and no drone could spot us in this tangle. When we reached the overgrown path, I used my fork to help push our way through the thick shrubs and vines. I felt thorns grip my sleeves, some piercing the skin beneath, and Flame's muffled yelps told me she was experiencing the same problem, but we pushed on regardless. The biggest risk was if we bled and left a trail behind us.

We soon arrived at the footbridge, which had a steep set of stairs on either side to allow barges to pass underneath. The river was already quite narrow here. At a guess, crossing the bridge would take roughly five seconds.

We halted under the last shrub.

'Drones?' Flame asked.

We both looked up, searching every inch of sky.

'None,' I said. 'There's no track along the river. Nowhere for a patrol except on the water.'

'Let's go forward, heads low.'

I nodded and started creeping towards the bridge, looking left and right nervously as more of the river came into view. My stomach tightened as I crawled up the stairs, and I'm sure Flame's was the same—nerves and hunger wringing our insides.

'Let's run across the top,' I suggested, taking off and then huddling as I reached the stairs on the other side. It might have been too much. We were well past a little paranoid by now. But the last thing we wanted was to take a bullet on the bridge or have a drone detect us and have enough time to zoom in.

Under the canopy of the woods, we turned and looked back, as though expecting to hear the beating of boots on the path or the whir of drones echoing up from the riverbank.

Silence.

'We did it!' Flame whispered, and the glint in her green eyes was more exciting to me than any blazing car.

'We did, didn't we? With a helping hand from the folks at the asylum.'

She laughed, then pursed her lips, realising it had been a little loud.

'A quick sip of water before we push on to the mill?' I asked.

She licked her lips. 'Two sips, Flicker. I need two!'

'Fair enough.'

We sat on the trunk of a fallen tree and took our bottles from our backpacks. A cool breeze soughed through the branches overhead, and we looked up to see yellowing leaves rustling.

'It's just the wind,' I told her as our eyes met, and I slipped my hood off for the first time that day, eager to cool down a little and feel whatever breeze flowed at ground level caress my head.

She did the same, and sipped her water.

'I'm going to think every unexpected noise is a drone from now on,' she said.

I drank.

'We need to get to this mill, eat a little, and try to sleep. I can't go on like this much longer.'

'You're right,' I said. 'We need to stay strong. Do you know

38

what food he gave us?'

'I hope it's that cake you owe me.'

I grinned, but it soon drooped to a frown. My home. My books. All my gear. Here we were, fugitives in the woods with only a backpack each, and my fork, of course.

'After the mill?' I asked. 'What shall we do?'

'We'll keep going,' she replied, shrugging. 'Further away from the city. Wherever our feet take us.'

I took a sip and screwed the lid back on my flask.

'I brought this on you.'

'Yes.' She shrugged. 'Yes, you did. You made me a fugitive when you stumbled into my life last night. You gave me no choice but to flee with you. But tomorrow—if we're still alive—we'll leave the mill and keep walking. If I stay by your side tomorrow, it will be of my own choosing.'

I said nothing, and she took her second sip of water.

'First things first,' she declared, standing up. 'We need to find this watermill.'

Before setting off, I studied the area around the trunk. Confident we hadn't left any trace of our presence, we continued on our journey, with Flame taking the lead this time.

We made our way slowly and in silence, our footsteps barely audible above the rustling of leaves. My legs ached and my arms stung a little from the thorns, but my mind was growing calmer. The drones that haunted my thoughts were fading away, replaced by the question Flame had brought up, about what tomorrow would bring.

I watched the rise and fall of her taut buttocks through her soiled tracksuit bottoms and smiled at how the dappled sunlight that managed to penetrate the canopy in places brushed her short brown hair, making it glow.

'We're almost there,' I said, roughly an hour after crossing the bridge.

'I can't see it,' Flame replied, turning to look back at me.

'The water flows faster here; unnaturally so. That's got to be the result of where it's channelled through the wheel of the mill.'

She stopped and looked at the river, nodding.

'I didn't know you were a watermill expert.'

'There's a picture of one in one of my old books.'

She tipped her head to one side and offered me a sad smile. 'The books in your house?'

'That's right. The books in the house I can never go back to.'

'You'll find more. There must be books...' She hesitated.

'Wherever we're going,' I finished for her.

'Yeah. I mean, for all we know, there may be more books in the countryside than in the city.'

I doubted it but appreciated her optimism.

She started walking again, eager to be safely stowed away in the mill. The path soon veered left and opened onto a small flat area of rocky land jutting into the river. It formed a landing of sorts; a triangle of hewn flagstone with the mill where the furthest point should have been, projecting into the river. There was a single, low doorway with a wooden door speckled with iron rivets. Directly above it, a small grimy window, set in a slate roof, watched the approach. On the upstream side of the building, steep and narrow stone stairs went down to the river, providing a simple dock for small boats bringing goods from inland. Fresh produce. Food. I could just imagine a flat-bottomed wooden barge from days long gone accosting here and crates of carrots, potatoes, spinach, and eggs being hauled onto the landing, and grain, of course, for the mill.

Flame was on the downstream side of the mill, looking back along the river. She had her back to me, but I could still sense her fear. She then looked down to where the water rushed boisterously from the mouth of the trough.

I walked over, wanting so much to put my arm around her, but I didn't dare. Instead, I shared my thoughts with her.

'There are stairs and a mooring ring on the other side. It must be where boats with provisions stopped when the mill was functioning. Have you ever eaten an egg?'

She turned to me and stared blankly, then tilted her head up and squinted, searching her memory.

'There's egg in a lot of packaged supplies, I suppose, like in cakes.' She smiled.

'That didn't quite go to plan, did it? It was a bad move. If only we'd gone to your digs and not mine.'

'Ifs and buts,' she mused. 'Anyway, I'm not sure real eggs are used to make them.'

'I ate one once.'

She raised her eyebrows. 'An actual egg?'

'An actual egg. I cracked it open and poured it into a frying pan. A bit of the shell fell in but it didn't matter. I just spat it out later.'

'But there are no chickens.'

'Not in the city, but I'd heard stories about them still being kept in the countryside, and not just by food corporations, but by families and communities. They eat the eggs themselves on special occasions but generally sell them for a fortune to the rich. That's how I came to eat one.'

'Oh, you're actually loaded,' she teased. 'All this burning cars and running from drones is your way of pissing daddy off.'

We laughed. 'I once raided a flat with terrible security when the owners were out and there was an egg in the fridge. I could hardly believe it and knew it was worth the risk. I fried and ate it right there in their kitchen.'

'How did you know how?'

'Guess how!' I said, winking.

'Ah, you saw it in a book.'

'I wonder if we'll find things like that. Chickens and eggs. I wonder if there are fish to be caught.'

'Fish?' Flame asked, looking at me as though I were crazy. 'They're extinct, aren't they?'

I just looked at the water, twisting and gushing, roaring as it flowed. Bubbles rose to the surface further along, before it became calm again.

Flame looked to the sky. 'Let's get inside the mill and eat our rations, even if they're not fish and eggs.'

I tried the door, which was unlocked, as promised. It took some effort to push it open and it grated against the stone floor. Once Flame was inside, I pushed it closed again. The building was small with the lower floor holding the ancient machinery and not much room to spare. There was no furniture to speak of and no indication that any cooking had taken place. Daylight and a feeble draught entered through several small openings in the far wall. The inert wheel could be glimpsed through these openings, as well as the river and the bank on the other side.

'There's not much here,' I observed.

'Perhaps that's intentional to avoid raising suspicions if a patrol decides to take a peek inside.'

To our right, in the corner, the ladder led up through a wide hole in the warped wooden floor. The disproportionate size of the hole compared to the ladder, and the fact that it was perfectly round, gave the impression a spiral staircase had once stood there.

'Ladies first,' I said, and she glared at me, but I caught her smile as she turned and started up the ladder.

Once the floor was at eye level, she paused to look around, then looked down to me. 'You'll get a sore neck if you stand there like that all day. Are you coming up or what?'

I joined her up there, and we found ourselves standing, heads bowed because of the low frame and ceiling, in front of a wall that crossed the building in the middle, stretching from just past the window overlooking the approach to the river side. There were stacks of empty crates and boxes lined against the wall.

'A fake wall. That's what he said, isn't it?' I asked.

'I think so. Fake or false or artificial—something along those lines. I guess it either swings in or slides away.'

I inspected the wall near the window, looking for a handle or switch.

'I think I've found it,' Flame said, kneeling in front of one of the crates. She reached in and turned a knob, and over the constant background noise of rushing water, we heard a faint click.

She looked at me, mouth open in awe.

I grinned back at her. It was pretty exciting after all. We'd gone from being hunted by drones within the city limits to unlocking a secret room in a forgotten watermill, all in one morning.

'See how the wall is in three panels? I think we need to push the panel you're in front of but where it meets the middle one. I think that's where the click came from.'

She stood up and took a couple of steps to her left, then pushed firmly with both hands near where the panels joined.

Nothing happened.

'Nope,' she said, frowning and looking the wall up and down.

'Maybe it was the middle panel,' I said, walking over to her. We pushed the right-hand side of the middle panel and breathed a sigh of relief as it swung inwards.

The room was completely dark, so I took my torch and switched it on.

'Not bad,' Flame said. 'The floor is clean.'

'Four sleeping bags,' I observed.

'What's this bag hanging from a rafter?'

I pointed my torch at it.

'Food?' she asked.

It was a bundle wrapped up in a net and attached to the rafter by a rope.

'Or a small child's body?' I wondered.

'Very funny,' she said, but she clearly wasn't amused.

Asking myself whether I had indeed meant it as a joke, I reached out and tentatively opened the bundle.

My grin must have been a mile wide.

'Food!' she sang.

'Nuts, dried fruit, muesli bars, apple juice poppers, and tinned beans.'

Flame bit her bottom lip.

'What's in our rations?'

She took her package from her backpack and opened it.

'The same!' she almost yelled.

We laughed.

'It doesn't matter,' I said. 'Let's eat!'

We sat on a sleeping bag and dug into the rations, but I slowed down after just a handful or nuts and a muesli bar.

'You're done already?'

'Yeah. You too by the look of it. Maybe our stomachs have shrunk.'

Flame shrugged. 'I feel like a bath and some sleep.'

'If you can bear the cold, we could have a dip in the river, but best do it quietly and stay close to the mill.'

She finished her muesli bar. 'We're going to need new clothes soon.'

'I don't know if that's likely tomorrow. It'd be nice to have clean clothes, but it's probably too late to wash what we're wearing today and have them dry by morning. We'd have to stay here all day tomorrow and spend a second night.'

'No way. We need to push on.'

I nodded. 'Should we wash separately?'

'Why? Got something to be ashamed of?'

'No, that's not what I meant. I'm just being a gentleman.'

'Relax. I'm just messing with you.' She flashed me a playful smile, but her eyes told a different story. She was worried and full of doubt. Here she was, a young woman stranded in an abandoned mill with a man she didn't know. We were strangers flung together by circumstance. That look in her eyes told me she already felt naked and vulnerable. I understood then, in that very moment, that the further away from the threat of capture we moved, the more she would start to wonder whether she could trust me, as though the absence of drones and patrols, rather than diminishing her fear, merely made room in her mind for a new one. It was only natural. We'd faced the same challenges all our lives and both knew that trust was a hard-earned honour.

'Flicker?'

'Yeah?'

She clapped in front of my face. 'Can you stop staring at me?'

'Sorry. I didn't mean to.'

'What were you thinking? Was it what I said? I was just joking.'

I didn't know what to say—how to put what I was thinking into words—but the words ended up forming themselves.

'I know you were joking. The thing is, behind that, there's more to it. We're lost, and confused, and tired, and possibly on the verge of the biggest change either of us has ever been through. We don't know what lies ahead.'

Those green eyes were shining now. Tears were welling. I felt like telling her there was no need to put on a brave face, to pretend to be unbreakable and in control. But I didn't want her to cry. I didn't want to strip her bare.

'I got you into this mess, and I just want you to know that I'll be by your side for as long as it takes us to get out of it. I'll be your rock, steadfast and stubborn. You don't know me, but you will, and that doubt in your eyes will fade away.'

The tears came rolling down her cheeks, leaving a trail of dust, and she launched herself at me, throwing her arms around my neck.

Once the tears had stopped, she lifted her face from my shoulder, where my shirt was now damp and clinging to my skin, and moved her lips to my ear to whisper a question.

'Will you wash me?'

4. The Marshlands

Our sleep was deep that night, and the few times I woke, the sound of rushing water soon drew me back in. Flame had pulled her sleeping bag up next to mine at some stage during the night. I felt her face nuzzled against my back.

The room was utterly dark and there was no way of knowing when dawn broke, but I began to stir when I heard birdsong breaking through the rumble of the river. It was a magical moment, hidden from the world, without a fleck of light, yet knowing that a new day was dawning as I listened to the melody of the birds and the harmony of the water. While I listened, eyes closed because it made no difference, I thought about that world outside. There was beauty in it, but it came in glimpses. When you looked away, wretchedness engulfed it, and the beauty had often vanished into thin air by the time you looked back the same way. That was the hold fire had on me, the beauty of its ferocity, the vigour in its dance, the flair with which it consumed ugliness. In a crumbling city, it was the only rebellious form of ruin, the sole way of accelerating compliant collapse in a brief expression of magnificent fury. Fire is a backlash in a world in breakdown. Even once the flames have died down, the charred remains with twisted metal and warped plastic are darkly beautiful.

Would I continue my war wherever we were heading? Or was it a world without icons of power? Would the urge fade away?

'Are you awake?' Flame whispered.

'I'm listening to dawn's music.'

'It's lovely, isn't it?' She reached out for me and a hand fell upon my shoulder. 'I wonder what today will bring.'

'We'll do what we can. We'll keep our heads low and our eyes

46

peeled. If the day brings us food and clean clothes, it will be a fine one.'

'And no drones or patrols.'

'With a safe nest to lay our heads before nightfall.'

'We should get started if we're going to achieve all that,' she said, squeezing my shoulder.

'Let's go. We can stop for a light breakfast later.'

It would be lying to say we left the mill without some reluctance. We'd felt safe there. After an unforgettable day, we'd spent an entirely different yet equally memorable night. Neither of us would ever forget that ancient building.

'We can always come back,' she said softly when I turned to look over my shoulder one last time before the path led us into the woodlands.

'Perhaps we will one day. For old times' sake.'

Then again, perhaps we wouldn't get the chance.

We walked more slowly that day, wanting to let our sore legs take it easy. We didn't know when they would have to leap into action again, carrying us to safety. One step after the other, we followed the path until it dwindled away, and then we made a decision which way to go, avoiding where the thickets made progress impractical. There were clearings every now and then, although it was unclear to us why no trees grew in those places. Rock beds just below the surface? Invisible pollution in the soil? We crossed these clearings quickly, glancing skyward, but there were never any drones, just the occasional bird of prey.

The cycle continued, and the awareness that we were helplessly lost deepened with every change of direction, with every stretch of overgrown path we took, and every broken fence we climbed over. The first major difficulty was when we came across a creek, presumably a tributary to the river. It was only a few feet wide, but the water was muddy and sluggish. We stopped for a rest there and ate a light breakfast from our rations, sitting under the leafiest tree along the bank.

'No towns or roads. No farmland,' Flame mused, staring across the creek. There was woodland on the other side, but the trees were smaller and grew more sparsely. 'We can't keep on like this.'

'There must be people out here,' I replied, but my words lacked conviction.

'Should we cross the creek or follow it, Flicker?'

Cross or follow? It was the flip of a coin. We couldn't know if it would make any difference one way or the other.

'Follow it upstream,' I answered without quite knowing why.

'That's what I was thinking as well. There's more chance of a settlement near a source of fresh water.'

It made sense. It had to be the best bet. So we followed the creek upstream, weaving our way through the woods.

Judging by the sun, it must have been around midday when the land sloped downwards quite suddenly and the creek that had been to our left spread out before us. There were no more trees, just a broad and open expanse stretching out to the horizon.

'What is it?' I asked.

Her face was blank. She was trying to make sense of this new landscape.

'I've never seen anything like it before,' she said. 'It looks like long grass growing in water.'

I sighed, but a distant structure caught my eye and made me draw a sharp breath. 'Is that a building?' I pointed towards the horizon, slightly to our left, with my fork.

She placed a hand over her eyes to block out the sun and squinted. 'I think you're right! One small building. It might be a house. I can't see anyone around it.'

'It must be abandoned, surely. I can't imagine people living in the middle of this flooded land. It must be on some kind of island. This must be a marsh.'

Flame looked at me blankly. 'A marsh?'

'I read about it in a book. It's what you call land covered with water, but quite shallow, not like a river, and plants grow in it.'

Flame slapped her face, and when she looked at her hand, she saw a spot of blood on the palm. 'And mosquitoes,' she replied, frowning.

'Much of Europe was covered in marshland in ancient times before being dried for farming. Rising sea levels coupled with the abandonment of agricultural management and maintenance after The Breakdown has led to an increase in this wet land. That must be what this is—marshland.'

48

'You must miss your books?'

'I do. I wonder if there are some inside,' I replied, gazing at the distant edifice.

'I wouldn't count on it,' she said. 'Not here.' She slapped her neck and grimaced. 'We don't have much choice though, do we? It's the first form of potential shelter we've seen since leaving the mill.' There was already a hint of nostalgia in her voice. 'Why aren't they biting you?'

'My blood mustn't be as sweet as yours.'

The grimace turned to a smile for an instant.

'I wonder how deep it is,' I said, stepping closer to the water's edge, but my shoes began sinking deeper into the spongy earth with each step. It was immediately obvious that I'd be knee-high in mud before even reaching the water. We were going to have to find another way. The only option was to head right and follow the perimeter of the marshland in search of an elevated road or dyke.

The rushes were tall and we had to walk up to higher land every now and then in order to see over their swaying tops and keep track of where the building was. At one point, it seemed we were moving away from it, but the distance decreased again further along, giving the impression that time and space were somehow scheming against us. It was a disconcerting and demoralising process, making us feel that we were playing a geographical game of cat and mouse. Our complete ignorance of this environment was draining us.

Little by little, the mosquitoes began to realise that I was fair game, even though Flame remained their target of choice, and every dozen or so steps, one of us stood in a pothole and had to carefully wiggle a foot out again so as not to lose a shoe. The sodden earth would then fill in again with a slurping sound. We were sweating in that humid air, our clothes clinging to our skin, and if we'd wanted a change of clothes back at the mill, we didn't even dare dream of it now. All that mattered was reaching that forgotten building somehow, and hoping it would provide shelter for the night. We had enough rations left for another meal and neither of us was in the mood to eat before reaching our goal.

The sun was beating down on us through a thin veil of cloud.

Birds of prey soared high above, descending in circles and swooping into the marshes when they'd caught sight of a promising morsel. I wondered what it was they were hunting, and whether I'd be quick enough to kill anything worth eating with my gardening fork if the opportunity arose. It occurred to me that I should have had the foresight to bring some kindling from the woods. There was nothing here dry enough to burn. The landscape to our right was now desolated plains, only distinguishable from the marshland because it was higher and the grass shorter. It was too late to turn back now, unless we couldn't reach the building and were forced to struggle all the way back to the woods to make camp—out of range for the mosquitoes, or so I wanted to believe.

Our sense of despair was drawing us irreversibly close to madness when Flame breathed a heavy sigh of relief and I knew she'd spotted a path of some kind.

'There!' she called, her voice so loud against the silence of the marshland that it seemed to boom all the way to the horizon.

I placed a finger to my lips. Paranoia? Perhaps. We hadn't seen a drone all day, but the element of surprise was the only weapon we had—other than Flame's knife, and my fork and hammer. If that building was occupied, as unlikely as it seemed, I didn't want them to hear us coming.

The passage through the rushes was high enough to be solid underfoot, and surprisingly dry. It was wide enough for us to walk along single-file and appeared to be as straight as an arrow. It was like floating in the air compared to the slog we'd endured. At the end, which looked to be a twenty-minute walk away, a corner of the building peeped out from behind the wall of rushes to our left. Only open sky could be seen beyond it, confirming my suspicion that it had been built on the highest point in the marshland.

'We should have a plan of approach,' Flame pointed out as we started along the passage. She was right, of course.

I turned my head a little and spoke over my shoulder. 'Once we get to the end, we'll stick close to the rushes to stay hidden from view and listen for a minute or two. If we don't hear anyone, I'll sneak up to the house for a closer look and you stay back to keep an eye out. How does that sound?'

'That seems sensible.'

We did just that. As we reached the end, we stayed close to the side of the passage and stopped.

'It's a chapel,' Flame whispered.

I don't think either of us was expecting that—here, in the middle of a vast marsh, far from human settlement. It was a small structure, made of stone and showing only minor signs of subsidence, with a hairline crack or two reaching up from the foundations. The entrance was facing us; a simple wooden door in an arched doorway with a rusted steel ring pull. The roof was also made of stone and a small section appeared to have collapsed—mosquito access, I immediately thought.

'It's a strange place for a chapel, isn't it?' Flame said, looking around nervously.

It must have been contagious, because I found myself looking over my shoulder, back along the empty passage.

'I suppose it is,' I agreed. 'But we don't know how old it is or how the landscape may have changed over the years. The marshland probably didn't cover such a broad area at some point in the past. This island may have merely been a small mound in the middle of a village. The marshland may have drowned the ruins of houses and workshops.'

Flame stared at the rushes and reeds, imagining that other time, a world away. Dragonflies hovered and navigated their way through the wetland plants, at perfect ease within their natural habitat. Watching them, I hoped beyond all hope that drone technology would never come close to imitating their movement.

'You've slept in a chapel before?' she asked. 'They make great hideaways. Hardly anyone ever uses them. The problem is most seem to be bolted shut.'

'I've heard they're used as warehouses, but by whom and for what, I don't know.'

'That's in the city,' she said. 'I doubt this one's used for storage.'

'Let's find out,' I said. 'I'll try to door.'

She waited while I jogged over to the chapel and pushed the door with one hand. It moved a little but then jammed. I dropped my fork and pushed at it with both hands, putting all my strength and weight into the effort. It swung inwards and I stumbled inside, losing my balance.

I heard her laugh, but a second later she was behind me, taking up my fork.

'That was one ungodly entrance!'

I got to my feet and reached out for my weapon even though there was clearly no one inside. That old gardening fork was all I had to make me feel safe since fleeing the greenhouses. I suspected it wouldn't be long before I was sleeping with my fingers wrapped around its shaft.

The shattered remains of two double-arched stained-glass windows punctuated the grimy whitewashed chapel walls, one pair on either side. Mosquito nets had been fixed over the windows, mimicking the countless cobwebs filling the corners between vaulted ceiling and walls, and hanging like grey ghosts in twists and clumps. Only three pews remained, placed facing each other to form a triangle. The chapel was otherwise bare, except for a long table covered with a dusty burgundy tablecloth at the other end, where the altar should have been. There had been a large stained-glass window behind the altar but it was boarded up and bore a message crudely written in white paint.

Congratulations, fugitives from the city. You've done well to make it this far. May you continue to avoid capture and The Esplanade.

We exchanged glances, then looked around the chapel again, half-expecting a gang of desperate fugitives to suddenly appear, but there was nowhere anyone could be hidden, except perhaps under the altar table.

'It's as though it was written specifically for us,' Flame said, knowing I was thinking the very same thing.

'Troubling, isn't it? And yet reassuring. We're not alone. We aren't the first to have come this way. The message, the pews, and the netting over the windows mean others like us have stayed here. But it's been some time, I'd wager.'

'I agree. That's all we know. We don't know what happened to them afterwards. We don't know whether they made it much further. They could be...' She nodded back towards the door, leaving her sentence unfinished.

'They could be where?'

She flashed me a look of annoyance. 'Out there.'

'Oh, I think I see what you mean. Their bodies might in the marshes.'

'They could have been ambushed here and their bodies dumped in the water. No one would ever find them. There are probably eels and the like swarming in there. Only scattered bones would be left, lodged in the mud at the bottom.'

Flame was opening a darker side to her psyche to me. She was quite right, of course. It was a definite possibility.

'Or they might have continued along the passage on the other side of the chapel and arrived somewhere safer and more comfortable. Take the nets over the windows, for example. It's unlikely they would have had that on them the first time they got here. They would have come back and put them up with the intention of spending the night on more than one occasion. Why? Well, that's another question.'

She shrugged, but didn't appear convinced. 'Sure. That's all very well, Flicker, but we don't know they weren't set upon on the third or thirteenth night staying here.'

Another fair point. The fact of the matter was that we didn't know anything at all. I turned my attention back to the message. 'Where's The Esplanade?'

She shook her head. 'What's an esplanade?'

'We need to find some old books for you. I hope we do one day. An esplanade is a wide street along the coast, usually near a beach. It's where people used to go on holidays. Perhaps the Overclass still does. They had shops, hotels, restaurants, bars, and casinos.'

'What's so terrible about that?' she asked, frowning. 'Why would the patrols take prisoners there?'

'No idea,' I said. 'No idea at all. It might be the nickname of a prison on the coast. What's peculiar to me is that the message doesn't tell us which way to go from here. Are we to assume that since the writer assumes we have arrived from the city, it's expected we will continue along the passage on the other side?'

'That makes sense. Or perhaps the message is merely a ploy—a word of encouragement to lull us into a false sense of security.'

She really was showing me her darker side. Could it be the influence of the marshland, the dread it evoked in two beings who had no experience of such terrain? In any case, I was lucid enough to realise her trepidation could very well turn out to be a lifesaving quality.

'Do we risk it? If we don't sleep here tonight, we have to trudge all the way back to the woodlands.'

'Out of the question,' she replied sternly. 'We'll block the door from the inside somehow and sleep under the table. That will hide us from view and give us a fighting chance if taken by surprise.'

'And the tablecloth will help protect us from mosquitoes as well.'

That observation brought a reassuring smile to her lips. The bloodsuckers were an ever-present threat, and one that would only worsen after nightfall.

'I'd kill for a bath and some clean clothes right now. I'll clean up in here and try to make ourselves as comfortable as possible. You have a look around outside in case there's anything of use to us.'

'Yes, ma'am,' I said, with a quick salute, and gripping my fork firmly, I left the chapel.

Walking around that small island—for that's what it was in a way, even though the dyke passed through it—I realised I was alone for the first time since meeting Flame. She was only a matter of yards away, inside the chapel, but all the same, we weren't together. We couldn't see each other. Except for when we had to relieve ourselves, we'd been together all the time. I wondered if she too was thinking about that as she cleaned the chapel up a little. What was going through her head—dark thoughts about our predicament, the one I'd thrust upon her, or was there a glimmer of hope in her heart? Was she picturing the skeletal remains of our predecessors at the bottom of the marshes, or was she dreaming about a better place, one that could become a real home—the first we'd ever know?

I walked around the chapel, but there was nothing at all. I took a few steps along the passage leading on from the island. It was clearly longer than the one along which we'd arrived because I couldn't see the end. As far as I could see, there were two unbroken walls of rushes that merged together at the end. The passage had been built perfectly straight. It had surely been a very long time ago, as long ago as the chapel, unless the building had been erected at a time when this really was an island.

These days belonged to the forces of destruction, not construction. The Breakdown had put an end to all that. Only the luxury residences of the city centre and the infrastructure of the administration were being built now, along with a select number of manufacturing plants, particularly in the field of aerial surveillance. The rest of the world was in tatters.

It's hard to say how long I stayed there, staring into the distance, but when I emerged from my thoughts, I realised I was sitting on the ground, cradling my fork like a baby. There were at least two mosquitoes on me and I brushed them away absentmindedly, almost gently.

There were so many questions churning in my head, and so much uncertainty. Attempting to answer them was pointless. I needed to keep my focus—to look after Flame. I was the one who had dragged her into this mess. Now, she was all I had. I owed her my life, and I...well, I cared about her more than I'd ever cared about anyone before. That was what it boiled down to, wasn't it? As terrifyingly simple as that. We had to look out for each other. That meant, first and foremost, staying on our guard, and nestling out of sight and holed up to sleep. It also meant staying strong, mentally and physically, finding clean water, food, clothes, and somewhere to eventually settle down. Not here.

I slapped a mosquito on my neck and got to my feet, then looked along the passage we would take in the morning. It was long but flat and straight—an easy walk.

Flame appeared at the doorway and shook the burgundy tablecloth, sending a cloud of dust into the air. 'It's important for us to have a moment alone from time to time.'

I smiled, knowing she could tell I'd been thinking just that.

'Were you meditating?'

'I guess you could call it meditation. I was trying to set goals, short-term and long-term. It feels like that's called for.'

'Was I in there somewhere—one of these *goals*?'

I walked over to her, grabbed the tablecloth, and wrapped it around her. 'First priority.'

She leaned back into my arms.

We jammed the three pews up against the door that night, and although the barricade wouldn't prevent a determined intruder from getting in, it would cause enough delay and noise to give us warning. We sat on one of them while we ate our rations and sipped water, making sure to leave some for the next day.

'We have to find food and water tomorrow,' Flame said between mouthfuls of nuts. 'We need to leave here at daybreak and keep going until we find provisions.'

There was a more optimistic note to her voice now than when we'd arrived. The tiring trudge and confusing terrain had taken its toll earlier. The air was cooler now, so much so that I wondered whether we'd have rain during the night, and we had some food in our stomachs. The tablecloth was wrapped around us, so we only had to keep mosquitoes off our faces.

'We will,' I told her. 'I'm sure we will. This marshland is fertile and a good source of water. That means there's bound to be farmland nearby. Tomorrow will be a better day.'

'Are you tired?'

'Not really. I'm comfortable sitting here on the pew with you.'

'Let's talk then.'

'Aren't we now?'

'I mean *really* talk.'

I frowned, not entirely sure of her meaning.

'Tell me who you are,' she said. 'Who is Flicker?'

I drew a deep breath. Where to begin?

'Who am I?' I asked myself—not for the first time. 'Now, that *is* a tricky question. Where do I begin? First, I have a question for you, because I don't know how old you are and would never ask a lady that question.'

'A lady?' She laughed. 'Your nose isn't working too well.'

'All I can smell is marshland.'

'I don't know how old I am,' she said, and I nodded. No one really knew.

'Do you remember The Breakdown?'

'I was so young.' She paused, lost in thought. 'I think I remember. Well, I'm not sure if I remember or whether I've heard so much about it that I imagine I remember—do you get what I mean?'

'I do,' I reassured her. 'It's pretty much the same for me, but I have vague memories from just before, when the city was reaching breaking point. I remember living in a high-rise building. Every flat was occupied. There were so many people back then. That sticks in the mind. The city was populated in those days—probably overpopulated. I suppose that was part of the problem. Thousands of people were crammed into that block of flats, while a fifteen-minute walk away, there were immense mansions inhabited by solitary widows or rich playboys. I remember thinking it should have been the opposite—working families in big houses and individuals in flats. That would have made more sense. It was a powder keg. That's what it was. There was no more work but we weren't paid if we didn't work. That didn't make sense either. Infrastructure was crumbling and the streets were filthy, but there was no work. Even as I child, I understood that it was an untenable situation.

'There were riots. I don't know how they started, but that hardly mattered, it could have been one of a thousand sparks that ignited the powder keg. The riots were quashed. Machines, like bulldozers, were sent in to scoop people up and carry them away. It went on for what I thought was a matter of months, but you know how time stretches for children. It was certainly a few days, or weeks, at most.'

'That was what triggered The Breakdown?'

'I think so. The population suddenly dropped. My building collapsed, or was demolished. Ever since, the world has been as we know it.' I shrugged. What else was there to say? I didn't understand it any more than she did. 'I became a rat. A dreg. I was aware of that and I hated it bitterly. That's when I decided I had to fight back. I wanted to burn the whole fucking world to the ground.'

I paused, hesitating in my admission.

'I'd always been fascinated by fire. Almost perversely.'

Her eyes widened. 'What does that mean?'

I couldn't tell her how it made me feel. The intimate details of the effect it sometimes had on me. But she understood and pursed her lips together to repress a grin.

Then it dawned on me. 'You're like me, aren't you? We're the same, Flame.'

She blushed.

'It was a powerful weapon at my disposal. I knew it would be my signature.'

'Fire is pure, raw energy, destroying all that is hideous in the most beautiful of ways—a dance and a song that is timeless and universal in its anger and rebellion.'

'Yes!' I gasped. 'That's it, Flame. Say that again!'

She did.

'And you always did it alone?' she asked.

'It was personal. I raided warehouses and went exploring with my companions, but fire was mine alone.'

'We need to discover the truth one day, about what happened to our family and friends. We owe it to them.'

'You're right. We do, and we will. What about you? What do you remember about the girl you were, Cara?'

Her eyes went far away, and although I followed her gaze to a dark corner of the chapel, I could not see what she saw.

'Cara was—a lost child,' she whispered, and those last three words spoke themselves, so that she listened to them as I did. 'Fire wasn't so personal for me at first, I suppose.' She paused and looked at me. 'There was someone else.'

'A boyfriend?'

She nodded. 'Our relationship wasn't perfect, but he used to always light the evening fire. It was one of his duties in our circle of friends. I don't whether it was him I fell for, or the fire, but every evening I'd watch him and it made me smile—at first.'

'What happened?'

'I soon discovered that I wasn't the only girl he made feel special.'

'He was leading a double life?'

'Right under my nose, with a girl I considered my sister.'

'That's horrible,' I said. 'Did they at least have the decency to leave your group?'

'They were taken by a patrol one night during a raid that went wrong.'

We sat in silence. I wanted to ask her if she still thought about him, despite how he'd treated her, but I didn't really want to know. I decided to change the subject instead.

'Do you remember your family?'

A veil of darkness dropped over her face and I regretted my question immediately. I yearned to take it back, but words spoken can never be undone.

'Another time, perhaps?' I said softly, laying a hand on her knee under the tablecloth.

'Let's get some sleep,' she said, and carried the tablecloth over to the chancel, where she draped it over the table. We crawled under and stretched out on the makeshift mattress of dry rushes and reeds that she'd prepared earlier. It would serve as our bed for the night—our nest in the chapel.

5. Ghost Town

We left at dawn, accompanied by a harmonious soundtrack of toad song. The marshes were alive in the cool morning air. The ground was damp with dew, and robins flitted about among the rushes, chasing insects. It was an encouraging start to the day.

While we'd left the sleeping bags at the mill, not wanting to steal from those who'd aided us, we decided it wouldn't be greatly inconveniencing anyone to take the tablecloth. It could prove handy, and probably wouldn't be missed at all. Rolled up tightly, it slipped easily into my backpack.

The walk along the path was easy going. We kept up a good pace, knowing we had to keep moving until we found food and shelter. We didn't know what the lay of the land would be like later, so figured it was best to make quickly while we could.

'I think I can see the end,' Flame said about forty minutes in.

I stopped for a minute. The sun was behind us and the rushes flanking us shone golden brown. I saw open land, green and flat, in the distance.

'No sign of settlement from here,' I observed.

'But it seems to be a clear field—cultivated land, perhaps, like you said last night.'

'Let's hope so.'

We picked up our pace again and reached the field a quarter of an hour later, stepping out past the last rushes cautiously and hopefully.

The land stretched gently downhill. It was covered with short grass but there were no animals that we could see. Further back, it rose slightly into a range of low hills, on top of which ran the towers of high-voltage power lines, one bent in the middle, making it look like the crooked finger of a gigantic buried robot.

To the left, southwards, I guessed, the fields stretched out but were overgrown in places with brambles and bushes. To the right, I glimpsed a swerving band of black between two rocky knolls. It was immediately clear what it was. There was no mistaking it.

I was about to ask Flame if she'd noticed it but she got in first.

'A road! We've found a road!'

I breathed a sigh of relief. Where it went hardly mattered. It was a road, so it had to lead us *somewhere*.

'We'll need to stay more alert than ever,' she said. 'Eyes and ears honed.'

The road was a single carriageway with one lane in each direction. After winding its way between the rocky knolls, it ran straight downhill, delineating the field from which we'd approached on one side and passing a quarry further along on the other. Where it reached the hills, it began to wind again, climbing the gentlest slopes.

'It hasn't been maintained,' Flame observed as we began the downhill stretch, sticking close to the side and ready to hide in the deep ditch, clogged with brambles and weeds, if a vehicle approached.

The surface of the road was pockmarked and uneven, and the white line was almost entirely faded along most of the length. As we passed the old quarry, I recognised the same type of stone used for the chapel in its two jagged cuts.

No vehicle came along the road as we followed it down and then up into the hills. At the highest point, the high-voltage lines stretched overhead, but one had snapped off and lay halfway across the road. There was clearly no current, but we gave it a wide berth all the same.

It was there, where the road flattened out along a ridge, that we realised we were about to enter a town. There was a sign leaning towards the road about three hundred feet ahead, perilously close to falling over. A multicoloured design represented the globe and beneath it were five red letters—*TOTAL*.

'Do you know what a TOTAL is?' I asked.

'Never heard of it. It must be a shop of some kind—clothes, hopefully.'

We stopped in front, taking in the details and drawing our conclusions. Four pumps were in place, but one of them no longer had a hose and nozzle attached like the other three.

'It was a business for putting fuel in vehicles?' Flame asked.

'By the look of it. I think they called them "service stations". Completely useless.'

It was the first I'd seen. I'd siphoned petrol out of cars but never witnessed it being put in except from a jerry can.

The building itself wasn't in bad condition, apart from the usual signs of abandonment—the drift of leaves on the flat roof, the searching tendrils of brambles and ivy along the side, reaching towards the pumps across the asphalt. The wide windows, while grimy, were unbroken. It was at that eerie stage between desertion and decay, as though suddenly seeing someone there behind the counter remained a distinct possibility.

I motioned with my fork, no doubt looking like a poor man's general unenthusiastically ordering a peasant army to charge. Nevertheless, Flame followed me, slowly but without hesitation. The glass door swung open without complaint and we found ourselves in a showroom full of shelves—empty shelves.

'I wonder what they used to sell here,' Flame said. 'If people came here to get petrol from the pumps, why does it look like a shop inside?'

'There's a coffee machine. I've seen them in old railway stations. You used to be able to put coins in the slot and the machine would make a coffee for you.'

'Serious?'

'That's what I understand. The instructions are written on it.'

'If only it was in working order.'

'Not without electricity.'

'And coffee,' she added poignantly.

We checked behind the counter but there was nothing of interest. I looked everywhere in the building, trying to find jerry cans of fuel or matches, but it was not to be.

'Power lines down. No fuel,' I said. 'This is a town with no vehicles.'

'Or people,' Flame added, heading for the door. 'Ready to go? I'm eager to try our luck closer to the centre.'

As we advanced, our suspicions were confirmed. The entire town had been abandoned, or cleared out. The houses were in a state of decay with front gardens overgrown jungles, brick walls cracked or collapsed, roof tiles missing, and chimney stacks crumbling. *The King's Head* was like a mausoleum.

'A pub, Flame. A real pub. It's like we've just stepped back in time.'

'To think people used to drink beer for hours in places like this. I can't even remember the last time I managed to score myself a single bottle.'

'Is it worth a look, do you think?'

'Without a doubt,' she said. 'Fingers crossed.'

We laughed as we stepped inside, the smell of dank wood filling our nostrils. It turned out we hadn't crossed our fingers earnestly enough, because the bar fridges and shelves were all bare.

'This must be what traditional pubs were like,' Flame said, walking around slowly and looking everywhere in amazement. There were photographs on the walls of what looked like sports teams. In the largest of them, a group of solid men with thick necks and rough but happy faces stood on a podium. One held a shield over his head and the others were pumping their fists in the air.

'Look at this, Flame. Look how strong these men were.'

'That's impressive. They must have eaten well. Do we know what year it is?'

I studied the photograph but saw no indication of the year.

'It might have been before meat ran out. They definitely look like they had a high-protein diet.'

'I'd say so,' I said. 'Either meat or protein supplements.'

'Do you know what sport it is?'

I didn't. There was no ball in the shot, but when I inspected similar photos, I saw an elongated ball, not a round one like the footballs I'd already come across long ago raiding old Decathlon warehouses.

'I don't know, but I'd guess it involved quite violent contact, judging by their faces and physiques.'

There were also shots of people drinking together—happy

people in a crowded pub. It was this very one presumably, although so much had changed.

Around the other side of the L-shaped room was a fireplace. There was no firewood or kindling, no pokers or tongs, no log grate. In fact, wherever I looked, I found no items made principally of metal. Anything of practical use had been taken. Above the fireplace, there was a stag's head—magnificent in this setting but of no conceivable practical importance outside of it.

It was safe to assume we would later discover the same trend all around the town. Was it then a matter of the inhabitants leaving in an organised manner, with time to prepare their departure and pack their belongings, or had these objects been removed over time by fugitives like ourselves?

'If only I could see what your glassy eyes have seen,' I told the stag's head. 'You must have witnessed it all.'

'You need some rest, Flicker.'

I turned to find Flame watching me, eyebrows raised.

'I do. We both do. I was just trying to get my head around what happened here.'

'I know. So am I. Why was the whole town abandoned? There are no signs of violence. You'd expect to find bullet holes in the walls or smashed windows and furniture if there had been a crackdown. It looks more like everyone simply upped and left.'

'That's the impression I get as well. Or perhaps they were forcibly removed in such a methodical way that resistance wasn't even possible.'

'Let's look upstairs.'

I followed her up the dusty wooden staircase and into a hall. On the right, there were three open doors. Flame glanced into the first room, then entered. I was right behind her, my fork at the ready. Sticking it into a human being was an entirely different matter to bringing down a drone, but with each passing day, I could feel my survival instincts growing.

It was a bedroom, presumably that of the couple who had owned the pub. Peeling wallpaper with red roses on a white background now stained with patches of mildew covered the room. The blithe prettiness it evoked made it look absurd in this forgotten corner of a dead town, and yet, despite that, it continued to produce a pleasant result. It *was* pretty, despite its poor condition, because it had been chosen by someone with the sole intention of creating a feeling of comfort and contentment. In a way, the wallpaper was in itself a symbol of resistance.

Flame read my thoughts. 'This room exists in some kind of alternate dimension.'

Below the window was a double bed with a mattress and what appeared to be a clean sheet tucked in under the corners. Although it didn't smell very fresh, I knew we would have no trouble at all sleeping on it. Three candles, not new but still usable, sat in saucers on a small table against the wall. On the other side of the bed stood a fine hardwood wardrobe with a key in the lock. Flame opened it, and what she saw made her draw a deep breath.

'Tell me it's good news, please,' I begged her.

'It is. Oh, it is!'

It was the happiest I'd heard her. Her voice was so sweet and cheerful. I straightened my back and smiled—a load taken off my shoulders.

'We've been hired!'

'What are you on about?'

'Have a look,' she said and laughed.

There were no clothes hangers in the wardrobe. There wasn't even a rod, but there were several vacuum storage bags piled on the wardrobe floor and they were packed full of black T-shirts with the name of the pub printed in a circle and the profile of a crowned head in the middle.

Flame started opening them and checking the sizes. There were also hoodies. It was like how Christmas is supposed to be—how it was in books.

'All we need now is safe drinking water, food, and water to wash with.'

'Let's change later,' she said. 'There's no point in putting clean clothes on dirty bodies.'

The next room along was an old bathroom. There were off-white tiles on the floor and covering three quarters of the height of the walls. Flame tried the tap, just on the off chance, but there was no water.

'I could hook it up to a reservoir and collect rain water, assuming we find the right material.'

Flame tilted her head to one side and narrowed her eyes.

'What did I say?'

'Oh, nothing. It's just that it sounds like you've already decided this is going to be our new home. Were you planning on discussing this with me? I mean, I'm not your wife, so there's no obligation, but I thought it might be the type of decision we could make together.'

'Merely projecting. I want us to be as comfortable as we can be. However you look at it, this town is the best prospect we've come across so far. If we choose one building here to fix up a little, we can use it as a base to keep exploring. That way, we can spend a few days scouting, then come back here for some rest. The weather is fine now but we'll need to be sheltered come winter, and it could take weeks of work to get an old building into shape. We're going to have to grow and store food as well.'

'You've got it all worked out, haven't you? Welcome to Flickerton, population two. Here's a tricky one for you. Who's going to deliver the babies? Can you handle that all on your own?'

I wasn't sure whether she was joking. I was starting to get a grasp on her acerbic sense of humour but couldn't always be sure. She relished that confusion. The only option was to play along.

'You want to have my babies, do you?'

She punched me in the shoulder. 'Whose else am I likely to have here?'

'Good point. After the night at the mill, one might already be on the way.'

She shook her head. 'I don't think so. Not the right time of month. I'll know in a couple of days.'

I must have been frowning because her jaw dropped. Then she bit her bottom lip, repressing the urge to laugh.

'I'm missing something here,' was all I managed to say.

'Yes, my lad. Yes, you are. All these books you've read—none of them were about, I don't know, biology?'

'Not specifically about women.'

66

Her cheeks turned pink.

'How long have you been with a woman before?'

'Just from time to time, when it was convenient. I've had a couple of...girlfriends, I guess you could say. But I've never *lived* with a woman before.'

'When it was convenient for her?' Flame asked, grinning.

'Sure. Well, convenient for both of us. Listen, are you going to enlighten me or just make fun?' I was feeling a little annoyed but equally pleased to see her having a laugh, even if it was at my expense.

'I think I'm just going to make fun of you for the moment!' she said, then forced her lips closed. 'This *is* pretty funny. Please just let me enjoy the moment. I'll enlighten you tonight. In any case, those XS T-shirts are mine. I'm going to need them.' She laughed again. 'Let's forget plumbing for a minute. I'm with you, Flicker. *The King's Head* isn't looking too bad for the moment, but we need to keep exploring.'

I nodded.

'This bathtub,' she said, bending over. 'Yeah. The plug seems to be in good nick. If we find a source of water and a bucket or some other kind of container—perfect. What about the cabinet over the basin? What's in it?'

I opened it. 'One small spider.'

'Ah, ok. Come on—let's move on to the last room.'

It was a second bedroom, this one with two single beds. There were no mattresses. Smaller and easier to carry away on foot? Definitely. It was a corner room with two windows and there was a fire engine toy box on the floor. I looked inside but found only a few figurines of rare or extinct animals, like a lion, a wolf, and a cow.

Flame moved from the side window—which provided a view of the slate roof of the single-storey building next door—to the rear window. I joined her and together we stood without speaking for a minute.

When we turned to look at each other, we laughed.

There had been a courtyard below the window. A beer garden was what they used to call it. A scattering of plastic chairs and tables covered in cobwebs remained. Beyond that was a thin stretch of garden ending at a stone wall several hundred yards down. What we could tell had once been a charming and well-kept garden was now an overgrown tangle. But growing within the mess of vines and weeds were edible plants. Even without the helping hand of a gardener, they had followed the seasons and grown unfettered.

Flame was the first to break the silence. 'Cherry tomatoes!'

'It's unbelievable!' I almost shouted. 'They've taken control of the herb garden, but the mint is counter-attacking.'

She laughed, and kissed my dirty cheek.

'There's a huge rosemary bush in the herb garden. Apples further back. We'll need to pick them quickly before they rot. I think we should cover them with a net to keep the birds off.'

'I guess so. We'll have to find one somewhere. Can you see any vegetables?'

'I think there are potatoes further back but it's hard to tell from here. We need to take a closer look. This gardening fork might come in handy for more than just crashing drones after all!'

We found enough potatoes for several meals, as well as courgettes. We brought them, along with a handful of the cherry tomatoes, into the kitchen, which lay between the garden and the bar. All the metal utensils had been taken, but there were plastic containers—one which could serve as a bucket—and Flame had her knife.

'I think we're doing all right,' I told her. 'But if we want to have potatoes tonight, we're going to need to cook them. Without gas or electricity, we can't do that. The only other option is fire. There's enough dry material in the garden for that, but if a surveillance drone happens to pass overhead, we're finished.'

'We could wait until after dark and the smoke can't be seen so easily, but then we'd have to make sure the fire can't be detected from the sky.'

'That's no problem—we have the fireplace.'

'Right,' Flame said. 'What else do we need then? A pot and water to boil.'

'I've added it to the shopping list,' I said, tapping my temple. 'A pot, netting for the apple tree, water, any other food or clothing we can lay our hands on, and we're going to need more matches

68

and batteries for my torch. Anything else?'

'They're the priorities.'

'We mustn't let our guard down. We need to remember to keep scanning the sky whenever we're in the street and to exercise caution entering buildings. We can't be sure that whatever happened here is one hundred percent over.'

'Understood. We might find better weapons while we're doing the grocery shopping.'

'That would be good,' I agreed.

We checked the length of the street as we left the pub, then scrutinised the sky. Nothing. It was cloudy and humid, and there was the smell and feel of rain in the air. More than the previous night, I hoped. A decent downpour would be a double blessing, providing us with a good wash while drastically reducing the chances of aerial surveillance.

The high street reminded us of the older boroughs in the city, except that the latter were hives of activity with squatters constantly wheeling and dealing. Drones and cameras were part of the landscape there, and patrols were commonplace. If you kept your head down and stayed out of trouble, your existence was tolerated. The problem was, it was increasingly difficult to scrape by without sticking your neck out, and some of us could no longer resist the temptation to lash out—to kick against the pricks. Some of us, well, we simply couldn't resist that omnipresent urge to watch it all go up in fucking flames.

There would be no burning here, because there were no ostentatious symbols of corruption and wealth. Nothing to waste. No one left to despise. Was that what had happened? Were we in the heart of a vanquished rebel stronghold? It didn't look it, but maybe that was the point. Had *The King's Head* been a hotbed of resistance with those sportsmen its guerrillas?

The more I thought about it, the more I saw raging flames. It wasn't too bad yet, but I knew the night would come when I'd have to set fire to something. The desire would build to the point it became overwhelming.

'There's a supermarket,' Flame said. 'It's worth a try.'

And indeed it was. As expected, the shelves were mostly bare, but there was enough left to make it a gold mine for us. We took a plastic basket each and started collecting what we needed.

'This jar of pasta sauce has an expiry date of February next year. When would that make its delivery here?'

'I think it's usually good for three or four years unopened,' Flame said. 'Do you think it's been that long?'

'It's hard to say, isn't it? The pub garden definitely hasn't been looked after in well over a year, maybe more. It could be as many as three, I guess.'

'This supermarket was better stocked than any I've seen in the city. It's as though the supply chain wasn't as severely affected here.'

'Perhaps they had one of their own.'

'I wonder. That might explain it. They might have drawn attention to themselves. If people in the city knew about this place, they'd be rushing here in the thousands.'

I took a bottle of olive oil. It had been years since I'd been fortunate enough to come across some while raiding a rich administrator's home. I'd heard that with the way the climate is heating up, wine and olive oil would become staples here one day, but temperature doesn't do the job on its own without infrastructure, know-how, and cooperation. I thought about those fields we'd passed yesterday after leaving the marshes. I'm sure cows could have lived there. That would mean milk and meat. But were there any cows left, and who remembered how to tend to them even if there were?

'I've found pasta and rice,' Flame chirped.

'Excellent. No sign of a pot?'

She shook her head. 'We'll have to go through some houses later.'

'Lentils, chickpeas, and semolina,' Flame went on. 'This is heaven!'

I pinched myself. 'No, not dreaming.'

Flame laughed and then glanced at the door before looking around the shop. 'What if it's all part of an elaborate trap?'

'Not their style.'

I strolled every aisle swinging my basket merrily in one hand and holding the fork in the other, knowing I'd feel naked without it. As I passed ridiculous signs for two-for-one deals and promotions at twenty percent off, I chuckled and gave them a jab. It was a rather small supermarket, compared to those with sliding doors that had once been automatic close to the ring road, but it was a veritable treasure trove for us.

Once our baskets were as full as could be without risking an avalanche of jars, tins, and packets, we decided to take them back to the pub before heading out on our next foray.

The cloud cover was increasing by the minute and a cool breeze was blowing. This caused subtle movements along the street that put us on edge. A sudden gust sent leaves scuttling across the street and a branch rubbed against the top of a brick wall. Useless overhead power lines swayed and rusty garden gates groaned. These normally innocent stirrings and noises would make any human activity or the arrival of a drone more difficult to detect.

We entered the first house after the supermarket. The front was hidden from the street by a low stone wall with a fence built on top. There had been a gate in the past, as witnessed by the latch on one post and two hinges on the other, but now we found only a short gravel path hidden beneath a carpet of thistles, clover, and bindweed. We climbed the three stone steps leading to the white porch and front door.

'Locked,' I whispered to Flame.

She stared at the handle for a moment. 'It's not a deadlock. It must have been locked with a key.'

'It's not important. I think I'm becoming paranoid.'

'That's not a bad thing,' she reminded me. 'But honestly, we don't know how the town was evacuated. It's a natural reaction to lock your house whenever you leave. What if the inhabitants were at the pub when they were rounded up or had to run? They would have locked the door when they left the house, the same as any other day.'

'It would be absurd to think anyone is in there,' I replied, noticing I was keeping my voice down all the same. 'This is a very good sign though, Flame.'

She bit her bottom lip. 'It is. The house is secure. It's likely I'll find a pot or two in there, and plenty of other goodies besides.'

There were windows on either side of the porch, too high to be reached from the ground. I handed Flame my fork and clambered across from the porch, testing one after the other. But neither could be opened. I unzipped my backpack, took my hammer, and tugged out the burgundy tablecloth.

'I'm going to smash this window,' I warned—just to be safe and avoid taking her by surprise.

I bundled the tablecloth up with one fist, used my knees to brace myself against the wall, and hit the bundled cloth with the hammer. The pane shattered almost soundlessly with just a tinkle as shards landed on the floor inside. I pulled the window open and climbed in, then reached for the fork before helping Flame inside.

We drew a deep breath of musty air and studied the living room. When I turned to look at Flame's face, I saw she was as much in awe as I was. We were in a museum. It was as simple as that. The house was a snapshot of country life a few years ago. This was not the home of a state official or regime collaborator. It was not luxurious or extravagant. But I felt sure the same thoughts were going through her mind, and she confirmed it when eventually she spoke. 'They were better off than the city folk. Charming simplicity. Quiet comfort.'

'You can tell it was a real home here. It looks like a place you could live, not just use as a den.'

There were tapestries on the walls, framed by cobwebs, and two fabric sofas. A low table sat between the sofas, but it didn't look like it had been used for meals, unless people had sat on the floor to eat in this area. There were shelves with odds and ends, including figurines and dolls, mugs and bowls, and—

'Books!'

'Later!' Flame snapped before I got any ideas. 'Let's remember our shopping list. Where's the kitchen?'

It was as well stocked as we'd hoped. Pots. Pans. Cutlery. Plates. I held my breath as I opened the pantry.

'Jackpot! Flame!'

She hurried over and covered her mouth to stop herself from screaming. It was full of goods we'd only dreamed of before! A dozen jars of honey. I'd read that bees had almost become extinct not so long ago, but that must have changed after The

Breakdown, with fewer people in the way and nature taking control again. There were more woodlands and marshes, wild flowers and brambles. There was no shortage of bees any longer, but honey is another story, isn't it? You needed people to collect it. It was an art, really, and a dead one. That's what I'd thought, but I'd clearly been wrong.

'Whisky!' I said, with hesitant excitement, not quite trusting my eyes. So, very carefully, I lifted the bottle. 'Highland Park! I stole a bottle of this once from a widow's mansion. It's not produced nowadays. The Scots didn't escape The Breakdown either, even if they proved more resilient than us. It's unopened, so it's the real deal, not moonshine.'

'Cases of red wine and rosé as well, and curry paste, dried beans, more olive oil, and salt.'

'Stay here, Flame. I'm going to check the rest of the house. I'm starting to think we need to have a little chat together.'

'A change of heart? I'm with you. Check the bathroom and bedrooms and let me know.'

The instant I saw the bathroom, I was sold. There was more mildew on the tiled walls than at the pub but that was easily fixed because there were cleaning products and rags under the basin. When I turned the tap in the bathtub, a trickle of water came out. It was enough to tell me the pipe was hooked up to a reservoir. The lack of pressure indicated that either there was practically no water left, which would be strange considering none had been used in years, or that there was a blockage somewhere. I turned the tap on and off a few times in quick succession and the trickle grew a little. I rinsed the tub and put the plug in the hole.

I tried the flush on the toilet but it didn't work. Not a problem. Everyone I knew had been using dry toilets since we could remember. Changing that habit was of no great import. The rare occasions on which I'd been able to flush my shit away had been when nature called during raids on luxury flats.

I looked out the small bathroom window and noted that it overlooked the loading bay of the supermarket, where stacks of pallets palely imitated the towering skeletons of city buildings.

I moved on to the bedrooms. There were three, and they were all furnished. Sheets lay rumpled on the beds, as though their occupants had left that very morning without bothering to make them. There were sheets and pillow slips in a chest at the foot of the bed in the master bedroom, and clothes in the wardrobe.

In the third bedroom, which had by all appearances been used as a kind of storage area, I looked out the rear window. The land fell sharply, so much so that I was looking down onto the roof of the house behind ours. A water tank sat on a platform at the rear of it. I realised this was the other side of the ridge the town stood on—the opposite side from the road to the marshes.

I gazed into the distance. So far away I couldn't be sure my eyes weren't betraying me, the land seemed to end and give way to an expanse of dark blue.

'The sea?'

Or was it just the sky, dark on the horizon, beyond the cloud front?

'Daydreaming?' Flame asked, her voice warm. It had become the voice of a woman who was content.

'I think that's the sea.'

She stared at the horizon.

'It does look like how I've always imagined the coast to be. It's not a smooth curve like the horizon, but comes in and out irregularly. That dark blue between the clouds and the earth. Yes. I think you're right.'

I put an arm around her and she let herself sink into my embrace.

'This change of heart you mentioned.'

'I think we'd be better here,' I said.

She hummed into my chest.

'My idea was to sleep here, and wash here, but to use the pub as our garden and kitchen. That way, if smoke or the smell of cooking attracted attention, we wouldn't be caught off guard while we slept. We could come here after dark, as quiet as mice, and keep it as our most secret and safest of places. From here, we'd be able to prepare expeditions further afield.'

'We could go to the sea, walk across the sand, and put our feet in the salt water. That must be the most surreal feeling. I knew a girl who had done that once,' she said, the warmth and optimism in her voice turning cold at the end. *Once* came out as a forlorn whisper.

'We'll do that,' I told her, holding her tight. 'And we'll do it often. This is the beginning of a new era. We'll find others in the same boat as us, but we'll take it step by step, not revealing our home, taking all the pains necessary to keep it our secret. We won't trust anyone but each other until we're both absolutely convinced that we can. We'll always speak openly with each other and make our decisions together.'

'That's a promise?'

'I swear it if you do.'

'I do.'

'This is a new life. A better one.'

She looked into my eyes, trying to measure my confidence. I don't think she was convinced—I certainly wasn't—but she pretended she was, and I pretended she believed I was. What else could we do?

'I have a suggestion for you,' she said. 'We get ready for the night. I noticed you got the tap running. We have a bath here and put some of those clean clothes on. After sunset, we do a spot of cooking in the pub, once we've barricaded the door. Later, we come back here, open a bottle of wine—you might need that whisky—and I give you an eye-opening lesson on biology so you know what I mean when I talk to you about "the time of the month". What do you say?'

Obviously, I said I agreed.

6. The Quiet Life

The next day, we set about making the town our own, knowing that whatever renovations we undertook had to remain as near to imperceptible as possible from the street and air. We started in our house, as we immediately began to call it. Flame cleaned every room, wiping dust away and rearranging to suit her whim, while I worked in the bathroom, clearing the bathtub tap.

After a light lunch, we went to the pub garden and started putting it into order, making sure each useful plant enjoyed the best conditions we could provide. Trying to pull every weed out of the garden would have been a mammoth job and probably not of any great advantage—not to mention the fact it would have risked making our presence obvious to a drone pilot worth his salt. We made a point of clearing away the thickest weeds, like bindweed and large thistles, in places where they were smothering the plants we needed. As we worked, we picked the ripest berries and I dug up a fine batch of potatoes.

'There's so much mint,' Flame pointed out. 'We could never eat all of it. Do you know what I want to do with it?'

I shook my head and smiled at her enthusiasm.

'A handful of leaves crushed in our bathwater would be like heaven.'

'Oh, that does sound lovely. I'd never have thought of it.'

'A woman's touch.'

'That's definitely what's been missing from my life.'

That made her laughed. 'Even after last night's lesson?'

'Even after that,' I assured her.

Once the garden was looking more manageable, we lay down for a while until the first raindrops announced the downpour we'd been expecting. That night, we ate mashed potatoes seasoned with fresh herbs, then crept back to the house. The first day of our quiet new life had gone off without a hitch. Before going to sleep, we discussed our plan for the morning and decided we ought to get to know the town better. We needed to carry out a full reconnaissance of every house, shop, and workshop in town and keep an inventory of what equipment could be found where for future reference.

I was the first to stir in the morning, slipping out of bed quietly and heading straight for the living room to have a look at the book collection. There were hardbacks and paperbacks of all sorts. Several of the older books had no spine or cover at all, so I had to very carefully pull them out to see what they were about. The most recent books looked like they'd been published in the last few years, but I knew that wasn't possible. At least, I assumed it wasn't. Most likely, they just hadn't been read yet. I checked the colophon of several and found they had been printed in the first half of the 21st century, thus placing them in the period leading up to The Breakdown. Had I been born then? I really couldn't say. In any case, I grouped these books together, regardless of subject matter or genre of fiction. I hoped they contained information that would prove pertinent to the world today. The majority of these more recent books were romance, as was obvious by their covers featuring bare-chested men or women in sexy underwear—the kind of impractical lingerie I'd never seen in reality. It certainly wasn't the type of fiction that generally interested me, but I found myself thinking about last night and what Flame had taught me about women. I realised there was probably a lot I didn't know about *the fairer sex*—a term I'd come across more than once in old-world dramas. I couldn't help but wonder whether these books could teach me more about her. Even if the world in these tales was at odds with our reality, there had to be some universal truths to be gleaned from them.

Almost everything I knew about the world came either from reading old books or narrowly escaping capture by patrols. Reading was definitely preferable at that moment in time, as the first rays of filtered sunlight shone over the fence and through the top of the living room window. A cool breeze, ever so soft, entered the room through the broken pane, and I reminded myself to take a rough measurement of it and try to find a similar pane and some putty or silicone during the day's scouting.

I sat back on the sofa, started reading a book called *Martin's Magic Touch*, whose cover sported a suave chap standing behind a woman in a black evening gown. He was holding the bottom of her right earlobe between a fingertip and a thumb, and judging by her expression, the effect it had on her was tremendous.

After three pages, I'd decided that despite the terrible writing, the book had two strengths—it was detailed in its descriptions and it was written by a woman. I made a mental note of an interesting technique I had to try on Flame when the timing was right.

I hadn't yet finished the fourth page when I heard footsteps coming from the bedroom and found myself pushing the book under the sofa without quite knowing why.

'Morning,' she said, looking out the window to where the band of sunlight was pouring over the top of the fence. 'I thought I'd find you here—but you're not reading. Nothing that interests you?'

'It's not that. There are plenty of interesting books, but I don't feel like reading right now. I was just enjoying the sunlight.'

She seemed to believe me and walked over to the bookshelf to glance at the titles, no doubt noticing I'd put a number of them into groups. When she turned to me, there was a cheeky grin on her face.

'There are a lot of romance novels here.'

'Yeah, I noticed.'

'They might teach you something useful for a change.'

It must have been my sheepish grin that made her laugh.

'It's a habit I should take up, I guess,' she mused. 'I've never been much into books, but maybe it's time.'

'It probably is,' I said. 'We've experienced incredible changes over the past few days, and we have plenty more in store. I'd say it's the perfect time to get into a good routine, and reading is part of that.'

She nodded.

'Do you remember learning to read?' I asked.

'Not really. It feels like something I've always known, but I suppose someone taught me.'

'It's the same for me. I sometimes get the feeling there were books all around me as a child, and then at some point in time, they simply vanished. I'm sure it wasn't anywhere near as abrupt as that, but I've been collecting them for as long as I can remember and I've noticed they've become harder to find over the years.'

She raised her eyebrows. 'Who knows? You might find more today if you're lucky.'

'I hope so. But first on my list of priorities is a pane the same size as this broken one.'

'You know how to fix it then?'

'It won't be a work of art, but if I find what I need, I can seal it up well enough to keep us warm when the nights grow cooler.'

'And if that fails, these erotic books of yours should help keep the temperature up.'

I stood and looked her in the eye before replying. 'You know what? I think they will.'

She bit her lip and turned her gaze back to the band of sunlight.

'Let's get ready,' I said. 'We can either start with the house next door and work our way further along the street or see what there is to be found at the end of the street and work our way back here.'

'I like the second option. Not sure why. It just sounds wiser. Can you give me ten minutes?'

'Ten minutes for what?'

She glared at me.

'*Of course*, Flame. That's what I wanted to say. *Yes. Of course.*'

'Much better.' The cheeky smile returned and she headed for the back door.

I prepared both our backpacks, adding a light lunch and filling our bottles with water we'd boiled the previous night. I decided to leave the gardening fork here, even though it bothered me to do so. It would only get in the way and I figured my hammer would be a more useful weapon if we were taken by surprise at close quarters.

Respecting what had already become unspoken protocol, Flame followed me out the front door and over to the gateway. She checked the sky while I peered out beyond the fence and made sure the street was empty. The sky wasn't so cloudy that morning, so we knew we had to watch out for drones.

'Do you think they're still looking for us?' I asked before stepping out onto the street.

'To be honest, I doubt it, but we need to tell ourselves they are. We can't afford to let our guard down.'

'That's what I figure too. Let's jog it to the end of the street. I'm guessing it's no further to the outskirts in this direction than back the way we came.'

We moved at a slow jog, past houses on either side of the street, and within a minute, we arrived at the town square. There had been another pub here, smaller than *The King's Head*, but probably busier. I could imagine a steady stream of locals popping in for a quick beer after attending to business. There was also an Indian restaurant, a handful of shops, the post office, and a church tower rose a little further off the square, from behind a row of terrace houses.

I saw on Flame's face the same surprise I must have worn on mine. The town was larger than we'd first thought. It certainly wasn't a mere village. A number of alleys branched off from the square and the main street turned at a sharp angle before disappearing downhill.

The square itself wasn't especially large. It was little more than an annexe off the main street and consisted of two wooden benches bolted to the ground and facing a bare plinth. A statue had apparently been demolished or dismantled, and the only trace of its existence left on the plinth was a small rectangular recess with a rusty spot in each corner. There was no way of knowing who had been honoured here, but after all, that hardly mattered to us. There were no great men or women any longer, and if there ever had been, they were certainly never the ones commemorated with a statue.

A change of plan was in order. There was no way we were going to be able to explore every building in town in a day, or even a week, and there was no reason to rush the process after all.

'Look at the state of the buildings around the square,' Flame said, keeping her voice low and pulling me protectively towards the wall of the closest building. 'All the windows are smashed or missing and most of them don't have doors or curtains.'

'We're not likely to find much here,' I agreed. 'It looks like there was a fire in the restaurant. And those boutiques have been ransacked.'

'We could climb the church tower,' Flame said. 'It will give us a view across town.'

'Sure. Lead the way.'

We checked the sky, then jogged across the square and over to the church. The building was still majestic, its ancient stone walls undamaged and its stained-glass windows miraculously intact. The ivy snaking its way up the stonework only added to its overall charm. The arched door hadn't been removed either. The two halves opened easily when I pushed them, offering no more than a timid creak of resistance.

We entered the once hallowed ground and I instantly felt a tinge of disappointment. 'I'd almost started to believe the church had been spared.'

Flame sighed. 'I know what you mean. It looked untouched from the outside.'

Little remained. There were no pews or candlesticks, nor an altar table. But the crucifix was still in place on the wall.

'Again the question about the order of events,' Flame said. She was standing beside me, and we were both looking at the crucifix.

'Only useful objects were taken. There was no spite or drive to destroy.'

'Yes. But when were they removed? Was it when the town was evacuated—if that's what happened—or did others come past later and take them?'

'Like we're doing.'

'Exactly. Like us. Except no one is here now. Why didn't they come back? Where did they go and why?'

'What about the missing statue? Why was it taken? I can't see how a statue could be useful.'

'It depends who it was,' she answered, shrugging.

I guessed that was it. The statue had either been taken out of admiration or destroyed out of contempt.

'We'll make sense of this, Flame. I really think we will. The more we explore the town, the more we'll come to understand it and piece together its story.' I turned and looked back towards the entrance. 'The stairs to the tower are over there.'

We jogged along the aisle, filling the air with echoing footfalls, and climbed the spiral staircase, steadying ourselves against the wall with one arm and brushing away cobwebs with the other. It must have looked as though we were performing some strange ritual or dance. And for all we knew of religion, dances of some kind may have played a part in church ceremony. We knew nothing of such matters. My restricted knowledge about churches was a mishmash of glimpses from history books. It was clear that religion had already been in decline well before The Breakdown, and although the church had been hand in glove with the state throughout most of history, this bond had weakened over the years. There had been no intentional destruction of churches. This fact indicated that either this privileged relationship hadn't entirely disappeared, or—and I suspect this is the more coherent conclusion—the influence of Christianity had become so minimal it wasn't considered a threat. Either way, churches today were havens for the homeless, who slept under the melancholy gaze of an emaciated man nailed to a cross. However distant and foreign this religion now felt to us, there was an uncanny feeling that this man, if he had been real at all, must have been very much like us.

The staircase came to an end and I opened the warped wooden door, which creaked but put up no fight. We found ourselves in the bell chamber and Flame stared at the six bells, losing herself in a kind of reverie. Despite the dust and cobwebs, their magnificence shone through. There was a louvre on each wall and enough filtered sunlight shone through the eastern one to make the metal shine and the dust and cobwebs sparkle.

'These are metal objects no one is likely to make off with,' Flame mused.

'It would take some doing to carry them down that staircase.' I looked at them more closely. 'It doesn't seem any attempt has been made to remove them from the beams. There's no damage. I doubt anyone else has set foot in this chamber in a long time.'

As we stood there staring at those extraordinary relics, it occurred to me that neither of us had ever actually seen anything remotely like them in our lives.

'Back in the days when couples would get married, they'd come to churches for the ceremony, and the bells would be rung,' Flame told me quietly, a pleasant dreamy note to her voice. She looked at me and smiled. 'Or so I've been told.'

I wanted to ask who had told her, but she would have offered that detail if she'd felt inclined to do so.

'I'd love to hear how they sound, calling across town and the surrounding countryside. It must be wonderful—a world away from security alarms and sirens.'

'Maybe we will one day, Flicker.' The hope in her voice made me feel stronger.

She turned her head and spoke more loudly. 'This ladder must lead to the roof.'

'There's nowhere else it could go. After you,' I said.

'Is this a thing between us now?' she asked, narrowing her eyes. 'Am I destined to always go up ladders before you?'

'Yes,' I replied. 'It's protocol. Hop to it!'

'Tell me if there's any leakage, won't you?' she added as she started up the ladder.

'What? Oh, right. Sure. It looks fine to me.'

She laughed all the way to the top.

The view over the battlements was stunning. We could see along the road into town, and down the sides of the ridge. The marshland and chapel could be seen in the distance, and the woodland beyond melded with the horizon.

'We couldn't see the church tower from the chapel but we can see the chapel from here. Strange, isn't it?' Flame wondered.

'I guess it is. Perhaps it's because we know the chapel is there, so we were expecting to see it.' I shrugged. 'And the sky is much clearer today as well.'

'That must be it.' She took a deep breath. The morning

sunlight warmed our faces while the cool breeze filled our lungs. It was so relaxing. And although it may not have been the highest either of us had ever been—because the ruins of residential towers in the city were on another scale altogether—the view from the church tower was undoubtedly the most beautiful we'd had.

I looked at Flame to ask her if she agreed, but there was no need. The simple look of childlike amazement on her tired, pretty face answered my question, and in that moment, I realised that there was still a scared and confused girl behind that tough exterior. I was seeing that girl now, but without the fear, and with the confusion pushed aside for a moment.

She blushed when she saw that I was looking at her, not admiring the landscape.

'Stop it!'

'Sorry. You just look so happy right now.'

'I am,' she said and turned to survey the countryside to the south. This was the other end of the ridge, where the main road snaked down sharply past houses that were almost completely overgrown with bindweed and ivy. Woodland and empty fields stretched out beyond them.

To the west, the land reached towards the same horizon we'd seen from the rear window of the house.

'It has to be the coast,' she said quietly, reading my thoughts. Then her expression changed, and following her gaze down to just in front of us, I saw why. Words had been painted along the lower part of the battlement, smaller than those in the chapel, but there was no doubt the same hand was behind them.

You're doing great. Don't stop. Not safe here. Go west.

'Not safe here?' Flame asked, but when she looked at me, she must have seen the same doubt in my eyes. Her smile had disappeared—replaced with a frown of betrayal.

'I feel safer here than I ever did in the city,' I said.

'We haven't seen a drone yet. There are no patrols. It's all ours,' she added, shaking her head. 'Why did we have to find this?'

'We don't know when it was written, Flame. There might have been a danger shortly after the town was evacuated. Perhaps patrols came back on a regular basis to ensure no attempts were made to repopulate. It doesn't necessarily mean there's any threat now.'

'That's right. We don't have to pack up and run just because of this, do we? We can't leave it all behind at the drop of a hat like that. We've found a new home here. We have everything we need. We can't give all that up!'

'Don't shout, Flame. Keep calm. I agree with you entirely. But it's a good reminder for us to stay alert. We can't afford to relax just yet.'

She breathed a sigh of relief and raised her eyes to take in the view to the west. 'I'd like to know why it tells us to go towards the coast though. What lies that way?'

'I can't see any buildings at all. Can you?'

'Fields and woods, and a few low hills. There don't appear to be any other towns.'

'We ignore it then?' I asked.

'Yeah. We ignore it. I mean, when we go on an expedition towards the coast, we'll see what's there. Who knows? We might find a better place. But we can't give up what we have here for no good reason.'

'It's settled then. We'll carry on as we are, taking all due precautions. Now, let's get back to today's priority—finding a nice pane to replace the one I smashed.'

Flame took one final glance at the painted words, stuck her chin up defiantly, and started back down the ladder.

7. The Warning

We didn't mention the warning for the rest of the day, by a kind of tacit agreement, but I'm sure it remained on her mind as much as it did on mine. It was a sense of betrayal that had fallen upon us, as ridiculous as that sounds. After all, the town had made no promises to us. It was nothing more than an abandoned stage where lives had once been played out—lives that had since moved elsewhere, or been taken elsewhere, and come to a brutal end for all we knew. Weary and desperate, we'd stumbled across this vestige by chance and allowed ourselves to be taken in by a promise that had never been made. There was no shortage of available shelter here, clothes, foodstuffs, and the means to grow more food, to cook it, and to store and boil water. There were even books. It felt too good to be true. But none of this had been offered. And so, what right did we have to consider the warning a betrayal by the town we wanted to call home? Nor could we rightly feel betrayed by its author, because whoever had written those words could only have done so with the best of intentions; what ulterior motive could there be in scaring us away from an unwanted town?

I found a pane the same size as our broken one in the garden shed of a house not far from the church, where the road dipped and weaved its way out of town. It was one of several spare panes stacked carefully on a workbench and covered in a blanket of dust and cobwebs. I also found an old pot of putty that I managed to knead into a workable state after leaving it to soak in water for a while.

Again, it had been easy. Too easy? That nagging doubt persisted. But we didn't want to come down from the cloud we were riding until we absolutely had to.

That evening, we sat by the fire at *The King's Head*, taking advantage of the warmth emitted by the glowing embers. The nights weren't yet cold enough to warrant keeping a fire burning once we'd finished cooking, and there was little point wasting precious wood on heating the voluminous pub when we'd leave its comfort for our unheated house before going to bed, but we enjoyed that luxury while we ate.

'This is delicious, Flame. You made it from what we have in the garden?'

'Mostly from the garden, but I bagged some other goodies during the day when you were busy hunting for the pane.'

She raised a spoonful of stew to her mouth and closed her eyes as she relished it.

'You found onions?'

She smiled once she'd finished her mouthful and raised her eyebrows as she opened her eyes. 'In the garden of the first house we checked after the church.'

But she turned to stare into the embers, and I understood why.

'The church,' I repeated, letting her know I followed her train of thought.

She sighed, turning back to me.

'I wish I hadn't seen it,' she said.

'Yeah, but we did. We saw the message, and I'm glad we saw it. Being aware of every detail of our surroundings can only be an advantage in the long term. The more pieces we pick up, the greater our chances of solving the puzzle.'

We kept eating, not wanting to let the stew go cold in our bowls, and I watched the embers as they slowly lost life with each passing minute. It saddened me, but the unleashing of fire leads inevitably to its eventual extinction.

'What *is* the puzzle, Flicker? I don't only mean about what happened here to make this a ghost town, although that has to be an important part of it. I'm talking about the big picture.'

'What is it? That's the question. I suppose it's to work out where we're going. Leaving the city was more than a physical journey—it was the beginning of an exploration of ourselves. Our experience of the world is so limited. We've been struggling to survive for as long as we can remember, and fighting against this world that doesn't value us. That's why we burn, isn't it? That's why we set fire to the icons of our oppression, and why we burn with anger inside.'

'But not here,' Flame said. 'The only fire you've lit here has been to cook. The church tower is the only symbol of authority in town and yet we felt safe there.'

'We did. Because the church hasn't represented oppression in living memory.'

'It's more than that though, isn't it? Putting history aside. We were happy and safe there, standing on that tower, because it was ours alone. We were Flicker and Flame on top of the world.'

'We were, weren't we? It was such a thrill.'

'That's why it hurt me to read those words. I hate whoever wrote them for the mere fact that the place chosen was up there on the tower.' She frowned at me. 'You must think I'm mad.'

'Not at all. You're perfectly sane. But you shouldn't hate the messenger because of the message, or because of the way it was conveyed. It had to be written somewhere it wouldn't be seen by drones, or by ground patrols, and you know I've been thinking about it all day, and I think it was written up there because the previous message was written in the marshland chapel. It seems a logical thing to do, keeping to a theme. Only, because the church is in the middle of a town, not the marshes, it would have been too risky writing the warning on the walls where a patrol might easily see it. The tower was much safer, low on the inside of a battlement where it would only be visible to someone standing in front of it. When you have drones at your disposal to undertake airborne surveillance, you don't need to send men clambering up church towers.'

'Well, I can't argue with your reasoning. All the same, we could have missed it. If it was genuinely written with the intention of saving us from a grave danger, it should have been somewhere we were sure to see it. It wasn't written in stone that we would climb to the top of the tower. It was my idea. If I hadn't suggested it, we wouldn't have come across the warning.'

'And yet you did.'

'What do you mean?'

'You *did* suggest it, and we climbed the tower. Like you say, it wasn't written in stone, but it happened.'

'Yes. That's true.' Flame looked into the embers and shuddered a little in spite of the warmth. 'Almost as though this person knows me better than I know myself.'

I took another spoonful of stew and thought about this unknown person, or people. 'Look at it this way, Flame. We found the message in the chapel, and the one on the church tower, and there may be more that we've missed along the way, although I can't imagine where, so the trail has worked. We're dealing with someone who's intelligent and who already knows the terrain. Agreed?'

She nodded and breathed a sigh of relief. 'You're right. If any harm had been intended, it would have happened by now.'

'That's what I figure.'

'By the same token, a rational person wouldn't warn of imaginary dangers,' she added.

'True.'

'So,' Flame said. 'We go on, one step at a time, playing it safe and watching our backs. We carry out our plan to explore the surrounding countryside and try to reach the coast. We keep our eyes peeled for more messages.'

'We need to have escape routes from here and from the house, and we need a meeting place in case we get split up.'

She stared at me wide-eyed, but then she relaxed and nodded her agreement.

'The church tower is out,' she said. 'If we get caught up there, we'll be trapped. We need somewhere close but not obvious.'

'The service station? It's away from the town centre, and both sides of the ridge—behind it and across the road—are heavily forested.'

'Do we know how to reach it from the garden, in case we have to make a hasty retreat from the rear of the pub?'

'Priority task tomorrow,' I replied. 'What about a meeting place from the house? The supermarket is too obvious.'

'Definitely not an option. We need somewhere safe we can reach from the back of the house, heading away from the road.'

'I haven't ventured down there yet. Did nature's call take you far this morning?'

'No further than the first barrage of brambles and nettles.'

'Right. I'll hack a passage through to the property line tomorrow and see where we can go from there.'

'Good,' she said, taking our empty bowls and placing them on the floor by her chair.

'Being clear on how to react if attacked will take a weight off our shoulders.'

'Even talking about it, strangely enough, makes me feel better.'

I saw a hint of the buoyancy Flame had shown that morning return. Talking about it was the key, without a doubt. Looking back, I think it was then—that particular day—that I began to understand one simple truth about couples. Talking about problems was the way to handle them. Flame and I needed each other. We no longer had anyone else, if we ever really had at all. I guess I suspected even then that we wouldn't always agree on major decisions, but thus far we had, and that was a foundation to build upon. And after all, I'd made a promise to her, back in the watermill, and already it was beginning to look like I could start to make good on it, to proclaim without a doubt that being forced to flee the city was a blessing in disguise. But the warning had reminded me not to be too hasty.

'Where are you, Flicker?'

I realised the dying embers had hypnotised me and that she'd been speaking.

'Sorry. You were saying?'

'I was saying we need more than just escape routes. We need to be ready to fight back. We don't know who or what is out here, so we need to be armed to the teeth, and we really ought to train on a daily basis.'

This enigmatic woman never failed to surprise me. At first, she had shown me a tough façade—a shell used to protect herself—and little by little, I'd come to see through it to find a vulnerable, sensitive girl, but what I needed to understand was that she was both, without any contradiction. She was what she needed to be according to any given situation. We were exactly the same in that regard. Here and now, with me, she was allowing herself to be the woman she wanted to be, without forgetting that she might have to raise the shield again at a moment's notice.

My grin must have been devilish and my admiration plain to see, because it filled her with fire. I had just enough time to brace myself as she lunged at me, but I caught her, and wrapped my arms around her. We kissed, and I felt the urge to go further, but I contented myself to hold her, letting her feel safe in my embrace. I thought about our first night together, back in the watermill—well, it was the second, but lying on the ground in a greenhouse, crammed between a metal table and a wheelbarrow, with a complete stranger who warned me not to get any "funny ideas" because "men are men" while drones and a patrol were tracking us didn't really count. No. The watermill was our first night together, and it was there that we started to get to know each other, and to trust each other. That had only been a few nights ago, but it felt like weeks already.

'What's on your mind?' she asked, holding my head between her hands and fixing me with those green eyes, as though daring me to lie.

'I was thinking about the mill.'

'I knew it!' she purred, almost victoriously. 'Wasn't it lovely, bathing in the river? We have our own bath now, of course, but I'd like to do that again one day.'

'The marshes aren't far.'

She laughed. 'Not quite the same.'

'It isn't, is it? You don't want slimy critters slithering where they're not welcome.'

She wriggled in my lap and grinned at me knowingly. 'No, I don't.'

'We'll bathe in the sea one day soon, before the winter.'

'We really should, as long as we stay close to land, just wading in the water. I'm not much of a swimmer, Flicker.'

'I'll teach you if you trust me.'

'You know I do.' She hesitated. 'But we'll see when we get there. The sea is a stranger to us. It may not be the same as swimming in the river.'

'We'll see,' I agreed.

'Would you like a special treat tonight?' she asked, then bit her bottom lip, taking delight in the perplexed look her question had put on my face.

'I'm not sure what you mean.'

'I think you are,' she teased. 'I'm talking about dessert.'

'Oh, yes—of course.'

She laughed and rushed into the kitchen, reappearing seconds later with a plastic container. 'Have a look at these plums. Once we've cleaned up here, why don't we take them back to the house and crack open one of those bottles of rosé?'

'You found plums,' I said, feigning enthusiasm, but she saw through it.

'Don't look so glum,' she told me, and frowned mockingly. 'It'll be the best dessert you've ever had. I promise.'

She took a plum from the container and placed it delicately between her lips.

I got up from my chair and drew a deep breath. 'I'll clean up!'

In less than five minutes, everything was back in its rightful place. I checked that the embers had safely died down. Of course, a close inspection of the pub would betray the fact that it had been occupied very recently. Tidying a room can never convincingly hide human activity. Undisturbed dust and cobwebs do that job best. Nevertheless, every night, we had to make a point of removing obvious signs of our presence to minimise the chances of attracting an unexpected visitor's scrutiny.

We hurried along the dark street and reached the house, our passage witnessed only by the stars that spattered the night sky.

I took a quick bath, barely noticing the biting cold of the water, while Flame opened a bottle of rosé and prepared the dessert.

It was scrumptious, just as she had promised, and we slept soundly, having passed a heavenly evening.

I must have slept longer than usual, because I stirred slowly the next morning. We hadn't finished the bottle of wine, but my mouth was dry and my mind a little dull. As Flame roused, I could tell she was in the same boat, unaccustomed as we both were to drinking.

'Good morning,' I said.

'Oh, hello. You slept in?'

'Yeah.'

She blinked. 'Had a good evening?'

'It was perfect.'

'Did we finish the bottle off?'

'We only had about half. Out of practice, I'd say.'

'We most decidedly are.'

We took our time getting out of bed. Once we'd drunk some water and were feeling more alert, I told Flame I'd go out back and have a look at how to tackle the problem of hacking a passage through the brambles. It only took a glance for me to realise I was going to need some kind of slashing implement, like a machete. But when I walked over to the side fence to relieve my bladder and happened to notice the poor state of the palings and nails, another angle occurred to me.

I pulled and twisted two palings until they could be easily parted—one to either side, like curtains—and stepped through. The rear of the supermarket was much less overgrown than our back garden. Only a few desperate vines and weeds grew from the cracks and potholes in the concrete surface. It had been a small car park, connected to the loading bay where the stacks of pallets we could see from the bathroom window stood.

The low dry-stone wall to the left separated the car park from what looked like a schoolyard. A high wire fence had fallen over and rested against the crossbar of a football goal. Only the tops of the goalposts were visible, indicating that the pitch was down lower, presumably built on a terrace like the house behind ours. Craning my neck, I saw a long slate roof interspersed with several chimney stacks.

It was a promising escape route. If we could slip through the side fence and take refuge in the school in an emergency, we could stay hidden in relative comfort. The only perceivable obstacle I could see was the fence, for although it had fallen over, climbing over it at night and in a hurry would be both a clumsy and dangerously noisy business. A pair of wire cutters would easily remedy that. All that was required was a small, neat opening for us to slip through.

I was tempted to go exploring immediately but I hadn't told Flame I'd leave the property. She would be expecting me to be close by. As minor as it seemed, ducking across a couple of property lines for a few minutes, I couldn't bring myself to do it. I knew I couldn't. It would be a breach of trust. And what if— just what if—something happened to Flame during that time?

I didn't have my fork or hammer with me either. I was completely unarmed. So I went back inside to tell Flame and fetch my gear.

'I'm coming with you,' she said, and grabbed her backpack.

'I had a feeling you'd want to.'

'There's no way I'm letting you wander off without me until we know more about our surroundings.'

I led the way through the side fence and across the car park. Once we'd jumped the wall, I saw that there was already enough of a gap under the wire for us to crawl through. I swung my backpack off and pushed it through along with my fork, and then I crawled under the fence using my forearms and knees to propel me. Flame followed suit, wriggling lithely, and we dropped off the top of the retaining wall and onto the football pitch, which was covered in tall grass. We dashed across it and slowed down as we reached the playground, drawing to a halt at the nearest door.

'How long?'

'No more than forty seconds from our fence to this door,' Flame guessed.

'Not bad, is it?'

'It should allow us to escape unseen if the house is broken into from the street.'

We looked around, starting with the sky. At ground level, the asphalt surface of the playground was cracked and warped but fragments of white paint were enough for us to put the dots together in our minds and picture where children had played hopscotch and escargot. A brick wall hid the house behind ours from view from the schoolyard on one side, and a steep embankment jutted up on the other. Along the base of this embankment was a rose garden, separated from the playground by the remnants of a low picket fence. The rose bushes were gnarled, snapped, and twisted, essentially indistinguishable from the brambles that smothered them, but a few pink flowers stood out stubbornly from the tangle.

'Would you like a rose, my dear?'

'Aren't you the hopeless romantic this morning?'

'*Hopeless romantic*—what's that supposed to mean?'

She just narrowed her eyes and nodded to herself.

'Fine. No roses for you then.'

'Hold your horses. I'd be happy to accept a rose, but not until we've explored the school. Business before pleasure.'

I looked around and realised I was frowning. 'Flame, there's something odd about this place.'

'There is, isn't there? But what is it?'

We both found ourselves scanning the sky, wondering if we'd subconsciously detected the presence of drones, but there was no noise at all, and the sky was clear. Not even a breeze. All was stillness and utter silence.

'Do you believe in ghosts, Flame?'

She stared at me. 'No, I do not, and neither do you.'

'You're right. Well, that rules that out. No phantom children playing hopscotch. But that's the kind of uncanny feeling we have, isn't it?'

'Yeah, more or less. There's something eerie about this place.'

'That's the word—*eerie*.'

We were lost in thought. Then it hit me.

'I think I know what it is.'

'Yes?'

'Did you ever explore the ruins of a school in the city?'

'A couple of times,' she answered, 'but I never found much. From what I recall, the buildings were mostly demolished. I've heard it said that schools were decommissioned around the time of The Breakdown—nobody seems to remember whether it was before, during, or after—and the buildings were either demolished or converted into luxury living quarters or private offices.'

'Exactly. I never went to school, or if I did, I was so young I can't remember. I was taught to read by older friends.'

There must have been a note of sadness in my voice, because she laid a hand on my shoulder.

'It was the same for you?' I asked.

'My mother—' she said before quickly removing her hand as

95

though regretting her words.

I didn't know what to say, instantly understanding that this was a talk she wasn't ready to have. But the silence that had fallen was unbearable, so I went to back to the point I was trying to make. 'This schoolyard—it's not in ruins. Not really. What am I trying to say?'

'Yeah, I get it, Flicker. That's why it's strange. It's no more in ruins than the rest of the town. It hasn't been abandoned for decades, like you'd expect a school to be.' She studied the playground and building again. 'It's been just a few years, the same as *The King's Head* and the supermarket, and everywhere else in town.'

We looked at each other as the significance of that observation sank in.

'It was in use up until the time it was evacuated,' she said.

I was lost for words.

'But how is that possible?' she said, asking my question for me.

'Yes. How? Did the town run the school independently?'

'If that was the case, it must have been without government permission, unless there were different rules outside the city.'

'Unlikely,' I said.

'They must have organised and funded it themselves.'

'And if they did,' I went on, 'that would have required a mindboggling degree of organisation.'

'This school is a piece of the puzzle, Flicker. It has to be.'

She was staring at the flecks of white paint on the ground, tracing lines in her mind. 'There's no doubt about it. The pieces are all here waiting to be put together.'

'I wonder what was being taught here.'

'Let's find out,' she said, snapping out of her trance and turning to the door. She tried the white aluminium handle and found that it offered no resistance. She opened the door and musty air greeted us.

The eeriness was even more intense inside the schoolhouse. I could almost hear the tapping of small shoes along the short corridor that led past two offices to the right and two classrooms to the left. At the end, a staircase running up the wall faced us.

'How about we start with the offices?' Flame suggested.

I followed her into the first. Sheets of paper covered the floor, many of them torn or crumpled into balls. There were balance sheets, correspondence between staff and parents, and lesson plans. All of them were hand-written, and they were barely legible for the most part. Nothing stood out as looking at all revolutionary. There were no manifestos against the regime or battle plans for an army of children. There were no sketches of homemade bombs or guides on how to sabotage surveillance equipment. We rifled through dozens of discarded documents.

'No pieces here,' Flame complained, scrunching a sheet into a ball and tossing it at a bare cork board.

'Maybe in the next office,' I replied.

But it was empty. There were no papers scattered across the floor or on the mouldy office chairs and dusty desks. Had any signs of rebellion or calumny been removed?

'That's all that remains,' Flame said, pointing at the wall.

It was an old map of Europe, complete with meaningless borders and obsolete flags. The most prominent flag of all was a blue one with a ring of stars.

'Do you think life's the same everywhere?' she asked.

I shrugged. 'We're barely more than a two-day walk from the city and it already feels like we've entered a foreign country. I can't even begin to imagine what's going on elsewhere.'

'Classrooms,' Flame said, but the word was uttered listlessly.

The empty desks and cobwebbed whiteboards came as no surprise. We decided to try the first floor.

'Do you know what else is peculiar?' she asked as we climbed the staircase.

'What?'

'This small town had enough children two or three years ago to have a school. How many children or teenagers do you know in the city?'

'Hardly any. Only the rich or insane have children,' I replied. 'Why was it different here?'

'It's hard to picture it,' she said. 'This town was so different from the city. Life must have been much more pleasant. But was it an exception here, or is the city the exception?'

I was speechless for a moment. 'That's a good question.' I

thought about it. 'My heart hopes it's the latter, but my mind tells me the former is more likely.'

There was one classroom upstairs, a large empty room with a raised platform at one end, and a final room that took my breath away—a library!

'Check it out!' I said once I'd caught my breath.

The shelves were still full of all kinds of books from adventure stories to picture books about science and geography.

'You've hit the jackpot!' Flame punched my arm.

'This is heaven,' I said. 'I don't mind that they're mostly children's books. There must be a wealth of knowledge in here.'

'A wealth of knowledge?'

'Yeah, that's a phrase—'

'—you read in a book,' she finished and laughed. 'You're an amazing man, Flicker. You really are!'

'Well, you're an amazing woman.'

We held each other's gaze, staring at each other with such intensity that it could only end one of two ways.

It ended with us bursting out laughing.

'You'll have to keep your reading for another day. I'm ready for my rose now.'

'Right. A rose for my fair lady, and then we need to think about improving our pathetically limited arsenal and finding an escape route from the pub to the service station before evening.'

'Best get moving then.'

I found a sharp piece of gravel near the embankment and cut the finest pink rose for Flame.

After passing by the house and leaving the rose there, we started venturing into garden sheds and only stopped when we had all the machetes and axes we could carry. We left our newfound weapons strategically located around the house and the pub, keeping only a machete each with us, then descended through the pub garden and hacked through the brambles and overgrown hedges that blocked us as we made an escape route. It ended up crossing several once private properties and a stretch of woodland before climbing back uphill to join the service station from the rear.

It was dark by the time we made it back to the pub and we

were dead tired, but we slept well that night, safe in the knowledge that our day's work had improved our defences and rendered our environment more familiar to us. The warning moved a little further back into the recesses of our minds. But it didn't fade away entirely. We didn't dare allow ourselves that foolish luxury.

8. The Night of the Hunt

We made new discoveries every day, and began, continued, or finished our various projects. It might be supposed that two fugitives from the city would find it unbearably lonely living in a ghost town with only each other for company. But we didn't. It was a topic we broached on occasion, and although we missed our friends, we doubted they had fared anywhere near as well as we had. We were frank with each other, as we had to be, well aware that our life together would sour without complete honesty. Letting go of our friends once and for all—mourning them—was the first step in that process. As inexperienced in serious relationships as we were, this need for openness struck us as blatantly obvious, especially in our situation, living in isolation. And yet, almost hypocritically perhaps, we also understood instinctively that not all truths needed to be voiced immediately. Flame had her secret garden—as I'd seen it described in one book—and even though I strongly believed it would help her to let me enter it, the decision was hers.

'One of the things that told me you were special, Flicker, was that you weren't intimidated by me that night in the greenhouse,' she said casually, and completely out of the blue, one evening.

Maybe time was warping my memory, or it could be that she hadn't been paying enough attention, but I'm quite sure I had felt a little intimidated by her, even though I couldn't quite put my finger on the reason why. Her knife had undoubtedly been part of the equation, and the fear of being spotted by drones and captured by the patrol also overshadowed any other feelings of unease.

'Why should I be intimidated by you?'

She shrugged.

100

'You weren't the most beautiful woman I'd ever seen in my life,' I informed her, adding a cheeky smile.

'I don't mean intimidated by my looks, you dickhead,' she replied, so stony-faced I could have placed her on the vacant plinth in the town square, and I wasn't sure whether her humour was becoming more caustic the longer she lived with me, or whether it was just shining through more clearly as we grew increasingly comfortable together.

'I know exactly what you mean and I accept your compliment,' I told her, watching her mask crack as she suppressed a laugh.

'It's just a problem I've had in the past.'

'For future reference, avoid threatening men with knives the morning after saving their lives, and don't accuse them of being pigs simply because of their gender.'

She glared at me, no humour of any kind on her face. 'I didn't do that!'

'I may be slightly exaggerating.'

'And what do you mean by *for future reference*?'

'I don't know, Flame. I hope I mean nothing by it.'

But I couldn't ignore the wounded look she now wore.

'Am I going to wake up alone one morning?'

'Only to find me reading erotic fiction in the living room,' I replied, eager to lighten the mood.

She smiled wanly. 'I'm serious, Flicker.'

'I will never abandon you. I've already promised that. That wasn't my meaning. It's just that, we've both lost everyone else we've ever had, and...' I didn't know how to finish my sentence. I didn't dare.

She took my hand and squeezed it.

'You can't imagine us growing old here together?' she asked.

'I've tried many times.'

'So have I. It's hard to do,' she admitted. 'Remember the man who helped us at the old asylum?'

'Yeah, I do,' I said. 'He was the oldest person I've seen in a long time, and yet, he can't be much over sixty.'

She nodded. 'There are no children or old people anywhere. In a few years' time, the world will be void of humans.'

'I'm not sure, Flame. The Overclass is still having children.

There are kids' bedrooms in some of the residences I break into. I find toys and children's clothes.'

'That's true. I've noticed those things,' she admitted.

We sat in silence, nursing our thoughts.

All we could do was take each day at a time, planning ahead for the short term. With winter on its way, we had to harvest what we could at the right time, making sure not to let a single fruit or vegetable go to waste. We'd try to get another crop of potatoes in before the first frost, and store whatever we could for the months ahead. There were also more repairs to be carried out in the pub and the house. Appropriate clothing wouldn't be an issue because we'd come across an abundance of winter clothes in houses around town.

Another objective while the weather was still mild was to carry out our expedition to the coast and back, which we estimated would take around four days. The first step to achieving this was making a simple tent by recuperating a tarpaulin in good condition and sewing loops into it through which rods or poles could be passed. It was a time-consuming process, but Flame surprised me with her skills as a seamstress.

I started keeping notes about each day's activities—a simple journal if you like. By the end of the twenty-seventh day since I'd started the journal, we were satisfied with our preparations for the winter and ready to embark on our expedition. We were merely waiting for the weather to improve after four days of constant drizzle. The warning came back to the forefront of our minds and we started wondering about the author again. Was this person still out there somewhere between this ridge and the coast? Or was it too late and we were the only people left alive beyond the city?

That evening, while Flame was in the pub kitchen preparing our evening meal and waiting for dusk before lighting the fire, and it was my turn to jog the length of town, which was now part of our regular fitness routine, the second question was answered.

It was my habit to do twenty push-ups at home, jog through town to the house where I'd found the window pane, do twenty chin-ups on the bough of a strong tree growing in the front

102

garden, and then sprint back up the slope to the church. I would then climb the church tower, enjoy the view and catch my breath for a few seconds, go back down to the road and run all the way to the service station, do another twenty push-ups, and sprint to the pub. It was enough to keep me in reasonable shape.

My routine, however, was interrupted that evening when I took in the view from the top of the church tower. At the foot of the ridge, on the western side, I saw movement. It was hard to say what it was at first, but it sent a shiver down my spine and set my heart racing.

It had to be a vehicle of some description. That much was clear. It was large and dark and moving faster than any living creature could run over what had to be rough terrain. Strangest of all was that there was no road as far as I could see. The land was hilly and sparsely wooded, and puffs of exhaust seemed to float into the air whenever it hit a rough patch. I couldn't imagine why anyone would be driving like that. The vehicle wasn't being driven towards any particular destination. I'd certainly never seen patrolmen acting in such a chaotic manner—an observation I should have found more reassuring than I did. And what were those smaller forms around the vehicle, trying to keep up with it? They could only be people.

I looked at the warning painted on the battlements and lost myself in thought for just a moment, but when I turned my attention back to the westerly view, I could tell that despite the seemingly random movements of the vehicle, it was getting closer to the foot of the ridge. Whether this was intentional or not, I had no idea. A few seconds later, it was so close it went out of view and I thought I could hear the faint rumbling of its engine, but I really couldn't be sure it wasn't my imagination.

That's when I drew a deep breath, took control of my senses, and hurried back to the pub.

Flame knew there was a problem as soon as she heard me rush inside.

'What's happened?' she asked before I'd even entered the kitchen.

I told her what I'd seen.

'No drones?'

'None at all. It's not a patrol. Like I said, as far as I could tell, there was one single vehicle and people following on foot.'

'We're not alone then,' she said quietly. Her face was pale and searching—so full of questions I couldn't answer.

'It appears not.'

Her blanched lips relaxed, then parted, and I noticed she was gripping the knife she'd been using to dice potatoes even more tightly than before. I guessed the one question she simply had to have answered before she could speak.

'Yes,' I said. 'They were heading this way. Whether they'll pass through town is another matter.'

'We have to assume they will. We have to play it safe.'

'No fire?'

'We can't risk it, can we?' she said. 'If they come along the road, they'll either see or smell the smoke. I suppose we could wait until well after dark. If they were already near the foot of the ridge when you left the church tower and coming this way, they'll be here any minute now, not in the middle of the night.'

I shrugged. All we could do was speculate. But we'd been warned, after all, and we were both fully aware that this was the greatest potential danger to face us since leaving the city. We had to err on the side of caution.

'I don't know if they have headlights. How they even found fuel out here is beyond me. In any case, we need to remain invisible tonight.'

'It's too late to go back to the house,' Flame pointed out. 'We can't risk meeting them on the road. I'll clean up, stow the food away, and we'll hide upstairs in the front room. That way, we'll have a view of the street. If they come this way, we can try to see who they are.'

'Sure. That's the best way to do it. Let's take a little food and water upstairs with us.'

We moved quickly, clearing everything away, and I checked that the front door was locked before we retreated upstairs. It wasn't pleasant by any means, having to hide like squatters in our pub. We'd already come to consider the entire town our own personal property, but in a matter of minutes, we had gone from lord and lady to frightened mice.

Flame pulled the curtains all but closed, leaving a gap just wide enough for us to peer down onto the road below. The sun was setting and darkness was falling upon the road like a shroud.

'Flame, I forgot my fork. It's at the house.'

She turned from the window and frowned at me. 'Why are you still favouring the fork? We have axes and machetes now.'

'I don't know really. It's a lucky charm, I suppose. It served me well against those drones back by the river.'

She turned back to the window. 'You need to be armed, Flicker.'

'My backpack is downstairs. I'll go down and get it. I've got my hammer in it. I'll bring a couple of axes up while I'm at it. Did we forget anything else?'

'I don't think so,' she said, not turning from the window. 'Do it quickly. They're not far away. I'm sure of it. I can hear a motor, and shouting. I can hear voices, Flicker.'

'Are you serious?'

She shot me a sharp look. 'Hurry up!'

It wasn't a figment of Flame's imagination after all. The low rumbling sound grew louder while I was downstairs. I glanced out onto the road and saw lights thrashing wildly from side to side, distant but drawing nearer. They couldn't be headlights judging by the way they were moving so erratically and yet they were approaching at speed. An image formed clearly in my mind; a vehicle with no headlights but with two or three passengers using powerful torches to light the way for the driver. And the way the beams of light were sweeping all over the place indicated that they weren't only being used to help the driver see where he was going, but also to find something.

I dashed upstairs to Flame as the rumbling of the vehicle's motor intensified and shouting reached my ears. It was terrifying howling and whooping, and there was a piercing scream of pure terror. I joined Flame at the window, her hands clinging to the curtains. She was trembling violently.

'What is it, Flicker?' she hissed. 'What's going on?'

'I think it's a hunt.'

'A hunt?'

The screeching of tyres rent the air, and while the lights

continued to thrash about, making us jerk back as they brushed the window, they were no longer drawing nearer.

'They've stopped,' she whispered.

The beastly howling and growling also ceased, but the calm was eerie now, broken only by the low rumbling of the motor and the searching lights dancing dementedly.

Flame was so surprised when the scream came that she pulled on the curtains and brought them tumbling down, leaving the streetscape in full view.

'Holy fuck!' she gasped.

The three hooded faces glowing behind the torches they held started howling again. They were standing on the back of a lorry, its black paintwork chipped and scarred with patches of rust and dents. The driver was no more than a vague shadowy outline. Two other figures were in front of the lorry and they'd just caught hold of a third—the young woman whose screams had caused Flame to bring the curtains down. They were trying to drag her back to the lorry now as it began moving again, edging forwards.

She was dressed in rags that barely covered her upper body, which glistened under the unrelenting drizzle. Her skin was milky, as though unaccustomed to sunlight, and her legs were covered in mud up to the thighs. Her face was ghostly pale, and her chestnut hair was clipped very short around the back and sides but kept longer on top with a straight fringe. One of them grabbed her by the hair where it was longest, at the crown of her head, and pulled her, making her scream even louder. It occurred to me it was as though this hooded man was leading her by a rope attached to her head—that her haircut had been designed to render it easy to catch and control her. It had probably been plaited and she'd undone it herself.

'She knows them, Flame. She was their prisoner and this is a failed escape attempt.'

'We have to stop this!'

'The two of us against six of them? It's sheer stupidity, Flame.'

She dropped to the floor, her fingers locked in her own hair, which she'd let grow since leaving the city, but which I was instantly sure she'd now cut again. 'I can't watch this!'

I kept my fury bottled up. What choice did we have? We'd be of no use to her dead.

'What are they doing to her?' she asked without looking up.

The howling continued as they hauled her over to the lorry, the two on the road taking her by the legs and two of the three on the tray pulling her up by one arm each. She kicked and thrashed but they dropped her onto the tray and the driver accelerated, leaving the two on the road to grab on and haul themselves up.

Flame forced herself to her feet and stared down at the road, but it was lost in darkness again, daring us to believe that what we'd witnessed hadn't merely been a hallucination. The only light we could perceive was a faint reddish line glowing in the distance, along the western horizon.

'We didn't help her!' Flame wailed, glaring at me, and the look in her eyes tore me apart.

I felt so guilty I thought I'd be sick, but there was no food in my stomach and the thought of eating disgusted me. Only the bottle of Highland Park downstairs was calling my name.

'We just hid here and let them kill her.' Her voice was low now. 'They'll gang-rape her, strangle her, and toss her body in a ditch.'

I wanted to take her in my arms, to make her feel safe, but I didn't dare. She was angry at me for not finding a way to save that poor woman, even though she knew we'd had no choice.

'I don't think so, Flame. They wanted her alive. She'd escaped and they were taking her back.'

'That's even worse,' she hissed. 'You heard her screams—the pure terror in her voice. They must be using her as a sex slave, Flicker. She'd be better off dead.'

I took a deep breath, trying to remain calm, searching within for some way to assuage my guilt. 'What could we have done? We couldn't have launched an attack on six armed men in a vehicle. Even if we'd somehow managed to kill five of them, but one had escaped, what would have happened? Tell me.'

'He'd have gone back to wherever he came from. For all we know, there's a whole tribe of these savages out there. They'd have come back here and hunted us down.'

'Yes, Flame. There you have it. That's why we did nothing. There's a world of difference between bravery and stupidity.'

107

'We forget about her then? We just pretend tonight didn't happen?'

'Ignoring this is not an option and you'll have no argument from me on that point. That much is clear.' I punched the wall, relishing the sharp pain. 'I need a whisky. I suggest you let me have one. Join me if you like. We take the risk of lighting a fire now that they've gone and sit ourselves down in front of it to talk this over.'

'You're right. We can't act rashly. We need to think this through and work out where to go from here.' She took a deep breath and stared into the empty street. 'You'd better pour two glasses.'

PART TWO

9: Trackers

Even a fire and a glass of whisky weren't going to be enough to settle our nerves entirely, but they could only help. Once I was confident the flames had taken hold and required no more fanning, I poured two generous measures and didn't speak until our glasses had kissed and we'd let the warming effect of the first sip soak in. Flame gasped a little, but her second sip went down more smoothly. She closed her eyes and relaxed.

'Where do we start?' I asked once she'd opened her eyes again. We were no strangers to tough times and we'd both witnessed terrible acts before, but I knew she was going to carry this one close to her heart for a long time—at least until we had some understanding of what had happened. For the first time since we could remember, life hadn't been so tough, and although neither of us had expected it to last indefinitely, reality had bitten particularly hard that night. Our burgeoning idyll had been ripped apart.

'Before we make any decisions, we need some answers,' she said.

'We do. And before we can find answers, we need to ask the right questions. So, what are they?'

We both took another sip and stared into the fire.

'We come back to the warning,' she began. 'The danger is real. Is this what the warning was referring to?'

'Good question. I think, for the moment at least, we assume it was. After all, it's the only danger we've seen since we got here. We haven't even spotted a single drone.'

'That's right. It doesn't seem to be a warning about patrols. Which brings us to the next question,' she turned her gaze back to me.

'Who are they?' I asked.

'Yeah, Flicker. Who are these bastards?'

'It's like some kind of tribe. They were howling like wolves and grunting like wild boar. But they have a lorry in working order, and even though they were all over the place, at least one of them knows how to drive off-road in wet conditions without losing control. I don't even know anyone who can drive properly. It also means they have fuel and oil and whatever else you need to keep a vehicle running. Then, there's the woman's hair. Did you notice that?'

'I noticed they were dragging her by it! Fucking pigs!'

I drew a deep breath, pushing back the wave of anger welling inside me. 'It's just an impression, of course, but the way her hair was cut looked intentional. It was short around the sides and longer on top. Not many women have long hair, do they? The one who took her by the hair was doing it like he was used to it, like a gardener might handle a wheelbarrow. Do you get what I'm saying? I think she'd already been in their possession, and they'd been forcing her to grow her hair long on purpose.'

'*Possession*, Flicker? *Possession?*'

'Well, *under their care* hardly seems appropriate.'

'It's horrible. Disgusting. I can't bear it.'

'I'm sorry, but you're going to have to. We need to explore this in detail if we want to even imagine being of any use to that poor woman.'

Flame took another sip—almost draining her glass, exhaled, then nodded.

'You're saying that they're organised, and possibly involved in...' She couldn't bring herself to say it.

'We don't know what they're doing, Flame, but it's safe to say they're holding people against their will. That's the key, you see. We're not dealing with a handful of fugitives. There's got to be a larger community out there with a hierarchical structure and impressive organisational skills.'

'Is this The Esplanade? What was the message in the chapel?

Congratulations on making it this far and on avoiding being sent to The Esplanade. That was the gist of it.'

'Is that where they're from?' I wondered. 'It could very well be. If that's so, the fact that that note of congratulations is still valid at this moment in time is a victory in itself.'

She sighed. 'So true. I wonder whether the author of those messages ended up getting captured.'

'There's a good chance. Was the town attacked and enslaved by this group? If so, they're very powerful indeed. Or were they themselves the inhabitants and the authorities expelled them because they caught wind of what was happening here and didn't like it?'

'Or neither?'

'Or neither,' I agreed, staring into what was left of my whisky. 'What we do know is that we have to find this place. An esplanade is usually a wide, maintained path along a body of water.'

'The sea?'

'Most likely.'

'In that case, we don't need to change our plan. We go ahead with the expedition.'

I gulped my whisky down. 'All right. That's what we'll do. After all, we don't have much choice. We're going to need to be extremely careful. If we're going to try to trace the lorry, we'll need to leave soon. With all the rain we've had, there'll be plenty of tyre tracks, or rather, muddy ruts.'

Flame looked at our empty glasses, then back at me. 'One more glass. After that, we close our eyes and try to get some rest. We'll take a chance and sleep here tonight. In the morning, we finish our preparations and start walking.'

I held out my glass.

Our sleep was light that night, but we were content to lie there on makeshift beds in front of the fire, knowing it would be a comfort we were going to miss.

Once we could tell it was daylight outside, we got up and made ourselves a filling breakfast. It was still drizzling but there was no holding off any longer. It was time to get moving. We finished

111

getting ready and inspected the road outside the pub, hoping to find clues of some description, but found nothing.

'If I go to the top of the church tower, I should be able to remember where I first saw the vehicle. I'll try to identify a landmark we can home in on, like a tree or a rock. If that works, we might be able to find their tracks.'

'It's our best bet,' Flame agreed.

We left our gear in the church and climbed the tower with nothing but my hammer and her knife—just in case. Not far from where I was sure I'd spotted the lorry was what looked like a pile of rocks, but I think it was actually one large rock with a cracked and worn surface. It was hard to judge from several miles away, but it looked to be roughly the height and width of a football goal.

'Light lunch there?' Flame asked.

'If we don't get lost along the way.'

'The sky looks clearer near the horizon. I think we'll have better weather by evening.'

'Let's do it,' I said, starting back down the tower.

We followed the road out of town, past the house where I'd found the window pane. We barely noticed the drizzle from under our hoods, with our faces tilted downwards most of the time to check our footing. We no longer bothered watching out for drones.

When a long muddy track through an ancient farm appeared on the right, I knew we had to take it to keep heading in the right direction.

'Are you serious?'

'I'm afraid so. It has to be the shortest route west to where the rock is.'

She sighed.

Long grass grew on either side, stretching out towards an old cowshed and rusty silo to the right and a crumbling stone cottage to the left.

'We'll walk on this side, where the grass is a little shorter and the ground doesn't seem to be too soft.'

'You and the driver must be brothers.'

'What?'

'Open your eyes, Flicker.'

I looked where she was pointing, and there was no doubt about it. The tracks could only have been made by our black lorry.

'I'd say we're heading the right way.'

The track led us straight ahead, up and over a low rise in the land, and when we reached the end, about ten minutes later, we found ourselves facing marshland with an uncovered road crossing our path.

'It's not as deep as the marshland on the eastern side,' Flame said.

'No, but too deep for a vehicle. Left or right?'

'I can't see your rock from here.'

Neither could I. There was no potential vantage point nearby either.

'The land to the left looks lower,' Flame pointed out.

'Your call. Let's go right.'

We followed the uncovered road for about a mile, noticing faint patches of mud but unsure they'd been left by a vehicle. We stopped when we saw a tiny wood shack by a small body of water. There were trees growing around it but not completely obscuring the view.

'If I can climb onto the roof, I might be able to spot the rock.'

The shack stood close to the water's edge and was closed on three sides but only half-closed on the side facing the lake. It had been a hunting shack, and I figured it may still have been in use. I looked inside before climbing onto it but found nothing to confirm my suspicion.

'I can see it,' I called down to Flame. 'It's closer than I thought. We'll stay on the road a little longer and try to head west in half a mile.'

It didn't feel like we were walking uphill, but after ten minutes, when we stepped through a break in the ditch following the road and the corresponding gap between the birches, oaks, and elms lining either side, we realised we had a clear view across a wide dale. There were groves scattered across the dale, slowly reclaiming land from the rolling stretches of tall grass that had undoubtedly been agricultural land before The Breakdown. It would only be a matter of time before these groves expanded to the point of reaching each other, like long-lost friends, once again making them worthy of being considered a proper forest.

'Spot on,' Flame said with an almost gleeful note to her voice, and she pointed to where two deep furrows with a sodden mix of brown and golden leaves, acorns, and grass stalks squashed in them marred the earth. 'We're becoming pretty good trackers.'

'It's a skill we're going to need out here. Our survival depends on it.'

'And hers.'

I looked up at her, peering out from under my hood, through the drizzle. Any hint of glee had vanished. 'You really think we can rescue her, don't you?'

'I don't know, but we'd never forgive ourselves if we didn't try.'

I nodded, turning my attention back to the view for a moment. With every passing day, the world was growing increasingly golden brown, with spectacular flashes of red here and there. Not far downhill, half a huge oak tree stood defiantly while the other half lay on the ground, partially hidden in the sea of long grass.

'If we ever make it back home, we need to add this area to our list of usual sites.'

'We have such a list?'

'We'll start one. Look at all the quality firewood here. It's a long haul but one I'm willing to make. I could store some at the bottom of the ridge, in a house near the church, and bring up enough for a couple of nights as required.'

'Sure. Do you know much about mushrooms?' she asked.

'No. You?'

She shook her head.

'Risky business. Wouldn't it be embarrassing to survive everything we've survived only to cark it because we picked the wrong fungi for dinner?'

'Hardly embarrassing. It's unlikely our bodies would ever be found.'

'A good if not particularly reassuring point, Flame. All the same, I think we should stick to eating what we know. I must admit, though, that hunting shack, if that's what they're called, has given me some ideas. If we happen to find a gun and ammunition one day and I manage to shoot a duck, would you be able to work out how to cook it?'

She stared at me as though I were insane, but I could tell she was giving it some thought.

'That's all very theoretical, and I really don't know. I'm not sure I could eat a living creature. That's kind of disgusting.'

'People used to do it all the time, and it wouldn't be a *living* creature when we ate it.'

'Find your gun first and then we'll see. Or, if you're as clever as all that, why don't you make a crossbow?'

I'd had friends who'd manufactured their own crossbows, and clearly Flame had as well. It was definitely a worthwhile project to consider, for both defensive purposes and hunting.

'Footprints,' Flame said, snapping me out of my dreams about what a roasted duck would smell and taste like.

'Several. Those smaller ones look like they were made by bare feet.'

'The woman.'

We looked more closely. It was hard to make much out, since the drizzle had turned the footprints into little more than a string of tiny puddles. The rounded form of the smaller ones bore witness to the balls of running feet plunging into the mud. It must have been hell for her. There were two or three other distinct boot prints. Although the pattern of treading couldn't be distinguished, the size, shape, and depth indicated different individuals. It all matched perfectly with what we'd witnessed.

'You can see where the grass was flattened by the lorry,' I pointed out. 'I'm surprised they didn't get bogged.'

'Maybe they did but with five of them pushing were able to get out of it. That would explain why it took so long for them to catch up with her on foot.'

'True,' I said, lost in thought.

'What are you thinking?'

'I'm thinking they can't be that far away. This damp terrain with few covered roads. The fuel they'd have needed to struggle through it. I didn't notice any jerry cans on the tray. Then you

115

think about the distance we've walked this morning. We're doing fine, I guess, but we're reasonably fit after all, and yet, I'm starting to feel a little tired. There's a problem here. It doesn't gel. I'm not making much sense, am I?'

'No. You are. You're saying she can't have run a whole lot further than where we stand—in any case, not as far as from the coast, however far that is precisely. I mean, it's definitely not over the next hill.'

'Exactly. So that means that if our esplanade is along the coast, as it must be—unless it's a misnomer—it's probably not where they're from. Does that seem like sound reasoning to you, or am I completely missing something?'

'It makes complete sense. It's quite—what's the word?'

'Perspicacious?'

Flame laughed. 'You and your books. I think I was going to say *insightful.*'

'That'll do me. This brings up a whole lot of new questions though.'

'It does. If they're not from The Esplanade, who is? Is it another danger, or are they part of one greater whole?'

'Yes,' I said, staring down past the split oak and along to where the land rose again into low hills. It was on that slope that I saw the weather-beaten rock.

'If we don't keep moving, I'm going to take my bags off,' Flame said. 'I'd rather we stick to the plan and have a rest at the rock. It can't be more than ten or fifteen minutes from here.'

'Unless we find a river at the bottom of this dale, but it doesn't look like it from here.'

'Fingers crossed. Let's go.' Flame took the lead, walking carefully to the end of the muddy track and following the trail of flattened grass down past the oak.

It took over twenty minutes to reach the rock. The tracks disappeared at the bottom of the dale, where a rough riverbed stretched out across our path, running down to where the marshland we'd seen earlier lay. There was only a narrow stream meandering through a maze of rocks and mats of branches and weeds that had piled up over time. Frogs or toads, I couldn't tell which, chirped a constant tune.

We were able to cross the stream by stepping carefully from one rock to another, ever so slowly, testing our footing before putting all our weight down.

'No bridge in sight,' Flame pointed out, once we'd reached the other side. 'If the rain picks up again while we're on this side, we may not be able to cross again when we want to go home.'

'Something to keep in mind,' I agreed. 'We might need to go further north, towards the source of the stream. It's not much of a river, and judging by the way it winds down from those hills, we should be able to join the ridge from the service station end.'

'The other option is to build a raft to cross the marsh and bring us straight back to the track through the farm.'

'Let's see how it pans out,' I said. 'The sun will be out this afternoon. We'll see what weather tomorrow brings. Now, getting back to the task at hand, we can see the tyre tracks again over there.' I pointed to the north-west, to where the land rose softly out of the rocky riverbed and up to a pass between two hills. 'There has to be a track through there.'

'Let's keep moving, unless you're hungry.'

'Not really. I'd rather keep going. We're too exposed here, and we'll get cold if we stop for too long.'

We trudged up the slope, so sure the lorry had passed this way that we barely even paid attention to the tracks. Apart from a lone bird of prey circling high overhead and rainclouds floating away towards the city, nothing else moved.

The dirt track snaked through the gap, lush undergrowth hanging down from the sides. The surface was hard and covered in gravel, making our footsteps crunch and echo. When I looked at Flame's face, I could see she didn't like it any more than I did. We were sitting ducks.

But we soon reached the other end the passage, and for the first time that day, rays of sunlight touched our faces. In the distance, clearer now but still not perfectly distinct, we saw the deep blue of the sea. White peaks and ephemeral sparks of light reassured us that we weren't mistaken.

'It looks so close,' Flame said.

'It does, but that looks much closer.'

She followed my gaze to the left, very slightly downwards, to where a shelf stuck out from the hillside. When I turned back to her, I saw the very same mix of surprise, apprehension, and wonder that I felt mirrored on her face. Those keen green eyes were staring from under the black hood. For nestled there on the hillside were the ruins of a castle.

10. The Stronghold

'That's a castle,' Flame whispered, trying to convince herself. 'It's a real castle, isn't it?'

'I think so. I've never seen one before either.'

'I know, but you must have read about them. There must be descriptions and illustrations in some of those old books you're constantly hoarding.'

'Hoarding? You make me sound like a dragon.'

Flame laughed. 'If only you were.'

I imagined gliding down from where we stood, breathing fire on my enemies.

'I've read about castles and seen pictures,' I told her. 'That's true. But seeing one for real is different. I can't recall a picture of a castle nestled halfway down a hillside like this one. I've read about the one that was in the city in mediaeval times. All trace of it disappeared centuries ago. It's probably buried under the ruins of a twentieth-century car park now. That seems to be the fate of most historic monuments, doesn't it?'

'I guess so,' Flame said. 'A lot of concrete flowed in the twentieth-century, smothering and encasing everything that had been built before it. People must have believed the world had some kind of grand future back then.'

'Either that or they were covering it with one gigantic funeral slab.'

'None of that out here though. This is the real world.'

'That it is, and so, that is probably a real castle. I had no idea there was one out here.'

'It must have been built to protect the passage through the hills and control access to the farmland and town on the other side.'

'It must have also served as a lookout to keep an eye on the coast, allowing warning of the approach of an enemy fleet to quickly reach the city.'

'Quickly?' Flame asked. 'It was no walk in the park for us. Perhaps the roads were better in those days.'

'It's possible, you know. They would have had an abundance of horses.'

'Before the last one was eaten?'

'Long before that time,' I mused, staring down at the stronghold. 'Just look at it, Flame. The wall is cracked and some of the battlements have collapsed, but it must have formed a perfect semicircular barrier originally. Look at the keep, towering near the outer edge, and the gatehouse facing us.'

'Not entirely mediaeval, are they?'

'No, they're most certainly not.'

Five solar panels stood diagonally atop the keep, facing west but leaning inwards, and there was a raised platform the size of large dining table with what looked like an armchair positioned in the middle of it, but it was hard to be sure from so far away. The structure was by no means in sound condition either. Part of the far side of the keep had collapsed—peeled away like shed skin. I couldn't tell how severe the damage was or what repairs had been made from this angle, but a low parapet of sacks or sandbags, about fifteen or twenty wide and three or four high separated the flat roof of the keep from what was probably a terrifying sheer drop.

'What's the gate made of, Flicker? Can you make it out?'

I looked down at the gatehouse. 'I'd say it's normal wire fencing, like around the schoolyard. Not as sturdy as a proper wrought-iron gate.'

'You wouldn't need a battering ram to break in.'

'No, you wouldn't. Can you see the top of something familiar over the wall to the left of the gatehouse?'

'Yeah, I noticed that,' Flame said, almost hissing.

I remembered last night's terrible scene as I stared at the black cabin roof with patches of rust.

'Can you see anyone? I can't.'

She shook her head. 'No one at all. There's a small glass or transparent plastic structure in the middle of the courtyard,

120

behind the lorry. I'd say it's a greenhouse.'

'That would make sense.'

'What do we do now?'

'Above all, what we don't do is go rushing into that death trap.'

'Absolutely not,' Flame replied. 'We're going to need to think this through. We should set up camp nearby, but well away from this track, and out of sight of the castle. If they spot us, we're done for. Once we're all ready for the evening, we find a safe and reasonably comfortable nook with a clear view of the castle, as close as we can get without putting ourselves in danger, and we sit and wait. We need to know how many they are, how they're equipped, and what they're doing. What do you think?'

'We're on the same wavelength, Flame. That's the way to go about it. At any rate, we don't have much of a choice. Short of an army, our hands are tied. Launching an attack would be utter madness.'

'We've always embraced stealth, haven't we? It's what we do best.'

She knew it as well as I did. Keeping our heads down had certainly kept us alive so far. "Keep it down, but don't bury it in the sand"—or something along those lines. That's about the best advice I'd ever been given, and I couldn't even remember who gave it to me.

'Let's get moving,' I said.

We clambered up off the track, which must have continued downhill before branching off towards the castle, and worked our way through thickets and bracken.

'This looks good,' Flame said after a couple of minutes, pointing to a hollow with a rocky bottom. It was mostly free of vegetation and the ground appeared not to be overly damp. Water evidently drained through the rocks. I followed her down into the depression, which was about half my height deep, and we stamped our feet to check that the ground was solid.

'We can move these rocks around to make a flat surface to put the tent on,' I said.

'We should check around first though, just to avoid any other surprises. We need to be sure we can move from a vantage point over the castle back here in the dark without getting lost.'

'Good thinking. Let's leave our belongings here though.'

Flame followed me back out of the hollow and through thickets beyond which we could see the sky. As we advanced, the sea came into view, and then the castle, still to our left but much closer now. We crouched at a ledge from which the view was clear, allowing us to see most of the courtyard within the walls. The lorry and greenhouse were in full view, and we could see that the door to the keep was closed.

'There are targets along the wall,' Flame whispered, out of instinct more than any real necessity.

'I wish I had a pair of binoculars. Can you see any arrows?'

She shook her head. 'It's impossible to tell from here.'

'That's something to keep in mind in any case. If they have targets, they're trained in the use of long-range weapons.'

She groaned.

'I know. A daunting prospect.'

'There isn't much else in the courtyard,' she said. 'There are stacks of firewood, and a kind of lean-to against part of the wall behind the greenhouse.'

'It looks like it might be a workshop.'

'You wouldn't think they'd leave their stronghold completely unmanned during the day while they go hunting and gathering, would you?'

'That's just what I was wondering. It doesn't strike me as being a particularly smart thing to do. Then again, we don't know if they've ever felt threatened. That wire fence wouldn't hold attackers off for long. They would have built a more substantial barrier if they were concerned about an assault. Who from though? We haven't seen drones or patrols out this way, so perhaps they've been living here unchallenged for years without any cause for concern.'

'This woman must be with them wherever they are,' Flame said.

'She must be, along with how many others?' I asked. 'Let's get the tent put up, eat a little, and come back here later.'

Flame sighed, and I knew she hated the idea of biding our time while the poor woman was out there somewhere, being manhandled and abused. But we both knew we'd only have one shot at getting this right. The slightest sign of our presence and the element of surprise—the only advantage we had—would be lost.

We put the tent up without any problems and I was relieved to find it couldn't be seen from outside the hollow.

'I'm going to have a very light lunch, Flame. I'm more tired and thirsty than hungry.'

'Me too. Let's have a snack, lay everything we might need during the night out so it's easy to find in the dark, and stretch out for a few minutes. We're no use to anyone exhausted. Should we take turns at the lookout?'

'If you like. I don't want to risk falling asleep just now anyway. I mostly want to lie down and stretch my legs out a bit. How about you get some proper rest while I do the first watch?'

'Thanks, Flicker. I need that.'

'On one condition though.'

'Your kindness is conditional now, is it?'

'A quick leg massage.'

'A quick leg massage, is it?' She laughed. 'I haven't heard it called that before.'

'No innuendo. I swear. My legs are pretty stiff. They're all I need massaged—for the moment. No ulterior motive.'

'Fine.'

'But I want you to rub hard.'

'You're terrible!' She waggled a finger at me. 'I will—but I really don't know how we can joke like this while the world is going crazy around us.'

'Well, you have to laugh to keep insanity at bay. I guess it's a survival mechanism.'

'It must be. In any case, as I said, we're not going to be much use to anyone if we don't take care of ourselves, so you've got yourself a deal. Food first though.'

We savoured every mouthful of our light lunch, taking our time and eating in silence except to ask each other if we wanted this, that, or the other. I was sure Flame was thinking about the horrible scene that had out played out before our eyes from the pub window. For my part, my mind was on the stronghold and its occupants. Who were they? How many were they? How were they armed? What form of social structure and repartition of roles did they have? Above all, what kind of chance did we stand against them?

Once we'd finished eating, I lay on my back and Flame began. She worked the soles of my feet, kneading them like putty, and massaged my ankles. Once my feet were tender, she pressed her fingertips into my shins, following the outer edge of the bone. She burrowed them into the muscles, making the soreness grow before it faded.

'Roll over,' she then said.

It was amazing. Her fingers could feel where I was tight. She had obviously given massages many times before, but I told myself I didn't need to know when or to whom. All that mattered was that she was taking care of me. She was transferring her energy to me and taking my stiffness upon herself.

She was using her thumbs now, digging them into each calf and working them in a circular motion, all the way up to behind my knees, over and over. Low groans of pleasure escaped my mouth and she let out a little laugh of satisfaction. For the first time, I realised just how much strength she had in her hands. It occurred to me that they were powerful enough to strangle a man, should the need arise one day. A strange thought to have during such a heavenly experience, but it was one that comforted me greatly.

She started kneading my hamstrings with her fists, pushing and twisting so that her knuckles squeezed the stiffness away, but they weren't as sore as my calves had been.

'Would you like me to return the favour?' I asked after a few minutes.

'Later tonight.'

'Thanks, Flame. You've obviously massaged before.'

'Never such wonderfully muscular legs as yours,' she said, giving me a cheeky wink, and I wondered if that was true.

'Did someone teach you?'

She looked at me, nodded, and smiled faintly. I'd seen that look before.

'It was amazing.'

'Yeah, I could tell you liked it. Do you think you can walk or have I melted your legs?'

'I should be able to make it to the cliff edge.'

'Do be careful.'

'Why? Do you need me?' I teased.

But her face was deadly serious now. 'I do, Flicker. For the first time since I can remember, I know I couldn't possibly go on alone. I need you.'

We kissed, and time froze, but her hands—not her lips—filled my mind.

'It's the same for me,' I said when she pulled away to catch her breath. 'While you were massaging me, do you know what I was thinking?'

'Tell me.'

'That your hands are strong. I think there's probably enough strength in them to strangle a man.'

'And that reassures you, in case you're not there to look after me one day?'

I nodded.

'I'd rather not find out. So please be careful—now, tomorrow, and always.'

'I'm not going to put a foot wrong. You're counting on me, and she's counting on us, even though she doesn't know it. I can promise you I won't fall down the cliff unless someone pushes me. On that topic, make sure you have a weapon within easy reach while you take your nap. I doubt anyone could reach the tent without me hearing them from the lookout, but you never know.'

'Of course, Flicker. Get going now, and come back when you've had enough. Oh, and wake me up gently or you risk feeling my steely grip around your neck.'

I took my backpack, returned to the lookout, and settled into the very same position I'd taken earlier. It took no more than a few seconds to ascertain that nothing had changed except the position of the sun. The castle was as it had been before in every detail. All I could do was sit back and make myself as comfortable as possible, my backpack wedged against the jagged rock behind me.

I closed my eyes and let my thoughts drift, like the clouds

sailing in from the sea. I knew I wouldn't fall asleep, because tired as I was, and even though my legs felt lighter after Flame's massage, I was still in a rather uncomfortable position. I imagined walking into the sea, the feel of salt water between my toes, and the splash of waves around my knees. I'd seen sketches of sea creatures and marine plants in old books. There weren't only fish, but also crabs and lobsters, shellfish, and jellyfish. There were these extraordinary sea stars as well, and seahorses. In the most recently published book on the subject I'd come across, dating from around 2030, from memory, the author explained that most species of whales previously on the brink of extinction were now only considered to be endangered. But what had happened since then? Had the population continued to grow to the point that the oceans were now swarming with whales? I knew that dipping my feet in the water wouldn't magically infuse me with an understanding of this unknown world, and that I'd be lucky to discover seaweed and shells washed up on the beach, but I wanted to see whatever I could with my own eyes and hold Flame by the hand as we walked across the sand and stepped into the water.

I opened my eyes and peered out to sea, where the sun was sinking ever lower. I realised it would look bigger and redder as it reached the horizon, before its perfect circle was broken and it disappeared from view. It would be a spectacle on another scale altogether compared to any sunset I'd seen before.

Below me, nothing stirred. The castle stood there as it had for centuries. It would have appeared abandoned and forgotten if not for those tell-tale signs of occupation. This was a waiting game, and so I waited. Life was a waiting game. That's all it had ever been in the city, at least. Waiting for night. Waiting for the drones and patrols to move along. Waiting for the right moment to leap into action. Waiting for the opportunity to light a match and let fire consume its prey.

I took a sip of water, then got up and walked back from the ledge a little. I stretched, relieved my bladder, and had a look around, wondering if there might be a sign of past human activity on the ridge—but there wasn't even a bottle cap or half-buried plastic wrapper.

I went back to the lookout, sat down, and closed my eyes again.

Some time later, a sound caused me to open my eyes. It had come from a distance and was faint but unmistakable—a kind of metallic rattle.

My attention was brought immediately to the gatehouse, and there I saw more than thirty people about to enter the stronghold. They were all on foot, about half of them carrying large baskets, and two carrying something hanging from a long pole they held horizontally, one at either end. A wild animal? So, these people were hunters, and consequently meat-eaters. The realisation filled me with a sense of awe, or rather, an unsettling sense of admiration tinged with apprehension. The other dozen or so were armed. Some carried what looked like clubs from where I sat and others had what could only be bows strapped over their shoulders. Two archers held the wire gates open while the others stood behind the slaves, waiting for them to enter first. I watched as the group went into the courtyard and the gate was closed behind them.

It was then that I noticed a figure standing at the entrance to the keep. It was so unexpected I leaned back a little, hoping I hadn't been spotted, but there was no reason to think that was the case. I was high on the ridge and certainly indistinguishable from the rocks and bushes around me. The figure remained there, no doubt watching the arrival of the group. Whoever it was had been there all along, inside the castle.

I don't know how I knew it—there was obviously something in the stance—but even from so far away, I could tell this was their leader, not merely a guard left to watch over the stronghold while the others were out. It begged several questions. First of all, what kind of system did they have in place? The use of slave labour prohibited anything remotely democratic in nature. Were we witnessing the dawn of a new feudal age?

The figure descended the stairs from the door to the keep and the others stood to attention.

Whatever title the leader held, there was something else I was now almost certain of, even from here. Their leader was not a king.

I watched that figure, trying to make out every detail and interpret every movement despite the distance. There was no mistaking it. The way she walked. The majestic posture. Confidence and elegance.

The idea seemed absurd, but that didn't mean it couldn't be so. In this ruined castle, reigning over an almost empty realm, was I witnessing the first queen this land had known in living memory?

I watched, as much in fascination as with a kind of slow-brewing fear. This band of warriors showed signs of discipline. It could be seen in the way they were standing, facing their queen. They were undoubtedly listening to her thank them for their work and congratulate them on the success of the day's hunt.

'Flame needs to see this,' I whispered to myself, as though actually saying the words would help break the spell and force me to take my eyes off the scene and rush back to the tent.

It must have worked, because I found myself running back to her, but I entered the tent slowly, not wanting to alarm her.

She was already awake, and spoke first.

'They've returned?'

She didn't wait for my reply, already pushing me out of the tent.

We hurried back to the lookout and found them still in the courtyard.

'Can you see the one at the bottom of the stairs?' I asked.

Flame stared in silence for a minute, before turning to me. 'She's their leader?'

'Yeah, I think so. She must be their queen.'

'Their *queen*? What in the world are you talking about? I must have massaged you too hard.'

'How else would you describe her?'

She looked again and eventually shrugged. 'I don't know. She's their leader. That's obvious enough. What are the two with the pole carrying?'

'I think it's an animal.'

'That's what I think too. That means they're hunters. They have bows, Flicker!'

'I know. I saw them.'

'This is bad.'

'Yeah. We should give up and head back to the town.'

She turned to me and stared into my eyes, then relaxed. 'I almost believed you for a second.'

'Really? Are you serious, Flame?'

'Almost,' she repeated. 'Just for a fraction of a second.'

'You should know me better than that by now. I'm not giving up on her—on *them*. There's no going back. I often spare a thought for all my lost friends, and for yours, Flame, even though I didn't know them.'

She put a hand on my shoulder. 'I know you do. It's the same for me. Sometimes at night, while I'm waiting for sleep to come, I think about them—your friends and mine, and all of those we never even knew—and I wonder what happened to them all.'

I drew her close and she rested her head on my shoulder.

'You're telling yourself,' she said softly into my ear, 'that by freeing these slaves, you're making up for not being able to save your friends.'

'In a way, I am. Yeah. I know it's not our fault. None of it is. We have no control over what happens in this world. We didn't make it how it is.'

'But you feel like that's changing now?'

'That must be it. I suppose. I don't really know. Do you? After finding our new home, I started to think we could find meaning in the little everyday triumphs. Creative purpose instead of hatred and destruction. Fixing the window to our home replaced smashing a windscreen. Eating a meal together by the fireplace replaced setting fire to a luxury car.'

'But that's not enough for you?'

'I don't know. Is it for you?'

'I'm not sure either. I think it could be, but not if it means turning our backs on others. We can't change the world, but we have to strive not to become what we despise about it. The city may be far behind us now, but what's happening in that castle is too close to home. You don't fix the failures of the past by reproducing them on a smaller scale. This is what gives our lives meaning right now, making us not just fugitives, but rebels. If we make it back to our new home at the end of it all, we'll know we really deserved it.'

We turned our attention back to the courtyard.

'We're going to have to come up with a hell of a clever plan, Flame.'

The queen was making her way slowly up the stairs, followed by the two slaves with the hunted beast and the two warriors who had opened and closed the wire gate. These warriors closed the door to the keep behind them, while the other warriors ushered the remaining slaves from the courtyard in another direction, out of sight.

After several minutes, we realised that was going to be all we'd see for the day.

'Let's watch them again in the morning,' Flame said. 'Early.'

'Yes. It'll be dark soon.'

'Flicker, look at the sun!'

'I was wondering when you'd notice,' I said, putting an arm around her, and we watched wide-eyed as fire kissed water.

11. Cat

'How did you sleep?'

Flamed rolled over to face me and offered a groan as a reply.

'That bad, huh? Pretty much the same for me. It wasn't the return to sleeping on a rough surface though. At least, I don't think so.'

'You were dreaming up a plan?'

'The castle was definitely on my mind, but I'm pretty sure it was those owls that kept waking me.'

'Is that what they were?'

'What else could be hooting in the middle of the night?'

'I have no idea. I'm not even sure I've heard owls before. I thought they were extinct.'

'Some species probably are, but I've slept in hidden spots in the city where there are owls. A lot of animals that were on the brink of extinction before The Breakdown are making a resurgence now that there's less human activity and the forests are growing back. I was thinking about that yesterday at the lookout, wondering what kind of creatures live in the sea.'

'We'll get there, Flicker. We'll put our feet in the salt water one day.'

It was still dark inside the tent, with only a faint luminosity perceptible through the fabric, but we easily found the clothes we'd laid out yesterday. We dressed warmly, knowing the dawn air outside would be a sudden change from the comfortable temperature inside the tent. Falling sick was the last thing we needed.

Flame unfastened the six cord loops she'd made to keep the tent closed and insulated at night and peeped outside. The coast clear, she left the tent and started stretching while I crawled out

131

after her.

'Better?' I asked.

'Much better. We need to make sure we keep moving. Going back and forth from tent to lookout won't be good for us.'

'That's why we need to take turns. If nothing's happening down there at the moment, I'll stay and you can go for a walk, but not too far.'

'I can try to find a source of fresh water.'

We walked towards the lookout.

'That would be perfect. Talking about water, I get the feeling rainclouds are heading in from the west.'

'The sky's not as blue as yesterday. I was hoping we could enjoy another romantic sunset together.'

'That would be lovely. Followed by another massage?'

'Sounds like heaven. I'll give you some more pointers though. A woman's not a drone, Flicker! You need to balance strength with tenderness.'

'I'm a willing student. Wait! Look!'

We crouched on the ledge and watched the comings and goings in the courtyard. The sun's rays hadn't yet reached the western slope of the hill and wouldn't for many minutes more, but there was enough morning light to make out the figures of the warriors and the workers.

'No sign of our queen,' I observed.

'I imagine she has the privilege of sleeping in,' Flame replied, a hint of bitterness in her voice.

'That's the impression I get. It's bizarre when you think about it. We've gone from a city where people like us are considered excess population to a microcosm where they're used as slaves.'

'What's wrong with people?' Flame asked. 'What's wrong with *her*, this queen? I thought women were better than that.'

'You really think gender makes a difference?'

'Of course, Flicker. You don't understand. Despite all the books you've read, and all the big words you know—like "microgasm"—you don't understand some basic truths.'

'Microcosm.'

'Whatever!' she hissed.

'Sorry,' I said.

'You don't need to be sorry. It's not your fault. In fact, it's one of the things I love about you. The fact that you don't think it's more surprising that a woman can be cruel and arrogant than a man is itself due to the fact that you're a good man.'

I must have been frowning.

'Does that make sense?'

'Ah, perhaps. I really don't know, Flame. You have a lot to teach me about these things. We've clearly established that.'

She smiled. 'We have, haven't we? Well, there are some things I didn't have to teach you.'

I tried not to grin. 'On that topic—'

She placed a finger over my lips and shushed me. 'We'll talk about that later. Back to the task at hand.'

We looked down into the courtyard. There was still no sign of the queen, but a handful of the warriors was now lined up facing the targets and drawing bows.

'That's one question answered beyond a doubt,' Flame said. 'They use bows.'

'I can't see where the arrows are landing.'

'Wait a second. We'll soon see.'

Having fired several volleys, the archers advanced in a line to their targets and reached out, plucking from near the centre of each one.

'Not bad at all,' Flame whispered lowly.

'So, this is the biggest danger for us. We have to think about techniques and tools that will protect us from their arrows.'

'Noted. Look what's happening now. The others are getting ready to leave. If the archers stay, that means the slaves won't have as many warriors accompanying them as yesterday.'

'What exactly are you suggesting, Flame?'

'We could try to follow from a distance and take advantage of having fewer eyes that risk catching sight of us.'

'I like the idea, but we have to promise each other we'll keep our heads cool. We don't know what we'll see. If there's any violence, we have to resist the temptation to act. We mustn't let our emotions get the better of us. It was hard enough watching from the pub window.'

'There is no way in the world I'm letting my emotions betray me, Flicker. I won't give that bitch and her pigs the satisfaction.'

I looked at Flame's face and the calmness of expression that accompanied those vicious words reassured me.

'They're leaving,' I said, and we heard the faint rattle of the gate. 'All of the workers and one, two, three...eight warriors. None of the warriors have bows. They mustn't be planning on hunting today. Yesterday's catch is probably enough meat for them for the moment, especially if the workers don't get to eat any.'

'Couldn't they overpower them?'

'It's hard to say. They're unarmed, and we don't know what physical condition they're in. We don't know their history either —what the punishment is for a failed uprising. You're right about following them. There's only so much we can learn from up here. We need to find out exactly what's going on. We have what it takes to move noiselessly and remain undetected.'

'Let's get moving then,' Flame said. 'Are you armed?'

'No. You?'

'I have knives on me.'

I raised my brow.

'Hurry up, Flicker. Go and grab a weapon from the tent. No backpack today, then we'll head down the track.'

I moved swiftly, and took only my hammer, so as to stay as light and unhindered as possible.

We jogged back to the main track, clambered down onto it, and continued jogging downhill, slowing to a walk as we approached where a branch cut south towards the castle.

There was no cause to speak. We were thinking the same thing. We had to remain quiet, catch our breath so we could hear more clearly, and try to work out whether the group had already gone by. We had to stay behind them, not get caught in front. We were tailing them, not setting an ambush.

We stared into each other's eyes for an instant and slowed our breathing. She pointed to her ear, and I shrugged in reply. I couldn't hear anything beyond the normal sounds of the woods.

We kept waiting, then she pointed to her ear again, her eyes wide this time, and I nodded and pointed to the left, to where a thick tangle of ivy enshrouded the half-moon trunk of a dead oak.

We hid inside the trunk, wrapped together tight so our shoulders and elbows, or any other part of our bodies, couldn't be seen protruding from behind the ivy curtain. I'll never forget that moment, whether it was the thrill of danger, or simply the magic of holding Flame against me in that primal setting. I kissed her passionately and she melted. I wanted her so much, but the voices were growing louder. It wasn't constant chatter, but they spoke every now and then, and it made me wonder who was talking. Were the slaves allowed to talk among themselves? Or were the guards communicating with them, or with each other?

When the footsteps became audible, it was easier to judge how close they were.

The sound of those shuffling feet was unsettling. Here we were in these woods, miles from the city, and all these feet were stomping, scuffing, and dragging on the ground so close behind us, just out of view. I realised I could hardly remember the last time I'd been near so many people.

The footsteps grew to a crescendo and eventually faded away without another word being heard.

After a while, Flame took a cautious peep and scampered back onto the track.

I joined her, and we looked to where the track disappeared around a gradual bend. The canopy was so thick with golden and brown leaves it looked like a tunnel.

We started walking, taking our time because the group hadn't been moving at much of a pace. Further along, the woods thinned out a little, which was bad news for us, but we soon understood why. There had been a small town here at some point in the past. Nothing anywhere near as old as the castle. These ruins were crumbled brick cottages. There were five or six on either side of the track. Only one still had half a roof intact, and it was this cottage that had a crooked television aerial hanging impotently from the side of its broken chimney stack.

Flame noticed it too. 'Early twenty-first century?'

'At a guess. This isn't like our town, is it?'

'No. This place has been in ruins much longer. It's a different story here,' she said. 'The street was covered at one point. There

135

are patches of asphalt under the dirt.'

'This was the end of a road leading inland from the sea. I bet you it connects with at least one main road following the coast to the south and linked to other roads heading back inland again, eventually providing access to our town.'

'I think you're right. But none of that helps explain where they're finding food around here. Are they farming?'

'We'll soon know.'

The landscape opened out a little past the ruins, and to our right, there was a broad field with a farm remarkably similar to the one we'd passed leaving town, when we followed the lorry tracks through the mud. The silo was identical in every way except for the pattern of the rust and the angle at which it was leaning. There was a cowshed beside it and a stone farmhouse nearby.

'They're not here.'

'No,' I said. 'I'd expected them to be. This is the perfect place to grow crops. Too close to the castle?'

We turned around and looked back at the hill. The sun was rising behind it, ready to battle the incoming rainclouds from the sea. A battle it couldn't win. We could see the top of the keep through the trees covering the hillside.

'That might be the reason, but the chain gate doesn't fit with an attempt to hide from danger,' Flame reminded me.

'I don't like this one little bit. They were moving slowly. We shouldn't have lost them. It feels like a trap.'

'No, it can't be. They have no idea we're here.'

'Where are they then? Is there another path we've missed?'

We turned all around, scouring the countryside as far as we could see, and glad the archers were at the castle.

'There they are!' Flame whispered, and we immediately realised our mistake. They'd taken a path through the field on the opposite side of the road from the farm. It was really no more than a trail beaten by regular use and we wouldn't have noticed it at all if they hadn't still been in sight. The group was only a couple of hundred yards away but moving southwards with their backs to us. Two guards were at the rear. It was hard to tell if they were part of the party that had captured the woman outside the pub, but they were dressed much the same. They wore black tracksuits, like us, but unlike the other night, their hoods were down. There was also some discolouration to their clothes as though they had been patched and mended. It made sense. So far from an inhabited town and wealthy residents, they wouldn't have been able to steal clothes very often.

Because their hoods were down, we could see that the guards' heads were shaven. This appeared to be a major distinguishing feature between them and the slaves, whose hair was close-cropped around the sides and—like I'd suspected—plaited on top like a rein. The guard to the left had a long gleaming scar on the back of his head, like a giant pink slug. It crossed diagonally from above his right ear down towards the lobe of his left ear. Both held what I'd taken to be clubs in their right hands and what I now could tell would be better described as wooden batons or truncheons, designed to subdue without inflicting too much damage. After all, what use was an injured slave?

'Can you see the pale slave?' Flame whispered.

I looked past the broad backs of the guards at the slaves. They were dressed in what amounted to rags, but which after a moment of reflection, I understood had been white or light grey tracksuits, to help make them stand out. None of this had been clear from up on the ledge, but now, so close to them, it made perfect sense. The tracksuits were supposed to denote rank in this neo-feudal society.

I glimpsed the swanlike neck and milky shoulders of the slave Flame was referring to. She was just in front of the two rearguards. The others weren't nearly so pale.

'What do you make of it?' I asked.

'It's her, the one we saw.'

'And?'

'And, well, she's much paler than the others. Uncommonly paler, I'd say. So she has been out of the sun for some time.'

'Yes. And she's walking right in front of the guards.'

'Yes, and that's because they're keeping a close eye on her. Why? Because she has tried to escape before. Several times. And that's why she's pale. She tried to escape and was locked away inside the castle. Then? Well, she was released at the end of her sentence but ran away again, and now they're just going to watch her closely while she works instead of locking her up and not getting any use out of her.'

I nodded. 'That has to be it. It all fits together.'

'Which means saving her will be harder than saving any of the others.'

'I'm not sure. In a way, it does, because they're watching her carefully, but it also means she's motivated. At the first sniff of freedom, she'll bolt. The others may be more hesitant.'

'Let's follow.'

They were out of sight now, over a slight rise in the field, so we crossed the road, keeping our heads down, and started along the trail. Once we could see them again, it became clear what the day's work involved. They'd doubled back to the left and were at the edge of the woods that climbed the hill. Two enormous elms lay on a clear patch of land that had already been tidied up in preparation. The trunks had been cut into sections, using a two-man saw most likely. Today's job was to chop and gather.

Two of the slaves had axes. They were young men, possibly still teenagers, and they were wafer-thin and haggard beyond their years. One had red hair, the likes of which I hadn't seen in a long time, and the other had dark skin and black hair. The rest of the slaves were all girls or young women, and they carried baskets or sacks.

'They're not using the lorry to collect wood,' Flame said. 'Is fuel too precious?'

I nodded. 'Not too precious to be used to catch slaves but too precious to be used to help them do their work.'

'Flicker, let's hide behind this holly bush.'

We nestled into place between the branches, taking care not to get caught up in the jagged leaves, and tried to make sure we were hidden from view from behind as well as in front.

One of the guards at the head of the group spoke and the two boys started chopping wood. The women stood watching at first while the guards shouted insults at the boys and laughed at them.

After a minute, one of the guards shoved the redheaded boy to the ground, grabbed his axe, and brandished it threateningly. I felt Flame grab my arm and dig her fingers in, but the guard swung the axe down against a section of trunk. An almighty crack boomed through the air.

'Like that, you pathetic piece of shit!'

He then tossed the axe back at the slave boy, who jumped up and got back to work, putting a lot more effort into each swing.

As the wood was cut into manageable lengths, the women moved in and started filling their baskets.

'What do the women do once their baskets are full?' Flame asked. 'They'll have to return to the castle with each load.'

'I wonder. They can't just sit around waiting all day, can they?'

Our question was answered about five minutes later. While the other guards mocked and spat at the slave boys, one called out the names of four women who had filled their baskets before waving towards the road. An instant later, they were heading back in our general direction.

'What do we do?' Flame whispered frantically.

I froze.

'Flicker!'

'We stay here and don't move an inch. Put your hood up, hunch up, but keep your eyes on them.'

The rainclouds were overhead now. That came as a blessing, reducing visibility a little. Peering out from under my hood, I watched the group follow the trail. One guard with four women. This told me they didn't generally have trouble keeping them under the thumb, because four young women used to the hard life could in all likelihood overcome a man, especially since this particular one didn't give the impression he was the toughest of the bunch, like the two rearguards did. Were they complacent? Had the taste for freedom been beaten out of them? Had they been brainwashed into thinking this was normal? I tried to get a look at their faces as they passed, but I couldn't read their expressions. No joy, of course. No boiling resentment either. No hint of rebellion. They looked tired and vacant.

The guard's truncheon tapped against his left shoulder as he walked, ready to spring into action. The silent threat was enough to keep the women in line.

'What would happen if—?' Flame whispered once they'd passed, knowing I'd understand her unfinished question.

'I thought today was just reconnaissance?'

'It's just a question. One guard. We could take him easily. We don't know when an opportunity like this will pop up again. So, what would happen? Would they run with us, or go into a state of panic?'

'Or turn on us?'

'Are you serious? Why would they do that?'

'I don't know, Flame. We don't know anything about them. All we know is that the only people we've ever been able to trust are our friends and family, and they're gone.'

She didn't say a word, but I could see a faraway look in her eyes.

'Am I wrong?'

'No, I guess not. Wait a second. There was someone. Yes, that's right. You're forgetting the old man who told us about the mill. If we hadn't trusted him, where would we be?'

I nodded. 'He saved our lives.'

'And we saved our own lives by choosing to trust him.'

'I'll bite. What if? So, what would be the first step? We'd have to jump him by surprise. If he has a chance to yell, we risk a company of archers rushing towards us down the hill.'

'Agreed. Do I slit his throat?'

'What?'

'That would be the easiest way of ensuring silence.'

I felt the blood rush out of my brain at that point.

'Are you going to throw up, Flicker?'

'No, of course not. You mean that though—what you just said? You're capable of simply running up behind him and slitting his throat?'

'If I ran up behind him, he'd probably hear me.'

'You know what I mean, Flame.'

'Yeah, I am. I'm capable of it. Do I disappoint you?'

I was speechless. Was she wrong? I guess I knew there was no other option—no place for pity against people like that.

'What if we can get information out of him?'

'Unlikely, and what would we do after he'd given it? Let him go?'

I shook my head and sighed.

'If the women aren't complete idiots,' Flame went on, 'they'll keep quiet, help us toss his body into a thick patch of brambles or ivy, and follow us back to the tent. We'd have enough time to start our journey back to the town before his disappearance is noticed, and we'd take a route impracticable for the lorry.'

I was about to agree when I caught a movement out of the corner of my eye.

'Quiet!' I whispered.

Through the holly branches, we could see two more people moving away from the worksite, heading along the trail.

I felt Flame tap my shoulder.

It was her, the recaptured woman. One guard just for her.

We remained motionless as they drew nearer and a chill went through my body as she looked our way. I could swear her dark eyes connected with mine for a fleeting moment before she turned her gaze back to the road ahead.

Flame released a breath.

We watched them as they moved further away, walking side by side, with the guard to her right. His pink scar was a sadistic grin and his long, thick truncheon rested on his broad right shoulder. Our eyes, however, homed in on her, and I'm sure we both saw that most subtle of gestures. Her tracksuit bottoms were tattered and we could see her left cheek where part of the seat had been torn away. It was milky beneath a smear of dirt. She held her left hand against that cheek and beckoned with her fingers.

'Change of plan,' Flame said excitedly.

'You bet. This is the way to go. She's a sharp one.'

'We can't risk them catching up with the first group. We need to attack where the road ends, as they pass the last ruined cottage.'

I checked that no one else was about to leave the worksite then crawled out of the holly bush. Flame was right behind me. We kept our heads low as we headed towards the road and we stuck close to the ruined cottages.

The slave didn't take the risk of looking back even once. She would be hoping we were there, closing the gap, and she'd be ready to act the second we pounced.

We kept to where the ground was soft, ignoring the mud

141

covering our shoes and trouser legs almost up to our knees. There were enough gaps in the low brick wall delineating what had once been front gardens for us to hide quickly if need be. Avoiding the brambles in the process would be another matter. But the guard and his slave were walking in the middle of the road, and although she was clearly letting her bare feet drag ever so slightly with each step, it was the noise made by the heavy, crunching footsteps of the solid man in his hiking boots that provided the cover we needed. I'd rarely seen such a muscular build, in fact. These warriors, while lacking the technology and arsenal at the disposal of the patrols, made up for it in sheer physical power. I remembered the hunted animal and couldn't help but think their diet played a role, in addition to whatever training they did.

Today, however, Flame and I were the hunters. We exchanged glances, knowing this was the time to close the gap and run at him the moment he showed any sign of acknowledging our presence.

But that's not how it was to play out.

'What's he doing?' Flame whispered, gripping my arm.

We crouched and froze, backs against the wall, but they weren't turning around. He wouldn't see us.

'No!' the slave hissed.

His only reply was to tug her plait harder, holding it like a rein, the way I'd seen knights do in the illustrations of books about the Middle Ages. I recalled one of the words used over and over again in those books. *Chivalry*. Unsure it had ever really existed, I was certain there was none on display here—this monster was not the knight in shining armour of fables.

He was in front of her now, pulling her off the road and into the undergrowth, his left hand never letting go of her hair and his right holding the truncheon erect, ready to strike.

'I'm still sore!'

He laughed.

'He's going to rape her!' Flame hissed.

'Not today,' I whispered. 'Never again. Breathe, Flame. Don't forget what we said about our emotions.'

The slave, despite what she was going through, set the

142

example. She kept a level head and acted in a way that struck me with awe. I don't think I've ever seen or ever will see such pure grit in the face of horror in my life.

As he tugged her through the undergrowth, brambles catching her bare feet, she somehow managed to turn her head sideways for a second before he pulled harder. It was enough for her to spot us, as though she'd known just where to look. Her left hand swung casually back behind the exposed cheek and she flashed her fingers and thumb three times.

'Did you see that?' Flame asked, her whisper electric now.

'I did. I can hardly believe it, but I did.'

'She wants us to wait fifteen seconds.'

'I know what she's thinking. We're to attack him at his most vulnerable, the moment he goes to enter her. Do you follow? Can you hold off until then?'

'Flicker, a woman like that—the rush she gives me! Yeah, I can do anything.'

'Let's move in closer.'

I checked behind us. No one. We walked across the road, heads down, and up to the trunk of the biggest tree.

He hadn't taken her far into the woods. Getting caught apparently wasn't of great concern. She was on all fours, her skinny arse hypnotising him, and we could hear her whimpering lowly. He was leaning over her, pulling his tracksuit bottoms down awkwardly with his right hand, having dropped his truncheon on the ground. His left hand was still tugging at her hair.

'It still hurts,' the slave groaned. 'Let me suck you this time.'

He tugged her hair again and laughed at her yelp of pain. 'It's not your mouth I want to fill.'

'Fucking pig!' Flame whispered, her lips against my ear. The venom in her voice was so bitter I no longer doubted those shocking words about being able to cut a man's throat. This was a fear and a terror women carried with them all the time—a grim shadow lurking around every corner. While it had always outraged me in a distant and ethical sense, it was visceral for Flame. I could now truly appreciate why she always carried a knife hidden on her person. I wondered whether she had ever

143

been—but now wasn't the time.

'Your knife is out?'

'Yes.'

'I'll crack his skull. If it doesn't end him, you go for his throat.'

She released a heavy breath in my ear and I dashed forward, leaping over brambles and fallen branches, landing my feet on thick patches of ivy where I could. My hammer was above my head, ready to come crashing down with all the might I could muster. This would be a fight to the death. There would be no question of holding back.

He spun around, wide-eyed surprise immediately turning into a ferocious grimace. She then spun, unable to use her legs with her tracksuit bottoms around her ankles. Instead, she pushed behind his knees with her hands, bringing him to a kneeling position. I brought my hammer crashing down, aiming for his forehead, but he dodged and it landed on his right shoulder. Roaring with pain, he dropped to his left to grab his truncheon, but the slave got it first. She rolled away, got to her feet, and pulled her tattered tracksuit bottoms up.

Flame was on him now, and her knife flashed at his throat, cutting skin, but he had her at arm's length, avoiding a deep slice. He then pushed her with all his strength, sending her flying. She landed heavily on her back.

I swung my hammer horizontally as he sprang to his feet, tracksuit bottoms still around his ankles, but he blocked with his left arm, growled like a beast, and smashed his right fist into my face.

For what I thought was a matter of several seconds, all I could remember was struggling to get to my feet and trying to get my bearings. I had to ignore the sharp pain in my nose. I was aware of Flame beside me, also finding her feet again.

It had only been two or three seconds though, because the warrior was pulling his bottoms up to his waist. Realising I'd managed to keep my hammer firmly in hand, I lunged forward, but before I could swing, the slave brought the truncheon crashing into his head from behind, dropping him to his knees again.

I stopped as he twisted to face her, and Flame did the same, coming to a halt beside me.

She swung again, a loud crack ringing out, and the last move he made was to clutch her left ankle in an attempt to pull her down, but she kept her balance and struck several light blows in quick succession like slaps. Left. Right. Left. Right. Left.

His hands dropped to the ground, and his head turned in circles, the slick scar now covered in blood.

She raised the truncheon over her head with both hands, shot us a wide, trembling grin that sent a shiver down my spine, and pounded the crown of his head with the weapon.

There was a frightful crack and his body went limp.

She looked at us and sighed.

'Is he dead?' Flame asked, speaking to her for the first time.

She shrugged and looked down at his inert body, then raised the truncheon above her head and brought it slamming down again for good measure. Her plait jumped on her head and another sickening crack echoed through the woods.

'Thank you,' she said, her voice dull, almost incongruously pitiful. 'No. That sounds absurd. I'll never be able to thank you enough.'

'You can thank us later,' was all I could think of to say. 'We need to get away while we can.'

Flame was the first to move. I fell in behind, and the slave—no longer one—stuck close to me. Where the track branched right, Flame slowed down, peered along its length to make sure the first group wasn't already on its return trip, then jogged uphill, only slowing to a walk when it was time to climb up off the track and seek the safety of our tent.

Once inside, we sat in silence, catching our breaths and trying to gather our thoughts. We looked at each, bewildered, as though wondering whether what had just happened was real.

Flame spoke first. 'Are you hurt?'

But the woman looked at me, a deep frown scoring her face. After an uncomfortable moment, she turned her gaze on Flame.

'You're safe now,' Flame said softly.

'I'll be fine.' It was barely more than a whisper. 'Let's not talk about it now. We can talk later. The two of us.'

'I understand,' I said, feeling strangely guilty.

'My name is Flame, and this is Flicker—he's a good man.'

Tears welled in her eyes, but she smiled as she looked from Flame to me and back again.

With a voice that was soft and melodious, belonging more, I thought, to the woman she wanted to be than the one the world had made her, she told us her name.

'My name is Catriona, but you call me Cat.'

'Well, you certainly have claws,' I said, and I was glad to hear them both laugh.

12. The Lady

'We're not safe here,' Flame said, the very act of laughing snapping her back to the gravity of our situation. 'We have to get back to the town.'

'The abandoned town on the next ridge? Is that where you're from?'

'It's where we live now,' Flame said. 'We're from the city, but we escaped.'

'I've never been there. What's it like? It mustn't be any better than here if you had to run.'

'It's terrible—a nightmare of a different kind, I suppose. You have to keep your head down if you want to make it, and we're not so good at doing that.'

'Are you serious? You were sure as hell good at it today. I was mad impressed!'

'The feeling's entirely mutual, I assure you,' I said.

'Does he always talk with grand words like that?' Cat asked Flame.

We laughed again, enjoying how good it felt for an instant.

'Thanks,' Cat said.

'Where are you from?' I asked.

'The coast. It must have been about a year ago that they started rounding us up and we had to flee. I guess the same kind of deal goes on in the city. That's what it sounds like. Only it didn't matter about keeping your head down or not. They started grabbing everyone who wasn't part of the Overclass—or whatever it's called—or didn't work for them. Useless people, I mean.'

'Who was going after you?' Flame asked. 'State patrols?'

'Yeah. They started tracking us down with drones, flushing us out of hiding or trapping us in. The patrols would then close in and haul everyone away—so we ran inland. Not many of us made it.' She stopped and wiped tears away. 'Those who did, well, they hid in the woods where the drones couldn't find us and the patrols didn't bother chasing.'

'Only to be captured by these monsters,' Flame said, shaking her head.

'There were five or six of us. We didn't hear them coming. No drones or flashing lights. One morning, after a few days walking, they were there, surrounding us, armed with bows and sticks. We were exhausted and not used to fighting. We had no choice but to surrender. They marched us to the castle where there were already other slaves. The worst part of all was knowing we probably would have starved to death without them, and that they know it too.'

'You've been a slave for a year?'

'About that, but it seems like much longer. It's torture.'

We didn't say a word.

'They won't take me alive again. I swear it!'

'So do we,' Flame replied. 'They'll never lay their filthy hands on you again.'

'Do you know what happens to those who are caught by the patrols?' I asked.

'They take them further south along the coast. That's what everyone says at least. They take them to The Esplanade.'

Flame and I exchanged glances.

'It was a seaside resort before The Breakdown. Luxury hotels. Fast boats and cars. Expensive clothes boutiques. Casinos. All that kind of jazz. Hard to imagine, hey?'

'And now?' I asked.

She frowned and shook her head. 'No one knows. What I mean is, well, I don't know anyone who has been there and made it back.'

'There's a message on the church tower in town, and another one in the chapel in the marshes.'

'The marshes?'

'Further inland. Never mind. The thing is,' Flame said, 'the message in the chapel mentions avoiding The Esplanade, and the one in the chapel tells fugitives to keep heading west. We don't know what to make of them. Heading west led us to the castle. Is it a trap?'

She thought about it for a while. 'It's not her style.'

'The queen?' Flame asked.

Cat smiled, but it soon faded.

'She'd like that. You two would amuse her.' She shrugged. 'At least for a short while. She doesn't call herself a queen, even if she acts like one—a fucking evil one. She makes us call her Lady Armstrong. Can you believe the bitch? She's no lady, and she must be about the only person still using a family name.'

'I suppose she wouldn't have kept it if it was Cockburn or something like that,' Flame said. 'Armstrong commands respect.'

'Is there a Lord Armstrong?' I asked.

Cat stared at me. 'Of course not. Are people getting married again in the city?'

'No one we know,' Flame answered. 'Listen, we should get moving, shouldn't we?'

Cat looked at me and I knew what she was thinking.

'We're safer here for now,' I suggested.

'What?' Flame shook her head. 'Have you gone mad?'

'He's right, Flame,' Cat said. 'The town is the first place they'll go. They would never imagine we'd stay here, close to the castle. They'll be expecting us to run as far away as we can, and not to lose a second going about it.'

'But how long do we stay?'

'All day and all night, depending on how things pan out. It will give us a chance to keep track of their movements. I think the best time to move would be before dawn,' Cat said.

Flame considered the plan for a moment. 'You'll wake us up, Flicker.'

'No problem.'

'If we can sleep at all,' Cat said. 'I'm a bit shaken.'

'You must be,' Flame whispered. 'Had you ever, you know— done that before?'

'No way. I can hardly believe it happened.' She was struggling to stop herself from shaking. 'I now know I have it in me.'

'You sure do,' I said. 'You fucking destroyed him.'

149

Flame's glare made me shut up.

'I felt so calm and in control at the time.'

I remembered the terrifying way she'd grinned at us.

'We start before dawn,' Cat said, changing the subject back. 'We get to the town and barricade a building, getting ready for an eventual attack. The pub, for example.'

'The pub or the school,' Flame said.

'The school's better,' I said. 'The pub's comfortable but not as safe a place to hide.'

Cat's eyes lit up. 'Is that where you were? Did you see us?'

'We saw everything,' Flame admitted, her voice heavy with guilt. 'I felt like being sick. We're so sorry, aren't we?'

I nodded and was about to speak, but Cat jumped in.

'Oh, but you were right! They would have caught you too. You stayed hidden and then came looking for me. That decision was what allowed you to save me. Now, we'll do that again. We'll take care of ourselves first, and when we can, we'll save the others— even if it's one by one.'

A tear of relief trickled down each cheek when she saw we were nodding.

'What was I saying before?' she asked, drying those tears.

'About the message,' I reminded her. 'We don't know who wrote it.'

'Yes—the message. That's right. It's not that bitch's style, and it's definitely not typical state tactics. It doesn't sound like a trap to me. I'd say a fugitive from the city, like you two, found a safe haven near the coast and went back to leave directions for others.'

'That was my first impression,' I said. 'You don't have any idea where such a place might be?'

'You kidding? If I knew there was a safe community where I'd be free and respected, I would have run that way on all three of my previous escape attempts.'

'We have to find this haven,' Flame said.

'We do,' Cat agreed. 'One day.'

'If it still exists,' I said. 'Yeah, we have to try. We have to know.'

'Cat,' Flame spoke softly, signalling a change of subject, 'did he do that often?'

She stared at her feet. 'Every few days. Whenever we were alone. He usually did it at the same spot. That's why I beckoned you after seeing you crouched in the holly. You hid yourselves well, but I know this area like the back of my hand and I'm always on the lookout for a chance to leg it. There was something about the holly bush that looked odd and made me look that little bit closer. You saw my hand?'

'We did,' Flame confirmed.

'We all have keen eyes. We're like hawks,' she said.

'I think we were going to follow regardless,' I volunteered. 'We recognised you.'

'Something along the lines of, "That miserable looking creature, Flame. That's the one."'

'You're going to look fantastic before you know it,' I told her. 'There's no doubt about it.'

Flame shot me a take-it-easy look, but I just smiled back at her. If Cat noticed, she pretended not to. It brought a slight blush to her pale cheeks, which did us all a world of good to see.

As she parted her lips to speak again, sadness returned to her eyes. She made a point of holding back her tears.

'You can't imagine how hard I was hoping you'd follow, but at the same time, I somehow knew you were there without having to take the risk of looking back. I couldn't. He would have noticed. You saw him. It took three of us and his ankles pretty much bound to beat him.'

'Fucking monster!' Flame hissed.

'He is. Oh, that he is. When I was in the cell after my last escape, he came to me every second or third night.'

'He stayed with you?'

'Fuck no! He wouldn't be allowed to. They distil spirits, you see, and get to eat meat. That's why they're not skinny like us. We only get potatoes and cabbage—mushrooms if we're lucky and we've worked extra hard. Anyway, he'd come after a bellyful and a few drinks. Lady Armstrong didn't want to know about those kinds of goings-on. Maybe she didn't know. But I'm sure the other soldiers knew and had a laugh about it between themselves. I'm not the only woman who got raped, but he got

151

me because I was trouble and he's the nastiest fucker.'

'*Was*,' I corrected her.

'Yeah.' She breathed a sigh of relief and wiped her eyes. '*Was*.'

'What if you'd fallen pregnant?' Flame asked.

'I'm not allowed to,' she said. 'Only two slaves have that privilege.' She spat the last word out.

'That's the rule? Why two?'

'They're the two most docile cows, and the Lady has promised them easy domestic duties if they have children.'

'Yes, but it could have happened,' Flame insisted. 'It probably would have eventually.'

'No,' Cat said sharply.

Flame didn't understand.

'You really don't get it, do you?' she asked Flame, and the tears couldn't be held back this time.

'I'm going to leave you two for a while,' I said. 'I won't be far.'

Cat smiled. 'You *are* a good man, aren't you?'

'I try.'

I shot a glance at Flame as I left and the look of disgust on her face told me she now understood.

'I'm so sorry,' she whispered.

I probably shouldn't have gone to the lookout, but I was curious and knew how to stay hidden.

Down at the gatehouse, one group was arriving while another in the courtyard was stacking the last logs from their baskets against the wall. No panic. No alarm. No haste.

As I sat, I touched my nose tenderly, then squeezed it lightly between thumb and forefinger. It was swollen, but not too bad, and it hadn't bled much. I'd been careful running up the hill to make sure I didn't leave drops of blood on the track, but I wasn't so sure about Cat. Her feet, as tough as they were after a year of slavery, had been scratched by the brambles when she got dragged off the road. They weren't bleeding now, but if they had been where we left the track at the top of the ridge, we were in trouble. I had to go back and check while I could still do so safely.

I got up, moved slowly away from the ledge, and backtracked, studying the ground closely. Satisfied there were no blood drops,

I went straight back to the lookout.

As the two groups crossed paths, the guards stopped and spoke. There were some gestures and what looked like shrugging and headshaking. This was it—they'd noticed the disappearance. I was sure that had to be it. They then went on their separate ways.

I started to doze off waiting, and wondered whether Flame and Cat were having a bite to eat in the tent or crying their hearts out. Either way, I had no appetite at all, and even less desire to disturb them.

Whether I'd actually fallen asleep or not, I can't say, but a thunderous sound made me sit up and grab my hammer, which lay beside me. I then drew a deep breath and took hold of myself, realising I was in no immediate danger.

The sound had come from the castle, calling out through the air, and I quickly realised what it was—a mighty blast from a horn. Looking down, I saw a figure on the keep, standing by the low parapet of sandbags along the crumbled flank.

The horn sounded again, its call rising to the clouds that had been threatening rain all day, and descending to the woods and plains below. Rain now wouldn't make for a comfortable night but it would certainly hinder the search for Cat.

Would they suspect she hadn't acted alone? I went through the fight in my head, trying to recall every strike and parry. My hammer had hit his shoulder. Of that I was sure. But if they did happen to remove his clothing to check his body, would it appear obvious a hammer had caused whatever mark there was? It didn't seem likely. He'd been killed with his own truncheon, by Cat. And Flame? That was the problem. She'd cut him. Her knife had kissed his throat. Neither of them, especially not the troublesome Cat, should have been carrying a knife of any description. If the guard had had one, he definitely would have produced it after Cat snatched his truncheon.

That clue alone would tell them she hadn't acted alone, confirming what was obvious—that no matter how desperate and driven she was, she couldn't have disarmed their fiercest warrior and battered him to death with his own weapon.

'Be that as it may,' I told myself. 'They've never seen us before.

They don't know who we are or where we are.'

Footsteps crunched behind me. I glanced over my shoulder and sighed.

'Talking to yourself?' Flame asked, crouching behind me. 'First sign of madness—isn't that what they say?'

'I'm only at my first sign?' I quipped. 'In that case, I'm not doing too bad.'

The horn sounded a third time, drowning her laughter.

'This racket must mean they've found him.' She peered down at the keep. 'Cat's in the tent. Her feet were in a pretty bad way. You saw. I've cleaned them up a little and she's confident it's no problem for the walk back to town.'

'Good. How is she otherwise?'

'She'll be fine, I think. Give her time, and some space.'

'Space?'

'Well, she knows you're not a threat, but a lot of men have hurt her, deeply. It's best not to surprise her or touch her.'

I raised my eyebrows. 'Flame, I wasn't planning on touching her. You know that, right?'

'I know. What I mean is—oh, I don't know really. She's confused.'

'I won't touch her and she won't touch me. Is that what you need to hear?'

Flame smiled. 'Yeah, I think it is.'

'Listen, I'm going to stay here a while. I'll stay out of sight and away from the ledge. I won't learn anything about their tactics hidden away in the tent. You should spend time with Cat. Get to know her if she wants to talk. Hold her if that's what she needs. Make her feel safe.'

She nodded.

'All I ask is that you bring me some water and a little food.'

'No problem.'

'Thanks.'

She crawled away from the lookout before straightening up and walking. I shuffled to the left so that a low branch from a conifer reached out between me and the open air beyond the ledge.

The figure remained on the keep but no longer blew the horn. I figured he was now acting as watchman, searching for signs of unusual activity. He was soon joined by Lady Armstrong, easily recognisable from a distance because she wore a dress, long and light blue. She also wore her hair long, I could tell. It was chestnut or an even darker shade of brown and reached all the way down to her waist. It was quite a sight, and I wondered how it must feel and smell. Did those special slaves, the two women allowed to fall pregnant, brush it and wash it in water scented with rose petals and aromatic herbs? If so, how could she live with herself, having her hair taken care of so extravagantly while the others had plaits designed to facilitate abuse and rape? No wonder Cat hated her so bitterly.

I turned my attention to ground level, where the slaves and their guards had arrived at the gatehouse. The two young men who had been cutting firewood were at the back of the group, swaying from side to side, struggling to carry the bloody body. Everyone entered and one guard walked around, evidently counting heads, making sure only Cat was missing. While he did this, the slaves carrying the body were instructed by another guard to place it in the middle of the courtyard. At the same time, several archers got onto the tray of the lorry and one climbed into the driver's seat.

Cat had gone one step too far. Murder. That's what they'd be calling it. Or maybe unlawful killing. No pulling of the hair or twisting of the arm this time. Cat was to come back with a volley of arrows sticking out of her skinny body. The final punishment. Her body penetrated one last time. It would be the ultimate warning to the others.

On the keep, Lady Armstrong and the guard crossed to the inside battlement in order to see what was happening below. They stood there, hardly moving. It may have been that she was now shouting instructions down to them, but if that were so, she was doing it without any gestures at all. The impression conveyed was rather one of simple observation. She was watching them to make sure they were acting in accordance with protocol, and there was no reason to think they weren't as far as I could tell.

It filled me with a sense of dread. These men who were capable of repugnant cruelty, of dragging a woman barefoot through thorny brambles to bugger her remorselessly, were also so well trained and organised that if you put them up in unarmed combat against a city patrol of similar numbers, I had no doubt they would be able to outmanoeuvre and massacre them.

I didn't hear the motor start up from where I was, but the lorry started forward and passed through the gateway. I counted four archers on the tray. A number of other warriors, both archers and truncheon-bearing, followed on foot. The gate was then closed.

Their thinking was clear—if my guess was right—the lorry would head towards the town, the same as last time, and those on foot would split up and search the woods starting from where the body was found.

It made perfect sense. With limited numbers, there wasn't much else they could do. They could hardly leave the Lady alone to face a potential uprising and they couldn't look everywhere.

It wasn't *everywhere* that interested me, however. It was *here*. We'd figured we were safe. Fugitives either run for their lives or go to ground, after all. When they hide, it's in low places like grottoes and gullies, not on the tops of ridges.

Flame arrived with some water and snacks, and she sat with me a while, snuggled up with her head on my shoulder. Cat was asleep. She'd held her, stroking her hair until she'd nodded off. That's how she always slept, she explained. The women were locked up in one chamber and the men in another. They fell asleep in each other's arms, like sisters, taking turns caressing each other. Nightmares were commonplace, so when one was troubled in their sleep, another would stroke her hand or gently rub her back, whispering that everything was going to be fine— lying to each other.

'Do you think she'll sleep tonight?'

'I don't know, Flicker. Will you?'

'I hope so, but I don't want to wake up late either. I need to be awake before dawn.'

'One of us will be.'

'I suppose so. There's a million times less risk they'll find us at night than during the day. They won't even bother after dark. It's pointless. Regardless of how tired we are, we have to move before dawn. When they find no sign of Cat in our town, they'll come back this way. They'll stop the hunt at dusk. A night's reprieve. But in all likelihood, they won't just give up. If they decide to launch a full day's search of the entire area around the castle tomorrow, we won't stand much of a chance.

'Flicker, don't worry. We move before dawn.' She paused and raised her head. 'Is that the lorry?'

I listened. It was. The humming grew louder as the vehicle reached the top of the ridge. I looked at Flame. We were both holding our breaths.

We relaxed when the low rumble started to fade.

'Flicker,' she whispered, then laughed, letting all the nerves out. 'We're doing this.'

'We are,' I replied, nodding. 'A hell of a day so far.'

'Oh yeah. It's certainly been one hell of a day. I'll never forget how she obliterated his head.'

'Me neither. Did it make you feel good, Flame?'

She looked into my eyes. 'That's the thing, isn't it? It was horrible, and I'm going to have nightmares about it, but that look on her face. That's an old word I'm sure you've read in one of your books—*floodgate*.'

'That's exactly it. She just let it all out.'

'Can you imagine what she went through? Have you thought about that?'

'You don't want me to think about that, Flame.'

She bit her bottom lip. 'No. Don't.'

I glanced back in the direction of the tent.

'I'm going to lie down beside her,' Flame said. 'If you get tired, come and lie next to me. I'll be in the middle.'

I nodded. 'You go and get some rest. Thanks for the food.'

Once Flame had left, I looked down at the keep, but my mind wandered, trying not to think about what she had so bizarrely brought up only to tell me I shouldn't think about it. The Lady was no longer there but her guard remained at his post, now looking out over the sandbag parapet. In the courtyard, the slaves were being put to other work. The two young men were now stacking wood next to the body.

I eventually closed my eyes and drifted off. When I opened them again, I saw no movement down in the castle. Raindrops were landing on the ground and leaves around me, but they were few and far between. That must have been what woke me.

I cleaned up around me, brushing all traces of food into the dirt just in case someone happened to walk by later. A lie-down in the tent was in order.

After relieving my bladder, I crawled into the tent as quietly as possible, not wanting to rouse Flame and Cat, who were curled up and sleeping soundly. There wasn't a lot of room left for me, but I didn't mind. I managed to stretch myself out as flat as a board and fell asleep listening to the raindrops.

It was growing dark when I woke again. I listened, thinking I could hear the lorry, but wasn't sure. If the sound of its motor was what had drawn me from my slumber, it was already too late. The lorry would be on its way down the track and out of earshot.

Flame and Cat were fast asleep, and I wasn't going to disturb them. I slipped out and proceeded carefully to the lookout. The sun was hidden behind thick cloud cover, but a faint glow close to where I knew the horizon to be told me it was almost dusk.

Before I reached the lookout, I noticed an orange, flickering glow coming from the castle and I recognised it immediately as my old friend, there in the midst of our enemy's stronghold.

It's hard to grasp the profound effect it had on me. It's a part of you or it isn't. For me, nothing was more familiar. It belonged to me. I wished I could smell it, hear it crackling, and feel its warmth against my skin. Fire. Not the timid fire we used for cooking in the pub. This was a blaze, rising like a pine tree in the very middle of the courtyard, and everyone was gathered around it—a silhouette or a shimmering apparition depending on where he or she stood.

I knelt at the edge and watched the fire dance.

Torchlight lit up the wire gate, and when a guard opened it, the lorry entered, halting at a safe distance.

'I want to see you burn,' I whispered, smiling as I imagined its tyres melting and bodywork buckling. This rust bucket was a far cry from the luxury automobiles of the city's high-end residential estates, but it was just as vile a symbol of greed and cruelty, and the castle was Paradise Towers with the veneer of civilisation and sophistication ripped away. Out here, forgotten or ignored by the machine trying to hold sway over a world it had failed, they could have been striving to build a better society. Instead, they had chosen brutality.

The archers joined the circle around the fire. I tried to make out Lady Armstrong, but if she was there—and surely she was— my view of her must have been obstructed by the blaze.

As I watched, the last faint glow faded from the sky, leaving these majestic flames and the flickering light they projected onto the gathering and the castle walls alone in a black void. I could only see my hands when I held them in front of me, silhouetted against the blaze. The edge of the lookout was indiscernible but I knew my way back to the tent, and if I took it slowly, paying attention to my footing, I'd be able to make it without getting lost or losing my balance. For the moment, however, I was staying put, allowing the primordial ballet of the funeral pyre to hold me spellbound.

He was in there, now taken by the fire—licked by flaming tongues and then consumed. I felt no guilt. None of us would ever forget his death, least of all Cat. The sight and sound of his skull cracking would haunt us on silent nights and lonely daytime moments when a seemingly unconnected detail would bring the devil back to life. The scratch of a thorn. The clang of the hammer's head on a nail. The simple act of having one's trousers dropped around the ankles. Would this change Flame's desire? Would she secretly distrust me at some level simply because I am, like he was, a man? Would living with Cat damage our relationship beyond repair? There were so many questions— there always had been, and as one was answered, another arose. But guilt? No question at all.

Raindrops landed on my hands, and when I raised my hooded face to the black sky, I felt them on my cheeks, my chin, and my sore nose. The rain was cold but pleasantly so.

Turning back to the twisting and twirling fire, I wondered why he had chosen the path of brutality. Why had he chosen to partake in this travesty? Why had he supported this Lady? Why did they give her their fealty, these warriors? Did she hold them together, preventing the pack from tearing each other apart, using the slave not only for work but as a vent for their bestial yearnings? All this, I longed to fathom.

The rain was pouring down now and the funeral party dispersed. It was only a matter of time before the rain won the battle and vanquished the fire. I didn't want to witness such ignominy, so I cautiously began the journey through the darkness to the tent.

13. Payback

Cat whimpered and moaned in fits and starts throughout the night, and whenever she did and Flame could tell I was awake, perhaps by my breathing, she'd feel for my hand and squeeze it, silently sharing her sadness for our companion.

Despite my fatigue, simply being able to lie there out of harm's way recharged me—that and the prospect of a bath and a decent meal at home before strengthening our defences and revising our contingency plans. The image of the funeral pyre played against my eyelids, the warmest of embraces from the oldest of friends. I wondered whether I ought to tell Cat in the morning, unsure whether the knowledge her tormentor had been burned in a funeral ceremony would provide relief or hurt her further due to the honour inevitably bestowed in the very performance of it.

It was dark when I crawled out of the tent, but I could sense the approaching dawn, and lying awake had become unbearable. The ground was damp but not sodden, which was as I'd expected considering the heavy rain hadn't lasted long. The ford we'd crossed while tracking the lorry was on my mind. We'd have to get to the other side regardless of how powerful the stream may be. There was no room for invention. We had to get back by the shortest route, and the only one we knew.

I scanned the sky to the east. The faintest hint of light was lingering just beyond the horizon. It was the perfect time to get moving.

I popped my head into the tent and gently shook Flame by the leg, hoping she wouldn't wake up with a start and plant her knife in my hand.

'Time to go?' she whispered, her voice calm and clear, and I was sure she'd already been awake.

'The sooner, the better.'

Flame rolled over and must have been searching for Cat's shoulder or arm, avoiding her hair, even though I suspected they'd already undone her plait.

'Cat,' she whispered. 'It's Flame.'

She groaned a little and then took in a sharp breath.

'Cat, you're in the tent with me. It's Flame.'

'Hi, Flame. I'm all right. Thank you. Is, ah, your boyfriend ready?'

'My boyfriend?' Flame laughed.

'Oh, isn't he?'

'Well, Flame, am I?'

'I'm sorry. This is no way to wake up,' Cat said. 'I'm putting too much pressure on you. The thing is—'

'You forgot his name,' Flame interrupted. 'It's Flicker. Don't worry. He's not offended, is he?'

'I'll get over it. What I hope neither of you has forgotten is that we decided to get moving before dawn.'

'We've not,' Flame assured me. 'Are we taking the tent?'

'Best not leave it here if we plan on saving the other slaves. We might want to use the lookout again, and if they stumble across it, that's the end of that.'

'And the end of us,' Cat added.

Flame grabbed our backpacks and I took the tent down and rolled it up.

'We walk in single file. Stay close until there's more daylight so we don't get lost,' I instructed them.

'Loud and clear,' Flame said.

'Got it, Flicker,' Cat said.

We headed to the track and felt our way down onto it before starting down the eastern side of the ridge.

We kept looking over our shoulders as we progressed but never caught sight of the lorry. Once we'd reached the church, we slowed our pace and showed Cat which buildings we'd searched and what we'd found.

'The view from the top of the church tower is breathtaking,' I told her. 'It's from there I spotted the lorry chasing you.'

'It must have been a hell of a sight.' She turned her gaze from

162

the tower to me. 'They'll come back here. There's no doubt about it.' Her voice was melancholic. 'You realise that, don't you?'

'They won't take you, Cat,' Flame said, putting a hand on her shoulder.

'No, they won't even try. This time, they'll loose their arrows on me. I'll have crossed that thin line in their minds from useless dead to unbearable alive.'

'That's the big worry, Flame. We saw them training. Their aim is spot on.'

'Flicker!' Flame snapped.

'He's right,' Cat said. 'There's no point tiptoeing around it. I may as well have a target painted on my back. We have to be ready for them.'

'Let's clean ourselves up first and have a proper feed. Two of us can get on with fortifying the school and gathering weapons while the other keeps watch from the church tower,' Flame suggested. 'Flicker, could you do the first watch?'

'No problem. In fact, I think I should have a quick wash, put on some dry clothes, and grab a bite to take up the tower with me. That way, you two can get yourselves sorted knowing we won't be taken by surprise.'

'I'll show Cat the house and pub. New clothes are in order, and hopefully we can find her a pair of shoes.'

Once I was ready, I returned to the church and climbed the tower. I read the painted message again, and again wondered what had become of its author. Clouds were still floating in from the west, but they were thinner and sparser now, allowing the sun to light up patches of the landscape. It wouldn't last though, judging by the grey veil that obscured the distant coast and horizon. I scoured the countryside all the way up to where I knew the passage to the castle began, even though I couldn't make it out. A black form moving quickly caught my eye but its speed indicated a low-flying bird.

I leaned against the battlements and ate beans from a tin, enjoying every spoonful and hoping beyond hope the Lady would elect to cut her losses and let the wild world exact its

163

revenge upon Cat on her behalf.

It was hours later, after changing position a dozen times and intermittently walking down the tower and back up again to keep myself warm and awake, that I spotted them. I'd been on the verge of jogging to the school to tell Flame I was going stir-crazy and ask her to do a shift, so fed up I'd grown of being perched up there on that stone nest.

A knot formed in my stomach.

But the party hadn't taken the expected route along the track from the ridge. They weren't advancing past the cracked rock and crossing the stream at the ford as we had. They were approaching from further south. It was an area I thought impassable and marshy but they were moving without hesitation, albeit slowly, following a path known to them. They were too far away to count, but I'd have said between five and seven, and there was no lorry.

What was I to make of it? I sat to think, leaning against the battlements. There was no need to rush to tell the women without delay. We had some time. First, I needed to think. They hadn't taken the lorry because this wasn't a matter of hunting down Cat, hot on her heels. Unlike last time, they were too late to know where she was. This was a thorough search, not a high-speed chase. They'd already come here last night and left empty-handed, so there was no immediate reason to expect Cat would be here today. Using the lorry under such circumstances would waste fuel and risk eliminating the element of surprise. They were better off on foot, aiming to catch her unawares. Were they low on fuel? That could also have been a factor behind the decision.

It was only a matter of time before they passed through the town. They'd arrive from the south, pass the church and the square, and continue along the road. Would they venture off it and search buildings further back, like the school? It was unlikely, especially considering the time. They couldn't conduct a full search of every nook and cranny in town and return to the castle by nightfall, even taking the most direct route. Impossible. Pure and simple. And so, if we'd left no indication whatsoever of our presence, we were safe.

I got up and checked their progress. They were now veering

towards the southern approach to town. They would shortly move out of sight as they drew closer and reach the church in about forty-five minutes.

It was time to warn Flame and Cat, make any final preparations, and hide ourselves away in the schoolhouse.

I made my way down from the tower, left the church, and jogged along the road to the school. The grass on the football pitch was soaking wet, but by running around the perimeter, I was able to stay dry. It didn't look like any alterations had been made to building. I opened the door, walked along the corridor past the two classrooms and two offices, and—supposing the women were on the first floor—headed for the stairs.

'Watch your step, honey,' Flame called, mocking me, and Cat encouraged her by laughing.

I looked up and immediately understood the reason behind the warning. Lined along the balustrade, placed so that our hands could push one each directly onto an encroaching group with a high likelihood of hitting each member, were six large terracotta flower pots.

'That's enough to give them a bad headache,' I said.

'A headache,' Flame said, popping up from behind the balustrade, 'and severe burns.'

Cat appeared beside her, sporting a wide grin, but I could tell by their glistening eyes that both of them had been crying shortly before my arrival. 'I'm calling it Flame's grill,' she chirped.

'I like it!' I assured them, continuing up the stairs. 'What's in them?'

'Strips of rags soaked in white spirits.'

'Where did you find that?'

'In a storage room full of painting equipment.'

'Excellent. You'll need wicks and matches.'

'It's all sorted, Flicker,' Flame said. 'No sign of them?'

I gave them a meaningful look, raising my eyebrows.

'Shit!' Cat hissed. 'How many?'

'Between five and seven. They're on foot.'

'Stop, Flicker!' Cat yelled.

I stopped just as I was about to arrive at the top of stairs and looked at my feet to see a tripwire stretched out in line with my ankles. I gave it a kick to test it and found it held its own. Looking around the corner to the right as I stepped over it, I could see the end tied around a screw in the wall.

'I'm impressed. There's no indication of our presence outside or downstairs, so their guard will be down. If they somehow survive the cascade of flaming oil on the stairs, they'll trip at the top and either go tumbling back down or fall flat on their faces and give us a chance to crack their skulls open before they even know what's hit them.'

'That's the idea,' Flame said.

'You've planned an escape route, I take it? The fire could spread throughout the school.'

'The thought never crossed our minds,' Flame said, her voice soaked in sarcasm. She shot a glance at Cat and rolled her eyes, and together they giggled and walked away.

'Follow us,' Flame said.

I was starting to feel outnumbered already and found myself wondering whether living with two women was destined to be more complicated than I'd anticipated. More importantly, I had to ask myself whether it would be more dangerous, lowering our chances of survival. But the answer had to be a resounding no. The way Cat had turned on her captor and beat him to death quelled any doubts. She was a killer, and she was going to do whatever she could to stay alive, keep us alive, and use our freedom to save the others. If she was going to lose the plot, it would have happened long ago. She would have given up after the first escape attempt—after she'd first been brutalised. Cat would always be damaged, but she wasn't going to break.

Flame turned to me as we walked and gave me a wink that said it all. She was thanking me for playing along and letting them have their fun with me. They were bonding. The tears, the jokes, the making fun of me, the setting of deadly traps—it was all part of Cat's healing process. It was a process Flame had launched, perhaps purely instinctively, for our new companion's benefit, and I had a role to play. All I had to do was appear strong and stable without being a threat. In a way, I had to allow myself to be a vent for Cat's frustrations.

'You with us, Flicker?' Flame asked over her shoulder as they entered a classroom.

'All the way,' I told her.

A barricade of desks stacked two high blocked direct access to the room. The top desks were upturned, their legs sticking into the air. Upon passing through the door, you were immediately forced to look left and right to decide which way to turn. The barricade touched the wall to the right, therefore leading you to the left in order to go around the barricade. The makeshift battlements would slow potential attackers unfamiliar with the layout. It was simple but ingenious, and made archers effectively obsolete.

Behind the barricade, a stash of weapons, bedding, food, and utensils for eating were laid out, and a battered aluminium ladder lay along the floor under the window.

'It's long enough to reach the ground,' Flame answered before I could ask.

'Perfect,' I said, walking over to the other window and smiling when I saw it provided a clear view of the football pitch—the most likely approach. 'Let's run through the drill together so we all know exactly what to do if they set foot on school property.'

We rehearsed a combination of attacks based on every imaginable eventuality, all taking into consideration the fact that if they were indeed to enter the school at all, they could only reach the classroom we were in by climbing the stairs as we had. Likewise, they'd have to enter from the playground door, because the main entrance to the school was bolted shut. They couldn't get through there without pummelling the door with a ram. We would only be in real trouble if they somehow worked out where we were and one or more of them stood guard outside the windows, preventing us from safely leaving by means of the ladder. If this were to happen, and a fire spread from the staircase, we would find ourselves trapped.

Going over every eventuality in such a way was most likely bordering on the neurotic, but there wasn't much else to do, stuck there in the schoolhouse, so we figured it was better to be safe than sorry.

The Total station that had been our first glimpse of the town was where we would flee if need be. But if they tracked us there?

What then?

'I'll stay by the rear window until it's too dark to see,' I volunteered.

Flame and Cat started preparing what would be yet another cold meal, talking lowly as they did so.

'Your story is amazing,' Cat said. 'I'm so sorry I came crashing into your lives like I did, just when you were starting to settle down.'

'I told you I don't want to hear nonsense like that, Cat. Don't say you're sorry. Right, Flicker?'

'Right,' I said. 'I don't want to hear it. Not ever. There's no reason to apologise. No one should have to go through what you have. It's absolutely inhuman and we won't rest until every slave is freed.'

'Thank you so much.'

'No need for that either, Cat. We're doing what's right, and that's all there is to it.'

She closed her eyes and smiled. When she opened them again, I could tell she was ready to change the topic. 'Tell me, does everyone have fire names in the city?'

'No,' Flame told her, 'but most people have a nickname. I guess it's part of our "amazing story", as you call it.'

'A firestarter love story,' Cat announced.

'It's hard to explain if you've never been there,' I said, 'but the city is a wasteland—all abandoned office buildings, derelict houses, and ruined infrastructure with pockets of obscene luxury near the centre. You want to start a fire pretty much everywhere you look.'

Cat nodded. 'It makes sense. I think I understand. I want to see the castle burn to the ground.'

We thought about that for a while, and without taking my eyes off the football pitch, I visualised the lorry burning.

'Have you ever started a fire, Cat?' I asked. 'I mean a genuine raging blaze.'

'No. I can't say I have.'

'You have to try it. You really do. It's so exciting.'

'How does it make you feel?'

'Thrilled,' Flame said. 'It's so exciting. You feel like the most

168

powerful person alive. It makes your skin tingle all over.'

'All over?' Cat asked.

I turned to look at them and nodded at Flame when our eyes met. Cat's demeanour changed from genial and curious to distant and dreamy.

'It's the best therapy,' I said, and watched her smile. But when I turned back to the window, it was my expression that altered, and I must have let out a low groan or a gasp.

'What is it?' Cat asked, jumping up and rushing over to my side.

'I think I saw movement.' But no sooner had I spoken than I began to question it. It could have been a trick of the light, or perhaps a breeze had picked up since I'd been inside and what I saw was no more than a twig sent scuttling by.

'What kind of movement?' Flame asked, joining us.

'It might have been nothing. Stay calm.'

'*You* stay calm,' she countered, her voice level.

I drew a deep breath, released it, and nodded. She was right.

'I can't see—' But Cat stopped midsentence.

Flame and I followed her frozen gaze.

'The supermarket car park,' I said. 'I saw a shaved head.'

'We can't both have had the same hallucination,' whispered Cat, barely moving her lips.

We stared at the horizon offered by the stone wall. A moment later, all three of us took a short, sharp breath, and Flame's hand clawed my upper arm, fingertips digging into my triceps. The head had come back into view.

It was a skin dome at first, but then the entire head rose into our field of vision, followed by the neck and shoulders clad in black.

'Is he alone?'

Flame's question was answered immediately as another bust appeared—this one carrying a bow. They were drawing nearer the low wall, slowly, and turning their heads from side to side as though examining the ground at their feet. We could now see almost down to their waists, which indicated they were inches away from the wall.

'Flame?' I asked, my voice deep with concern.

169

'I swear, Flicker, I don't know.'

'That's where we crossed the wall, isn't it?' Cat said.

'I guess. Flicker must have as well.'

'More or less. I think I crossed a little further along towards the northern end.'

'What are they looking for?' Cat wondered.

'They must have noticed something out of place,' I said. 'Scuff marks on the wall. Flakes of brittle stone chipped away. It's hard to believe they could be such good trackers though.'

My instincts told me to turn away from the window and look inside for a clue. Regardless of their admittedly impressive training and skills, the notion that these louts could home in on a flake of stone at the very spot where Flame and Cat had just happened to climb the wall was simply too frightening to accept. Not even drones could do that. There had to be a more logical explanation. They had picked up a trail the nature of which was unknown to us.

I walked over to where Flame and Cat had been sitting and chatting while they'd started to prepare the evening's meal. There were two baskets full of tins, packets, and jars, and some cooking utensils.

'Did you take these chickpeas from the supermarket?'

'Why?'

'Did you, Flame?'

'Yeah, I did. They should still be good to eat and I figured if we need to get out of town, they might come in handy once we have a chance to boil water.'

I held the ripped packet up for her to see. It was almost empty.

'Oh, shit!' Flame said, her eyes pleading.

'That's the trail they've found.'

Cat stared at the packet, her mouth wide open.

'I didn't notice, Flicker,' Flame admitted. 'Fuck, I didn't notice! How stupid of me!'

'It's my fault,' Cat said. 'I'm so sorry. It was me who wanted to take them in the first place.'

'But I was the one carrying them.'

'Forget it,' I said softly. 'It's too late now.' I walked back to the window. 'What's done is done.'

There were now five of them standing by the wall.

Flame and Cat had fallen silent.

'Forget about it, both of you. If it's not the last mistake you ever make, it won't matter. We need to stay focused now if we're going to survive.'

Without warning, the five hunters lifted their heads and looked straight at the window.

14. Stairs and Ladders

We fell back into the room, stunned, and kept our heads low.

'Did they see us?' Cat gasped.

Soft evening sunlight entered the room through the opposite window, so there was a real possibility we'd been visible as faint silhouettes.

'I'll look,' I offered, and crawled up to the window. I raised my head just enough to see out over the sill. 'It's on! They're climbing the wall. They're not looking at the window any more but they're coming this way. There are five of them. Three are archers and two are carrying axes. It's going down!'

'To the stairs,' Flame said, her voice level again. 'We follow the plan, attack when all five are on the stairs, and Flicker is first to take care of whoever reaches the top.'

We moved into position. Once Flame had doused the rags in each pot with more white spirits, we stood there at the balustrade in perfect silence, wicks and matches ready, waiting to hear the door open.

Time dragged its heels. We looked at each other, putting on brave faces and forcing ourselves to maintain our composure. The key was to make sure our nerves didn't prevent us from keeping our hands steady. If we couldn't light the wicks and then quickly light the pots, we wouldn't stand a chance.

They still hadn't arrived. Why? Perhaps they hadn't seen us at the window after all. The trail of spilt chickpeas may have ended, or at least become scattered and undetectable in the long grass.

We waited in silence, and when we heard the door open, we looked at each other to be sure all three of us had heard. We had —it was easy to tell from the fear written on our faces and the way we were all holding our matches and wicks at the ready. Our hands were rock solid. We each held a matchbox in one hand and two matches in the other—the second to avoid fumbling in the box if the first went out before it could be applied to the wick, which was draped over a wrist.

I couldn't hear footsteps, but we were peering carefully over the pots and down onto the staircase.

The first came into view. He was carrying an axe. I was sure the archers would have been smart enough to put their bows aside and arm themselves with a weapon more suited to close combat. They would be at the rear, following the two with axes.

We stepped back from the balustrade and listened. A first pair of footsteps on the stairs. Now a second. But then nothing. Silence.

I turned to Flame beside me and Cat beside her. Four eyes full of panic. Flame flicked her gaze at the pots, and I understood. She was worried they'd looked up and seen them. If they got suspicious and decided to storm up the stairs, we wouldn't have time to react.

We listened but there wasn't a sound. My heart was pounding in my chest and I wasn't sure how much longer I could stay in control. But I had to. We had to hold fire. We needed all five of them on the stairs before we attacked.

I raised my match to my nose and looked at the women, our signal to be ready to strike, then I pointed it at my right eye and towards the staircase.

Flame nodded, and I think a shiver ran through her at the same time.

I moved my head forward and looked down. Two faces about halfway up the stairs were looking straight back at me.

'Now!' I yelled, the element of surprise lost, and they struck their matches.

The two axemen rushed up the stairs, and I knew it was too late for me to light my pot. I pushed it unlit and hit the second one on the shoulder. He roared like a demented beast and dropped to his knees. Before he could get up, Flame and Cat had lit their pots and pushed them over, Flame's aimed at him. I didn't see exactly what happened because I was already reaching to the ground to take my axe, ready to engage the first attacker who'd almost reached the top of the stairs, but I saw the flash of flames against the wall of the stairwell and heard the roar of fire sucking in air. My opponent tripped on the wire but didn't come crashing to the ground, instead stumbling a few steps and using his axe to prop himself up as he found his footing.

He snarled at me and nodded his approval—the traps clearly to his liking. No doubt all the more because he hadn't succumbed to them.

'You should have been one of us!' he jeered.

'Never!' I hissed.

'Your loss!' His axe was above his head now and he brought it arcing down at me. I stepped aside and it struck the floor with an appalling clang. The image of the warrior Cat had slain flashed through my mind. I stepped forward and kicked him square in the stomach, sending him lurching backwards, gasping for breath. I raised my axe high and brought it crashing down, but he shuffled further back along the corridor, forcing me to bring my axe up over my head again. I swung but was bumped by Flame as she moved in beside me, making me miss.

Despite the conflagration on the stairs, one of them had managed to reach the top. I caught sight of him and his gleaming machete out of the corner of my eye. I wasn't counting on the trip wire and wasn't going to take any chances with Flame, so I rushed to the top of the stairs, raising my axe as I did so, shoved Flame aside, and took advantage of my higher position to bring the axe crashing down on his head. It split his skull open and I turned away from the atrocious sight as he fell back into the flames. My body shuddered but I kept a tight grip on the handle and ignored the gore on the head of the axe.

Flame and Cat had launched themselves at the first attacker and were stabbing unsuccessfully at him. He'd lost hold of his axe but they couldn't overpower him. He grabbed Flame's head with a great paw of a hand and slammed it against the wall, laughing as she dropped to the floor. Cat let loose a piercing scream and slashed at his face, slicing a long gash in his left cheek. He slammed his fist on top of her head, bringing her to her knees, and kicked her in the chest, sending her sprawling onto the floor.

Riding a wave of rage, I surged forward and swung at him, landing my axe on his head. It stunned him, giving me enough time to raise it again and strike again, delivering the deathblow. The sickening crack rang out and he collapsed.

I looked at Flame and was relieved to see she was moving. If nothing else, she would be concussed and confused. I needed to get her back to the classroom.

'The flames are dying down!' Cat called from behind me.

I'd just killed two people. It hadn't sunk in yet, and maybe never really would. I was horrified and thrilled at the same time, but above all, I felt so powerful.

'There are three more down there somewhere.'

'Two,' Cat told me.

'Of course, the second attacker had been armed with a machete. The second one with an axe had never made it up the stairs. I peered over the balustrade, too late to hear Cat's warning, and as I glimpsed the two smouldering corpses on the stairs, an arrow whizzed past my ear.

'Two archers down there,' Cat said. 'And the fire's dying down.'

I looked at Flame, squirming on the floor next to the body. She was going to have a splitting headache for quite some time. She was in no state to keep fighting.

'How are you?' I asked Cat, but her expression said it all.

The two archers weren't going to take any risks. They had us cornered, and they'd move in when they were ready. Only, they didn't know about the ladder.

'Do you have more white spirits?'

She nodded, taking a plastic bottle from the ground. 'A little.'

I crawled closer to her. 'Keep the fire going,' I whispered. 'I'll see how Flame is doing. If she's up to it, I'll get her down the ladder. You follow us and we get away from here.'

I was afraid Cat would argue with me, insisting we fight to the end, but that brute had hurt her, and she knew I couldn't look after the two of them and take on two experienced archers at the same time.

She pulled herself to her feet and approached the balustrade with the bottle. I didn't stop to watch the blaze burst into life

175

again. I ran over to Flame and took her head in my hands.

'Flame, can you hear me?'

'Yes, I can—that son of a bitch!'

'He's dead. I cracked his skull. But listen, Flame, we need to go.'

'The ladder?' she asked, her eyes searching mine and locking on them. A good sign.

'Yes, I'll help you.'

She pushed herself to her feet and let me guide her through to the classroom.

'Cat! Where's Cat?'

'She's coming. Don't worry.'

I led her around the school-desk barricade and lowered her to the floor by the window, then I opened the window and slid the ladder down.

'We'll wait for Cat outside,' I told her.

'Our food?'

'No, Flame. Only weapons. We have to travel light.'

I climbed out the window and started down the ladder a couple of rungs. Flame steadied herself in the window frame and I guided her feet onto the ladder, helping her find each rung until we reached the ground.

The sun was setting. Darkness would soon embrace us, making our path more difficult but infinitely less dangerous.

'Where is she?' Flame asked, tense in my arms.

'She'll be here any second now,' I reassured her, looking up at the window. But the longer I stared at it, the more I began to doubt.

'We've abandoned her, Flicker!'

Had we? In the heat of the moment, it had seemed the most sensible course of action, but I now wondered whether I'd instinctively put Cat at risk in order to make sure Flame survived. Had I left her to die?

My gaze stayed fixed on the window. 'What are you doing, Cat?' I whispered to myself.

She'd been alone on the first floor and knew the way around the barricade in the classroom. Nothing had been blocking her path.

'Come on, Cat!' Flame hissed.

'Get out of there!' I spat at the window.

The tension was unbearable. We held each other tight.

My whole body relaxed, and so did Flame's, when we saw Cat's hands on the window sill. She climbed out and made her way lithely down the ladder, jumping off at the end.

'Let's go!' she said, and smiled at Flame as she wrapped one arm around her. 'You're holding up great, girl. You're a hell of a fighter.'

We pushed on and I looked back once to make sure we hadn't been spotted as we fled the school property and followed the escape route to the Total station.

'Our town, Flicker,' Flame said quietly. 'Our town no longer. We can never come back.'

'Yes, we will. We'll come back one day, but not until we've defeated the Lady,' Cat said.

'You know what I'm never doing again?' I asked them.

'What's that?' Cat took the bait.

I held my tongue, letting the suspense build.

'Tell us!' Flame urged.

'I'm never ever eating chickpeas again.'

We laughed, despite it all, and it felt absolutely fantastic.

15. The Promised Land

Night had engulfed us by the time we reached the service station. We took refuge in the backroom. I sat with my back against the wall and Flame stretched out with her head in my lap so I could comfort her. Cat lay beside us.

'What happens tomorrow?' Cat asked. 'They'll be camping here in town tonight and they'll start looking again in the morning.'

'Or they'll get back to the castle as fast as they can and they'll all come back here in the lorry,' I suggested.

'Either way, we have to leave before dawn again,' Cat said.

'We don't really have any choice, and this time we'll have no food with us.'

'Where do we go?'

'We need to find others like us,' I told her. 'We can't go on alone like this.'

'You're suggesting we head for the coast?'

'Yes, but giving the castle a wide berth, heading north first.'

'Without any food or water? We're already tired and hungry. And where will we sleep? It's getting cold at night.'

She was right. Living like fugitives was one thing, but trying to survive like wild animals was another altogether.

'There's a track leading from the woods behind us past the pub. I could make it, even in the dark, and bring warm clothes and enough food and water for a couple of days.'

'I'm not sure I like that very much. What if they're hunkering down in the pub as we speak?'

'Then I'll return empty-handed and we'll be in exactly the same predicament as right now.'

'What do you think, Flame?' Cat asked.

'I think she's asleep. Listen, there's not much choice, Cat.'

'Are you up to it?'

'I am. After what we've just been through, I know I can do more than I ever thought possible. Tired or not, I'm up to it.'

Cat slid across beside me and felt for Flame's head. I helped her gently hold Flame's head while I slid away and she took my place.

'Thanks, Cat. She's going to have a nasty bump but she seems fine otherwise,' I whispered.

'Be careful, Flicker.'

'I'll be careful.'

It was frustrating trying to find my way through the dark. It was a moonless and starless night but I remembered the path I'd cleared and I eventually reached the pub. I saw no sign of the archers and wondered where they'd decided to spend the night. Surely they hadn't camped in the school with the smell of their comrades' roasted flesh in the air. Or had they become so far-removed from humanity that such details hardly bothered them?

I had free reign in the pub but wasted no time gathering as much as I could carry all the same. I was eager to get back to the service station.

Once I'd made it back, I called softly to Cat but got no answer. Good on them, being able to sleep. I didn't think it would come so easily to me, and I couldn't stand the thought of staying in that backroom. I needed air, even if it was cold. I wrapped myself up in warm clothes, went outside, and sat against a tree.

I dipped in and out of sleep, and as soon as the first glow of morning light reached me through the forest behind the service station, I woke Flame and Cat, apologising profusely but insisting we had to move. At first, Flame wasn't happy that I'd gone to the pub, leaving her and Cat alone, but she was soon won over by having water and tinned beans for breakfast and clean clothes for the journey.

We walked the road out of town to the north but left it near the fallen power line, where it led back towards the marshland and the chapel. We hiked through woodlands, keeping the sun at our backs, and after every obstacle, we tried to veer back to a north-westerly direction.

We took regular breaks, but didn't stop for long each time. We wanted to make as much ground as possible, aware that the further we walked, the greater were our chances of finding a building of some description. But shortly before nightfall, we discovered a shallow grotto in the side of a hill and knew we had to stop there. There wouldn't be better pickings.

'It's enough to keep the rain off us,' Flame said, and I had to admire her capacity to look on the bright side. Then again, we were alive, and the day's walk, however strenuous for her, reassured me that her sore head wasn't anything more serious than that. Our lot could have been immeasurably worse.

Cat was also looking good, I thought. We'd both offered Flame a helping hand and a shoulder to lean on throughout the day, but it didn't seem to have taken a toll on her. She hadn't complained once. I suppose it was relative to her. After all the suffering she'd experienced, this was probably a walk in the park.

'There's enough room for the three of us,' she pointed out, taking a fallen branch and sweeping away a layer of dirt and debris to make our nest as comfortable as could be.

'You're holding up amazingly well,' I told her.

She looked at me before speaking—there was something enigmatic in her gaze. 'Thanks, Flicker. I slept well last night, strangely enough. You know what I think it is? I think sometimes it's better to be exhausted. You don't feel so scared, or sore, or hungry when all your mind wants is to sleep.'

'I was out like a light,' Flame added.

'You had it in you to get back on your feet after what happened to you and push yourself to get down the ladder. That was what really counted—getting out of there,' Cat replied.

'Are you sure there's enough room for the three of us?' I asked Cat. 'I can find somewhere else. It's no skin off my nose.'

She shook her head. 'It's going to rain tonight. I can tell. We'll squeeze in together.'

'I just want you to feel safe.'

Cat stopped brushing away the dirt, straightened up, and turned to me. There was hidden fire in those eyes, dark like

180

charred wood, but the slightest breeze could stoke them into burning embers again. She must have seen the dismay I felt on my face and she relaxed, her slender shoulders that belied her strength dropping as she sighed.

'Flicker, I can't stand your pity.' She paused, and as ironic as it was, I couldn't help but feel sorry for her as she struggled to say what I could see coming. All she needed me to do was keep my mouth shut.

Flame was standing there in silence, looking from one of us to the other. There was a faint smile on her lips, which I found unsettling considering the awkwardness of the exchange, but then I understood the reason behind it. It was Flame's seemingly inappropriate smile that told me what was really happening.

This was Cat healing herself.

'I'm listening,' I said, and nothing more.

'I don't have your fine words, but I'll try.' She paused, gathering her thoughts, and I wanted to tell her not to bother with fine words but to merely speak from the heart. But she found them. 'I'm not a delicate little flower. I won't perish with the first frost of winter. I'm stronger than you can ever imagine, Flicker. I'm not a fragile little girl, and if I ever was one, she died long before I was enslaved. You're a good man and I trust you with every fibre of my being.'

She turned to Flame, her head tilted to one side, and on her face was an expression I could only describe as apologetic.

Flame started to cry, and when she turned to me and saw my confusion, that pleased her greatly, making her smile broadly as she began to wipe her tears away.

Cat drew a deep breath and turned back to me, holding my gaze, her eyes now pleading. 'I will never forget what they did to me—what *he* did to me—but it has nothing to do with you. It's not your guilt. I don't blame you for their vileness.'

I couldn't help but wonder whether it was true and I couldn't hold her gaze any longer.

'Look at me,' she said, quietly but sternly. It was an order. 'I don't blame you,' she repeated slowly, 'and I don't fear you.'

'Good,' I said.

'I feel safe with you. Both of you.' She turned to Flame, who couldn't stop crying, and now there were tears welling in Cat's eyes. 'The moment I saw you hiding in the holly bush, I felt it in my bones. I could just tell this was the day it would all be turned on its head—the day I stopped running and started to fight back.'

Her tears were flowing now, streaking her pale cheeks. She wiped them away, sniffed, and put on a stony expression, reminding me of the white marble statue I'd seen one day in the foyer of an abandoned residential tower.

She drew a deep breath and I could see she didn't want to cry while she spoke the next words.

Flame wiped her face and straightened her back, resolute that she would stand with dignity, for Cat's sake.

'I will never forget, but I don't want you to remind me,' she told me. 'I don't want you to be afraid to touch me or lie next to me. We can't travel through the wilderness like that. We can't live like that.'

I nodded, and I wanted to thank her, but it wasn't what she needed.

'What goes on in our heads is hard to control. We all know that. I can't tell you what to think or feel, Flicker, but I want to ask you a favour. I beg you. When you look at me, try not to think about that.' She broke eye contact with me, looked at Flame to make sure she wasn't crying, and forced herself to look me in the eye again.

'I promise,' I told her.

She sighed, then started laughing, and Flame threw her arms around her, laughing with her, knowing that if they stopped, they'd start crying again.

'Hug her, you idiot!' Flame yelled at me, and their laughter grew as I wrapped my arms around both of them.

'Are we feeling safe enough to light a fire tonight?' I asked, eager to cut the tension I still felt, even though they were now as light and serene as butterflies.

'We should,' Flame said. 'A hot meal is in order. After all, we're celebrating tonight.'

'We are, aren't we?' Cat said. 'We do have a lot to celebrate.'

They were right, of course. I reached into my backpack and

produced two bottles.

'Flicker!' Cat gasped.

I shrugged. 'Well, you can't have a proper party without whisky and wine.'

They laughed. 'I guess not,' Flame said. 'I'll have wine.'

'Same for me,' Cat said.

'Good, because I only found two cups at the pub. We left the others in the classroom. I'll have to drink from the whisky bottle.'

'Go easy,' Flame warned me. 'One of us with a sore head is plenty.'

'How is it? Feeling any better?' Cat asked. 'The bump hasn't gone down yet.'

'No, it hasn't.' Flame touched her head gingerly. 'But I'm not feeling too bad. A decent meal will help.'

I poured their wine, took a swig of whisky, and set about gathering whatever dry wood I could find. Once there was enough for our immediate needs, I enjoyed another sip and took pleasure in starting the fire.

'We covered a lot of ground today,' I said, once the fire was going.

'How far do you think we are?' Flame asked.

'From where?'

'From the town. From the castle. From the coast.'

'Hard to say. We're further from the town than the castle is— that's for sure—and we're a long way from the castle in terms of walking distance because the landscape between us and it is hilly.'

'The walk from the castle to the coast takes almost a full day, but it's probably even further from here because there's a peninsula on the north coast,' Cat explained.

'What if we're wrong?' Flame asked.

'No promised land, you mean?'

'Yeah, Flicker. What if there really is no one else between here and the coast? What if the castle is all there is?'

'There has to be others,' Cat said. 'Away from the city, and the castle, and The Esplanade. Someone wrote the message you saw.'

'We'll reach the coast tomorrow?' Flame asked.

'We might,' Cat said. 'If we leave early. The land is heavily wooded but much flatter, as far as I know.'

'Let's eat,' Flame said. 'Flicker, more wine.'

We ate well, and slept well, huddled together as the fire died down.

I woke first, and the damp cold drove me out of the shallow grotto. I jogged on the spot and did stretches to warm my body. It would be a dark day but it wasn't raining at the moment, even though it had during the night and probably would again.

Once I'd got my blood flowing, I went over to Flame and gently shook her.

She groaned as she opened her eyes. 'Give me a minute, will you? Just one minute.'

'Of course.'

She didn't need reminding. A minute later, she crawled out of the grotto and walked over to me.

'I'm so proud of you,' she said.

'You are?'

'You bet, Flicker,' she said, looking back at the grotto. 'She needs your support, and you're giving her what she needs.'

'But last night?'

'Exactly. What she said last night was as much for her benefit as for yours. You did what she needed.'

'I didn't do anything.'

'For all your books and big words, you're still just a dumb man, aren't you? You were there, and you listened. That means the world to her. That's what she needed. She also needs to sleep a little longer. Five or ten minutes. That's enough. Can you do that for her?'

'We can wait ten minutes.'

'Good,' Flame said, a mischievous gleam in her green eyes. She took me by the hand and led me away into the trees.

When we returned, about ten minutes later, Cat was awake but hadn't yet emerged from the grotto. She raised her head but pretended not to have noticed our brief excursion.

'Morning,' she chirped. 'I'm ready.'

We gathered our belongings and set off, all three of us feeling lighter and more energetic than the previous morning.

184

It was tough terrain and we spent the first couple of hours searching for a way around rocky outcrops, fallen trees, and impassable thickets. Little by little, however, the going got easier as the hills flattened out.

We walked all day, only stopping to drink some water. The woods gave way to fields of tall grass. The sky was heavily clouded and a fine drizzle fell incessantly, but we could see where the sun was in hiding, and we let it guide us.

No sign of a town anywhere. Not even ruins. We could glimpse the towers that had once stretched power lines between them here and there, and we passed the skeletal remains of a tractor at one stage. But that was all. No revived village. No rebel encampment.

The wind was picking up, pushing us as if to hold us back—or to tell us we were going the wrong way—and my determination began to waver. My will to believe faltered.

Nevertheless, we pushed on, because there was no alternative. There was no turning back.

The wind's determination didn't waver, only intensifying with each step we took, and it was oddly invigorating with its energy and crispness. It was somehow foreign, telling of a world we'd never set foot in before. It was unlike any wind I'd even known before. I couldn't quite put my finger on it.

So when Flame pointed ahead and excitedly told us to look, I think I knew what it was before my eyes confirmed it.

'The sea!' I gasped, gazing at where the land ended beyond a row of enormous pines that waved in the wind, welcoming us. It was as simple as that—the land ended and the sea began.

16. On a Beach

We ran in a frenzy past the swaying pines, stumbling in the soft sand, falling to our hands and knees, but getting up again and breaking into a run each time. Even Cat, who knew the coast well, ran with us, soaking up the excitement. She'd been separated from the sea for over a year. It must have been like finding a long-lost friend.

As the sand became more solid, set heavy with water, we ran faster, leaving a trail of deep footprints behind us.

'Shoes!' Cat yelled, roaring with laughter. 'Don't get your shoes wet!'

We stopped, dropped our backpacks, fumbled to get our shoes off, and pulled the legs of our trousers up to our knees. Then we sprinted again, rushing towards the foam-crested waves crashing onto the beach. Once we were in the water, almost up to our knees, Flame squealed.

'Cold, isn't it?' Cat yelled from behind us. She'd taken her shoes off and was walking slowly into the water.

'Freezing!' Flame shouted, then burst out laughing. She jumped up and down a few times before running back onto the sand. 'It's exhilarating!'

'Can you smell it, Flame?' I asked. 'Can you smell the salt in the air? That's what makes it so strange. Isn't it just the best air you've ever breathed?'

In fact, you hardly needed to breathe at all. The wind seemed to make its own way into your lungs, filling you with energy and hope, and making you think you were soaring like an eagle.

'I've missed her so much,' Cat said. 'The sea. It's been so long. But she doesn't change one little bit. She's eternal.'

Flame walked along the beach, studying her feet and watching

186

how the sand squeezed up around them and wormed its way between her toes.

'It's like a massage,' she said. 'It oozes the same as mud but it feels pleasant.'

Cat laughed. 'Amazing, isn't it? I can't believe how excited you both are—and it's contagious. I can't remember the last time I just let it all out like this.'

'This is a dream, Cat,' I said, watching Flame as she trotted away along the sand. 'In the city, we hear stories about the sea, but no one has been here. Some people say it's a myth and tell you you're stupid if you believe it exists.'

Cat was lost for words.

'There are shells everywhere!' Flame called back. 'They're just lying here on the sand.'

'That's what they do,' Cat replied with a laugh.

'Gather some for me, Flicker. I want them as souvenirs. Choose five for me.'

I started wandering slowly after her, marvelling at those works of art, fashioned by sea and offered to the land—a courting ritual that had been performed every day since the dawn of time. There was seaweed and jellyfish washed up on the beach as well. I'd seen pictures of them, of course, but I hadn't realised they had such a strong and peculiar smell. It was neither appealing nor repulsive. It belonged to a world all of its own. It was part of the smell of the sea.

The clouds had started to disperse, whisked away by the growing wind, not so much being swept towards the east as appearing to simply dissipate into the heavens. The cold and distant light of the waning sun was bidding us farewell.

'You've found five shells?' Cat asked.

I showed her. Two brilliant white ones like broad fans. One was conical and red, and slightly twisted like a flame. The other two were dark and glossy, shaped like tiny ears.

'We should go now. It will be dark soon. We can come back tomorrow,' Cat said.

She was right. We had to find shelter for the night. I called to Flame and waved for her to come back to us. She'd wandered a long way away now. She turned, and as she did so, a movement caught my eye. Not far from her, behind the dunes.

'Run!' I shouted.

She looked all around, confused, and saw what I saw.

'Hurry!' Cat yelled.

Flame sprinted towards me and the figure that had been watching sprang forth and ran after her. All along the dune, others emerged and closed in on us.

'Who are they?' I asked, but Cat didn't answer. She produced her knife and assumed a crouching stance, ready to fight. I ran back to where I'd left my axe, along with my backpack and shoes.

I was about to run over to Flame, but she had almost reached us and the man chasing her was jogging now. He looked relieved.

'Stop!' he called, but his words weren't directed at us.

The others obeyed immediately, slowing to a walk and stopping several feet from us. There were ten of them.

'Who are you?' a woman asked, but our tongues were tied, and how could we even begin to answer such a question.

They could see our fear change to pure awe.

These people were neither state patrols nor slave drivers. The three women and seven men were unlike anyone we'd ever seen. Their clothes and equipment were foreign to us, as though they belonged to a different culture, but there were no cultures these days. We were all in the same boat. You were either working for the broken system or doing whatever you could to exist in the shadows. It was more or less a rule, and if there was an exception to it, the only contender we'd come across was the Lady. No— these people were like us. That much was immediately clear. The difference was that they were getting it right. Their clothes were clean but original—the fruit of skilled handiwork, not tracksuits stolen from a shipping container or an abandoned warehouse. And they were armed with real weapons. Several had pole-arms over eight feet long with hooked ends or serrated edges. The length of the shafts and curious shapes of the heads made my thoughts turn immediately to drones. These were most definitely weapons designed to ensnare and destroy low-flying drones. Two women, including the one who had addressed us, carried crossbows made of polished oak. The mechanism looked simple enough, and I didn't doubt the effectiveness.

'Who are you?' she asked again, her crossbow resting on her left shoulder, the colour of the oak matching that of her long fawn brown hair. 'Where are you from?'

'We're lost. We're from the city,' I answered, indicating myself and Flame, 'and she's from the coast to the south.'

'From the coast?' she asked Cat for confirmation.

Cat nodded.

'That's impossible. You're lying!' one of the men said, stepping closer. He had short sandy hair pushed up into a crest, and like several of them, he wore thick welding goggles with round lenses. His jacket and gloves were made of animal skins sewn deftly together—black hair with white specks—and he gripped a pole-arm with a central spike and three hooks curving downwards. The weapon reminded me of sketches of exotic flowers.

'It was possible until about a year ago,' Cat replied calmly, staring him down and I suspect wanting him to understand that she'd met worse.

'You're saying you're from The Esplanade?' the woman asked.

'Not that far south. There was at least one town between here and there. That's where I'm from originally, but I fled when the patrols moved in. We all did. The patrols switched from a strategy of suppression to one of removal. I suppose it was a kind of purge. In any case, we weren't hanging around to find out. We ran for our lives, my friends and I, only to get caught in Lady Armstrong's net.'

'Lady Armstrong?' the woman asked, unsure whether to laugh at the absurd title.

'It's no joke,' Cat said darkly, looking around at her audience. 'She's the lady of the castle where the hills rise in the east. She made slaves of us all.'

'You were a slave?' she asked, astonished.

They all murmured.

'Yes, and these two rescued me.'

She raised her eyebrows.

Another man spoke, disbelief written on his face. 'You're telling us there's another community, unknown to the authorities, and that they use slavery.'

189

'I don't believe them,' someone said.

'Why would we lie?' Flame asked.

'How many are in this castle?' the man with the sandy crest asked.

'Seventeen slaves. Well, sixteen now that I've escaped. They're kept under guard by—how many warriors now?'

'We've killed four,' I reminded her.

'You've killed four of these warriors?' the woman asked.

'Cat beat one to death, Flame set one on fire, and I killed two with this axe.'

The group raised a cheer, and the woman laughed and shook her head in amazement.

'That leaves how many in the service of this so-called lady?' she asked.

'Nine or ten, I think,' Cat said.

'Is that all?' a man asked, scoffing.

'There are only ten of you,' I pointed out.

'Only ten of us!' the woman laughed, and the others joined her. 'What do we think?'

'I like them!' someone shouted.

'We can't leave them to die.'

'We need people like them. Fighters.'

'My name is Arden, by the way. What were your names again?'

I told her.

'Well, we welcome you, Flicker, Flame, and Cat. We'll spare all the introductions for later,' she told us. 'We can't stay on the beach.'

'It's getting dark,' I agreed.

'It is, but that's not the big problem. Drones are used to keep an eye on the coast. We're exposed here.'

'Why did you come here then, to the beach?' Flame asked.

'We were hunting when we saw you. It was pretty funny, I have to say. You had no idea.'

'Hunting?'

'Yes.'

'You eat meat?'

They burst out laughing.

'Come on. Let's go. You can tell us all about your adventures later. You have no idea how lucky you are we spotted you before a drone did! Once one of those is on your tail, there's no shaking it off.'

'We've been through that,' I told her. 'We met while hiding from drones. We'll tell you all about it. Where do you live?'

'Where do we live? In the woods, of course. We live where no drone can find us—in Newton.'

Before I could say another word, someone shouted, 'Drone!'

To the south, a black speck could just be made out against the wispy clouds.

'See what I mean?' Arden told us. 'Speak of the devil.'

They started jogging back to the dunes. We grabbed our belongings and followed.

'The promised land?' Flame asked as we ran.

'We'll soon find out,' I said.

17. Newton

The walk to Newton couldn't have taken us much more than half an hour, moving at a leisurely pace through the woods. Our rescuers—for we couldn't consider them anything else—chatted as they walked, talking to each other and introducing themselves to us. I caught one or two eyeing us cautiously, perhaps wondering if we really were who we said, then seeming to relax when a friend reassured them. I could understand their wariness, I suppose, but who else could we be, other than Flame, Cat, and Flicker? Who were we anyway? We were and always had been just like them—nobodies. The biggest difference being the fact that they had got themselves organised. While the rest of us were city rats or feudal beasts of burden, they were wolves.

To be honest, it felt a little surreal, walking through the forest with this—what were they, a brotherhood? Yes. A band of brothers. I'd read that term in a very old book long ago, but it had stayed with me, as though waiting for the right situation to be used. And so this band of brothers and sisters advanced through the trees and undergrowth as the wan shadows cast by the setting sun grew longer, and what struck me most was the notion that this was *their* land. After running off the beach and under cover, they had immediately and simultaneously relaxed, as though they knew instinctively where they were in danger and where they were safe. Here, we were in their domain, and no one was to be feared.

'Do you feel it, Flame?' I asked once there was a pause in the conversation she was having with Cat and Arden.

'The weightlessness?' she replied.

'That's it, Flame. That's the very word. They're light. There's no crushing weight, always looking to the sky or behind your back. I don't think I've ever felt so safe. It's almost—I don't know how to put it.'

Cat joined the conversation. 'It's almost suspicious.'

I shrugged.

'I can understand that, Flicker,' Arden said. 'But you have to realise that we're the ones taking a risk on you, just as we have with every one of us at one point or another.'

'You were all like us?' Cat asked. 'Well, like Flicker and Flame, I mean. My story's quite different.'

'We all come from elsewhere, but no one here comes from as far as the city. There used to be towns all along the peninsula, but they grew rebellious after The Breakdown and were cleared out, one after the other, over the years.'

'Cleared out?' I asked, thinking about our town—the one we had thought of just a few days ago as our home but could now only dream of returning to if Lady Armstrong's rule came to an end.

'Cleared out,' she repeated, frowning. 'The patrols moved in and carted everyone away. The names of the towns were taken down from council buildings and businesses. Street signs and statues were removed. Any trace of history or identity disappeared, leaving faceless ghost towns.'

I looked at Flame and she replied with a faint, melancholy smile. One question answered—one of so very many.

'You don't know about one town, south-west of here, with a message written on the church tower?'

Arden raised her eyebrows. 'I don't think so. Is it near this castle where slaves are kept?' There was venom in her voice.

'Not far. A little further inland. About half a day's walk from the castle.'

'We can ask everyone later, but if anyone had discovered a message on a church tower, we'd all know about it. What kind of message was it?'

I told her what it said, and told her about the one in the chapel.

'It certainly sounds like a reference to Newton. There's nowhere else safe around here.' She frowned. 'I'm glad it led you to us, but I can't say I like it. It's a risk, leaving an open trace like that.'

She was lost in thought for a minute, then called to one of the others. 'Oak!'

A broad-shouldered man whose grizzled beard was worn on a leathery face joined us.

'How are our newcomers faring?' he asked, raising his left hand, palm upturned, by way of greeting. In his right hand, he held a pole-arm. Its curved axe was fashioned into a hook at the back, and I could imagine this powerful man catching a drone with the hook and casting it adroitly to the ground before raising his weapon with a twist to bring the cutting edge around, ready to come crashing down to chop the rotors.

'We're faring well,' Flame replied. 'We're very grateful.'

'There's no call for any of that,' he said. 'We look out for each other in Newton. We work together. Not to say we don't have our differences now and then.'

'Who's your leader?' Cat asked.

They shook their heads.

'We work together, Cat,' Arden said. 'We make decisions together, and on the rare occasion tensions rise, the big boys like our Oak here have a way of calming everyone down.'

He laughed.

'Oak was one of the founder's of Newton. He's from a village north of here.'

A shadow passed over his face.

'Do you remember there was a girl from the city once?'

The shadow gone, a smile touched his lips for the briefest of instants.

'I remember, Arden. Her name was Echo. What about her?'

'She was always talking about helping fugitives from the city to find us. Did she ever talk about messages?'

'Messages? What do you mean?'

'Our new friends saw messages on walls telling people to keep heading west, to find safety and avoid The Esplanade.'

'That could have been her. She wanted friends from the city to find their way to us. She had a sister back there. Once or twice, she disappeared for a couple of days at a time without telling us.'

He paused, lost in the past.

'If she wrote these messages,' he went on, his voice full of

194

sadness, 'well, it's a little ironic, I guess.'

We didn't dare ask him more. His grief was palpable and Echo's fate was clear enough. Whether she was the one who had written the messages, we'd probably never know. It didn't really matter anyway. If it wasn't her, it was another lost soul.

'One more question for the moment,' Flame asked.

'You can ask as many as you like,' Arden told her. 'Mind you, we'll expect the same from you once we're in town and all settled. That will be in a few seconds.'

We looked ahead through the gloom and could make out a high fence made of wicker or thin branches woven tightly together.

'What happens at The Esplanade?'

Oak and Arden laughed, as did a couple of others who I realised had been listening, but it was empty and uncomfortable laughter.

'That's the question everyone wants answered,' Oak said.

A gate was opened ahead of us and we entered Newton. The wicker fence was curved and seemed to entirely surround the town. More than a dozen wooden buildings stood along the fence and one large square hall was in the centre of the town. They all had flat roofs upon which vines and creepers grew, hanging over the edges.

'Camouflage,' I said.

'Impressed?' Oak asked me.

'Most definitely.'

'Not foolproof but it must be effective from high above.'

'You're still here,' I said. 'That means it works.'

'Exactly.'

The double doors to the hall opened and lamplight flooded out onto the ground, creating a path through the growing dark.

'How was your hunt?' a voice called from the doorway.

'We got a little distracted,' someone said. 'No quarry, but we tracked down a trio of fugitives.'

A wave of sound rose from inside the hall—voices chatting.

'How was yours?'

'One kill. Enough to welcome the newcomers. Are they safe?'

'We think so,' Arden answered, giving us a wink, as we

followed the others into the hall.

The air was warm inside and chased the chill of the sea from our bodies. Lanterns were burning in the four corners and a fire was roaring in the middle under a metal cone which I could tell had been cut and fashioned into shape from a shipping container. This crude chimney rose to the ceiling and stood on four stone pillars about six-feet high. Where the fire blazed, on blackened ground between the pillars, an animal and a pot hung from chains attached to a metal frame. The strange smell of roasting flesh filled the air. But what made our jaws drop more than any of that were the people all around, staring at us from where they sat on mats and skins. There were twenty or so of them, including one baby and a dark-haired girl of no more than ten. Newton was home to at least thirty souls. Plus three.

'Everyone,' Arden announced, 'meet Flicker, Flame, and Cat.'

A chorus of hellos and welcomes greeted us.

'We won't burden them with trying to remember everyone's name,' the man with the sandy crest told the gathering. 'But when you speak to them, please introduce yourself.' He turned to us, removing his goggles, and looked at each of us in turn portentously. 'I am named Dray.'

'Come and sit by the fire,' one woman said convivially. She was sitting on the skin of an animal. The woman next to her beckoned. 'I'm Tara and this is Heather.'

We joined them and I couldn't help but notice that the one called Tara kept glancing at Cat with a look of keen interest.

'What did you catch?' I asked, looking at the animal on the fire.

'Some kind of dog,' Heather told us.

'You eat dogs?' Flame asked, unable to conceal her surprise.

The women shrugged. 'Don't you?'

'We've never eaten meat,' Cat replied.

The gathering gasped.

'Meat is a delicacy for us. Try it if you like. It's up to you,' said Oak, who was now sitting with the girl and a beautiful woman with long dark hair and a dress the colour the setting sun had been that first night camped overlooking the castle. Adorning her ample bosom was a necklace of white seashells, gleaming under the light of the fire. I tried not to stare, but when I turned to Cat and Flame, I saw they were making no attempt whatsoever to conceal their wonder. I don't think it was so much her beauty itself that dazzled us, but rather the simplicity and grace that accompanied it. There was an otherworldly aspect—a whisper of a forgotten age.

'Dahlia,' she said, her voice a soothing counterbalance to Oak's, 'and this is our daughter, Blossom. I'm the seamstress.'

She was looking at our tracksuits and I could feel her measuring and dressing us with her eyes.

'Blossom and I don't eat dog,' she continued. 'It's up to you to do as you please. We're free here.'

'There's a vegetable stew in the pot. It's plenty filling,' Oak added.

'Are you ready to tell us your story?' Arden asked, handing us metal goblets. 'You drink beer?' she asked with a smile.

We thanked her and looked at each other, wondering where to start.

'Start with your story,' Cat told me.

And so I began, describing life in the city, telling them about how Flame had helped me hide from the drones. As I spoke, questions were asked, and Dray prompted those who forgot to give their names.

'It's the main act of rebellion in the city, starting fires?' asked Lark, a teenager with a thick mop of brown hair and the promise of a moustache on his lip. I wasn't worried about answering his question truthfully, because in his eyes was the glint of keen interest, not a look of concern. They were all listening intently.

'It's our way,' I said, looking at Flame. 'I think, somehow, we knew each other even before we met. It's as though the fires we lit were our signatures.'

I wasn't sure they'd understand, but a lot of heads were nodding, and I noticed Dahlia and Arden gave Flame a kind of dreamy look as though what I'd just said was wildly romantic. The smile on Flame's face told me she felt that way too. Maybe our story was romantic, after all. We'd been so preoccupied with surviving that we hadn't noticed—at least, I hadn't.

'Everyone handles living in the city differently,' Flame joined in. 'Vandalism is common. When you're surrounded by ruins all

197

day and all night, you can't help but feel furious when you come across a luxury car. It looks so out-of-place and provocative. Flicker and I used fire to release our rage.'

'It's the most appropriate weapon,' I said. 'It destroys, but it's so beautiful and full of energy while doing so. I think that's what it is that pulls us in.'

'It puts you in a trance,' Flame added. 'Out here, where the woods have reclaimed the land, it's probably not easy to understand. The environment, although tough, is pleasant here. I'm not sure I'm making sense. What I mean is that the urge to watch the world burn follows your every step in the city. It's an urge that hasn't followed us here.'

I went on to tell them about the ring road, the old asylum, the mill, and the chapel. I took note of their expressions when I mentioned the message. Blank faces and shrugs. Flame told them about the town, and she turned to Cat when she reached that fateful night.

'I can take over,' Cat assured us. 'They need to know.'

But before Cat could begin, Tara, despite being seated next to us, spoke loudly so that the assembly could hear.

'They have a vehicle?'

We confirmed.

'How is it possible?' Dray asked, but out of astonishment this time, not accusation.

'Where did they find fuel?' Oak asked.

Muttering and speculation filled the air.

'Listen, everyone,' Arden called out. 'We'll have time to talk about that later. There are decisions to be put to the vote. Let Cat tell the story of the hardship she's endured.'

Cat began with the clearing out of the coast—a tale which echoed their own experiences—and recounted the story as she had to us. She told them of the abuse she'd been subjected to, without going into details.

As Cat spoke, raised eyebrows and hushed comments gave way to angry frowns and loud protestations. Tara and Heather had placed one hand each on Cat's shoulders, and although I don't think Cat felt comfortable about it, she made no move to brush them off. Meanwhile, Arden and a couple of others who'd been at the beach were walking around with jugs of beer, refilling our goblets.

'You are three very remarkable people,' Dahlia said once Cat's voice had faded away, giving the impression her tale had come to an end.

We thanked her, unsure how to appropriately respond to such a compliment.

'This,' Flame said, spreading her hands to indicate the hall and the thirty-odd inhabitants of Newton gathered within, 'is remarkable to us. This is the first time we've been in a truly self-sufficient community.'

Arden poured us beer. 'That means you're staying?'

'If you'll have us,' Flame replied.

Her reply was met with a heart-warming cheer from the assembly.

'Welcome to Newton,' Dray said. 'You are very welcome indeed. Unfortunately, your news is not. This Lady in her castle can't go on enslaving our brothers and sisters. If we're to bring the tyrant down one day, we'll need every willing fighter we can find.'

'You hold that hope?' I asked.

'It's the only one worth fighting for, Flicker, my friend.'

There was malice in his eyes and in his voice—malice I'd earlier taken to be directed at us—these three newcomers who'd walked onto their land. Now, I saw it for what it was. He despised the regime and its insidious drones, like the rest of us did, but he'd been afraid we weren't who we'd claimed to be. He wanted to believe we could play a role in the battles to come.

'The way I see it,' he continued, 'is that if we can't overthrow this lady in the ruins, we'll never be able to destroy The Esplanade.'

And like that, his ambitious plan was announced to us—not just his either, because not a single voice contradicted him. It was their shared goal—the destruction of The Esplanade, whatever it was, and whatever that entailed.

I looked at Flame, a mix of apprehension and anticipation on her face. Cat, for her part, was smiling—a dark smile, no doubt with the delicious taste of revenge on her tongue, but her eyes spoke of hope. Staring at the fire, I was sure she was seeing her friends.

'We have much to discuss,' Oak said loudly, glancing about the hall. 'But not on empty stomachs. Carver, give me a hand with the dog.'

Disgusting as the idea of eating a dog was, once Oak and Carver had taken it off the fire and placed it on a long wooden table, I decided I would try it.

'I'm going to taste it, Flame,' I told her quietly, although Cat, Tara, and Heather could hear me all the same.

She gave me a vacant stare. 'You want me to as well?'

'Suit yourself. Honestly. I just want to show them I'm willing to adapt to their lifestyle and traditions. If we're going to wage war together, we have to form a close bond, and eating what they eat is part of that. One of us should do it, and I'm prepared to be that one.'

'What do you think?' Flame asked Cat.

'I'm curious,' she said. 'Lady Armstrong and her men eat meat. Whatever they can hunt, they cook it and feast on it, whether dog, boar, rabbit, or duck. The slaves never had any. It might sound stupid, but partaking in this meal is like slapping that bitch's face.'

'That doesn't sound stupid at all,' Flame replied. 'You'd be doing what she forbade.'

'You heard what Dahlia said. You do as you like,' I said.

Heather leaned forward and spoke in Flame's ear. From what I gather, she told Flame she'd eat her portion if she didn't like it.

'I'll try it,' Flame decided.

'Carver!' Heather called out, and when he looked up from the dog, she held up three fingers and then held her thumb and forefinger ever so slightly apart.

He nodded and the others laughed.

'You'll see,' someone called out. 'It's delicious!'

The newcomers were served first, their portions small, as requested, and everyone watched them unashamedly while Carver continued cutting thin slices and several others filled and distributed bowls of meat and stew.

I tasted the meat first, holding the thin slice with my fingers.

My expression must have said it all, for a cheer filled the air, and several of the younger men barked excitedly. I gave Flame and Cat a nod of approval and looked around the hall, soaking up the swell of appreciation. Best of all, Dray caught my eye and gave me a thumbs-up.

'It really is delicious,' Cat announced. 'Unlike any food I've ever eaten, but really good.' She turned to Flame, who hadn't yet tasted it.

Flame nibbled the end of her slice. At first, her brow was creased and her lips were pressed firmly together, but she soon relaxed, and after swallowing called out, 'Delicious!'

'Serve them a decent portion, Carver!' Oak shouted, getting to his feet. He'd already finished his serving of dog and had drained his bowl of stew. 'Now, it's time to talk business.'

He was met with murmured agreement.

'It's been a long time since we had to fight hand-to-hand, hasn't it?'

'Not since those three patrolmen tried to arrest us on the beach,' Dray answered. 'You remember, Oak? You, me, and Arden.'

'I'll never forget. It must have been over a year ago.' He turned to Cat. 'It makes me wonder whether it was around the same time your town was cleared out. These three were in a speedboat. They might have followed the coast north, searching for your lot.'

'What happened?' I asked.

'I'm glad you asked,' Oak replied dramatically, and he grinned at his comrades, who were all giving their undivided attention. Shouts of encouragement filled the hall. 'Three against three it was,' he began. 'They were armed with pistols, but they were intent on taking us alive, and that, you see, was their first mistake. They got too close.'

'I hid my crossbow when I saw the boat heading straight towards us,' Arden said. 'It was too late to run because they'd spotted us and it was the beach where we found you. Too close to Newton. That's the main reason we avoid that beach now. Anyway, we had no choice. They couldn't live.'

Everyone was listening intently, even though they must have

heard the story a thousand times.

'So, like I was saying, I hid my crossbow under fishing nets, and the boys buried their pole-arms in the sand. If they'd had binoculars fixed on us, it would have been a completely different story.'

'I'll never forget the way Arden moved,' Oak said, looking at her with admiration. I glanced at Dahlia but detected no hint of jealousy on her face. 'She's always been one of our best hunters, but this wasn't the same as tracking down a wild animal. A boar can charge at you, but it can't analyse the subtleties of your facial expressions or body language. Arden's every movement was like that of a trained soldier.'

'It happened so quickly,' she said. 'I don't remember thinking about what I was doing. It was instinctive.'

'You have the instincts of a natural-born killer, Arden,' Dray announced.

Arden turned to him, frowning faintly.

'That's nothing to be ashamed of,' he explained. 'Not in these times.'

'We had no choice,' Oak explained, for her benefit as much as for ours. 'We couldn't risk Newton's existence being revealed. All three of us realised this inside us—what's the word?'

'Viscerally,' I suggested.

Oak grinned at me. '*Viscerally*. That's it, Flicker. That means "in the guts", right?'

'Exactly.'

'Our warrior poet,' he announced, bowing his powerful head and shoulders to me. If I was the poet, he was without doubt the master storyteller. 'Listen carefully so that you may tell the tale to others. What happened is this—the patrol boat landed on the beach and the three clowns jumped from the bow onto the sand. Thinking we were unarmed, they twirled their batons as they approached and left their pistols holstered. One of them started on about how the beach was out-of-bounds and how we'd have to be taken to a secure location, while the others leered, whacking their batons against their palms.'

Oak strode back and forth, working the crowd.

'That was as much as we were going to take. I moved in on the

202

one who'd been blabbering, effectively blocking Arden from his line of sight. Dray pretended to play it cool, telling me to take it easy, but the other two stepped up and raised their batons. They didn't even get one hit in. Arden had whipped her crossbow out from under the net and the first I knew about it was when I saw the bolt smack bang in the middle of his forehead. He dropped to the sand. The other two clowns were stunned just long enough for us to pull our pole-arms out of the sand. We had to take a couple of steps back to put them to use. That gave them the split second they needed to reach for their guns, but they didn't get a chance to shoot. We impaled them like boars good for a roasting.'

The audience listened in silence.

'What did you do with them?' Cat asked.

Oak shrugged. 'Sand is easy digging.'

'We kept the boat though,' Dray told us. 'It didn't appear to have any tracking device but we hid it in the woods away from town just to be sure.'

'You haven't used it?' I asked.

'Out of the question,' Dray said. 'Too risky.'

I'd figured as much.

'We need to make some decisions,' Arden said, getting the conversation back on track. 'We can get started right now, or we can hold off until tomorrow if our newcomers are tired.'

'I'm not tired,' Cat whispered to us eagerly.

'We're good,' Flame announced.

'In that case, the first and most significant decision to be made is whether we're prepared to risk our own lives laying siege to this castle.'

Without hesitation, an enthusiastic chorus of "for" came as her answer.

'Is anyone against?' Dray asked, surveying the assembly stony-faced.

Silence.

'This is who we are!' Oak told us proudly, and I could sense a swell of emotion rising in the big man. 'We'll never be slaves!'

The gathering cheered.

'Cat,' Arden said, 'how many slaves did you say there are and will they rise up if we penetrate this stronghold?'

'They will. I have no doubt about that. There are fourteen women and two men—well, adolescents.'

'The other women can fight like you?' Carver asked, looking up from the now clean dog bone in his hand.

'I wouldn't count on them being decisive in the battle,' Cat admitted, 'but they'll rise up if they can and they'll run wherever we tell them to go.'

'The warriors are about ten?' Dray asked.

'Yes. There are nine or ten of them left, including archers, and they know how to fight. They're hideous beasts!'

'You're safe now,' Dahlia said, sensing Cat's growing distress. She was unaccustomed to drinking and the beer was letting her emotions flow after being bottled up for so long.

Tara and Heather whispered soothing words to her and Cat thanked them.

'What's the next step?' Carver asked. 'We'll need a tight group of leaders for the expedition. The three newcomers know the lay of the land better than any of us. Oak, Dray, and Arden are best qualified to get us prepared for battle. What does everyone think?'

Everyone agreed, and so, just like that, our war cabinet of three women and three men was formed. Oak, Dray, and Arden looked at us, and we nodded our consent.

'Tomorrow, we'll get started making preparations,' Arden said. 'We have enough crossbows, but we'll need plenty of bolts, and we'll need more pole-arms and shorter weapons.'

'Shields as well,' Dray added. 'We're going to have to make shields.'

'I can do that,' another young man sitting next to Lark called out.

'Good, Sylvan,' Oak said. 'Your woodworking skills will come in handy there. Let me know if you need help with metalwork.'

'We'll need details on the castle, Cat,' Arden said. 'I have pencils and cloth you can use to draw a sketch.'

Cat nodded.

'I suggest one more round of beer and then we call it a night,' Dray said. 'Tomorrow will be a busy day.'

Arden approached us. 'What are your sleeping arrangements?' she asked uncomfortably.

'What do you mean?' Flame asked.

'I mean—well, do you usually all sleep together?

'Well, we have been since we met,' Flame said.

'Cat can stay with us,' Tara suggested.

'Seriously?' Heather asked her friend, disapproval in her tone.

'She needs to be shown a little tenderness,' Tara replied. 'Have a heart, Heather!'

'I'm not sure Cat is interested in your tenderness,' Arden said.

'I'm used to sleeping with other women,' Cat explained.

'Yes,' Arden replied cautiously, 'but Tara and Heather are very close.'

The two women in question giggled.

'Oh, I see,' Cat said with an awkward laugh. 'I don't know. I just want to sleep, and I don't want to cause any problems or be a hassle.'

'It's no problem, Cat. We all just want to stay warm and feel safe.'

'Do you have a brush? Can you do my hair?'

'We absolutely can,' Tara said.

Cat turned to us and shrugged.

'We don't have a spare cottage that's suitable for sleeping in at the moment,' Arden said, turning to us, 'but I'm one of the few who live alone. You should stay with me. I have an extra quilt you can use. Dahlia made it. It's very special to me, but you're a very special couple.'

'Thank you,' Flame said soberly. 'It would be an honour, wouldn't it, Flicker?'

'An honour,' I echoed.

'That's sorted then,' Arden chirped, and she took our goblets to serve the last drinks.

PART THREE

18. On the Warpath

In the morning, Arden roused us gently from our sleep. It was a little disconcerting, to be frank, not being the first awake for a change, but she had a gentle manner for a woman capable of putting a crossbow bolt in the middle of a man's forehead.

'Did you sleep well?'

'Better than we have in a long time,' Flame answered.

'If you'd told me I was destined to sleep like that this time yesterday, I'd have said you were off your rocker,' I told her.

'I'm very glad. I trust Cat was treated well. Tara and Heather are lovely, even if Tara can be a little overbearing at times.'

'Cat can take care of herself,' Flame said. 'She could certainly do with a sister or two right now.'

'That's what she's found in those two. Can I ask? Well, I get the impression she was treated horrifically.'

'She was,' Flame said. 'She was abused by one of them in particular. The one she beat to death with his own club.'

'Good for her. No one will ever abuse her again. Not while I'm alive.'

'We'll never let that happen again,' I promised.

'Let's have some breakfast and get to work,' Arden said. 'The sooner we're geared up, the sooner we can lay waste to this damned castle and get back to our usual routine. We had a play lined up for tonight, but that will have to be put off.'

'A play?'

'We don't get bored here in Newton. There's entertainment every third or fourth night. We're particularly fond of theatre and could do with a wordsmith to write dialogue, Flicker. We have magic shows, as well, and various displays of skill. Colby, for example, is an expert knife thrower. You'll soon know more than you want to about everyone. Don't worry about that.'

We followed her to the hall, where everyone was taking a handful of hard biscuits from a basket and filling their goblets with water.

'We have fruit and all kinds of berries when they're in season, but the biscuits get us through the winter.'

We tasted them and hummed our approval.

'You grow wheat and oats?' I asked.

'We grow them in a wild plantation about a half-hour from here. We let different types of cereal grow in the tall grass. From a distance, you can't tell the fields are cultivated.'

'Clever,' I said.

'It's basically the first rule we have. Any activity that could be detected by drones needs to be kept at least a half-hour walk from town. The only obvious exception is the dinner fire. We only eat a hot meal at night though, in order to lower the likelihood of the smoke being spotted.'

'We did that too back in the abandoned town,' I told her.

'You're both clever too. Of course you are. You wouldn't have avoided capture for so long otherwise.'

'I guess you're right,' Flame replied. 'We were just doing whatever we could to survive.'

'Do you think you'll want to go back there, once we've defeated this Lady Armstrong?'

That was a question that had crossed my mind a hundred times the previous night. The warm welcome was unlike any I'd ever experienced, and I assumed it was the same for Flame. My friends back in the city had stuck by me, just as I'd stuck by them, and yet here the bond was clearly so much stronger. The unanimous decision to wage war on an unknown enemy, risking their own lives for those of complete strangers, had bowled me over. I don't think any of us would have so readily agreed to that in the city. And yet, despite the camaraderie and the safety life in Newton would offer, I wondered whether we'd eventually yearn to be alone. Time would tell, if time was to be our ally.

'*If* we defeat her,' I said.

Arden scanned the hall, and I could read the concern on her face.

Oak must have seen it too, because he strolled over to us, bidding a good morning to those he passed, and lay a strong hand on Arden's shoulder.

'Morning all. Arden, don't count your dead before a fight has even begun.'

'I don't want *any* dead, Oak,' she said quietly. 'I don't want *you* dead. You have a woman who loves you dearly and a daughter who needs you by her side. I'd never be able to look them in the eye again if I came back and you didn't.'

'That's why we need a brilliant plan of attack. Is Cat here?'

We looked around but couldn't see her.

'Tara kept her up all night?'

'Stop it!' Arden whispered. 'It's not funny.'

'Well, these two are having trouble hiding their smirks.'

I had to admit I was.

'We'll take her to do sketches of the castle once she's scoffed down a couple of biscuits—she needs fattening up, the scrawny thing.'

'The weak point is the gatehouse,' I told him. 'The main entrance is a wire fence. It rattles noisily when opened, but if we cut the chain in the dead of the night, we might be able to get inside unnoticed.'

'I have bolt cutters.'

'Perfect.'

'They have a night watchman?'

'I doubt it,' I said. 'Cat might know for certain, but I don't think they do. The castle is set up as a prison—keeping the slaves in, not others out.'

'Do you know where the slaves sleep?'

We shook our heads.

'We haven't been inside,' Flame explained. 'Cat knows.'

'Here she is,' Arden said.

Cat, Tara, and Heather walked in and came straight over to us.

'Sleep well?' Oak asked, a mere hint of cheekiness in his voice.

'Very well,' Cat said, ignoring it. 'I don't think I've ever felt so safe.'

'That's what we want to hear,' Arden told her. 'I see you have your goblet from last night. Tara and Heather told you the drill?'

'Yeah, a handful of biscuits, plenty of water, and then we get to work.'

Arden smiled. 'Your job this morning is information.'

'I'm good to go,' Cat replied enthusiastically. 'I don't eat much in the morning.'

'It's up to you,' Oak said, looking her up and down.

She knew what he was thinking. 'Well, maybe one or two then.'

'That's the spirit,' he said. 'They're full of oats and seeds. Fuel for your motor.'

'Dray's over there talking to Sylvan,' Arden said. 'They must be discussing shields. We'll go back to my quarters and get started. Oak, maybe you can check in with Dray and then both join us when you're ready?'

'Will do,' he said and took his leave.

'What about us?' Heather asked, straightening her grey pelt tunic before crossing her arms.

'Are you two planning on fighting?' Arden asked.

They stared at her wide-eyed.

'Isn't everyone?' Tara asked.

'Of course not.'

'What do you mean?'

'I mean we can't all go. Dahlia and Blossom are obviously staying here. The same goes for Brianna. She has a baby.'

I wondered who the father was.

'Carver's boy,' Arden said, turning her head towards us.

'Yeah, but we're going, Arden,' Tara said firmly. 'We can fight.'

'Fine, girls. Go and talk to Dray.'

'Do we have to?' Heather asked.

'If you want to fight, you'll need weapons and training. Dray will sort you out. He's not a monster.'

'He hates us,' Heather said.

209

'He can be a dick sometimes and he doesn't understand you, but he doesn't hate you. Tell him to train you when he's ready. He won't kill you. He might, however, give you what you need to stay alive.'

'I guess we can hardly go into battle together if we can't even talk to each other,' Heather said, unfolding her arms.

'It could be the dawn of a deep and meaningful friendship.'

'Let's not get carried away,' Tara warned, rolling her eyes.

We returned to Arden's and watched as Cat sketched the castle for us. I helped her with the details I was more familiar with from above—the sandbags and raised platform on the keep. It was a part of the castle Cat had never set foot in.

'The Lady's quarters are in the keep?' Arden asked.

'Yes, and the door is locked at night, I believe,' Cat told her. 'This door to the right provides access to our chambers.'

'Also locked?'

'Every door is locked at night. You can count on that.'

'I wonder whether an attack at night really is the best approach,' Arden said. 'If the slaves are set to work outside the castle during the day, it would be much less dangerous to ambush their guards then.'

'That's a point,' Flame said. 'But we can't be sure they'll be working outside the day we march.'

'Most of our work is away from the castle. It's highly unusual we spend an entire day inside the walls.'

'Very promising,' Arden said.

Oak arrived with Dray. They sat with us on the floor and immediately set to studying Cat's sketch.

'So, Dray?' Arden asked.

'Sorry. Hello.'

'Yes. You forgot to say hello, but my *so* was with regards to Tara and Heather.'

'Oh, right. Well, they'll be up to it.'

Arden nodded. That was Dray—straight to the point.

'Cat tells us the slaves work beyond the castle walls every day.'

'Is that so?' Oak mused. 'Meaning a daytime attack would be more advantageous.'

'It also means the Lady might lock herself away in the castle with her best warriors,' Dray pointed out.

'Is our main aim to kill her or to free the slaves?' Arden asked.

'I was planning on both,' Dray said drily.

'How many of them guard the slaves at work, Cat?' Oak asked.

'Nearly all of them. She has one or two stay with her. Her favourites.'

'She can't hold a castle against us with one or two, Dray,' Oak said.

'No, I suppose she can't. We'll need broad shields we can carry over our heads while we break down doors. If the two she has with her are archers, they could wreak havoc from above.'

'They are,' Cat said. 'They're excellent archers.'

'If we take them on in a field or woodlands, we have to slaughter them all,' Dray told us. 'You all understand that, don't you?'

At first, no one replied, so I nodded.

'We can't let word reach the castle ahead of us, giving her time to put defences into place. I want as many of us as possible to walk back through the gates of Newton.'

'We all do.' Arden agreed. 'I want everyone to come home.'

'If we don't make any mistakes, it's by no means impossible,' he said, considering each of us solemnly. 'The six of us have that terrible shared shadow.'

He was met with blank faces, but then I understood.

'We've taken lives,' I said.

'That's it, Flicker. We've killed fellow humans. Speaking for myself, it doesn't haunt me.' He studied our expressions. 'We've done it once, and we know we can do it again. We did it to survive, and survival isn't a battle won once. It's a constant struggle.'

'The others?' Oak asked.

'That's what we don't know,' Dray went on. 'We don't know how they'll react once the heat is on. I've told Tara and Heather I want to train them in pole-arms. They're not bad hunters but they'll need to handle their weapons with more confidence and ease. They both have a good sense of direction, so I'd like them to lead the slaves back to Newton as quickly as possible. The sooner they're all out of the way, the less hazardous and messy it will be for us.'

'Sylvan and Carver will hold their own,' Oak said.

'I hope so,' Dray said. 'Carver—yes. I don't know about Sylvan.'

'What's the plan for today?' Arden asked. 'We need to get weapons and shields sorted.'

'I'll get back to Sylvan to tell him we need one broad siege shield,' Dray informed us. 'He's already started with personal shields. How many of us will be fighting?'

'We need to work that out,' Arden said. 'Twenty at most.'

Dray whistled lowly. 'Will we all need shields?'

'I won't,' Arden said. 'My crossbow and bolts are all I need.'

'And the hunting knife you keep strapped to your ankle.'

'And that little darling,' she confirmed. 'Tara and Heather won't be able to juggle shields and pole-arms.'

'No, they won't,' Arden agreed. 'Fern won't need one either. She's like me—nothing but her crossbow.'

'What's your weapon, Flicker?' Oak asked.

'Fire.' I shrugged.

They laughed.

'You can take all the matches you want but you might need another weapon. You have an axe. Are you happy with that?'

I thought about it. 'I think I am. I've got my axe and a hammer.'

'You won't be able to carry a shield either then.'

'Cat and Flame should have one,' Arden said. 'They'll need weapons as well. Maces?'

We looked at each other and nodded.

'We'll aim for ten shields then,' Dray said.

'Crossbow bolts, Oak?'

'We have dozens. Even if there were only nine or ten each, it's more than overkill for the likes of you and Fern.'

'I have a question,' Cat said.

'Ask, Cat,' Arden urged her. 'Speak your mind.'

'How long will it take?'

'Eager, aren't you?' Dray asked, a wicked twist to his lips. 'Three days, at least. It takes time to manufacture shields and weapons.'

Cat sighed.

'I know every minute your sisters remain in captivity must be torture for you, Cat,' Arden said tenderly. 'That's the very reason we can't rush our preparations. The element of surprise is on our side, but we can only play that hand once. There's no room for mistakes. We'll keep you busy so the wait doesn't seem so long, and we'll be on the warpath before you know it.'

19. The Siege

As it turned out, the three days did fly by, and it was with a curious combination of excitement and foreboding that we readied ourselves for the expedition that morning. We were eighteen in total, putting us at twice the expected number the Lady had at her disposal.

We backtracked along the route that had led us to the beach from the hills and turned southwards at the point where we estimated we were in line with the castle. It was tough going, hiking up and down the hills, climbing over rocky outcrops and squeezing single-file through narrow cracks, but when I saw the derelict farm across the field below us, I knew it had paid off.

'That's where they were working the day we rescued Cat,' I told the others. 'Cutting wood not far past that old farm.'

We stayed close together—Dray, Oak, Arden, Flame, Cat, and myself. We six were at the head of the warband, peering down past stony trunks and bare branches beyond which the land opened out and flattened.

'Let's take a closer look,' Dray said, and I was about to start down the hill when I realised he was reaching into a pocket.

'Binoculars!' I said.

He grinned. 'Small but powerful. I found this little treasure on a trawler that washed up on the coast north of town a few years ago. They're not much use in the woods, but they'll prove mighty handy today.'

He moved a little ahead of us, further down the slope, looking for a clear view of the backdrop to the farm, and raised the binoculars to his yes.

'What can you see?' Oak called, keeping his voice low and soft.

Dray didn't answer at first. He was scanning slowly from right to left, which gave the impression there was no sign of human activity. He turned and shook his head.

'Best you stay ahead, Dray, and have a look every now and then,' Arden suggested.

'Will do,' he replied. 'Flicker, you said you can see the top of the keep from the farmhouse?'

'That's right.'

'Once we're out in the open,' Dray said, 'we'll have to advance quickly to the farmhouse and stay close to the walls on this side. That way, we won't be visible from the keep. Once we're all positioned there, Flicker and I can jog ahead to the spot where he and Flame were hiding when they saw the slaves cutting wood. With Cat's escape and their routine disrupted, they may still be there finishing the job.'

'If not,' Arden said, 'we'll start towards the castle, with you two staying ahead.'

'Agreed,' Dray said.

Without turning around or saying a word, Oak raised a hand and waved forwards. We all started moving again, following Dray downhill.

Once we'd passed the last trunks, Dray sprinted forward.

I tried to keep up with him but he was just too fast, even with his pole-arm raised clear of the ground. Like me, he'd chosen not to carry a shield, preferring to remain unencumbered. The arm holding it didn't waver as he ran. The other, he pumped backwards and forwards.

I held my axe close to the head and was able to run naturally with arms moving, but he still arrived at the farmhouse a good three seconds before me.

He turned around and shot me a victorious grin.

The others were right behind us, some carrying unmarked shields of wood, which provided excellent camouflage in the forested areas. Sylvan and Carver were at the rear, carrying the siege shield, and Tara and Heather were just ahead of them.

I stayed behind Dray as he edged up to the corner of the stone farmhouse and peered around, raising his binoculars. I could tell he'd pointed them in the direction of the castle.

He turned to me and frowned. 'That podium or whatever it is

215

up there,' he said, not finishing his question or observation.

'Strange, isn't it? The keep is high enough for a good view across the surrounding area.'

'Why does she need one then?' he asked.

'To be higher than others standing on the keep,' I suggested.

Dray stared at me blankly.

'But why would she want that?' I wondered.

'This is a very dangerous woman we're dealing with,' Dray whispered. 'Didn't Cat tell you about this podium?'

I shook my head. 'Slaves don't go up there. I don't think she knows much about it.'

He looked at me but didn't speak—a dark expression on his face.

'You think you know?'

'I've seen atrocities, Flicker. I've known horrors worse than you can fathom. I can tell by your eyes. The eyes reflect what they've seen. In my life before Newton, I witnessed unspeakable depravity committed by people who'd left any hint of humanity behind. I know, because I almost became one of them. It took a huge amount of courage and stubbornness not to follow them down a dark path. Not everyone has those two qualities, but I did. I still do, and I think you might.'

I didn't know what to say. Was he right? Did I?

'There's pain in Cat's eyes,' he went on, keeping his voice low, 'but I'm not certain she's the one who has suffered the most within that stronghold.'

'You think the platform is used as a kind of theatre box and the roof of the keep is the stage—one where atrocities of some description are carried out?'

Dray raised his sandy eyebrows. 'Flicker, I think we need to watch our step with this *Lady* and we need to end this conversation now.' He glanced over my shoulder. 'They're starting to get impatient. Best not make everyone more nervous than they already are. We may outnumber them two-to-one on paper, but unless my imagination has caused me to misinterpret the reason for having that platform up there, this battle isn't going to be a walk in the park.'

I drew a deep breath. 'Let's go. The holly bush,' I reminded him, turning back to Flame and the others and giving them three hand signs—two fingers running, flat palm to tell them to wait, and a thumbs-up for good measure.

Dray dashed down and across the road, this time holding his pole-arm horizontally to avoid it being seen from the cutting site. He had no problem spotting the holly bush and swerved smoothly towards it, but instead of crouching behind it, he pulled up beside it and stood quite casually.

'No one,' he said, looking at the clear area. 'Instead of disrupting proceedings, I get the impression Cat's escape did the contrary.'

The site was clear of wood. All that remained was a muddy patch of trampled grass, leaves, and twigs.

Dray had his binoculars out again and was surveying the surrounding area. I doubted he'd spot anyone I couldn't see with the naked eye.

'Nowhere to be seen,' he said, putting them away again.

'In that case, we have to lay siege.'

He stared into my eyes again, making me aware that the words I had uttered weren't to be taken lightly, particularly in light of the hushed conversation we'd had a minute earlier.

We have to lay siege.

They were extraordinary words. There was no doubt about that. Only days ago, it was a sentence I'd never have imagined coming from my lips. What did I know of sieges and battles? What did any of us know?

We looked back at the farmhouse. From this angle, we could see the others waiting patiently, watching our every move.

'There are a couple of things we need to get clear between us before we go any further, Flicker.'

I could tell what was coming. His every thought hung heavy in the air around me. The more I got to know Dray, the more I was in awe of him. It was that terrible awe occupying the place where fear met admiration. This man, whom I would never truly like— let alone call a friend, was as steadfast as he was dreadful. He could be counted on.

'Once we've engaged them in battle, there's no going back,' I said. 'We can't hesitate, we can't retreat, and we can't show mercy. We crush them or we die.'

He closed his eyes and bowed his head. 'I'm glad you're here, Flicker. I'm honoured to fight alongside you.'

'I'm sorry we brought this upon you.'

'Don't say that. You can't ever say that. We couldn't hide in the woods like squirrels all our lives. You found the castle, and we found you. If I believed in fate, I'd be tempted to admit a hand had guided us. But all I believe in is fighting what the world has become, and if we can't do that today—and win—our lives are meaningless.'

'I suppose that's why Flame and I rescued Cat in the first place. We knew we had to. Turning our backs on her and pretending that night had never happened wasn't an option.'

'Then we understand each other,' he said. 'On the topic of decisions, we need to decide whether we wait for dark, as planned, or attack now.'

'Both options have their advantages and disadvantages. A night attack would catch them by surprise, but it would make ushering the slaves to safety more difficult.'

'That's the main issue,' he agreed. 'I overlooked it at first when I suggested attacking by night. At best, Cat knows the castle as well as they do. The rest of us will be lost.'

'We'll also be hungry and tired by nightfall,' I added. 'Dusk is still a few hours away.'

'Of course, if we win decisively and kill them all, we could stay the night. We wouldn't have to move the slaves out until morning. Some might even want to stay and built their own community.'

He made a good point.

'For now, we need to close in,' I suggested. 'Once we reach where the track branches right, the two of us can go ahead and find out what's happening inside.'

'Agreed,' he said.

We jogged back to the road and signalled for the others to follow, then kept moving quickly past the ruins of the cottages, not slowing our pace until we were sure everyone was out of sight of the keep.

Flame and Cat caught up with us before we reached the track

218

to the castle.

'We're not attacking now, are we?' Flame asked, trying to hide her fear but unable to prevent her voice from trembling a little.

'Before we do, we need to work out where they are,' I told her. 'Where else could they be working, Cat?'

'It depends what they're doing.' She shrugged. 'If they're hunting or gathering nuts, they could be anywhere in the woods.'

'But they always enter through the gatehouse?' Dray asked.

'Yes,' she said. 'It's the most convenient entrance. Otherwise, you need to clamber over rubble and climb sections of wall. They wouldn't do that unless there was an obstacle preventing them from using the gate.

'Flicker and I will have a look,' Dray said. 'Cat, I'm going to leave my pole-arm with you. It'll only risk attracting attention and get in the way. Flicker, stay with me and have your axe at the ready. Flame, make sure we have someone keeping an eye on the rear.'

'Fern, Carver, and Sylvan are watching out.'

'Good,' Dray said. 'Wish us luck.'

We walked along the track in silence, listening for voices or any sounds of movement other than birdsong. We were quite exposed, the trees having lost all but the most stubborn of leaves, but we stayed to the right-hand side of the track, closest to the keep. This was where the thin skyward-reaching branches provided what little cover there was to be had. We glanced up there every few paces but could see no watchman standing guard.

The gatehouse then came into view, but from our position, we could see only the distant hillside through the wire.

'Where are they?' Dray asked lowly.

We listened but there was only the faint background provided by carefree birds, chirping merrily.

'How close should we go?' I asked. 'All the way?'

He looked at me, sandy eyebrows raised, then flashed a smile. 'All the way,' he echoed.

And so we did, taking our time, one step after the other so as to avoid making undue noise. The castle walls loomed above us and the keep rose into the sky to our right.

'Could she be there alone, our so-called Lady?' Dray asked.

'If she is?'

'I won't tell Flame.' He winked.

'What? No, Dray. That's not who we are.'

'I was joking, you idiot.' He laughed under his breath. 'You should have seen your face.'

But with each step, I found myself asking that question. Was she alone? If she saw us and there wasn't time to tell the others, what would we do? Could I cut her down with my axe, just like that?

I didn't have to wait long for the answer. A horn blast rent the air and I turned immediately to the keep. I could hardly believe we'd been spotted and thought he must have caught sight of the others, but he was facing us, looking down as he blew the horn.

'Fuck!' Dray yelled. 'Where did he come from?'

'I can't see anyone else,' I said, glancing all around.

'We have to get in, Flicker! Oak and Arden will be charging up here already. We need to get that gate open!'

I surged up to the gate, raising my axe and bringing it crashing down onto the lock in one smooth movement. The entire gate shuddered and rattled loudly, but the lock didn't break. I swung again and again in rapid succession, but to no avail.

'The hinges!' Dray yelled, his voice drowned by the second horn blast. I looked where he was pointing and I saw what he meant. While the lock and chain had withstood my repeated attacks, the two hinges to the right had been displaced from their sockets in the crumbling stone of the gatehouse. I lifted my axe, aimed it at the gap between the top hinge and the stone, and swung.

With a loud clang, the hinge snapped off the stonework and dropped towards us. We stepped out of the way.

There was no need to break the lower hinge. Dray had slipped his welding goggles on—ready for battle—and was already pulling at the gate, twisting it down to the ground.

The others arrived.

'Hands away!' Oak yelled, and Dray moved back while dozens of feet trampled on the wire gate, flattening it as they entered the courtyard.

'Your pole-arm, Dray!' Cat said, shoving it into his hand.

'Where are they?'

'One on the keep,' I said, looking up, and I was immediately glad I had at that very moment. 'Archers!' I roared. 'Archers on the keep!'

The watchman had abandoned his horn in favour of his bow, and I could see that it was Lady Armstrong who was with him. They aimed and shot in perfect unison.

'Take cover!' someone yelled.

I didn't see where the arrows struck, but there were no cries of pain.

'Siege shield!' Dray shouted. 'Carver! Sylvan!'

They rushed over to Dray and marched towards the door to the keep, holding the shield over their heads.

Oak looked up at the keep and sidestepped. An arrow hit the ground where he'd been. He then ran over to the door—sledgehammer at the ready—and began pummelling at it while the others held the shield.

Lady Armstrong shot an arrow straight down but it failed to penetrate the thick shield. The watchman aimed straight at me, so I sprinted towards the lorry and crouched behind it. Cat, Flame, Arden, Tara, and Heather were also there. The others had taken cover in the gatehouse or behind the small workshop.

'Stay down until the door yields!' Arden whispered. 'We need to get inside before the others make it back here.'

We kept our heads low. Arden crawled towards the front of the lorry.

'Are they in range?' Tara asked.

'I think so.'

She stood, aimed, and released her bolt. I couldn't see what was happening but she ducked again and reloaded.

'Within range but he saw me coming.'

The cracking of wood from Oak's sledgehammer filled the air. It was only a matter of time.

Time, however, was running out. Screaming and roaring filled the gatehouse and I could see Fern aiming her crossbow down along the track. She shot and immediately reloaded, but I saw one of our men drop to the ground, an arrow sticking out of his chest. I couldn't tell who it was, but I saw Lark grab him by the arms and struggle to pull him backwards into the courtyard.

'No!' I yelled, but it was too late. An arrow from the keep hit Lark in the shoulder, making him drop the first victim. Another arrow hit the ground just short of them, then a third struck Lark in the temple. A hideous victory cry from the keep filled the air, and it soon became a fit of hysterical laughter.

Arden stood and shot again. The laughter became a roar of pain.

'Got him!' she said, dropping behind the lorry.

'Dead?' Cat asked.

'Out of action, for sure. She'll have to tend to him.'

No sooner had Arden spoken than we heard a dull thud, followed immediately by angry shouting. I looked instinctively at the gatehouse, where the enemy was being held off admirably for the time being—the result of superior numbers using shields and pole-arms effectively, while Fern and a man whose name I don't remember stayed at the rear and shot at the archers with their crossbows. But one of the voices I'd heard belonged to Oak. Its deep gruffness was unmistakable. The thud had come from the door to the keep.

I raised my head and peered over the tray of the lorry, first looking up to the top of the keep, but I couldn't see the Lady. I looked down and understood what had happened. There was a body on the ground near the door and the siege shield was lying next to it. Oak was pounding at the door with his sledgehammer, splintering wood with each strike, Dray was looking straight up at the top of the keep, and Carver and Sylvan were rubbing their heads.

'What's going on, Flicker?' Flame asked.

I ducked back down.

'I think she pushed him off the keep,' I said, not sounding too sure of myself.

'What?' Arden said. 'She pushed her own archer off?'

'Trying to stop Oak from breaking the door,' Tara said.

'That's what happened,' I said. 'Unless he jumped or fell by accident.'

'No,' Cat said. 'Arden injured him, so he was no longer any use as an archer. That's why she pushed him over the edge. Falling onto the shield was his last act of usefulness. That's what she's like—a heartless bitch!'

Arden stood up, crossbow ready. 'I can't see her up there.'

'She won't be far,' Cat said.

'She could have killed them.'

'Carver and Sylvan aren't looking too good, but they're alive. If Dray hadn't been holding the shield with them, the impact might have proved fatal.'

'We're in!' Oak roared.

We all stood up and saw him reach through a gaping hole in the door to raise the latch from the inside. He pulled the door open and stormed inside. Dray was right behind him but the other two were struggling and followed more slowly.

'Arden!' Fern called.

We all turned our attention to the gate and could see that our line was being pushed further into the courtyard.

'Coming!' Arden called back, already on her feet. I caught up with her.

'A few of them have got a hold of our pole-arms and are pushing the line back. We can't shoot them from this angle,' Fern explained.

'How many archers are there?' I asked.

'Only one now,' she said.

'Where is he?'

'Straight ahead down the track.'

'I'll get to the top of the keep and try to get a line of sight,' Arden said. 'Even if I can't hit him from there, I should be able to make myself enough of a hazard to stop him from bothering us.'

'The keep's clear?' Fern asked.

'Oak and Dray are in there with Carver and Sylvan. As far as we know, the Lady is alone.'

'How many are here?' Cat asked.

'We've counted seven.'

'Seven,' she repeated, frowning.

Arden dashed over to the keep, glancing up as she ran. But Lady Armstrong hadn't taken up her bow again. Had she escaped through some secret tunnel?

Cat, Flame, Tara, Heather, and I tried to help push back against the relentless heave coming from the other side by grasping the shaft of someone's pole-arm with one or both hands and trying to hold it steady. We were more numerous, but they were definitely stronger, and they were pushing in unison, reminding me of the way the waves crashed into the beach.

I could glimpse the one I was battling with through the gaps between shields and recognised him from the worksite the day we'd rescued Cat. A couple of them broke away from the pole-arms but stayed close to avoid the heads of the weapons. They started pounding against shields with their clubs and howling like wolves. The psychological effect of this change in tactic was more powerful than the physical.

'Hold firm!' I pleaded the line, suspecting that every one of us had just taken a step backwards.

The howling intensified.

'Where are the slaves?' Tara shouted.

'Gone!' Fern yelled back. 'They all took to the hills.'

'They all ran away?' Cat asked.

'Yeah. It seems you're one of a kind, Cat.'

I didn't hear Cat's reply, but I could tell her heart broke. If they'd had the courage to launch an attack from behind, the battle would already be over.

'Push harder!' Flame yelled.

A united groan came in reply and we pushed, but our determined step was met with a beastly roar from our enemy, and with a chorus of wolf howls and a frenzied battering of clubs against shields, they pushed us two steps back.

I looked up at the roof of the keep but there was no sign of Arden. Why was it taking so long?

'Flame, there's a problem in the keep. Oak and Dray should have caught Lady Armstrong by now and Arden should be up top.'

'What can we do?'

'I should go and have a look.'

'They can't be in any danger—five of them against her alone.'

'I'm not so sure she's alone,' I said. 'Cat!'

'Yeah?'

'One warrior isn't accounted for?'

'There were seven here and the archer Arden shot. But I think there should have been nine after the fight in the schoolhouse.'

'You'd better go,' Fern told us. 'The three of you. We'll try to hold them off. Come back with news as soon as you can. If we had Arden on the tower and the others somehow launching an attack from outside the walls, we'd have beaten them by now.'

'Right, let's move! Cat, you coming?'

We ran across the courtyard and past the dead archer to the shattered door, which hung open and useless. The hall was void of furnishing of any kind. There was only one large chest against the wall to the right. The walls were damp but clean. Without slave labour, there would have been moss and cobwebs everywhere.

It was when I turned left and saw the opening to the spiral staircase that I discovered my instinct was right. Sprawled across the first few steps were the bodies of Carver and Sylvan, twisted and bloodied. Flame and Cat froze beside me, gripping their weapons in terror.

'Their throats have been cut,' I whispered.

The women remained silent.

This was her work. After shoving the archer off the tower, she'd vanished. At first, I'd thought she must have taken an escape route out of the castle. But she wasn't that kind of woman, was she? She wasn't going to leave her castle alive. She'd hurried downstairs and hid in the chest. There was nowhere else. She'd held the chest only very slightly open—just enough to peep out. Dray and Oak had bounded up the stairs, but these poor souls, still half-dazed, had lagged behind. Lambs to the slaughter.

'Where are their weapons?' Flame asked.

Gone.

'I have to move them,' I said, already taking hold of Carver's feet and trying not to get blood on my hands. 'They're blocking the stairs.'

I dragged them both back into the hall, cringing at the sounds their bodies made as I dragged them across the stone floor.

Cat and Flame hadn't closed their eyes but they were trying to

225

look away. I was glad of that. I didn't want Flame keeping this image of me.

'Follow me,' I whispered. 'We take it slow and keep our eyes and ears open. We have to watch our backs.'

They nodded, their faces pale with shock, and I couldn't stop myself from looking at those slit throats and the rivers of blood that flowed together. She'd climbed out of the chest and approached them from behind—perhaps tiptoeing—in perfect silence. Two throats cut from behind. It was no mean feat.

I started up the stairs. There was no choice but to tread on blood on the first two or three, but I made sure I didn't slip.

Time had polished the stairs and worn them smooth. Each step was uneven with a central dip in the front where uncountable feet had landed over the centuries.

The staircase spiralled clockwise around a central column and gave access to the first floor, to which there was no door. I stepped over the threshold and down into the room.

The floor itself had been repaired recently using old planks of wood clearly taken from elsewhere—the timber old and grey but the floor perfectly flat. There was no one here but there were six single beds, their frames built from black tubular metal. The beds were made, with clean sheets tucked in neatly around mattress corners, fluffed pillows, and blankets folded neatly at the foot. It was somehow bizarre to see this attention to detail in such a savage environment. Wood was neatly stacked against the eastern wall, beside a fireplace with the remains of charred logs, and there was a narrow window in that wall. The opposite wall was a different story. There was no window at all in what was clearly a work in progress. A mishmash of material had been used to seal the gap left by the collapsed wall. Sheets of corrugated roofing metal were nailed to chipboard and lengths of tarpaulin hung from hooks, presumably for added insulation.

I pointed upwards and went back to the stairs.

The door to the next floor was ajar.

I raised a hand for Cat and Flame, indicating for them to wait, then approached the door carefully, my axe gripped in both hands with the head hovering over my right shoulder.

I didn't quite know what I was expecting—perhaps an arrow

with my name on it. It was with a keen sense of dread that I used my left foot to ease the door open.

It swung noiselessly.

No one. No arrow.

This room was much like the previous one, but I only counted four beds.

We moved up to the next floor, moving faster this time, because I was beginning to suspect they were all on top of the keep now—if they were still alive.

Arden, Dray, and Oak against the Lady and one of her guards? There could only be one left unaccounted for. At face value, the odds were good, but we were struggling to push an inferior number back at the gatehouse.

On the next two floors, I kicked the doors open, and on the final one before the roof, I didn't even allow myself an instant of awe at the luxurious furnishings surrounding a grand queen-size bed.

Cat, however, did. 'The evil bitch!'

When we reached the roof, we breathed a sigh of relief. Standing with their backs to us were Dray and Oak. They were alive.

They turned. Oak's face was a mask of terror that didn't ease upon seeing us, and Dray's was a portrait of hopelessness—of his worst expectations confirmed.

Beyond them, a solitary warrior stood with his chin raised in defiance. I recognised him as the one who had been walking next to Cat's guard on the way to the worksite.

At first, I didn't understand why they weren't fighting. As daunting as he was, Oak and Dray together could have easily defeated him.

But I was about to understand all too well.

'Welcome to the rooftop!' a woman's voice called from above.

We stepped out onto the roof and I lifted my gaze to the platform. There stood an old black armchair on it, probably an antique, with discoloured patches here and there where the leather had needed mending. Lady Armstrong sat there, her expression impassive on an unsettlingly pretty face. Her eyes were a warm shade of light brown but her regard was ice-cold, and her long dark hair was draped elegantly over her left shoulder, which was covered by a dun-coloured animal fur.

But what really caught my attention was her right hand. The arm was wrapped around Arden and the bloodied blade held in the right hand was pressed firmly against her throat.

20. His Brother's Keeper

'Cat's come home!' Lady Armstrong jeered. 'You couldn't stay away, could you? You know this is where you belong. There's a big bad world out there now, and it's getting worse every day. This is your home, isn't it? This is where you have structure and certainty.'

'This was never my home, you bitch!' Cat spat.

'Bitch, am I? How a little taste of freedom has loosened your tongue! You never dared call me that before.' She tutted. 'If I were you, I'd watch that mouth of yours. Don't presume to know how this scuffle will end. This mob you've somehow rounded up is beginning to tire. My soldiers are trained. They have endurance and patience. They'll overwhelm your rabble, Cat. Will you still call me a bitch then? Will that be your dying word?'

It was terrifying, the way this woman exuded authority. She had to be several years younger than the rest of us—certainly younger than Oak, Dray, Flame, and me, and perhaps roughly the same age as Cat and Arden. She was probably the junior of her loyal warrior, who stood there scowling at us, but his hardened features made guessing his age difficult. And yet, her presence was overshadowing. She commanded respect, almost as much as she induced a burning hatred.

Cat's reply sent a shiver down my spine. 'It probably will be, you fucked-up bitch!'

It was as though a spell had been broken.

'Leave Arden out of it,' Oak told her, his voice calm and strong. 'We'll come to an arrangement.'

'Arrangement?' Dray asked, whispering. 'With that creature?'

'Arden's coming home with us,' Oak answered.

229

'The only arrangement we can come to is for you to leave my home and never return,' Lady Armstrong said icily. 'I don't recall inviting you.'

'The slaves were invited?' Flame growled.

She glared down at her. 'They had a social contract with me. Security and sustenance in exchange for work.'

'A contract?' Cat hissed. 'We were prisoners.'

'True. You were,' she replied calmly. 'Look around yourself now, Cat.' She smiled mockingly. 'Where are they all? A little ironic, isn't it, that our repeat escaper is here at my feet while all the others have run for the hills? You've risked your lives today for a pack of cowards and deprived me of my workforce. Are you proud of yourselves?'

'We are,' I told her. 'We've already achieved one of our goals.'

Her smile couldn't have been more wicked, and yet I saw fear in her eyes.

'That goal is enough for today, is it not? This beautiful girl here doesn't deserve to be sacrificed for your second—less honourable—goal, does she?' She pouted in mock sadness.

We all stared at Arden, her lips pursed and her eyes staring at our feet. She was petrified.

The Lady's face brightened for an instant, as though she planned on changing the conversation to a more palatable topic.

'So, whose bitch is she anyway?'

'No one's,' Dray answered. 'She belongs to no one.'

'A woman after my own heart! I don't belong to anyone either, do I, Hunter? Well, not unless I'm feeling generous.'

He grinned and stuck his chin even further into the air, his nostrils flaring with pride.

'This castle isn't some temporary base. It's the heart of a dawning empire, and its future leader could quite possibly be Hunter's child.' She laid her left hand on her belly.

Cat gasped. I think we all did, but hers was the loudest.

'Can't you all see the sun sinking towards the deep green sea?'

It was getting lower, now hanging in the distance beyond the parapet of sandbags, but it remained bright enough despite the cloud cover to make our shadows stretch towards the inner edge of the keep.

'Now look to the east, where your mob is clinging to the last few feet of the gateway. They'll soon lose that grip and be sent scuttling into the courtyard. The writing is on the wall. Can't you read it, you idiots?'

She was convincing, but the setting sun was no more a sign of our defeat than of hers.

'What kind of arrangement do you suggest?' Dray asked, and I knew what he was thinking. The sooner we resolved the standoff here, the sooner we could put an end to the deadlock downstairs.

'Hunter wants to know who murdered his brother,' she said.

The warrior squared his broad shoulders, bare despite the cold. There was a club and a long machete on the floor behind him, but he was unarmed.

'Cat?' she asked. 'You must have seen it all. Who killed him?'

Cat looked at us, then turned back to Lady Armstrong. She was about to speak but I wasn't taking that chance.

'I did,' I said.

'Flicker!' Flame hissed.

'I thought as much,' Lady Armstrong said. 'This skinny girl couldn't have done it alone.'

'What's the deal?' I asked.

'Isn't it obvious?' she sneered. 'Hunter wants to avenge his brother's murder.'

'It wasn't murder! He was raping Cat!' Flame yelled.

Lady Armstrong raised her left hand and flicked it in the air, dismissing the trivial detail.

'What are the terms, Hunter?' she asked.

'It will be a fight to the death,' he growled. 'I avenge my brother, or I join him. We start unarmed. If we're both alive after five minutes, we choose one weapon each. Do you accept?'

I heard my voice say, 'I do.'

The Lady smiled pleasantly. 'If Hunter wins, you all leave immediately. Arden will be released once the rest of you have passed the gate. If Flicker—that's your ridiculous name, isn't it?—wins, we will leave the castle to you.'

'But we want you all dead!' Dray said, before spitting on the floor.

'If it's more bloodshed you crave, that is another path we can

231

walk together.'

I didn't hear every word that was spoken after that. What I do remember is staring at my opponent. There was a mix of fury and arrogance written on his worn face. His shoulders were broad and his bare arms were muscular, but he wasn't as impressive as his brother had been. I wondered whether he could pack as good a punch.

He was rocking his shaven head from side to side, stretching out the muscles, but his cruel eyes remained locked on mine.

It took some time before I realised Flame was talking to me. I broke his gaze to look at her.

'I don't want this,' she whispered.

'This is how it has to be,' I replied.

'But Flicker,' Cat began.

I raised my hand to silence her.

'We were all there. This is as much my fight as yours.'

'I love you, Flicker,' Flame mouthed.

I kissed her. 'I love you.'

'How touching!' Lady Armstrong declared. 'I'm sure she'll cherish her fond memories of you, even if the last ones aren't too pretty.'

Hunter laughed heartily.

'Who will keep time?' Oak asked.

'Why not you?' she replied. 'Give him the hourglass, Hunter.'

He walked across to the platform and took a small hourglass from behind the armchair. I also noticed the butt of Arden's crossbow sticking out.

It was then that I understood what had dawned on Dray back at the farmhouse. This wasn't the first time a fight to the death had taken place on the keep. The hourglass and the platform were kept up here for that very purpose. This was her way of settling differences and entertaining her black heart. Cat hadn't told us because she hadn't been aware of it. This wasn't slave business.

Our shadows were stretching ever longer as the sun sank, and I had to wonder whether I would be alive when it kissed the sea.

'Step forward, Flicker,' Lady Armstrong said. 'It won't hurt for long.'

They cheered for me, everyone but Arden, who was too scared to make a sound.

I could hear Dray's voice behind me. 'You've got it in you, Flicker. I failed to mention that when I told you what I saw in your eyes. Unleash the hell within.'

He was right. There *was* hellfire inside me. There always had been. Today, it had to burn more fiercely than ever before, and it would.

'Are you ready, timekeeper?' Lady Armstrong asked.

'Ready,' Oak growled.

'Hunter and Flicker?'

'Ready,' we chorused.

'Fight!'

He didn't waste a second, stepping forward with his fists up, ready to box. He was furious and he kept his eyes locked on mine. He was yearning to hurt me.

I reminded myself I wasn't a boxer, and my goal was neither to make him feel pain nor to provide entertainment. I needed to kill him.

No one uttered a word around us. Only the shouting from the pitched battle at the gatehouse reached our ears.

Hunter swung at me, but I ducked and then lunged, tackling him to the floor. I landed half on top of him—with my face on his abdomen—and crawled further up, but he placed his hands on my shoulders and lifted me off. I guessed his next move would be a crushing head butt, so I let myself drop away from him, then rolled to one side and got to my feet.

He drew a deep breath and walked slowly up to me this time, giving no indication of what he had in mind. I raised my fists to my face, hoping to trick him into thinking I'd punch, but I didn't know what I was going to do at all.

He swung a left hook at me, and I had to stumble back a couple of steps, but I immediately marched up to him, fists raised again. I struck at him, right and left, but he protected his head with his fists and kicked my left leg with his right.

I roared with pain and retreated, hoping he hadn't broken a bone. Yet somehow, rather than distracting me, the pain helped me keep focus. I had to do much better than that.

He attacked while I was still crouching a little and I guessed he was going to try to finish me off, knocking me out with a powerful kick to the head. But he was too fast for his own good. I watched his right leg out of the corner of my eye, ignoring the pain in my leg and the screams from Flame and Cat. When he was about to kick, I dropped to the left and stuck my right foot out to catch his left. There was nothing he could do. He tripped, only just managing to put his forearms in front of his face before it hit the floor.

Flame and Cat gasped.

I stumbled to my feet before he could and kicked him in the back, sending him crashing into Dray, who then shoved him back towards me with both hands.

'Careful!' Lady Armstrong warned, and even though I didn't take my eyes off Hunter, I could feel that bloodied blade pressed harder against Arden's throat.

Taking advantage of Dray's shove all the same, I punched Hunter in the face an instant before he flattened me. My head hit the floor and a searing pain filled it, but I kept my attention on my opponent, pushing him off me before he could react.

We both got to our feet and shook ourselves off, getting ready for what would be the next round. It was impossible to say how much time had passed without catching a glimpse of the hourglass, but it would have been a potentially fatal mistake to even try.

He was more wary of me now and must have realised that laying a knock-out punch to my head wasn't going to be easy. My leg no longer hurt too badly but I could tell I'd hurt him when I kicked his back. He wasn't letting on though, standing tall, shoulders back, trying to intimidate me.

We circled each other a couple of times, looking for an attack that would catch the other off guard, but we were starting to know each other now, and to understand how we thought and reacted. The fight was a conversation—one that revealed hidden aspects of our personalities that we likely didn't even recognise ourselves.

He decided on a direct tackle, running at me arms outspread, and instead of doing what I should have, which was to aim for a kick to the head, I braced myself to engage him. Our arms locked and I bitterly regretted not going for the kick. Was the killer instinct missing? If so, that was a weakness that would eventually prove fatal. I vowed not to hesitate next time. But locked together, hands clasped onto each other's shoulders and thumbs digging, feeling for the spot that would immobilise the other, we were engaged in a combat of strength. It was hard to say how long we stayed like that, each of us trying to drag the other down. It seemed like well over a minute.

I tried to draw him down to my right, groaning until there was no breath left, but he resisted. I drew in a deep breath as I felt him try the same manoeuvre, pulling me down to his right, and I wasn't sure I'd be able to withstand the pressure.

But I didn't have to.

'Time!' Oak boomed.

We push each other away and stood, gasping for air.

'Weapons!' he said, grinning. 'Play time is over!'

The sun was so low now it no longer shone onto the keep.

'What's happening down there?' I asked Oak.

'They won't be able to hold the gateway much longer.'

'Weapons?' Lady Armstrong asked.

'Machete,' Hunter said, staring straight at me.

I heard Flame and Cat gasp behind me.

'And you?'

'Fire,' I said.

'What? That's not a weapon.'

I looked up at her. 'It is. It's my choice. Fire is my weapon.'

'Prepare a torch, Hunter,' she ordered.

He narrowed his eyes at me before walking slowly to the far side of the platform to rummage in a chest. He came back with a torch, a small jerry can, and matches, which he dropped at my feet.

I gathered them and lit the torch.

The heat and the odour filled me with renewed force, making me feel lighter. The hiss of air being sucked into the flame roused me, making me hunger for destruction. I smiled. It must have been a maniacal smile, because when I looked at Hunter, I saw an expression of grave concern etched on his face.

He must have noticed that I saw fear in his eyes, because he took the machete and started twirling it around to intimidate me —and I have to admit, it worked. He was slicing a figure in the air between us. The whirring sound the machete made as it traced the infinity symbol through the air sent a chill through my body. But I wasn't planning on letting him reach me. My torch was longer than his machete, without including the flame itself, and I had to put that advantage to its fullest effect. If I failed to do that, he'd chop me to pieces.

The flame was burning furiously. It was hungry.

I drew a deep breath, sucking the familiar smell in and feeling the warmth of the fire against my face. I blew at the flame and stared past it at Hunter, watching the wild light flickering on his face.

I had a plan—the only one that could feasibly work with such a weapon. *My* weapon. My oldest friend. There would be no more hesitation.

'Fight to the death!' Lady Armstrong announced, her voice betraying her excitement.

He came at me fast this time, catching me off guard and preventing a counter-attack. He raised his machete to swipe at me diagonally from right to left, so I backed away, and kept backing away, holding the torch in front of me for protection. His swipe missed but he twisted his wrist and brought the machete swinging upwards at me, forcing me to back away even further. It occurred to me that I was dangerously close to the parapet.

I swiped at him with my torch, pretending to aim for his crotch, hoping only to provoke him even more.

It worked. He rushed me, forcing me against the sandbags, and I stretched out as far as I could, trying to take advantage of the extra reach I had, thrusting the torch at him. The flame reached its target and he released a blood-curdling scream that rang out across the hills.

He dropped the machete and raised his hands to what was left of his face.

I let go of the torch and grabbed him with both hands, pushing him up onto the parapet and wedging him on his back. All he

236

could do was thrash about blindly.

I avoided his flailing arms and shoved him with all my strength, sending him over the edge of the parapet.

The scream ended after a few seconds with a dull and sickening thud far below.

It had all happened so quickly, but not nearly as quickly as what happened next.

I turned to Flame, hoping we'd have a moment to hold each other and celebrate the fact that I was alive, but she was no longer looking at me. None of them were. Their gazes were fixed on the platform. They were shocked, but not horrified.

'Jump down, Arden!' Dray shouted.

I spun around to see her land on the roof, while up on the platform, Lady Armstrong's expression of stone shattered.

Arden ran straight towards Dray and Oak, seeking safety in their arms. She must have taken advantage of the instant Hunter had gone over the edge to act. Lady Armstrong would have been stunned and her right arm easy to push away. Now, she was furious, leaping down from the platform, knife clenched tightly.

Dray left Oak to hold Arden and lowered his pole-arm, but Arden wasn't the target. I was.

She came straight at me, seeming to float like a ghost along the floor, because her legs and feet were covered by her long scarlet dress. I didn't have time to retrieve either the torch or my axe, so I braced myself to take her on empty-handed.

But it was not to be. Cat intercepted, swinging her mace at the Lady, who deftly dodged the strike.

'You want to fight me, slave?'

'I want to kill you!' Cat hissed.

The Lady spread her arms wide, raising her slender shoulders and making the fur covering them look like it sighed. Then she adroitly tossed her knife from right hand to left and back again.

'But what will you do without me and my unborn child?' she asked, turning to us all. 'I'm the mother of a new world.'

'They don't want your world, you twisted bitch!' Cat yelled. 'It was a living hell here. Your reign of terror is over!'

'You'll end up at The Esplanade without me. You can count on that.'

'It can't be any worse than here,' Cat replied.

Lady Armstrong raised her eyebrows, then smiled cruelly. 'Can't it, Cat? You don't know what happens at The Esplanade, do you?' She laughed. 'I do, you fools. I know what lies in store for all of you.'

'What?' Flame asked.

'You don't want to know. It will drive you mad,' she said. 'It will push you over the edge.' She looked at the sandbag parapet.

'Tell us!' Flame yelled.

'Do you really want to know?'

This time, no one spoke.

She grinned as she looked at each of us in turn, taking delight in our bewilderment. Then, taking our silence as agreement, she told us.

The horror of her words left us thunderstruck.

'It's a lie!' Cat screamed, charging with her mace raised. But Lady Armstrong stopped the blow with her hands.

'It's the truth, whether you like it or not.' She ran to the inner side of the keep and looked down into the courtyard. 'I'm up here! Your Lady is in danger!'

Cat sprinted across to her, raising her mace again, and Lady Armstrong turned around as Cat swung. The mace struck her on the head and she dropped backwards onto a section of crumbled battlement. The top half of her body was hanging perilously over the edge.

Shouting could be heard from below, and as I rushed over, I heard another sound—the engine of the lorry.

By the time Flame and I had arrived, it was already too late. Cat had been trying to push the Lady over the edge, but in the struggle, she was stabbed several times.

'You bitch!' Cat hissed one last time as she slumped onto her former captor, her blood soaking the scarlet dress, and together, they slipped over the edge.

'Cat!' Flame screamed, dropping to her knees. 'No! Cat!'

But there was no point pleading with gravity.

I couldn't stop myself from looking down. The urge was too great.

They'd landed right next to the archer—three bodies now lay

sprawling by the stairs to the keep.

In the courtyard, the lorry was being driven around in circles. Lady Armstrong had been right. Her warriors had pushed their way back in, armed with superior discipline and strength.

Arden ran across the keep and took Flame in her arms, whispering that she was sorry, that she shouldn't have let herself get caught, and that it was all her fault. But Flame just wrapped her arms around her and cried.

'Flicker, leave them be!' Dray shouted. He was holding the torch in one hand and had his pole-arm and my axe in the other. 'We need to fight!'

We rushed down the stairs, using our shoulders to guide us against the walls more than relying on the light of the torch.

'Don't slip on the blood at the bottom!' I warned.

'Carver and Sylvan?' Oak asked.

'I'm afraid so,' I answered.

'She mentioned that,' he added darkly.

We rushed outside and tried to make sense of the scene. The lorry was still doing circles, with the three warriors on its tray shouting insults at the eight or so remaining Newtonians. The driver was trying to run over anyone in his path.

'We need to put the driver out of action!' Dray said.

'It's my turn to play the hero,' Oak announced, and he charged forward and tried to climb onto the lorry. A couple of others, seeing him, started cheering and followed suit. They hoisted themselves up onto the tray and the warriors tried to push them off again. The lorry hit a bump and two of them lost balance and tumbled off with two of ours, but Oak got up to the cabin and held tight. When the remaining warrior tried to hit him with his club, he kicked him hard, sending him hurtling along the tray. Dray killed the two who had fallen off with his pole-arm and I raced at an angle to intercept the lorry. I let go of my axe while I was running, and held the torch in one hand while I used the other to haul myself onto the tray.

'Get up here!' Oak yelled before leaning around to the already smashed driver's window. He started pounding the driver with his club.

I kicked the warrior on the tray to keep him down. This bought me enough time to work my way—practically crawling—towards Oak. When I reached him, I pulled myself up, holding the torch carefully, and he moved aside to make room for me.

'All yours, Flicker,' he boomed.

I tossed the torch into the cabin and the driver lost control, sending the lorry hurtling towards a section of wall. We held on tight, bracing for the impact.

Bang!

The shock was jarring and it took several seconds before Oak and I were able to get our heads straight enough to leap off the tray.

There was shouting and cheering all around. It sounded like a hundred voices, but I think there were only eight or nine of us left in the courtyard. I looked up at the keep, hoping Flame and Arden had witnessed the end of the battle, and was relieved to see their black silhouettes huddled together against the backdrop of the darkening sky.

When I looked back at the lorry, the cabin was fully ablaze— the driver's body slumped inside. Hungry flames had erupted from the smashed windows and windscreen and were licking the chipped black bodywork and rising into the chill night air. It was magnificent—just how I'd imagined.

Dray pulled the last warrior off the tray and brought his pole-arm down on him over and over again.

'Flicker, it's over,' Oak said loudly so he could be heard over the last warrior's final screams.

I stared into the flames. 'It is.'

'The time will come to celebrate, but we'll be faced with a sorry sight when the sun rises tomorrow.'

'I didn't think it would be like this, Oak. I really didn't.'

He sighed. 'I don't think any of us did.' He turned to Dray, who was giving the hacked-up body a kick for good measure. 'Except maybe him.'

All around the courtyard, the dead and wounded shimmered in the angry light, some motionless on the ground, others groaning in pain, and others trying to help them.

Dray limped over to us.

'You're hurt?' I asked him.

He shrugged. 'I don't even know when it happened. Probably just bruising. Don't worry about it. It means I'm still alive. Who's left?'

'That's the question,' Oak said. 'Where's Fern?' he called out, hoping she'd hear him.

'Dead,' a voice said from nearby. 'Fern, Grant, Xavier, Quark, Tara, and Heather—all dead.'

'Shit—' I heard myself whisper.

'We don't know who else didn't make it yet. They were vicious bastards!'

'That they were. Is that you, Raleigh?' Oak asked.

He approached and I recognised him even though we hadn't had the chance to get to know each other very well. Raleigh was one of the young men—barely in his twenties—who'd had no experience of fighting from what I gathered. Yet here he was, blood streaming from a gash on his head—despite his dogskin skullcap—and down past his chin. Only his welding goggles, which he had wiped clean, were untainted.

'How did that happen?' Dray asked, removing his own goggles and running a hand along the length of his sandy mane.

'I took a few blows to the head after they broke our line. We had to turn and run, most of us losing our weapons in the process. I had a hammer as a backup and charged one of them but he cracked me a solid blow on the head, following it up with another before I could fight back. Before I knew it, I was on the ground coming to. He must have been attacked by someone else or thought I was already dead. I don't know. Anyway, he was one of the three who eventually climbed onto the lorry.'

'You're tending to someone?' Dray asked, nodding towards where he'd been.

He shook his head slowly and removed his goggles. His eyes were red. 'I was trying to save Quark.'

Oak slumped beside me—his big shoulders sagging.

Three others approached, carrying someone in their arms, and Arden and Flame arrived in the courtyard.

'Everyone gather around!' Dray shouted, his voice echoing against the stone walls. 'It's time to do a headcount!'

'Who's that?' Arden asked, running up to the wounded person.

'Geordie,' he groaned in his distinctive accent. 'I feel like I got hit by a lorry.'

The three carrying him laughed. 'Funny that! You'll be right, mate,' one of them said.

Arden studied their faces in the firelight. 'Colby, Sparrow, and Hint. What a relief! Does anyone else need help?'

'There should be three more behind us,' Hint told her. 'Can you check?'

We all looked towards the easternmost wall and saw three figures stumbling towards us.

'Yes—you three get him inside,' Arden said. 'I'll help them. Dray, how about we get everyone inside and light a fire in the keep. It's not safe staying near the lorry.'

'You're right. It could blow up at any moment. We'll do a quick check to see if there's anyone else in need of help first.'

'Twelve,' Oak told Dray.

'Twelve out of eighteen,' he said. 'That's everyone accounted for according to what Raleigh reported. We came out of it better than them.'

'Cold comfort,' Oak grumbled. 'Let's do a quick check to make sure he didn't make a mistake.'

'I'll help Arden,' Flame said.

'I'll help you two,' I told Dray and Oak.

Now that the excitement and terror of the fray was over, it was hard to believe where we were, what we had done, and what we were doing. Looking back on it now, it feels like I was someone else—someone I didn't want to be. And yet, if the world was forcing me to be that person, I had to give in to him completely. I suppose that's what Dray had done. It was a matter of survival. There was no room in our lives for the luxury of self-reproach. We'd done what was required. I was a hero now, just as Cat was, and indeed all of us. We'd set the slaves free, and they hadn't hesitated to run. I wanted to hate them for their selfishness and cowardice, but I couldn't bring myself to do it. What did I know of their state of mind or what they'd been through? Not everyone was like Cat—that unbreakable resilience all the way to the bitter end. Or was it hatred that had seen her through and ushered in her demise?

242

I wanted to cry for her, but the tears wouldn't come. It wasn't yet the right time.

'Dead,' Dray muttered, inspecting Fern's body. She'd been run through with one of our own pole-arms. It stuck out of her chest at an angle. He went on to give an enemy body two heavy kicks. 'Dead,' he repeated.

And so that's where we were at—having invaded the castle and won, we now found ourselves checking that the bodies scattered around the courtyard really were dead, while the burning lorry roared and hissed into the cold night air and projected the dance of its firelight onto the walls.

Once we had fully ascertained there were no other survivors, I remembered the bodies on the ground floor of the keep.

'We'd better bring Carver and Sylvan outside,' I told them.

Oak hummed his agreement.

'Best get it done quickly,' Dray said, always aiming to be pragmatic, but I could tell by his voice that he was hurting. 'We'll pay our respects in the morning.'

When we entered the keep, we found Flame trying futilely to mop up all the blood with a blanket, but she hadn't touched their bodies.

'We'll take care of this, Flame,' I said. 'Are the others upstairs?'

'First floor. I'll help Arden with the others and light a fire. Can you light one on the second floor afterwards?'

'Will do,' I said. 'I'll also light one in her chamber.'

'Why?' Flame asked, dropping the blood-soaked blanket and looking confused.

'How many beds are there?' Oak asked.

'Six on the first floor, four on the second, and hers on the last one before the roof,' I said.

'You two are the only lovebirds here,' Oak said with a cheeky note that lifted our spirits a little.

'He's right, Flame.'

But she looked horrified. 'Wait a minute—no, I don't think I could sleep in her bed.'

'After everything you've done today that you never thought you could do?'

She looked at the swirls of blood smeared on the floor.

'Flame,' Dray said. 'I know I'm not the most sensitive soul in the world, but if I can offer you one word of advice, it's that we need to take care of ourselves as best we can tonight. We need to make sure we're warm and comfortable, and we have to keep an eye on Geordie. I'll help Arden do that. Whether any of us actually get any sleep, I don't know—probably not. What we need to do most of all, however hard it may be, is to leave our mourning for the morning.' He offered her the warmest smile he could manage. 'That's how I see it.'

Flame raised her eyebrows. 'This is a side of you I'd like to see more often, Dray.'

We laughed.

'I'll try. I promise.'

'Well said,' Oak told Dray, patting him on the shoulder. 'I don't know if any of you lot have much of an appetite, but I'm sure I can find some water and something to nibble around here. First, let's get these two outside while I've still got it in me. We'll give them a proper send-off tomorrow.' He drew a deep breath to avoid shedding tears.

'Let's get this over and done with,' Flame said, glancing at the blanket on the floor before hurrying upstairs.

We placed Carver and Sylvan next to Cat, laying her out on her back and closing her eyes while we were there. The archer and the Lady, we left as they were.

We then forced ourselves to keep moving. I went to light the fires while Dray and Oak began searching for provisions.

It was eerie on the second floor with those four impeccable beds waiting for their usual occupants. I couldn't help looking over my shoulder while I lit the fire, half-expecting them to come stumbling in, not quite dead after all. But the wood took to quickly. Once I was sure the fire wouldn't go out, I made my way up the spiral stairs to the Lady's chamber.

It wasn't so cold in there. The western wall had been repaired more painstakingly, and the long black drapes that covered it were in stark contrast with the tarpaulins on the lower levels. As I fanned the fire, I glanced around and knew Flame and I were bound to learn a lot about the room's former occupant by spending the night there.

The bed was placed with the head up against the northern wall, facing the door. In the eastern wall was the fireplace, which was connected to the chimney reaching from the ground floor, just like on the other floors. In the corner to my left, which must have been just below where the platform was on the roof, stood a desk with notebooks and a feather used for writing—I'm sure I'd read the word for this ancient instrument somewhere. There was a chair tucked under the desk.

I stopped fanning the fire, now crackling as it lapped a forked tongue around the topmost log from between the two beneath. As I stared at it, the lorry filled my mind. I saw the driver inside the cabin, being roasted alive, but when I tried to imagine his face, it was Hunter's I saw, with my torch thrust into it. It was a face that would haunt me forevermore.

I turned around. There were several fine animal skins on the floor in the middle of the chamber—whether they belonged to dogs, boar, or deer, I didn't know. Against the southern wall, between the door and the corner where the rebuilt western wall began, were an old wooden chest and a metal toolbox.

In the corner between the drape-covered western wall and the northern one, there was a dressing screen with a floral design printed or painted on it—pink roses, or faded red ones. Clothes were draped over a simple metal chair with a cushion, and a candelabrum stood by a small mirror hanging on the wall.

It looked how I'd always imagined the elegant chamber of a lady would be. Nothing about it shouted murderous slave-driving psychopath.

I had one desire at that moment, despite the state of physical and mental exhaustion I was in, despite the horror I had witnessed—and committed, and despite the sadness welling up inside me that I had to hold at bay until morning, as Dray had rightly advised. That overriding urge was to explore—to open those chests and sit at the desk and read the texts that dreadful hand—the very same that had held a knife at Arden's throat and plunged it repeatedly into Cat—had written. But I had to do it with Flame, if she was up to it.

I went downstairs to see how everyone was getting on and whether Oak and Dray had found some water.

'We found their kitchen,' Oak informed me when I arrived in the second-floor quarters. 'Had to break the door down to get in. There's also a small storage room connected to it. We found three jerry cans full of fuel in it.'

'Jackpot,' I said. 'We should take them back to Newton.'

'Nice up there in her chamber?' Dray asked, passing me a cup of water.

'Disgustingly so. I want to rummage around with Flame.'

'Not sure she'll be in the mood,' Oak quipped, giving her a sideways look.

She laughed. 'Not tonight. But when Flicker says "rummage", I suspect he's talking about insight into who she was and why she turned out the way she did.'

'I am indeed.'

'That could be useful,' Dray said. 'You'll report back in the morning, before we honour the lives of our fallen?'

I nodded, and we stood in silence for a moment.

'The wounded are downstairs?'

'Yes,' Flame said. 'We think they'll be fine. Arden's quite the nurse, as well as being an excellent hunter.'

'Some women have it all,' Dray replied sullenly.

'Let's get some rest then,' Oak said. 'We need to try, at least.'

'Tomorrow won't be easy,' Dray added. 'It will, however, be an important day. We've long been survivors, but we will wake as victors. We will be different people, and there's no looking back.'

He was right. Tomorrow would be the dawning of a new age.

21. Insight

'I can't decide whether this is a privilege I'm unworthy of or a punishment I suspect I deserve without knowing precisely why,' Flame told me as we entered Lady Armstrong's chamber.

'Neither,' I assured her. 'It's because we're a couple. That's all. It's that simple. I get the impression they give more weight to that here than people did in the city. I find it admirable. Even if Dray rubbed them up the wrong way, everyone recognised and respected Tara and Heather's relationship.'

'Don't say their names tonight, Flicker,' she begged me, her green eyes more sombre than I'd ever seen them before. 'I just can't.'

'Of course. I'm sorry.'

'She shouldn't have come,' Flame said, knowing I'd understand who she was talking about. 'She should have stayed in Newton and helped Dahlia with her work.'

She was fighting back tears, keeping them for the morning, but we both knew neither of us would get through the night without shedding a few.

'No one could have made her stay behind, Flame, even if they wanted to. This was her fight, first and foremost.'

'Get undressed and stand by the fire. I'll wipe you off,' she told me, keen to take our minds off the dead. 'Arden prepared these damp rags for us. She made one for everyone from an old tablecloth Oak and Dray found in the kitchen.'

She held the rags in front of the fire for a while to take the cold edge off them and I removed my bloodied clothes.

'Look at your leg,' she said, an expression somewhere between a frown and a smirk on her face.

I looked down at my left thigh, where Hunter had kicked me.

A reddish bruise covered the front just above the knee.

'Funny, is it?'

She looked me in the eye and said, 'You're alive. Let me laugh, will you?' Then she slapped the rag onto my face and wiped it clean. It felt good.

'Did you ever think we'd take control of a castle and sleep in the main chamber one day?' she asked, moving down to my aching arms.

'I most certainly did not,' I admitted. 'Then again, I couldn't have imagined I'd ever meet a woman like you not so long ago.'

'Was it fate that brought us together?' she wondered.

'Well, I don't know about fate but those tracker drones played a major role.'

She smiled, wiping my abdomen with long strokes all the way from chest to groin and noticing my involuntary reaction—one I couldn't prevent even though we both knew tonight would be a night of tenderness and consolation, and nothing more.

Once she'd cleaned my body, I undressed her, admiring the way the firelight caressed her skin, painting transient patterns. She hadn't been involved in much of the fighting, having been forced to watch on powerlessly as I duelled with Hunter, and for that I was grateful. There were the inevitable small bruises here and there on her body, but she was otherwise unharmed.

'Do you want me to clean your hair?'

'There's not much point. I'll have a proper bath when we get back to Newton. I want to keep growing it longer. What do you think?'

'I'd like to see that,' I said, wiping her face gently, following the contours of her nose, cheeks, and lips. 'Long like Arden's or really long like Dahlia's.'

'I'll start with Arden's length and then we'll see, I guess. I'll never be as beautiful as either of them anyhow.'

'What are you talking about? You're easily as beautiful as they are.'

'Even Dahlia?' she asked sceptically. 'You can't honestly tell me that.'

'Well, you're all beautiful in your own way. I'm no Oak either.'

She laughed. 'You're man enough for me. Dahlia can keep her

tree.'

I wiped her shoulders and her breasts, even though they were clean. I could feel the tension leave her body.

'It seems like it's been so long since we've slept alone together,' she said.

'Doesn't it? When in fact it was just a few days ago, in what we thought would be our new home.'

'We'll see what happens. I can't imagine leaving them after this. When you shed blood together, I guess you form a special bond. Like you said, Flicker, they're a band of brothers and sisters.'

'We're stronger together. That's for sure,' I said. 'But you know, I think this chamber is growing on me. Perhaps we could come back here from time to time. They used to have these "weekend getaways" back before The Breakdown. People would sometimes leave their usual houses and stay in the countryside on a Friday and Saturday night.'

Flame shook her head. 'They must have been happy times.'

I continued down, following her body as it curved between her legs.

'Here?'

'Softly,' she said, smiling but with a look of mild reproach in her voice.

I caressed her slowly and she groaned lowly for a moment before whispering, 'Not tonight, Flicker.'

'No. It's not right,' I agreed, moving down to her legs and then making my way back up behind her.

'You know you're perfect,' I whispered in her ear.

She grinned, then a darkness appeared and it melted into a frown. I knew exactly what she was thinking.

'Flame, stay by the fire,' I said more loudly, eager to lighten her mood.

I went over to the wooden chest and opened it.

'Just as I thought,' I said, taking a long, soft dressing gown for her. It was violet and smelled of dried herbs and wild flowers, with a vague hint of citrus and mint.

'Thank you,' she said, spreading her arms for me to put it on her. 'Is there anything for you?'

'I'll wrap myself in a blanket. That will do.'

She strolled over to the candelabrum and took it to the fire to light it.

Once I'd draped a blanket over my shoulders, I started looking through the metal toolbox. It was neatly arranged with a motley assortment of toiletries, accessories, and utensils that included hairbrushes, nail scissors, earrings, and daggers.

'Do you need earrings, Flame?'

She was standing by the dressing screen again and turned to look at me, eyebrows raised. 'You're asking me if I want to wear the earrings of the woman who—?' She couldn't bring herself to say it.

'Ah, yeah. Forget I asked.'

'Forgotten. Hey, do you know what's behind the screen?'

I said the first thing that came to mind. 'A bathtub?'

'Spot on. She must have had hot water carried up here to fill it.'

'All right for some, I guess,' I said, imagining her in there, and remembering that grin on Hunter's face when she suggested her unborn child could have been his. She must have known how to please men.

'Are you picturing her in there, Flicker?'

'I'm trying not to,' I replied, and it was true.

'Try harder,' was all she said, stony-faced.

There wasn't much to learn from what was in the toolbox other than what I already knew—that she paid careful attention to her physical appearance and didn't hesitate to stab people.

'What happened to her?' Flame asked, looking at herself in the mirror. 'How did she become a monster?'

'You heard what she said up there,' I said, looking up to the ceiling. 'She didn't consider herself a monster. She thought she was doing what had to be done.'

Flame spun around, readjusting her gown as though feeling cold or exposed, despite the fact that the chamber was slowly getting warmer.

'You didn't buy all that, did you?'

'I think that's what she believed. That's my point. In her mind, she was building an empire that would eventually be strong enough to confront the regime.'

'An empire built on slavery!' Flame almost shouted.

I shrugged. 'Like they all were back when the masses were still considered useful. She was a monster, and no one's going to argue with you about that, but if we're going to try to understand her, we can't ignore the point that she thought she was a good— a *magnificent*—leader.'

'I suppose so. We have to try to get inside her head.' She turned back to the mirror and stared into it, searching for that face it knew so intimately, but finding only her own reflected. 'She honestly believed she would be the founder of a great empire.'

'She was insane,' I said, walking over to Flame and holding her from behind.

She dropped her head back onto my shoulder.

'What she said about The Esplanade,' Flame began, and I could hear the dread in her heart carried in those words. 'It can't be true.'

She raised her head again and looked at my eyes in the mirror.

'We have to assume it is,' I said, and the hollowness in my voice chilled me.

'If that's so, our friends from the city—'

'It won't happen to us, Flame.'

'You don't know that.'

'We'll choose how the curtain falls. The only choice we have is whether to hide in the woods for as many years as we're to be allotted, knowing that a drone might locate us one day, or to discover The Esplanade for ourselves and watch it burn.'

'Even if it's the last thing we ever do?'

I nodded. 'Even if.'

'If she spoke the truth, we have no choice. We've both been fighters all our lives. That's who we are.'

'We're firestarters, and that's the ultimate target. It will be the biggest thrill of all.'

'I know you're right. We can't turn back now. We owe it to all those who didn't make it this far,' she said, still looking at our tired faces in the mirror.

I turned to look across the bed to the desk in the corner.

'Time to delve into that mind?' Flame asked.

I took the candelabrum and the metal chair and carried them to the desk.

'Look at all this paper stacked on the floor,' I said, pointing under the desk. 'There must be hundreds of sheets. I'm going to take it all back to Newton. Perhaps not tomorrow, but one day.'

'What are you planning on writing—your memoirs?'

I didn't answer. It was still the germ of an idea.

We sat there together in silence, looking over the desk, then Flame pulled the bottom notebook from a pile of five.

'Starting at the beginning?' I asked.

'That's my plan.'

There were several sheets of paper in front of me, bound together with string. I undid the bow and began reading, realising quickly that each page contained a list of tasks to be completed.

'You'll tell me if you read anything interesting?' I asked Flame.

'This is a private journal,' she said, keeping her eyes on the page. 'It sounds like she's from the north.'

'How far north?'

'She came from a town along the old border. When it was cleared out, some of the inhabitants fled north into the mountains, thinking it would be easier to hide there, but most of them came south where the winters wouldn't be so cold.'

'What mountains? I wonder if she means the highlands. That's a very long way.'

Flame shrugged. 'She came south with her father and brother.'

'What happened to them?'

Flame kept reading. 'It doesn't say, but she talks about building a new society to fight back. She says that's what they do—the people from the border. Her father had taught her and her brother to resist.' She kept reading. 'She's the only one left who can rise to the challenge.'

She paused, lost in thought.

'But why slavery?' I asked.

'No mention of that yet.'

I took the top notebook and started reading, figuring we could meet halfway between the beginning and the end of her story. I flicked through most of the pages, noticing her habit of detailing seemingly trivial events, but ones that obviously meant a lot to her—a woman intent on controlling every minute aspect of her burgeoning empire. Other passages were more revealing about her strategy and how she'd kept a tight rein over the men who served her. One particular passage in the second notebook I read caught my attention.

'Listen to this, Flame.'

'Yes?'

'These four illiterate and savage men I found living like fetid animals in the castle were about to rape me. I could see it in their eyes when they glanced at each other between the inane questions they were flinging at me. I could also tell which one was their leader, if such a title could be bestowed upon a brute like that. He would be the one to open proceedings. The others wouldn't surrender to their base urges until he had unleashed his beast within.'

'She was raped,' Flame said quietly, as though that explained it all.

'No,' I said, and continued reading aloud. 'I slashed his throat, pushed him to the ground and asked who was next. The look in their eyes was priceless. I knew I had to set the terms immediately. I had to earn their loyalty. I had to promise them a better life than the one they had. No big challenge. They would be the guardians and founders of my empire, placed above all those we would convince to join us.'

'Convince to join us,' Flame repeated, shaking her head. 'Their loyalty was kept through sex?'

'As long as I shared myself with each of them on different nights, and contingent upon their faithful service, they would remain committed to the cause. Most importantly, if I were to fall pregnant, not knowing who the father was, they would all be treated as the father to the heir. It was a simple plan, but it would work—them being simple men in search of a little pleasure and comfort in return for their allegiance.'

'Cunning,' Flame said. 'But—there's no way I could have done it.'

'Are you sure? You don't think you'd have done the same under the circumstances?'

'Sharing my bed with three of those brutes? The very thought of it disgusts me. I don't think I'd have even been capable of coming up with a scheme like that. She's a natural manipulator.'

'Yes. That's the picture I have of her. She was born to lead.'

'And born to come tumbling down,' Flame added. 'Cat was born to bring her down. We were merely the means.' She fell silent. She hadn't meant to speak her name. 'What do you think?'

'I'm not sure we were born to do this, that, or the other. It's our choice to make.'

I stood and walked to the window overlooking the courtyard. There was no sign of fire now. The lorry and the corpses of the fallen were lost in the cold void of night. I craned my neck to look up but saw no stars. I couldn't even make out where the hill ended and the open sky began.

'Let's try to see if there are any more in-depth references to The Esplanade and go to bed if there aren't.'

I paused by the fire, put another log on, and opened my blanket to let the heat brush my naked body and ease my stiff joints. Then I went back to the desk.

We flipped through the pages, scanning, but we turned to each other blank-faced in the end.

'It's as though she didn't dare write about it,' Flame mused. 'Did she say she'd been there?'

'She said she knew what happened there,' I said. 'I don't remember her saying how she knew.'

'How else could she know?'

'One of her warriors could have been there and escaped to tell the tale.'

Flame didn't reply.

'If that's what happened, that's encouraging.'

'How so?' she asked.

'It means we can go there and make it back alive.'

She went over to the fire, folded her arms, and gazed into it. 'The only place I want to go now is into that bed. I don't care whose ghosts are in there. We're alive. We're both alive tonight, and that's all that matters.'

She let the gown drop to the floor and climbed into the bed. 'Hold me in your arms.'

I did. I held her until she fell asleep.

22. The Funeral Pyre

We slept in fits and starts that night, waking each other without meaning to whenever we emerged from our troubled dreams. Sleeping in unfamiliar surroundings is often an uneasy affair, even when it has become a habit. When it's in the most comfortable bed you've ever known, with the embers of a fire within sight, the feeling is even stranger. You keep telling yourself you should be having the best night's sleep of your life. And yet, we tossed and turned, and sat up in the dark to watch the glowing embers stare back at us like the eyes of imps.

Lady Armstrong's presence was all around—it was as if she were there with us, haunting the chamber. I hadn't got close enough to smell her scent—perhaps I would be in the morning when the time came to put her on the funeral pyre—but the chamber had its own unique scent, that of the dried herbs and wild flowers that had soaked into the violet dressing gown. Her scent was surely the same, the aroma of various wild plants intermingled with her unique body odour.

Flame and I didn't speak during those moments when we were awake together, sensing that to utter a word would break the spell of sleep for the remainder of the night. Instead, I would put my arms around her and stroke her hair until I was quite certain she'd fallen asleep again.

I woke to hear her whimpering softly every now and then—as though she was crying in her dreams—but a kiss on the forehead or cheek made her stop.

I think we were both eager for dawn, no matter how sore and tired we were. We were looking forward to getting the harrowing day that awaited us over and done with.

When I noticed the wind was picking up, whistling beyond the imperfectly-fitted windows and making something tap behind the draped wall, I knew dawn was approaching. I slipped out of bed, donned the blanket like a cape, and went to the eastern window.

The outline of the hill was faint but unmistakeable. The first rays of the new day would already be brushing the treetops on the other side. I was torn between knowing Flame needed me by her side and the inexplicable urge to climb that final stretch of staircase to the roof of the keep, to observe the sun glide gracefully over the ridge and to see—as morbid as it would be—the carnage in the courtyard from above before inspecting it close-up at ground level.

I crept back to Flame, close enough to tell by her breathing that she was sleeping quite soundly, then tiptoed to where I thought the door to be, and found it.

It opened and closed with only the faintest creak.

The whistling of the wind was a steady howl on the roof, reminding me vaguely of the sound of machinery I'd sometimes heard in the city in powerhouses I'd wrongly assumed were abandoned. But on the roof, my blanket tightly wrapped around me, I was alone with the elements. The darkness was complete except for wan white and shades of grey in the eastern sky.

I stood in the middle of the roof, driven most likely by a semi-conscious awareness that being close to the sides was dangerous in the dark, especially when the keep had already claimed four lives. Standing there, where the fight to the death I could still hardly believe I'd won had begun, I ran through those terrible events in my mind, struggling to put them in the right order and asking myself if I'd made a mistake. The knife to Arden's throat had prevented us from acting freely. My duel with Hunter had been the only way out. But that's where the ifs began. If I hadn't chosen fire, would I have survived? If I hadn't succeeded in my plan to push him over the sandbag parapet, would Arden have had the chance to escape? If I hadn't made these decisions, would Cat be alive? Would Arden be dead? Would we all be dead?

The wind was biting my sore body through the blanket, so I stepped back into the shelter over the entrance to the stairwell.

The answers to these questions eluded me. Lady Armstrong

would never have left the castle alive. That I knew. And while she'd been delusional with regards to the grand scheme of things, she'd proved brilliant when it came to attending to details and analysing matters of a pressing nature. She'd been fully aware of her predicament and the outcome. There would have been only one objective in mind—not to go down alone, and who better to take with her than Cat, the rabble-rousing slave behind it all?

Perhaps I could have acted more decisively when Cat charged at her. I might have been able to save her. I'll never know. But it was their fight, not mine. Man against man. Woman against woman. It couldn't have been any other way.

'Flicker?'

I nearly jumped out of my skin.

'Oak?'

'I asked first,' he replied with a laugh, and I made room for him at the top of the stairs. 'Revisiting the battleground?'

'Running it all through my head.'

'I'll tell you the truth if you want to hear it.'

'Let me guess,' I said. 'You would have put your money on him, to use an obsolete expression.'

'Sorry, but that about sums it up. How wrong I was! You and your fire form a hell of an opponent. So, here you stand, a champion!'

'I don't feel like a champion.'

'What! You make me want to pummel you just for saying that. Dray's jealous as hell everyone's going to be talking about you from now on. I have to admit I would be as well if I believed in jealousy.'

'You would have massacred him,' I assured him.

'I know. I wouldn't have pussyfooted around like you did. That said, you got the job done. No one can fault you there. I don't think I would have tossed him over the side like that. You're a madman!' He laughed. 'And I mean that in the best of ways.'

'It was my fight. I did what I could.'

'It was, and Cat's was hers.'

I looked at him, but I don't think he could see my face in the dark.

'I was thinking about that.'

'Naturally. That's because you're a good man, Flicker—like me. Our problem is we doubt ourselves too much.'

'You doubt yourself?'

'Sure I do. I try to hide it though, for everyone else's sake. Good men do that too. I'm telling you now, you did what had to be done. You won your fight and somehow enabled Arden to save herself at the same time. If it had been me or Dray, it mightn't have ended like that. Cat chose to attack. It was her fight. She wanted revenge and she wanted it to be personal. It was her call—not yours, not mine.'

'Thanks, Oak.'

'There's no thanking about it, brother.' He gave me slap on the back that nearly knocked me over.

'Why did you come up here?' I asked.

'Couldn't stand being locked up with the snoring wounded any longer. You feeling better?'

'A little sore, but I'll be fine.'

'Sleep well in her chamber?'

'The bed's very comfortable. It was a peculiar experience all the same.'

'And?'

'And what? No, Oak, we just slept.'

He laughed into the wind. 'I wasn't asking about your intimate dealings. That's between you two, just as the spectacular sex I have with Dahlia is my private business. I'm asking about the rifling through the Lady's belongings.'

'Of course. I'm an idiot.'

I told him what we'd discovered, and he whistled lowly—almost imperceptibly against the wind—in all the right places.

'We could have used a woman like that,' Oak said once I'd finished. 'If only she hadn't been so messed up.'

'What she said about The Esplanade—do you think it's true?'

Oak didn't reply for a moment. Then he said, 'I think it probably is, Flicker. It fits their programme, doesn't it? They call the useless masses savages, even though they're the ones who made us this way. They hate us for what they made us. It's absurd. This, I guess, is their way of fixing the problem.'

I shivered and pulled the blanket tighter around me, but the cold remained.

'Talking about being good men, I suggest we go down to the courtyard and try to get it cleaned up before the women wake, and before the crows start looking for breakfast. Dray will be up soon. Arden too, I'd say.'

'The sooner, the better,' I said.

'You might want to sneak into the chamber and get dressed though. It looks like you're wearing a blanket. Or is that a trick of the light?'

'No trick,' I admitted with a laugh.

We went down the stairs and Oak waited outside the chamber while I got dressed.

'Flicker?' Flame whispered.

'I didn't want to disturb you. Go back to sleep.'

'I was already awake—more or less. What are you doing?'

'I'm with Oak. We're going to start making preparations.'

'I'll be down soon,' she said.

'Take your time. Wait for Arden. I'm sure she'll come to you once she's awake.'

'All right.'

I joined Oak on the stairs and we descended.

There was enough daylight to find our way around the courtyard. The lorry, breathing fire like a dragon after the battle, was now a blackened carcass, as lifeless as the body inside it and those scattered nearby.

'We should put the enemy dead in a pile,' I suggested, 'and arrange those of ours who aren't too badly disfigured. The others may want to see them. In the city, we don't have many dead. We disappear into thin air. Do you have a special ritual?'

'Like you said, Flicker, we try to make them presentable before lighting the fire. I was thinking we could pile the enemy onto the lorry, pack some wood under it, and set it alight again. We'll make a proper pyre for ours.'

'Ready when you are. Let's start with ours. I don't want Flame to see Cat crumpled at the foot of the keep when she comes down.'

We laid them out in the middle of the courtyard, closed their eyes, and did what we could to cover their wounds. Oak pulled the arrows out of Lark's shoulder and head. We both had to look away and take a step back to stop ourselves from being sick. We put Tara and Heather together, and I spread furs from an enemy warrior across their midsections to hide the horrendous wounds made by our pole-arms.

'Leave some work for us!' Dray called, striding up with Raleigh at his side.

'Plenty more to do,' Oak said. 'Are the girls up?'

'They're checking the patients.'

'Is Geordie all right?' I asked.

'Put it this way,' Dray said. 'He came out of it in better shape than the lorry.'

'On that topic,' Oak said. 'I was saying we should pile the enemy dead on the tray and build a pyre around it.'

'What not just leave them to rot?' Dray asked, shrugging.

'I'm not leaving anyone to rot,' Oak said sternly.

'For our sakes, not theirs, right?' Dray challenged.

'For ours,' Oak replied. 'To remind ourselves that we are and always will be better than them. We're not savages.'

'You heard the man, Rale. Let's toss them onto the tray.'

Once the only traces of battle left were patches of blood-stained earth and the troughs made by the lorry's tyres, we began stacking the pyres. Oak and I built the central one for our dead, and Dray and Raleigh set about building the enemy's. I kept four small bundles of arrows and splintered wood for kindling.

Oak stretched his back and arms, looking contemplatively at the broad pyre. It was about two feet high, six feet wide, and ten long. We didn't have enough ready wood to make it longer, which meant we wouldn't be able to lay the bodies out side by side.

'Let's pay our fallen friends the respect they deserve and get back to Newton,' Oak said loudly enough for Dray and Raleigh to hear.

'I'll go and see how they're doing inside,' Dray said.

Raleigh came over but stared forlornly at the seven bodies lined up on the ground.

'How's your head?' I asked him.

'It hurts,' he said, pulling his gaze away from the corpses. 'It means I'm alive.'

'It does,' Oak agreed.

'I hear we missed a legendary duel up there.'

'You've heard all about it?' I asked, looking at Oak.

'He's a hell of a storyteller, our Oak, even if it wasn't your standard bedtime story. All true? He has a habit of exaggerating.'

'I do not, and that'll be the last time I tell you a story if that's what you think, boy.'

'Did it involve a knife to Arden's throat, a flaming torch, and the Lady's champion being cast off the keep?'

'Yeah.'

'All true then.' I looked up. 'You couldn't see any of it from here.'

'I saw Cat and the Lady fall,' he said quietly. 'I'll never forget that.'

'There'll be no forgetting,' Oak said, 'but we'll all have to move on. This is only the lesser of two evils we've defeated.'

'They're coming,' I said. 'My vote is that we let Arden attend to proceedings if she's willing.'

'Seconded,' Oak said.

'She'll know what to say,' Raleigh added, staring at the bodies again.

'You and Flame should light the fires,' Oak said.

I nodded.

Flame and Arden had also donned the clothes they'd worn in battle. I knew Flame would have found the idea of wearing one of Lady Armstrong's dresses to the funeral repugnant.

'Good morning. Everyone well?' Oak asked.

His greeting was met with unenthusiastic replies, but no one dared complain. That would have been an affront to the memory of the dead.

He turned to Arden, and she took the cue.

'Gather around, everyone,' she instructed. 'Firstly, let me make it clear that this is a dark and difficult day for us all. There are no obligations or expectations. If you wish to see the deceased, you may do so now. If you would rather remember them as they were, full of life and determination, stand back. We will all honour them—' She paused, fighting back tears. 'We will each

261

honour them and say farewell in our own way.'

Flame approached the bodies, wiping her tears away as she stopped at Cat's feet. She turned to me briefly and nodded, acknowledging the effort I'd made to make her presentable. In a way, Cat was more dignified in death than she had been in life. I hated to think of it that way, but the impression was inescapable.

Arden also approached, kneeling to touch each of them softly on a foot or knee.

The men were more reticent, but they ended up following Flame and Arden's example.

'It will be a slow walk back to Newton but we must make it today,' Arden announced. 'Everyone will be waiting impatiently. We'll have time to reminisce around the fire tonight. What do you say?'

Everyone agreed. We were all eager to return to Newton.

'Dray,' Oak said, 'will you do the honours with me?'

He nodded solemnly and we watched as they began, lifting Lark and placing him on the pyre.

Once the dead were all arranged with as much decorum as conditions permitted, Oak turned to me. 'Flicker and Flame will now light the pyre.'

Flame wiped her tears away, and for an instant I thought she'd refuse, but she didn't. She knelt with me and we lit the first of the four bundles—one for each side of the pyre.

The flames rose quickly, sending smoke billowing into the sky, where it was carried on the wind. Another reason not to stay too much longer. The coast was a long way off, but if a drone happened to turn the right way for its camera to pick up the smoke, we'd be in trouble.

I left Flame there to watch our fire with the others while I went to the lorry to set it alight.

'Their lives were sacrificed for the worthiest of causes,' Arden continued, speaking loudly so all of us could hear over the wind and the growing roar of the fire. 'Our brothers and sisters gave their lives fighting so that others would be free of the shackles of oppression, and while we'd all like to lock a day like yesterday away in the vaults of our memories, never to be suffered again, we know that will not be the case—the war against tyranny is one we can only dream of winning, but one we must never dream of giving up.'

She looked around, smiling at us all, and nodded to me as I returned from the lorry—and she looked at that second fire over my shoulder, an expression not so much of hatred, but of bitter regret on her face.

'Goodbye, dear friends,' she spoke into the fire.

'Farewell, brothers and sisters. We'll be with you soon,' Dray said solemnly.

'No shackle will ever bind you,' Oak told them.

The two fires raged, their heat and strength making a mockery of the feeble rising sun. We stood mesmerised.

'Let's get ready for the trudge home,' Arden said eventually, breaking the spell. 'Everyone's going to jump on us for news, but your priority is to look after yourselves first. We'll get cleaned up and check your wounds. I'll announce who didn't make it back, though I guess it's hardly going to be necessary—they'll see who comes through the gate and who doesn't.'

23. The Map

We hardly spoke a word during the march home, only communicating for practical purposes. We took turns helping Geordie, who was badly bruised and limping heavily. The others were able to walk without difficulty, their injuries mostly to the head and arms. Raleigh had looked terrible after the battle, with blood covering his face, but his head wound wasn't so bad after all.

We took a less arduous route back to Newton and it was late afternoon by the time we arrived. Someone had been keeping watch and opened the gate for us as we approached. When we entered, everyone stopped what they were doing and crowded around, cheering and fussing and looking from one to the other, trying to work out who wasn't there.

Dahlia and Blossom ran out of their cottage, still clutching a quilt they'd been working on tight in their hands. They ran over to Oak, Dahlia's bosom bouncing and Blossom skipping with joy with a childish abandon I'd not yet seen in her. Dahlia wrapped her arms around her big man as best she could and kissed him passionately while Blossom hugged him from behind.

Everyone cheered, lost in that moment of pure relief and joy.

But it didn't last long.

'Tara and Heather?' someone asked.

Arden shook her head.

'They shouldn't have gone,' another voice said.

'It was their choice,' Dray replied. 'They insisted on fighting. No one forced them. They're together now, forevermore, and they died a heroic death.'

'Carver and Sylvan didn't make it?' Dahlia asked Oak, and he shook his head.

'Neither did Fern.'

'Fern's dead?' Dahlia asked, not wanting to believe him, and I saw the tears well in her beautiful eyes.

'Where's your friend?' someone asked Flame. 'Where's Cat?'

It was like pulling a trigger. She burst into tears.

The sight took a weight off my shoulders. She'd been keeping it all bottled up and I knew it couldn't go on like that. She had to let it out. But this feeling of relief on my part immediately gave way to a wave of guilt, and I had to tell myself the relief was normal—just as her tears were. Whatever we felt was a natural part of the grieving process.

'Listen to me,' Arden said loudly and firmly, and everyone fell silent. 'We will tell you what happened in detail around the fire tonight. We need to wash and rest, and I have to attend to the wounded. I know you're all impatient to hear our account of the battle, but you have to wait just a little longer. Know that we were victorious.'

They cheered again.

'One question first, Arden. Just one,' Dahlia said. 'We were all expecting you to bring the slaves here. Where are they?'

'They fled when the battle began.'

An uncomfortable silence fell, and I could feel all eyes turn to Flame and me, as though accusing us of their cowardice. After all, we were the ones who brought news of the castle's existence here with Cat in the first place.

'It's disappointing,' Dray announced, 'but it doesn't take away from our victory. We all fought bravely against an enemy that had to be annihilated. That is what matters. Tonight, we will eat and drink heartily, raise a toast to the fallen, and raise another to the future of Newton, home of the fearless rebels.'

They roared in response and Dray soaked up the praise.

'Have you hunted?' he asked once the cheering had subsided.

'We netted a few birds.'

'That will do nicely. Let us wash and rest,' Arden said. 'I'll put my crossbow to work hunting tomorrow.'

Everyone went back to their tasks.

Arden approached us and said quietly, 'Would you like to have Tara and Heather's cottage?'

The directness of the question took me by surprise, but she was right, we could have our own home. Arden was simply being practical. All the same, I could see it bothered Flame a great deal.

'I couldn't,' she said.

'It's up to you.'

'They're dead—'

'No, Flame,' Arden cut her short. 'They're not dead because of you. Chase that thought from your mind. The Lady and her men are the only ones responsible. We would have crossed paths with them eventually—of that, you can be sure—and if they'd found us and brought the fight to us on their terms, well, it could have turned out a lot worse. You and Flicker did what had to be done, and so did we. Now, go to your cottage and make yourselves at home. Draw and heat water for your bath and get some rest.'

'Thank you, Arden,' she said.

'There's no thanking about it. We're sisters now.'

Flame smiled and wiped tears from her cheeks.

'Look after her,' Arden told me. 'Look after each other and enjoy the good times while you can, because darker days than yesterday lie in wait. Of that, we can be sure.'

We bathed and rested, not falling asleep, but lying in our cottage and getting used to the idea that it was now ours. We were not thieves or imposters, but the worthy new occupants of the humble cottage. We told ourselves that as we lay there, holding each other, feeling both relieved and guilty, but above all thankful that we'd both made it back to Newton.

The festivities that night were a merry affair, everyone doing their best to set their sadness aside. Oak recounted the adventure in detail, holding his audience spellbound as he described the scene on top of the keep.

I could sense Dray's jealousy as they toasted my triumph, but he hid it behind smiles and cheers and the raising of his goblet in my honour.

There was plenty of bird meat for everyone. It tasted different from dog, and it was hard to say which we preferred, but we ate it and enjoyed it along with a generous serving of stew and plenty of beer.

It was growing late when Dray came to me and filled my goblet with beer. 'Can I borrow your champion for a minute, Flame?'

She hesitated before accepting.

'Come and talk to Oak with me.'

'What's going on, Dray?'

'I just want to strike while the iron's hot.'

His words sounded ominous, and I knew what he was going to suggest.

'Oak, let's talk,' he said quietly.

'What about?' Dahlia asked.

'Men's business,' Dray replied.

'Let's step outside,' Oak said.

We left the warmth of the hall for the chill silence of night.

'These slaves who disappeared into thin air,' Dray began. 'Where are they?'

'What does it matter?' Oak answered. 'You said so yourself, Dray. We went into battle and seized the day.'

'That's what I said and that's how I see it, but what happens to them? They're free now, but for how long? They have nowhere to go. They didn't stick around to see whether they could trust us. They probably think we're another band of rival slave drivers. The second they got a whiff of freedom, they legged it. But where will they go?'

'Perhaps they'll find the town where Flame and I were and stay there,' I said.

'You and Flame are smart. You made it all the way here from the city. Your friends from the city didn't. Where are they?'

'They're probably being transported to The Esplanade,' I told him, losing my patience and telling him what he wanted to hear.

'That's exactly right, and now we know what fate they'll meet there,' he went on. 'If they haven't been caught yet, they soon will be. I'd give them a day or two—a week at most. If we don't act quickly, we'll have saved them for nothing. I can't have that on my conscience. They're not fighters like us—the three of us in particular. Without our help, they're doomed.'

'We can't wander all over the countryside looking for them,' Oak said.

Dray reached into a pocket and removed a piece of paper, which he unfolded and held up for us to see. Despite the gloom,

I could make out what it was.

'A map?' Oak asked.

'You got it,' Dray replied, and he opened the door to the hall just enough to let a strip of lamplight seep out. He held the map under the light.

'I found it in the castle. See the red circle some way down the coast?'

'The Esplanade?' I asked.

'It has to be!' Dray said.

'What's all this?' Oak asked, indicating two lines that appeared to represent a long road stretching across the map from the red circle to the opposite side. At one point about halfway, two simple pictures had been sketched—an eye and a pistol.

'It's an access road leading from the city,' I said. 'Cameras and armed guards.'

'That's what I took it to be,' Dray said.

'Without a doubt,' Oak agreed.

'This is the supply chain,' Dray explained slowly, letting his words sink in. 'This is how The Esplanade's needs are met. Do you understand what I'm saying?'

'We can't risk going anywhere near this road,' I warned Dray.

He gave me a wicked smile. 'Out of the question. We approach along the coast—just the three of us. See the castle here? If this map is more or less to scale, we can estimate our distance from The Esplanade based on that.'

'A very long day's walk,' Oak suggested. 'Before the crack of dawn to an hour or so after dusk at this time of year.'

'That's what I figured,' Dray said, grinning. 'We're all in then?'

Oak eyed him suspiciously. 'When are we talking about?'

'There are lives at stake. This is no game,' Dray said.

'Tomorrow?' I asked, wide-eyed. 'There's no way Flame and Daphne will agree to that.'

'We can't tell anyone. I'll leave a note for Arden.'

Oak and I stared at each other.

'We have to strike while the iron is hot,' Dray practically hissed. 'We're either heroes or we're not—there's no middle path. We have to find out what it's like down there and lay the groundwork. The others need rest and aren't up to it. We need to

268

move fast and stay together. It's a job for the three of us.'

'I'm in,' I said, 'but if you come back without me, Flame will kill you.'

He saw I wasn't joking.

'She'll kill you on Daphne's behalf too.'

'We're all coming back, and we'll have a battle plan,' Dray answered, 'and you never know, maybe a new recruit or two.'

24. The Esplanade

Flame was sleeping more soundly than she had in days, making it easy to slip out of bed without waking her. I paused in the dark before leaving the cottage and swore an unspoken oath to her—I promised to be careful and do everything I could to make sure I came back in one piece. All the same, oath or no oath, I hated myself for going along with Dray's plan behind her back.

Oak and Dray were waiting outside the gate, whispering in the dark. The sky was still so black I couldn't even make out the bare branches overhead.

'Morning, Flicker,' Dray said, passing me one of the three pole-arms he must have planted by the gate during the night while everyone was enjoying the festivities in the hall. 'Not so windy today.'

The woods were indeed quiet. The stillness was disturbed only by the distant hooting of owls and the occasional snap as an acorn or twig dropped onto the thick carpet of leaves. There was no creaking of branches—the tell-tale sign of wind.

'No second thoughts?' Oak asked.

'Plenty,' I answered. 'But I'm here—like you two.'

'Let's get moving,' was all Dray said.

We made our way out into the open, following a path I had come to know by heart. The pale glow to the east told us dawn was approaching as we headed west to the beach where they'd found us days earlier—where we'd splashed in salt water for the very first time while Cat laughed at our childish excitement.

We followed the coast south, dipping inland whenever a cove or rocky headland hindered us, and we never stopped glancing at the sky, knowing we were entering drone territory once again.

It must have been close to noon when we stumbled across

what had once been a narrow road, the kind on which vehicles crossing paths would have to straddle the edge to avoid a head-on collision.

'We must be here,' Dray said, pointing to the map. A line from the east reached the coast and curved southwards through a town.

'That must be the town Cat comes from,' I said.

'Poor girl,' Oak muttered. 'Her friends might have gone there.'

'So close to The Esplanade?' Dray asked. 'That would be sheer insanity.'

'Let's find out,' I said.

The road was broken and rough, and there was a fine layer of sand covering it in places—sand that must have been brushed up from the beach during stormy weather. There were no tyre tracks anywhere, so no reason to think patrols had come this way in the last few days.

The first sign of the town was the abandoned campsite with its boom gate uselessly blocking access. The few remaining cabins were blackened from fire or stood drunkenly at an angle, and all were tangled in brambles.

We kept going and passed an empty signpost as we entered the town—another nameless settlement.

'Cleared out,' I said, not realising I'd spoken aloud at first.

Oak and Dray looked at me and nodded.

'We've been erased from history,' Dray said. 'We never lived at all.'

Every building faced the seafront across the now wider road. There had been hotels, restaurants, bars, and boutiques. We could only imagine what life must have been like before The Breakdown. Waking up and opening your hotel-room window to breathe the salty air. Watching happy people on one of those weekend getaways walk by as you drank a cold beer. Admiring the sunset while eating fish and chips, shooing the seagulls away. Children chasing the ice-cream van.

All those simple pleasures I'd read or heard about.

Not this eerie silence.

It hadn't always been like this.

A glint in the sky to the south caught my eye.

'Drone!' I snapped.

We dashed through the nearest doorway into some kind of foyer with a desk to one side and filthy red carpet on the floor. There were several doors further along on either side of an aisle. It reminded me of a derelict cinema I knew in the city, but this one looked much older, almost from another civilisation entirely. Had there been abandoned buildings before The Breakdown?

'We're more than two-thirds of the way to The Esplanade,' Dray pointed out.

'Are you thinking what I'm thinking?' I asked.

'That this is a good place to spend the night on our way back?'

'What do you say, Oak?'

He looked around. 'We could do a lot worse, I guess.'

We explored the cinema for a few minutes, choosing a spot to sleep so it would be easier to find in the dark.

'The drone should be gone now,' I said, 'but we're going to have to keep an eye on our backs for when it returns south.'

I went to the door and scanned the sky. It was clear as far as I could tell, with only gulls gliding under a patchwork of clouds through which timid blue penetrated here and there.

We followed the road out of town, veering away from the coast. There was a chapel similar to the one in the marshland and it reminded me of the night Flame and I had spent together with the pews stacked against the door and the old tablecloth wrapped around us to keep the mosquitoes from biting. We'd spoken about the past. It was the first time we'd started to get to know each other.

'Tell me who you are,' she'd said. 'Who is Flicker?'

We'd spoken about The Breakdown, and about solving the mystery of what happened to our family and friends. We'd read the writing on the wall—that reference to The Esplanade. The answer had been right there in front of us but hadn't yet been given meaning. Now, with every step I took, its significance was becoming more distinct.

What had I asked her about the past?

'What do you remember about Cara?' That was it.

I'd made a mistake, asking too soon and under the wrong circumstances. Even now, I didn't know if she'd be ready to talk about whatever it was that troubled her. Then, there was that night at the pub when the conversation had turned to the subject of reading and she'd let slip that it was her mother who'd taught her—a momentary lapse she'd immediately regretted.

What was the dark secret? Had her mother hurt her? Had her mother been hurt by someone else—her father? Or was it a painful memory, not a secret—a wound that wouldn't heal?

I wondered whether she'd ever tell me, and it hurt to think she felt she couldn't after everything we'd been through together. I wanted to know her inside out.

'The road follows this inlet and connects with the coast again a couple of miles along,' Dray said, and his words wrenched me out of my daydream.

We looked across the inlet beyond the chapel but saw no sign of the road on the other side. Rocks and trees blocked our view of the ground.

'After that, the road sticks to the coast all the way down.'

We kept moving and were pleased to find the map continued to prove true.

'They were a wily pack of wolves,' I said. 'I wonder why they drew the map, assuming they were the ones who did, of course. Were they planning on attacking The Esplanade?'

'I'd say so,' Dray answered. 'How and when is another question, but if she really was planning on building an empire of her own, destroying The Esplanade would have been a key part of her plan.'

We only stopped walking briefly to drink water and relieve our bladders, and I made a point of turning around every minute or two to check behind us for the drone. When I eventually caught sight of it, we hid behind the low wall of a front garden until it had passed.

We were grateful when the sun sank into the sea. There was sufficient moonlight to guide us but not so much as to render us easily perceptible from a distance, and already we could detect another powerful light—this one brushing the underside of the clouds.

Twenty minutes later, we reached a point where no more ruined beachfront houses lined the left-hand side of the road.

Low shrubs and thick tangles of bindweed and brambles grew over heaps of rubble before giving way to flat, clear land. I had the impression a long-abandoned demolition project had only reached this far. On the other side of the road, a seawall with stairs and slipways protected the land from the ocean.

'This is it!' Dray snarled. 'The Esplanade.'

We stopped and stared ahead. There was no missing it. Several hundred yards along the road, a white two-storey building shone like a beacon. We stood there bedazzled by its brilliance and I couldn't remember the last time I'd seen so many electric lights together—soft lighting through the windows, decorative strips of lighting under the eaves, and one spotlight in the ground near the entrance pointlessly sweeping the night sky. It was the most glaring icon of greed and opulence I'd even seen, and while it may have been at the centre of a bustling seaside town once, it stood proudly alone now, its arrogance bereft of an audience. Any other buildings had been bulldozed out of existence.

There was a vast car park on the far side and beyond it were two rows of street lamps with each lamp placed at an equal distance from the next. These rows stretched as far as I could see, and I knew it had to be the expressway from the city.

On this side of the building, between us and it, there were plants of various shapes—ovular, conical, and cubic—with soft spotlights angled up to illuminate them.

'It's one monstrously luxurious building in complete isolation,' I said.

'Not what I was expecting,' Oak admitted. 'It's not fortified as far as I can tell.'

'Why would it be?' Dray asked. 'The only practicable road from the city is guarded and all the towns around have been cleared out. They don't know about us.'

'That's the whole point of it, isn't it?' I said. 'This is their getaway from the city. This is where they can pretend there's nothing around except the ocean and vacant countryside. It's a physical and psychological escape from reality.'

'An escape from their guilt,' Oak said.

Dray turned to him, eyebrows raised, then I saw him scowl, his profile silhouetted against the bright light. 'You think they feel

274

guilt, these monsters?'

'It's a good question. We know next to nothing about them,' he replied.

'They're beyond guilt now, Oak,' I said. 'We know that much. Look at this place—it's a pleasure palace built on a foundation of misery and death.'

'This is where we end up,' Oak muttered bitterly. 'This is what awaits us all—only you can't see the darkness within for all the blinding light.'

'We'll bring the end,' Dray swore, his voice like granite. 'We're their apocalypse.'

It took me a moment to realise Dray was staring at me while I stared at The Esplanade.

'I can read your mind, Flicker,' he said, and there was a crazy edge to his voice that sent a shiver through me. But I realised it was a shiver of excitement, not dread. He noticed my reaction and grinned maniacally.

'So, tell me, what am I thinking?'

'You're seeing the whole wretched place go up in flames. The most ferocious and righteous fire you ever lit. A thrill a thousand times more intense than the best sex anyone could ever have.'

I looked him in the eye and he laughed.

'How close do we dare go?' Oak asked.

I scanned the sky, looking for the red light that gave drones away at night.

'I wouldn't worry about drones this close,' Dray said. 'They're used for coastal surveillance.'

'We can sneak into the garden to get a better look,' I said. 'No matter how safe they feel here, you can bet there'll be cameras on the building itself and possibly in the car park.'

The land between us and the garden was unnaturally flat and covered in grass. This soulless lawn, mowed to perfection, wiped out any trace of what had been here before. The vibrant seaside resort had been reduced to nothing, leaving only The Esplanade, as though the building had sucked up everything around it.

'We run to the nearest tree to start with,' Dray said.

Oak and I nodded, but Dray was already off.

'What took you so long?' he asked when I arrived a second or two later, immediately joined by Oak.

'My sore leg from single-handedly defeating a hardened warrior must have slowed me down.'

He laughed softly. 'Fuck, you got me there!'

'Enough messing about,' Oak warned us. 'Give me your pole-arm, Flicker. I'll hold it while you slip through the garden and try to get a look at the rear of the building.'

I slipped around the egg-shaped laurel we were hiding behind, crept across the serpentine path that led through the garden, and stopped at the last sculpted plant before the immense car park. A hundred cars could easily be accommodated, which seemed excessive for a hotel that couldn't have had more than thirty rooms. Only seven spaces were occupied. I moved along to a tall conical plant to my left and was able to get a better view of the back entrance to the building. There was a door halfway along with two large skips and a dustbin to one side of it. That was all. No other access. No windows. No one around. There were no vehicles moving along the access road as far as I could tell. If there was a holding facility for those captured by the patrols, it was either elsewhere, or inside The Esplanade.

It's impossible to describe how hard it was to resist the urge to run over to that door and try it. I imagined opening it to find the slaves huddled there in cells or chained to the walls. I'd usher them away through the garden and we'd disappear into the night. But it wasn't a risk I could take. I had no idea who was behind that door, or whether it was hooked up to an alarm system. For all I knew, one false move would have drones and security guards swarming everywhere.

I looked back at the egg-shaped laurel and could make out two heads protruding around the side.

We had to find a line of sight inside. There were windows on the side facing the garden and at the front. Soft light glowed through most of them, particularly at ground level.

I jogged back to Oak and Dray, took my pole-arm, and shared the details of the rear layout with them.

'That doesn't give us much to go on,' Dray said, 'but it's useful to know where the rear door is. We can assume the access for hotel and restaurant staff is by that door, and the main entrance

276

at the front is for guests.'

'We need to see the front,' I said.

Dray looked at Oak, then back to me. 'From the beach?'

'That's the only option.'

Dray handed his pole-arm to Oak and reached into a pocket for his binoculars. 'I'll do it. If you see me sprint along the road out of town, try to keep up.'

'Understood loud and clear,' Oak replied.

Dray dashed across the road and disappeared down the nearest stairs in the seawall.

'Flicker, do you think the guests know?'

It was a question I'd asked myself a dozen times since we'd first laid eyes on the extravagant monstrosity.

'That's been haunting me too, Oak. Put it this way—I've observed these people all my life. I've broken into their homes to take food and clothes, and I've seen them speed up when driving along streets where people like us live, even swerving to try to run us over. We mean absolutely nothing to them.'

'How did it come to this?'

I shook my head. None of us could adequately answer that one. There'd been no one to stop it. I guess that's what it boiled down to. The wheels had long been in motion and gathering speed. They'd only be stopped if an obstacle got in the way—and the resulting crash would be atrocious.

'I was hoping we'd save lives again tonight,' he said. 'We can't have come all this way only to turn our backs on whoever's in there.'

'Believe me, Oak, I feel the same, but we don't even know that there's anyone here to save tonight. We've no reason to think the slaves have been caught and brought here. There are no patrol vehicles at all.'

He sighed. 'I guess you're right.'

We heard the rapid fire of Dray's footsteps on the road.

'Two security guards in dinner suits at the top of the stairs,' he began. 'No patrols in sight. Two tables occupied in the restaurant. Three men drinking at one. A couple eating seafood at the other.'

Oak didn't say a word and I could see he was confused. I guess my expression was much the same. The only sound to be heard was the gentle lapping of waves on the beach.

'We're sure this is The Esplanade?' I asked after a moment.

'I'm not much good at reading but that's definitely what the blue lighting over the front entrance spells out,' Dray answered.

Silence again.

'Was she wrong?' Oak asked. 'Is everyone wrong?'

'No,' Dray said. 'It's all an illusion. Can't you two feel it?'

But we could, of course. It was all wrong—the bright lights and perfect gardens, the ridiculously flat lawn, the vacuum in which this ostentatious building stood, the expressway from the city leading to a vast car park that was almost entirely empty. It screamed wrong.

'I can feel it,' I said. 'We've just come on a quiet night.'

'We've seen enough,' Oak said. 'We need to sit down and talk this over. That cinema's calling our names.'

We jogged back along the road and slowed to a walk once we were in line with the end of the lawn.

I didn't take the torch from my backpack until we'd arrived in the cinema foyer. I led the way for Oak and Dray, heading to one of the spots we'd identified earlier as being a good place to sleep.

'They called this the projection room,' I told them, explaining what I'd read about cinemas.

The projector was there, intriguing and enigmatic, like a work of art we weren't equipped to make sense of. I held my torch to the window and we could see all the way down to the red curtain at the front. But it was his stomach that demanded Oak's attention. He opened a bag of nuts and seeds. It wasn't much of a meal but it would keep us from getting too hungry.

We sat on the floor and I reached into my backpack to take one of the candles I'd removed from the castle chamber. I lit it and placed it between us.

'That's handy,' Oak said. 'What else have you stashed in there?'

'A drop of whisky.'

'You're joking?'

I pulled the bottle out.

'He's not!' Dray gasped. 'Bravo! Where did you find that?'

'In the town we were in, east of the castle.'

'You'll have to take us there one day,' Oak said.

We laughed.

'I will.'

I took a swig and passed the bottle around.

'It's nice being together,' Oak said. 'The three of us. The whole community is counting on us to set an example.'

Dray took a swig. 'Us and Arden.'

'Everyone greatly admires her,' I said, 'and rightly so. You particularly, Dray.'

He looked me in the eye. 'It's that obvious, is it?'

I took the bottle from Oak and drank.

'She had a partner, didn't she?'

They looked at each other and the sorrow was palpable—but another emotion was stewing behind Dray's eyes.

'It's your tale to tell, Dray,' Oak said, his voice a low rumble.

Dray motioned for the bottle and took an aggressive swig.

'Ah, that hit the spot!' He shook his head and released a potent breath. 'I'm not usually one to unveil myself, Flicker—you'll have worked that out by now—but Newton is far too small for secrets. Everyone else knows what happened.' He paused, gaze fixed on the candle, the sole source of light in the projection room. 'She had a partner, and so did I.'

'I'm sorry,' I whispered, unsure how he'd react.

He shot me a faint smile before turning his focus back to the hypnotic flame.

'It all ties together, Flicker,' he continued, the light playing against his lips as he spoke. His eyes remained fixed.

'With The Esplanade, you mean?'

'What she told us—the Lady—in her final rant reminded me of what one of the patrolmen who carted our partners away had said. I didn't understand it at the time. I thought it was a cruel joke.' He paused. 'We knew it was a death sentence for them. No one comes back. But the Lady's revelation brought it all home. The pieces fell into place. In my mind's eye, I saw the scene again. I heard his sick remark and saw the cruel smile that accompanied it.'

'Do you recall the words?'

'More or less.' Dray looked up. 'He said they'd be put to good use. He didn't say "The Esplanade", of course. I guess they aren't authorised to acknowledge its existence. But he knew that we understood. He said they'd be very popular, especially her with her big tits.'

We sat in silence, and I felt the tide of anger swell up inside me as I joined Dray in staring at the flame, wishing it would expand and engulf the whole miserable world.

'You didn't know the true meaning of his words. You couldn't have. No one could have imagined.'

'No,' he said.

'Were you there, Oak?'

Dray answered. 'The four of us were together—I was with Arden and Horn, and my girl.' He paused. 'We called her Eclipse,' he said softly.

I didn't dare question him further. It was breaking his heart. That was plain to see. I'd taken Dray for unbreakable, and he was, but I'd misjudged the cause. It wasn't because life had hardened him, but because he was already broken. He had loved this girl with every fibre of his being and she'd been torn away from him. All that was left for him was to erase The Esplanade from the face of the earth, and it didn't matter to him one little bit if he went with it.

'They left you behind,' I said.

His face screwed up. 'And I'll hate myself for it till the day I die.' He drew a breath and released it, making the flame flicker. 'It was further north,' he said. 'We were following a road, looking for a good hunting ground. It was a stupid mistake. Horn's idea. By the time we heard the engine, it was already too late. We ran into the trees but Horn and Eclipse weren't as fast as Arden and I. There were three patrolmen, two young and fast, both carrying firearms. They were crack shots. Horn and Eclipse both took a bullet to the leg. Arden and I spun around to find them on their knees. One of the patrolmen holstered his gun, and mustering all his strength, he dragged them back to the road, pulling them by an arm each. His face turned red with the strain and he ignored their screams as brambles tore at them. I wanted to rush at him and stick my spear through him, but the other one had his gun levelled at me. Arden had her crossbow trained on him and could have taken him down, but she hesitated. Too risky. She hesitated for my sake.'

I passed him the whisky and he took a swig.

'I guess we thought we'd overcome them.' He shrugged. 'We assumed they'd want the four of us and that when they tried, Arden would kill one before the other could fire and I'd spear him. I don't know. It all happened so quickly. Before we knew it, Horn and Eclipse were in the vehicle, and we thought the fight was about to kick off. That's when the older one who hadn't chased us spoke and smiled that fucking evil smile I'll never get out of my head.' He took a breath and put his hands over his face. 'There was no fight—no second chance. He jumped into the vehicle and started driving while the other two shot at us, forcing us to dive for cover. Next thing we knew, they'd climbed into the vehicle beside the driver. Arden took a shot at the rear left tyre, but we saw the bolt ricochet to the side.'

He took another swig. 'Only a drop left. Sorry.'

'Finish it,' I told him, and he did.

'They took Horn and Eclipse and left us. I returned to the same spot to hunt for weeks after that, wondering whether they would come back to take me away. To be honest, I was hoping they would.'

Dray looked at Oak, then narrowed his eyes and looked at me, almost accusatorily, as though suggesting I'd somehow tricked him into baring his heart.

'That's why you two need to take care of yourselves,' he told us. 'I don't blame Arden and she doesn't blame me, but she blames herself, and I blame myself—and that guilt is a heavy burden to carry. I'm not a strong as she is. She's carrying on. Putting on a brave face. I try to do the same, but it's all an act. And before you ask, yes, we care about each other very deeply. She's all I have left to care about. But that's not enough, and we'll never be together. We're bound to our ghosts.'

We all three stared at the flame.

'You're one of the strongest people I've ever met,' I told him.

'It's a charade, Flicker. I hate to admit it, especially to you. It's not so much strength as the fact that I don't give a shit any more. It's not my lot to die an old man. None of us will. I don't want to waste away or be claimed by a fever. We can cry for Cat and for Fern, and all our lost friends, but they died fighting. Cat's death was the most glorious I've ever witnessed.'

He was right. It hurt to admit it, because Flame and I hadn't saved her from slavery with the intention of sending her straight to her death—but that's how it had played out, and that's what made her a legend. Whatever was to happen from here on, Cat's legend would never fade.

'In a way, I envy her,' Dray said, almost too softly to be heard. Then he said with more conviction, 'I hope I go down fighting like her, but before that, I have to live long enough to see The Esplanade burn to the ground.'

He placed a fingertip above the candle's flame and held it there for several seconds. His face remained impassive.

'Promise me that, Flicker. Swear that if anything happens to me, you'll see it done—your greatest inferno—your masterpiece.'

'I promise,' I said without hesitation, 'but I'm counting on you being there with me. Both of you.'

'Let's try to get a bit of shut-eye,' Oak suggested. 'You two lightweights may be used to running back and forth all over the countryside, but I've covered more ground in the last two days than I have in weeks. I think that's worn me out more than the actual fighting.'

We arranged backpacks and furs into pillows, I stood my torch within easy reach against the wall, and then I blew out the candle.

'Sweet dreams,' Dray said. 'Tomorrow, we'll call a meeting in the hall and start planning The Esplanade's destruction.'

I closed my eyes and tried not to imagine the horrible fate so many of our friends had met, but appalling images kept creeping into my mind, preventing me from falling asleep. Now that we knew what went on in there and had seen that grotesque palace with our own eyes, I was yearning—burning—to reduce it to nothing. The Esplanade was within our grasp, but we had to bide our time and gather our strength. At least, that's what I thought as I lay there waiting for sleep to claim me. I had no idea what was happening back in Newton, and just how soon it would all come to a head.

25. The Newsflash

There was no way of knowing when daylight had broken. The cinema, like every building along the coastal road, faced west, and the door to the projection room was at right angles to the corridor. When I was wide awake and couldn't bear lying in the dark any longer, I fumbled for the torch, pointed it to the floor at my feet as I switched it on, and made my way to the door.

A quick movement made my heart skip a beat, and I caught a shadow with a bushy tail disappear through the main entrance. A fox, I guessed, and for the first time in my life, I found myself seriously wondering what one would taste like.

A chill breeze filled the foyer, carrying the distinctive smell of seaweed I'd first discovered at the beach. I decided to follow my nose down to the sand, to splash water on my face, not caring how salty or cold it would be. I stopped at the entrance, and scanned the sky, looking for the glint of a drone in the morning sunlight. There were only gulls.

I descended the seawall stairs and ran to the water, which was much closer than it had been the other day—now covering most of the beach—and after checking the sky again, I cupped water in my hands and splashed it on my face.

The cold made me gasp, but it turned into a laugh. It felt so good to be alive. Every step we'd taken since leaving the city, no matter how difficult, had been one in the right direction. Unlike Dray, I considered The Esplanade a new beginning, not the end, and I dreaded the prospect of becoming like him—seeing what he had seen, and suffering as he had suffered.

I climbed the stairs back to street level and returned to the projection room. It was time to get moving.

They were awake and talking quietly.

'It's morning?' Oak asked.

'Well and truly. Ready?'

'We are,' Dray said. 'Let's make it home before dinnertime so we have a captive audience.'

But we didn't even make it to the point where the road became narrower and curved inland.

'What's going on?' Oak asked, and we stopped dead in our tracks. We immediately recognised the group heading southward along the coast. Their pole-arms glinted in the sun.

Dray turned around and studied the sky.

'No drones?' I asked, doing likewise.

'Not yet, but we need to get everyone into the cinema before we're spotted. What are they thinking, walking along the coast like that in broad daylight with their pole-arms stuck in the air? We need to move them along quickly.'

Oak waved them on, trying to get them to pick up their pace, but they'd already starting jogging slowly, which wasn't easy with all the equipment they appeared to be carrying. Dray took his binoculars to get a better look while we waited for them to reach us.

'There's no sign of Arden or Flame,' Dray said, lowering his binoculars and turning to me.

'What? Are you certain?'

'They might be at the back, but that's not Arden's style. I hope I'm wrong.'

I could feel a knot tightening in my stomach already, but what could possibly have happened? There'd been no survivors from the castle—we'd counted the bodies and I'd lit the funeral pyre myself. No patrols ventured that far off-road without good reason.

'The smoke, Dray. Was it a mistake lighting the pyres?'

He frowned but shook it off a moment later. 'I find that hard to believe, and even if a drone did spot the smoke and a patrol was sent out, that wouldn't lead them to Newton. There's no way.'

We looked into the air behind us again as they drew nearer,

panting from the strain of jogging under so much weight.

'Where are Arden and Flame?' I asked the instant they were within earshot.

'They're not with you?' Raleigh asked.

'Why the hell would they be with us?' Dray asked. 'Didn't Arden tell you about my note?'

'She did, but we couldn't just sit around while you three were risking your lives. She was pissed off with you, Dray. Flame as well,' he said, looking at me. 'We held an emergency meeting and decided to march south to try to find you in the morning. Arden and Flame left yesterday. They wanted to see if they could find the slaves before joining us on the coast.'

'They went back to the castle?'

'I don't know exactly. Flame was talking about the town where you lived before.'

'I don't like that,' I heard myself saying.

'They can look after themselves,' Oak told me. 'They'll catch up by nightfall.'

'Did you find The Esplanade?' Raleigh asked.

'We'll tell you about it once we're under cover. Follow us!'

We led them back to the cinema and gave everyone a moment to catch their breaths once we were in the foyer.

'What have you brought with you?' Oak asked.

'Food, drinks, jerry cans, and weapons.'

'Good show,' Oak said. 'Let's start with the first two.'

We shared our observations with them and their first reaction was much the same as ours had been.

'No patrol vehicles in the car park?' Sparrow asked, stroking his unkempt goatee.

'None. No sign of security other than the two guards on the door. That's it,' Dray confirmed.

'The sheer arrogance!' Raleigh spat.

'That's what we figured,' I said. 'It's as though the idea that anyone could know what they're doing or be in a position to pose a threat is so absurd it hasn't even occurred to them.'

'Could there be another reason?' Hint asked.

We hadn't even considered that.

'Like what?' Dray asked him, but I could tell by his voice he was dismissing the suggestion.

'I don't know,' Hint said, shrugging.

We sat in silence for a while and I wondered whether maybe Hint was onto something. Sparrow and a few of the others were looking all around the cinema foyer. They'd probably never seen anything like it before.

'How are Arden and Flame supposed to find us?' Dray asked no one in particular. 'They didn't think it through very well—chasing these slaves. There's no way of knowing which way they headed.'

'No,' I agreed, 'but if they reached the town, they'd stay there.'

'We need to have someone by the door at all times,' Dray said. 'Otherwise, they might walk past us and end up at The Esplanade alone.'

'I wonder how long it is from this town of yours to here,' Oak said.

'This road connects with the town,' I said. 'It has to. If they take the road south out of town, then turn west when they can, they'll arrive here eventually.'

'We sit tight here all day?' Raleigh asked.

'We don't have a choice, do we?' Dray said, looking around. 'Plenty of time for rummaging. There's no knowing what bits and bobs worth keeping are stashed in a place like this.'

I have to admit it did our bodies a world of good. After the ordeal of the battle and all the walking, we needed a day of rest. Oak was content to stretch out on the floor in the foyer with his hands behind his head and contemplate the ceiling. Though time-worn and faded, motifs could be made out. There were crowns, I thought—the symbol that had once adorned infrastructure all over this land. We used to joke about it in the city—The Once and Future King would come back to save us one day, giving us the strength and courage to overthrow the crippled regime. I only knew one Arthur back then, and he was no king. We were going to have to rely on our own strength and courage.

Raleigh took first watch by the door and Dray waltzed around impatiently, joining the rest of us in our exploration of the cinema every now and then. All the while, Arden and Flame were on my mind.

There wasn't much of use to be found concealed by the dust, cobwebs, and feathers from wayward birds. I found batteries that fit my torch and a few boxes of matches hidden alongside cleaning products. We soon tired of it and lounged around instead. I relieved Raleigh at the door and sat there staring at the sky, watching the gulls and the clouds for I don't know how long —and all the while, I was willing Flame to me.

That day dragged it heels, and as good as it was for the body, every hour was more torturous than the last for the mind. When Dray came to replace me at the door, the sun was already visible in the western sky. I told him not to worry and that I was happy to stay there, but he insisted, making it clear it was for my sake.

'They brought beer with them. Go and have a drop. It'll do you good. They'll be here by nightfall. No one knows Arden like I do. She'll be here, and Flame will be with her. Who knows who else they'll have—maybe a slave each for the lads?'

'You wouldn't joke about that if you knew what they'd been through,' I told him.

'I don't doubt what they've been through for a second. All the more reason. Let me laugh while I still can, Flicker.'

I gave him a slap on the arm. 'I'll bring you some beer.'

'Cheers.'

We limited ourselves to two goblets each, wanting to keep plenty aside for later that night when we'd be even thirstier, assuming we made it back alive.

The last rays of sunlight were shining up from behind the seawall and Oak was on watch when the calm came to an abrupt end.

'I hear a vehicle!' Oak shouted to us.

'Coming which way?' I asked immediately.

'Sounds like from the north,' he said, and peered along the length of the road. He turned back to us, eyes wide. 'Patrol vehicle approaching.'

'We have to stop it!' I yelled.

'You don't think—?' Dray asked me, cutting himself short.

'Maybe!'

I could tell Dray's mind was racing. We had to act fast. 'Wait until they've stopped to attack!' he snapped loudly enough for everyone in the foyer to hear. He then rushed past Oak, out onto the street, without taking his pole-arm with him.

'Shit!' Oak gasped, getting to his feet and making sure he remained out of sight. 'Arm yourselves and wait for my word!' he called into the foyer.

I watched Dray's performance through the doorway. It was thoroughly convincing. He'd obviously been paying attention during theatre nights. He turned right and looked along the road, pretending he'd just noticed the vehicle. I couldn't see his face, but I imagined the shocked expression he must have adopted. Then, as the vehicle drew closer and brakes screeched, he ran back into the cinema.

'Two of them!' he said, dashing over to take his pole-arm. 'Everyone out of sight!'

Oak sank back against the wall to one side of the door, far enough back for his pole-arm to be effective, and I took up position opposite. Dray joined me and everyone else hid where they could. Dray started to whisper something but ran out of time. The two patrolmen ran straight into the trap.

Oak struck first, thrusting the spike of his weapon into the side of the first one to enter. The patrolman managed to fire a shot as he dropped to the floor, and a shower of plaster fell from the ceiling. From the corner of my eye, I caught the others spring out of hiding and charge, but it would all be over by the time they reached us. Dray and I struck at the same time, impaling the second patrolman, who had turned to fire at Oak. He never got the chance. Oak brought his pole-arm down to catch the man's left wrist as he slumped to the ground.

Dray dropped to his knees, holding up a hand to make the others lay off. 'Do you know what happens in The Esplanade?' he asked.

'Yeah,' he rasped, and tried to grin, but coughed up blood instead. No other words would escape his lips.

Dray finished them both off with his spiked pole-arm, tossed it on the ground, and took their pistols. He handed one to me.

'You know how to use it, don't you?' he asked.

I shrugged. 'Aim and squeeze the trigger?'

'Basically. Just make sure the safety's off.' He showed me.

'Let's keep it on for the moment.'

I looked outside, left and right, and checked the sky for drones. 'The coast is clear.'

'Stay inside,' Dray said to the others.

The vehicle was still running, its motor grumbling lowly. It was a white lorry, spotlessly clean except for mud around the tyres and surrounding bodywork. PUBLIC CLEANING was printed on the sides in simple black letters.

We hurried around to the back and I opened the door with my left hand—pistol at the ready in my right.

'Flicker! I can't believe it!'

It was dark inside, but I recognised Flame's voice instantly.

'Is Arden in there?' Dray asked urgently.

'Yes, I'm here. We owe you our lives. Some of us more than once.' She laughed, and I could tell it was the kind of laugh that comes after a lot of crying.

'Come on out!' I said, helping Flame down, then Arden and the handful of slaves they'd brought with them. One, two, three, four, five, six, seven, eight, nine. 'Where are the others?'

'They didn't all stay together,' Arden said. 'We found this group in the church—in *your* church.'

'You let yourselves get caught by those two idiots?' Dray asked, looking at Arden with a mix of relief and disappointment.

'They caught us by surprise. Did you kill them?'

He nodded. 'Of course. We need to get this thing off the road and out of sight until after dark.'

'Do you know how to drive?' I asked him.

He shot me a wicked smile and a wink. 'Watch your step going into the cinema,' he told the women. 'Flicker, jump in with me.' He strode around to the driver's side and climbed in. I clambered up onto the passenger seat and watched him inspect the pedals and gearstick. The radio was on and a woman's voice was in the middle of a news update.

'Listen, Dray,' I told him.

He looked at me, then his eyes widened.

...the state of emergency was upgraded to its highest level and the board of administrators evacuated from the city as violence worsens. What began as isolated rioting has now consolidated into a general uprising. The rioting

began in September in response to the crackdown on public disorder following the arson attack on a vehicle belonging to a high-ranking public order coordinator. All available patrols have been deployed to prevent the occupation of central administration facilities.

'It's a fucking revolution!' Dray shouted. 'The city's fighting back!'

'Did you hear what she said, Dray?' I asked, and he must have seen how stunned I looked. He just stared at me, and then his jaw dropped.

'The arson attack against a car in September!' He punched me in the arm. 'That was you!'

'I think it must have been, but I don't know what month it is.'

'It's practically winter now,' Dray said. 'How long did you live in the town?'

I thought back to the journal I'd started, reminding myself to retrieve it from the house one day. I'd made thirty entries—of that I was quite certain. But we'd already been there several days prior to that. A week? Probably more. How many days had passed between the first night camped near the castle and now? I'd lost track. More than a week. All in all, it had been close to two months already since we'd fled the city.

'We were there for more than five weeks. It must have been early or mid-September when we left the city. The leaves were only just beginning to turn yellow. The reaction to the attack was so swift and relentless. I remember thinking at the time that I'd chosen the car of someone high up.'

'You've triggered a revolution, Flicker!' He shifted the lorry into gear and drove it slowly along the road, turning left onto a narrow side street, then left again into a vacant lot where two tall pine trees would provide adequate cover.

'That explains why there's so little security around The Esplanade,' I said. 'All forces have been sent to the city. Except for these two.'

'When she said the administrators had been evacuated from the city,' Dray said. 'You don't think they were brought here?'

'I'd say it's highly likely. They certainly seem to think The Esplanade is a safe location.'

...and concerns are growing that this unrest has now spread to the capital.

Authorities have instructed citizens to put their contingency plans into effect and warn that all unlawful behaviour will result in immediate incarceration.

Dray cut the engine. 'That's what they call it, Flicker. It's "immediate incarceration" for all us troublemakers and rabble-rousers. What do think about that?'

I reached into a pocket and took a box of matches. I shook it and watched Dray grin maniacally as the matches rattled around inside. '*This* is the only prison I'm aware of, but tonight, the inmates will be set free.'

26. Flicker's Masterpiece

We walked back to the cinema and I switched on my torch once we reached the entrance. The last glimmer of daylight was now sinking into the horizon. The bodies had already been removed and the floor cleaned as best it could. The foyer was empty and lost in darkness, but we could hear muffled voices coming from one of the rooms.

'That one,' Dray said, and I aimed the torch at his arm to see where he was pointing.

'It's us!' I said, opening the door. Not wanting to give Oak or any of the others a fright and end up like the patrolmen.

They were seated on the floor in front of the dusty red curtain, gathered around candles placed on the floor.

'Where did you put them?' Dray asked.

'Dragged them out the back door,' Raleigh answered. 'They should keep the foxes busy.'

'Good job,' Dray replied. 'How's everyone feeling? Arden and Flame? Ladies?'

'Ladies!' one of the slaves said, and the others laughed.

'Sorry. Poor choice of words.'

'I could get used to it. We haven't been called that in long time.'

'I don't think I've ever been called a lady,' another said. 'I don't think it's the word that best describes us.'

'It definitely isn't the title that suited the woman who enslaved you,' Arden said. 'I can think of one or two others—Psychobitch Armstrong, for example.'

There was a wave of laughter. That title was bound to stick.

'Every woman in Newton is a lady, really. The men respect us and treat us as equals—don't you?' She shot a warning glance all around. 'They know they'll end up with a crossbow bolt in the forehead if they don't.'

Laughter filled the room again, even though Arden was clearly only half joking.

'Talking about crossbows,' Dray said. 'I found this in the lorry.'

'I was worried they'd thrown it away.'

'Well, they would have if they'd counted on us rescuing you. Have our newcomers ever fought before?'

They shook their heads.

'I was thinking they should stay here, Dray,' Arden said, and I could tell by her voice she was worried how he'd react to the suggestion.

'I agree. Best hold the fort,' he said. 'You and Flame are up to it? There's no shame in staying here if not.'

I sat beside Flame and took her in my arms.

'We're fine. They didn't hurt us. We were worried about taking a bullet, but they didn't seem interested in shooting us. They wanted us alive.'

'Did they say anything?'

Arden glanced at Flame, her eyes haunted and face outlined by the candlelight. 'One of them made a remark about how we'd bring a smile to the lips of the board of administrators.'

'They know,' Dray said. 'The whole system's in on it. All that talk about imprisonment on the radio is a cruel joke—a coded message.'

'What radio?' Oak asked loudly, and everyone turned to Dray in anticipation. They probably couldn't remember the last time they'd heard a radio broadcast, and even if they had, there was only the one state-run station available. Whenever pirate radio had popped up in the city, drones had somehow tracked down the point of transmission and everyone involved had vanished into thin air.

Dray sat himself in the middle, next to the candles, and grinned mischievously at the party.

'Spit it out, man!' Oak said.

'We caught the latest news in the lorry,' Dray began, soaking up the expressions all around him.

'I haven't seen you look so happy in a long time,' Arden said warmly. 'It must be good news.'

Dray looked at me, and whatever jealousy he felt had disappeared. It was pure admiration I saw in his eyes.

'You all remember Flicker and Flame's first night with us, when they told us about how they met. They had to flee the city because Flicker lit a car on fire and a swarm of tracker drones arrived in record time.'

Everyone nodded, except the nine slaves, who turned to me wide-eyed, and Flame, who pulled away from me so she could look me in the eye, trying to uncover the secret before Dray revealed it.

'It seems Flicker picked the car belonging to a high-ranking official—who was it again, Flicker?'

'A public order coordinator, I think.'

I felt Flame shiver in my arms. 'You didn't!' she asked with a laugh.

'I didn't know at the time. You know how it is Flame, I saw that revolting symbol of superiority and the primal urge inside me did the rest. It had to burn!'

The air was filled with cheers and applause, as though our uproarious tale was far more entertaining than any film that had ever graced the screen in that room forgotten by time.

'That was almost two months ago now,' Arden pointed out. It's hardly breaking news.'

'That was the trigger,' Dray continued. 'Listen, everyone. Flicker's attack led to a widespread crackdown in the city. Unable to catch the perpetrator, they must have decided to take it out on everyone indiscriminately. That was a mistake. The whole city is kicking back and the uprising is spreading all over the country. The board of administrators has been evacuated.'

Another roar of cheers filled the room, and before I knew it, Flame had been torn from my arms and all the men except Dray had piled onto me, patting me on the back until I could hardly breathe. Then, I was up in the air, floating on a cloud of hands.

'Keep your strength, lads,' Dray said once the cheering had died down. They put me down. 'There may be revolution in the city, but our battle is yet to be fought. Arden, according to what you heard, the administrators are indeed at The Esplanade.'

'That's what he said, but Oak was telling us there's not much security in place.'

'We didn't see a lot last night, but we don't know who was inside the building.'

'And there's this expressway,' Arden reminded us. 'We don't know how far it is from the city to The Esplanade, but you can count on it being thirty minutes at most driving at top speed.'

'Don't forget tracker drones have infrared cameras,' Hint said. 'If they're deployed, they'll track us back here. We have to strike hard and fast. We won't be able to slug it out like at the castle or get caught up in a standoff.'

Dray turned to Arden and she understood. 'I'm not making that mistake again,' she assured us, 'and I doubt they'll be pulling knives on us—it'll be guns. Dray and Flicker have pistols. I have my crossbow. Does anyone else have a long-range weapon?'

'I have a spear,' Raleigh said.

'I've brought my throwing knives,' Colby said.

'Are we going inside?' Oak asked, looking at Arden, and I got the distinct feeling they'd been talking about it while Dray and I were parking the lorry.

'We need to know,' she said, 'and they need to know why we're there.'

No one spoke for a moment.

'They're all in on it, Arden,' Dray said. 'We know that.'

'They can't be,' she said with a stubborn frown on her face, and she shook her head. 'Not the guests who stay there. They wouldn't know.'

'I envy you, Arden. I really do.' He sighed. 'You want to ask them? Will you be able to tell if they're lying—if they refuse to confess?'

'Yes,' she said without hesitation. 'There's no knowing how they'll react or what words they'll use, but we'll be able to tell. I'll know.'

'If they express what you, Arden, believe is genuine surprise, we walk away? Is that it?'

She looked around, reading our faces as best she could in the candlelight.

'We could give them the choice to run.'

A murmur rose among the men.

'We can't slaughter innocent people,' she said.

'No, we can't,' Flame agreed.

'Innocent people,' Dray repeated pensively. 'I'll know if they lie. We're both very good judges of character. If they're in on it, there can be no mercy. Do we all agree on that?'

Everyone nodded.

'We need to take out any security quickly,' Oak said, 'before we give Arden and Dray a chance to confront any guests present.'

'Flame and I should be there as well,' I said. 'I don't doubt that you are excellent judges of character, Arden and Dray, but you have no experience of the urban Overclass. We do. They speak and act differently from us.'

'The four of us,' Arden said. 'What do you say, Dray?'

'Sounds good. Oak and Raleigh can watch our backs. Who'll stand guard at the back door?'

'I'll do that,' Hint volunteered. 'Sparrow and Colby, do you want to join me?'

They agreed.

'Now, about the lorry—' Oak began, and while they discussed tactics and the nine newcomers listened, occasionally whispering to each other and giggling, Arden turned to Flame and me.

She spoke softly. 'Flicker, your priority tonight, ahead of setting that damned place ablaze, is to keep Flame safe.'

I cocked my head to the side to look into Flame's eyes.

'Are you feeling unwell? You said the patrolmen didn't hurt you.'

'It's not that, Flicker. I'll explain later.'

I turned back to Arden, but her smile was enigmatic.

'I'll stay by her side.'

Arden winked at Flame.

'We're good to go then,' Oak announced. 'Everyone's ready?'

We all said, 'Yes.'

'Are we ready?' Oak asked again, yelling this time and holding a hand cupped around one ear.

'We're ready!' they shouted.

'Revolution!'

'Into the fray!'

Our roar filled the room.

'Ladies,' Dray said eventually. 'Stay here and keep us in your minds!'

'We will, Dray!' one of them replied. 'I'll be right here waiting for you.'

That raised a cheer from everyone. I noticed Dray glance at Arden and he saw the encouraging grin she gave him. He then jogged outside ahead of everyone else, presumably to get the lorry and back it up in line with the cinema entrance.

We waited outside, then Oak climbed in front with Dray while the rest of us crammed into the back with our weapons and equipment.

'Well, this is an experience, isn't it?' I asked everyone, hoping to ease our nerves a little. It was the first time most of us had been in the back of a vehicle—an experience we'd always been taught to dread.

Several minutes later, the road became smoother and Dray drew to a stop.

'It's on!' Raleigh announced. 'Let's all make it back this time.'

'Hear, hear,' Hint replied.

'Stay by my side,' I whispered to Flame. 'You'll tell me what this is all about if we make it through the night.'

'You don't have the faintest idea, do you?' she asked, then laughed at my blank expression. 'I'm never late, Flicker.'

I shrugged. I couldn't recall ever telling her off for not being on time. Anyway, it wasn't the moment to push the matter. My mind was on The Esplanade and it was filled with ravenous flames. We could hear shouting outside but couldn't make out the words. It grew louder and clearer the second Oak opened the door for us.

'Pistol ready, Flicker?' he asked quietly.

I nodded. The safety was off.

'Don't shoot unless you have to. We want to do this as quietly as we can.'

We hurried out and found ourselves right in front of The Esplanade, the left side of the lorry facing polished marble stairs at the top of which stood two guards dressed in dinner suits complete with black bow ties decorating their stout necks. Their wide-eyed gaze flashed back and forth between Dray and the rest of us as we joined him at the foot of the stairs.

'What's your business here?' one of them demanded. 'I won't ask again!'

The other spoke in low tones into a microphone clipped to his collar.

'We'd like to speak to the manager,' Dray said.

'Not possible,' he replied, scowling with contempt as he looked us over from head to toe.

'Move along now!' the other called out, not too loudly so as not to alert the patrons to the disturbance. 'This is your last chance to crawl back into whatever filthy cave you live in before a patrol arrives to haul you off to prison.'

'But they won't be here for a while, will they?' I asked. 'They're busy trying to quash the uprising in the city, and there's no prison. This is where we all end up.'

The twisted smile on their lips made me feel sick.

'The Esplanade is the terminus for scum like you.'

They reached into their dinner jackets in a movement they'd clearly rehearsed a thousand times but probably never needed to perform in earnest at The Esplanade. It was immediately answered by an order from Oak and we swiftly raised our arms.

'Stand down!' Dray shouted.

The guards, surprised by the pistols, spears, throwing knives, and crossbow aimed at them, stopped moving their hands and looked at each other.

I don't know precisely what it was, a glint of insanity in their eyes, or the sheer arrogance they exuded, but I grabbed Flame and pushed her behind me. Before the guards could level their guns at anyone, Raleigh's spear pierced the one who had spoken to us through the middle of his chest, followed immediately by a crossbow bolt in the throat. Another spear struck the other one at the same time as Colby sent a throwing knife spinning. He dropped to his knees howling.

The air seemed to freeze, and I think we were all horrified by what had just happened, but we couldn't afford to waste time.

Oak dashed up the stairs and cracked the skull of the second guard with a blow of his sledgehammer, then waved for the four of us to go inside.

'Hint, Sparrow, and Colby,' he said. 'Time to secure the rear.'

The manager and two members of staff were standing just behind the door, their faces blanched except for a tinge of blue from the illuminated sign over the entrance. Looking past them, I realised that the confrontation hadn't been noticed by the patrons, who were eating and drinking and chatting loudly.

'Let us in. We have a question to ask your diners,' I ordered the manager.

He was shaking his head but his lips were incapable of forming words.

'You don't have a choice,' I pointed out, trying to reassure him by speaking calmly.

He nodded reluctantly and motioned for the two employees to step aside.

We entered, refusing to be mesmerised by opulence on a scale we'd never seen before. The walls of the entrance were decorated with portraits of men and women I didn't recognise but assumed to be prominent government figures past and present.

When we stepped into the dining room, the chatting ceased, and one by one, every face turned to us—confusion, concern, or derision written on them. These people were impeccably clean and splendidly attired. The women had straight, shining hair, and wore brilliant earrings and necklaces. They stared at Flame and Arden with a look that was hard to decipher—not disgust or even disregard, but a form of eagerness. The men, for the most part, looked bewildered, unable to understand how the likes of us could be standing before them.

The manager eventually found his tongue for long enough to ask everyone's attention.

'Our apologies for the disruption, ladies and gentlemen,' I said. 'We've come here tonight because we've discovered the terrible truth about this restaurant and feel it is our duty to share it with you.'

They frowned, unsure where it was all going, but nobody spoke. They couldn't see that Dray and I had pistols, and Arden had left her crossbow outside. Nevertheless, they remained in their seats, ready to humour us. Several of them were eyeing the others mischievously, no doubt thinking it was a staged performance for their amusement.

'The Esplanade is considered the finest restaurant of all, which no doubt is why you are here, thoroughly enjoying your meals. It is the only establishment serving meat—*real* flesh.'

They nodded and made comments about the fact, praising The Esplanade's unique cuisine.

'What you almost certainly do not know is precisely what you are eating.'

At this point, the head chef appeared. He was a small man but a bold one, with curly dark hair under his toque and keen eyes. He strode up to me like a cock used to ruling his roost and glared at me, hands on narrow hips.

'What the fuck's going on?' he snarled, forgetting the register of language appropriate in the establishment.

'You know very well, chef! Tell them. Go on! What kind of meat have they been eating? What happened to my friends? What happens to those arrested by the patrols? What good use are the useless put to?'

The chef turned to his patrons and raised his hands in a gesture of mock surrender. 'Got me!' he shouted comically, turning back to me.

The diners laughed uneasily.

'There's no mystery there, whoever the fuck you think you are,' he went on. He turned to the diners again and grinned. 'We eat them, don't we?'

They burst out laughing. The women covered their mouths or clutched their pearls, embarrassed that an unspoken truth had been aired in such an indelicate way, but thoroughly amused all the same. A number of the men, rather than finding humour in the failed revelation, jabbed their forks into a piece of meat and continued eating provocatively.

I held my anger in as several men began making atrocious comments, encouraging the laughter of their fellow patrons.

'Not so useless after all!'

'It's the only way they can find themselves at a table at The Esplanade!'

One of the older women joined in the fun.

'The poor are delicious, sweet child!' She kissed her fingertips. 'So wonderfully gamy!'

'You're monsters!' Flame roared, and a heavy silence fell across the room. But it was short-lived, quickly replaced by a burst of laughter.

'We may be monsters, but you're animals!'

The laughter grew deafening. There was the slapping of hands on thighs and the thumping of fists on tables. All semblance of respectability was cast aside.

'Are the administrators here?' I asked, surveying the room and noticing the uncomfortable setting of brows and furtive sideways glances.

'Get out of my establishment!' the chef snarled. 'There's a patrol on the way. You'll end up tomorrow's special if you don't piss off right now!'

The patrons howled at that one and stared at us, licking their lips.

'Time to go,' I told Flame quietly.

The chef, manager, staff, and patrons watched us leave.

'They killed the guards,' one of the waiters whispered to the chef as we were leaving, and I heard his stomach-churning reply, telling the young man to drag their bodies into the kitchen.

The manager locked and barricaded the doors behind us and remained there, staring at us through the glass. I'll never forget the terror in his eyes when I came back from the lorry with wicks and the two remaining jerry cans, one of which I passed to Dray.

He spun around and rushed out of sight, thinking they'd be able to escape through the back door.

'Go to the back and tell them to light up,' I told Arden.

The others watched on as Dray and I splashed fuel all over the front entrance and along the wall of the building. Once we'd emptied our jerry cans, I took a box of matches from my pocket, grinned at Dray while I gave it a rattle, and started lighting our wicks. We cast them at the door until it exploded into flames, which quickly spread like wings. The door shattered and the fire entered the building, crawling along the floor and licking its way up the interior walls. I could imagine the flames incinerating those portraits of meaningless celebrities.

301

We howled into the night like wild animals, knowing that whatever lay ahead, that timeless moment was ours. We were savage beasts. Oak pounded his broad chest and Raleigh thrust his bloodied spear into the sky over and over again. Dray leered at the inferno.

I pulled Flame up against me and placed a hand below her belly, just above her mound—over the spot where I thought my seed had taken root. The beast in me now sensed what the rational mind had failed to understand.

We stared at the hungry fire which would consume those who would have devoured us, and I smiled as I studied the twisted tongues of fury. I felt a chill of immeasurable power course through my body, making me turn hard.

A window was opened on the first floor, further along from where the flames were already lapping. Through the thickening smoke, I recognised the chef. He was climbing out onto the sill, but Dray walked along until he was in line with him, raised his pistol, took aim, and fired. The chef dropped to the ground with a terrible thud that made the keep flash into my mind's eye once again, but my attention quickly returned to the fire, and I noticed my hand hadn't stopped caressing Flame, firmly but lovingly, making her melt under my touch. Her head rested upon my shoulder and she moaned softly.

Arden and the others joined us.

'No escape?' Dray asked.

'The entire back wall is alight,' Arden said, looking at the front of the building, 'the same as here. It's magnificent!'

There was an explosion of glass as the illuminated sign announcing *The Esplanade* shattered under the scorching heat.

Everyone cheered, and Flame trembled in my arms.

'Look at it, Flicker!' Dray shouted, and grinned at us, seeing how excited we both were. 'Your masterpiece!'

The fire was spreading faster than I'd expected, wrapping the building in a mortal embrace.

'We have to go!' Oak yelled.

He was right, of course. It wouldn't be long now before sirens filled the night air.

Dray climbed into the driver's seat.

'Get in, everyone!' Arden ordered. We hadn't spotted drones, but that didn't mean there weren't any. We'd have to hide the lorry and get into the cinema quickly.

We waited with Oak and Arden while the others got in.

'Time to go home, Flame,' I said, and I bent over until my mouth was level with her belly. 'This is a wild world we're bringing you into, my child, and one we have to burn down before we can start over again. Your mother and I don't know where we come from and we don't know where we're going. No one knows what tomorrow will bring, but I'm going to write a story for you—*our* story—and it will always be there for you, so you know where you come from. I want you to know who your parents were.'

Flame kissed my head. 'I'll tell you my story, Flicker, before you start. No more secrets. I'll share my memories about who Cara was—about the night her building collapsed and Flame was born.'

'When you're ready,' I told her, standing up. The blaze was reflected in her green eyes, but I could see the sorrow in her soul.

'Well, this is a surprise!' Oak said with a laugh.

'It's early days yet,' Arden warned him. 'We'll let Flame make the announcement when she's ready.'

Oak nodded and indicated that his lips were sealed.

I helped Flame into the lorry, and before I joined her, I took once final glance at the blaze, roaring into the night sky. In those cleansing flames, I saw forgiveness for all the mistakes I'd made and all the ordeals we'd been through. None of it mattered any longer. This was a new beginning. Every fire I'd ever lit had been leading up to this, my masterpiece—*Tyranny's Funeral Pyre*.

For news, reviews, competitions, author interviews, and exclusive excerpts

Visit our website
blackbeaconbooks.com

Like us on Facebook
facebook.com/BlackBeaconBooks

Join us on X
@BlackBeacons

Follow us on Goodreads
goodreads.com/author/show/20231552

Enjoy the photos on Instagram
instagram.com/blackbeaconbooks

Subscribe on Patreon
patreon.com/blackbeaconbooks

Also Available from Black Beacon Books

Fourteen terrifying tales of a ruined tomorrow! Was it nuclear war, an uncontrollable pandemic, or forces beyond our reckoning? Will we even know what happened once supply lines have been cut, radio silence has kicked in, and our world has come to a grinding halt? Who will have what it takes to carry on? Who will want to?

BLACK
BEACON
B O O K S

blackbeaconbooks.com

www.ingramcontent.com/pod-product-compliance
Lightning Source LLC
Chambersburg PA
CBHW020235180626
46810CB00006B/2197